T0023034

PRAISE FOR TAHOE DEE

"A SMART, INTRIGUING MYSTERY....

- Kirkus Reviews

"JAW-DROPPING INVESTIGATIVE SKILLS... DEEP, THOUGHTFUL AND COMPLEX" — Gloria Sinibaldi, Tahoe Mountain News

PRAISE FOR TAHOE SKYDROP

"ANOTHER IMPRESSIVE CASE FEATURING A DETECTIVE WHO REMAINS NOT ONLY DOGGED, BUT ALSO REFLECTIVE."

- Kirkus Reviews

"A SURPRISE TWIST WILL GIVE YOU AN EXTRA JOLT...a great addition to the Owen McKenna series." - Gloria Sinibaldi, Tahoe Mountain News

PRAISE FOR TAHOE PAYBACK

"AN ENGROSSING WHODUNIT" *- Kirkus Reviews*

"ANOTHER GREAT TODD BORG THRILLER *- Book Dilettante*

"FAST PACED, ABSORBING, MEMORABLE" *- Kittling: Books*
Borg's Tahoe Mystery series chosen by Kittling: Books as ONE OF THE TEN BEST MYSTERY SERIES

PRAISE FOR TAHOE DARK

"ONCE AGAIN, BORG HITS ALL THE RIGHT NOTES FOR FANS OF CLASSIC DETECTIVE FICTION in the mold of Dashiell Hammett, Raymond Chandler, Ross Macdonald, and Robert B. Parker."

- Kirkus Reviews

"TAHOE DARK IS PACKED WITH ACTION AND TWISTS. THE SURPRISES JUST KEEP ON COMING...THE FINAL SCENE IS ANOTHER TODD BORG MASTERPIECE." *- Silver's Reviews*

PRAISE FOR TAHOE BLUE FIRE

"A GRIPPING NARRATIVE...A HERO WHO WALKS CONFIDENTLY IN THE FOOTSTEPS OF SAM SPADE, PHILIP MARLOWE, AND LEW ARCHER" *- Kirkus Reviews*

"A THRILLING MYSTERY THAT IS DIFFICULT TO PUT DOWN ...EDGE OF YOUR SEAT ACTION" *– Silver's Reviews*

PRAISE FOR TAHOE GHOST BOAT

"THE OLD PULP SAVVY OF (ROSS) MACDONALD...REAL
SURPRISE AT THE END"   – *Kirkus Reviews*

"NAIL-BITING THRILLER...BOILING POT OF DRAMA"
                                       - Gloria Sinibaldi, Tahoe Daily Tribune

"BORG'S WRITING IS THE STUFF OF A HOLLYWOOD ACTION
BLOCKBUSTER"   – *Taylor Flynn, Tahoe Mountain News*

"ACTION-PACKED IS PUTTING IT MILDLY. PREPARE FOR FIRE-
WORKS"   – *Sunny Solomon, Bookin' With Sunny*

"I LOVED EVERY ROLLER COASTER RIDE IN THIS THRILLER
5+ OUT OF 5"   – *Harvee Lau, Book Dilettante*

PRAISE FOR TAHOE CHASE

"EXCITING, EXPLOSIVE, THOUGHTFUL, SOMETIMES FUNNY"
                            – *Ann Ronald, Bookin' With Sunny*

"OWEN McKENNA HAS HIS HANDS FULL IN ANOTHER THRILL-
ING ADVENTURE"   *- Harvee Lau, Book Dilettante*

PRAISE FOR TAHOE TRAP

"AN OPEN-THROTTLE RIDE"
                        - Wendy Schultz, Placerville Mountain Democrat

"A CONSTANTLY SURPRISING SERIES OF EVENTS INVOLVING
MURDER...and the final motivation of the killer comes as a major surprise.
(I love when that happens.)"   – *Yvette, In So Many Words*

"I LOVE TODD BORG'S BOOKS...There is the usual great twist ending
in Tahoe Trap that I never would have guessed"   – *JBronder Reviews*

"THE PLOTS ARE HIGH OCTANE AND THE ACTION IS FASTER
THAN A CHEETAH ON SPEED"   – *Cathy Cole, Kittling: Books*
"AN EXCITING MURDER MYSTERY... I watch for the ongoing develop-
ments of Jack Reacher, Joanna Brady, Dismas Hardy, Peter and Rina Decker,
and Alex Cross to name a few. But these days I look forward most to the
next installment of Owen McKenna."   *- China Gorman blog*

PRAISE FOR TAHOE HIJACK

"BEGINNING TO READ TAHOE HIJACK IS LIKE FLOOR-BOARDING A RACE CAR... RATING: A+"

- Cathy Cole, Kittling Books

"A THRILLING READ... any reader will find the pages of his thrillers impossible to stop turning"

- Caleb Cage, The Nevada Review

"THE BOOK CLIMAXES WITH A TWIST THE READER DOESN'T SEE COMING, WORTHY OF MICHAEL CONNELLY"

- Heather Gould, Tahoe Mountain News

"I HAD TO HOLD MY BREATH DURING THE LAST PART OF THIS FAST-PACED THRILLER"   *- Harvee Lau, Book Dilettante*

PRAISE FOR TAHOE HEAT

"IN TAHOE HEAT, BORG MASTERFULLY WRITES A SEQUENCE OF EVENTS SO INTENSE THAT IT BELONGS IN AN EARLY TOM CLANCY NOVEL"

- Caleb Cage, Nevada Review

"TAHOE HEAT IS A RIVETING THRILLER"

- John Burroughs, Midwest Book Review

"WILL KEEP READERS TURNING THE PAGES AS OWEN RACES TO CATCH A VICIOUS KILLER"

- Barbara Bibel, Booklist

"THE READER CAN'T HELP BUT ROOT FOR McKENNA AS THE BIG, GENEROUS, IRISH-BLOODED, STREET-WISE-YET-BOOK-SMART FORMER COP"

- Taylor Flynn, Tahoe Mountain News

PRAISE FOR TAHOE NIGHT

"BORG HAS WRITTEN ANOTHER WHITE-KNUCKLE THRILLER... A sure bet for mystery buffs waiting for the next Robert B. Parker and Lee Child novels"

- Jo Ann Vicarel, Library Journal

"AN ACTION-PACKED THRILLER WITH A NICE-GUY HERO, AN EVEN NICER DOG..."   *- Kirkus Reviews*

"A KILLER PLOT... EVERY ONE OF ITS 350 PAGES WANTS TO GET TURNED... *FAST*"

- Taylor Flynn, Tahoe Mountain News

"A FASCINATING STORY OF FORGERY, MURDER..."

- Nancy Hayden, Tahoe Daily Tribune

PRAISE FOR TAHOE AVALANCHE

ONE OF THE TOP 5 MYSTERIES OF THE YEAR!

- Gayle Wedgwood, Mystery News

"BORG IS A SUPERB STORYTELLER...A MASTER OF THE GENRE"

- Midwest Book Review

"EXPLODES INTO A COMPLEX PLOT THAT LEADS TO MURDER AND INTRIGUE"

- Nancy Hayden, Tahoe Daily Tribune

PRAISE FOR TAHOE SILENCE
WINNER, BEN FRANKLIN AWARD, BEST MYSTERY OF THE YEAR!

"A HEART-WRENCHING MYSTERY THAT IS ALSO ONE OF THE BEST NOVELS WRITTEN ABOUT AUTISM"

STARRED REVIEW - Jo Ann Vicarel, Library Journal

CHOSEN BY LIBRARY JOURNAL AS ONE OF THE FIVE BEST MYSTERIES OF THE YEAR

"THIS IS ONE ENGROSSING NOVEL...IT IS SUPERB"

- Gayle Wedgwood, Mystery News

"ANOTHER EXCITING ENTRY INTO THIS TOO-LITTLE-KNOWN SERIES"   *- Mary Frances Wilkens, Booklist*

PRAISE FOR TAHOE KILLSHOT

"BORG BELONGS ON THE BESTSELLER LISTS with Parker, Paretsky and Coben"   *- Merry Cutler, Annie's Book Stop, Sharon, Massachusetts*
"A GREAT READ!"   *-Shelley Glodowski, Midwest Book Review*

"A WONDERFUL BOOK"   *- Gayle Wedgwood, Mystery News*

Titles by Todd Borg

TAHOE HIT

by

Todd Borg

THRILLER PRESS

Thriller Press First Edition, August 2020

Library of Congress Control Number: 2020936889

ISBN: 978-1-931296-28-1

Cover design and map by Keith Carlson

Manufactured in the United States of America

For Kit

ACKNOWLEDGMENTS

Thanks so very much to my editors, Liz Johnston, Eric Berglund, Christel Hall, and my wife Kit. One simply cannot produce a story sufficiently free of mistakes without the help of good editors. More than finding mistakes, they made hundreds of suggestions for improving the story. I'm incredibly fortunate to have this expert crew.

As always, I get very excited when Keith Carlson shows me his new cover design for my next book. Each one is unique yet fits with all the others. This cover is beyond cool.

Reaching back 400 years, I want to thank Mr. William Shakespeare. All writers of English owe him gratitude for how he shaped our language and speech, invented countless compelling stories, phrases, descriptions, and new words. He was arguably the single most important writer in our language. As I constructed a story that connected to Hamlet, I was repeatedly amazed and humbled as I studied his words and technique. I hope I haven't mangled this story's Shakespearean connections too much.

Thanks again to all.

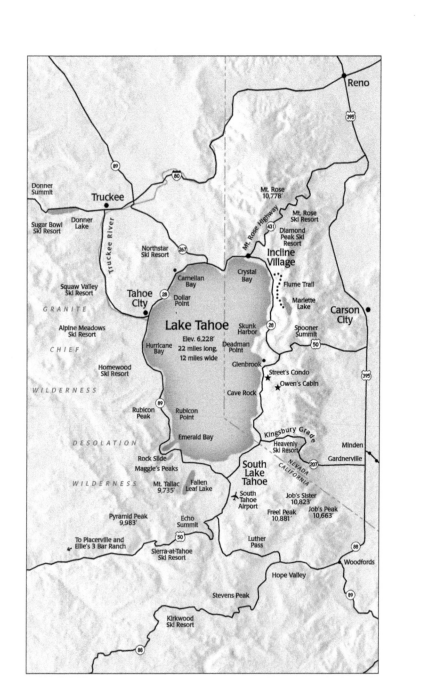

PROLOGUE

It was an ideal gathering for murder. A summer outdoor party. Twilight moving toward dark. Live music. Lots of people, loud with enthusiastic conversation.

The evening festivities sprawled out from the West Shore mansion on Lake Tahoe. Gas torches on 8-foot posts outlined the lawn and the swimming pool, and stretched in a line all the way out to the end of the pier. They looped in tight formation around the gazebo at the pier's end.

The pool glowed the iridescent blue green of a Caribbean lagoon with a white sand bottom. Around the pool were numerous garden fountains lit by submerged lights of a deeper marine blue. Stretching across the lawn were a dozen tables, each draped in white linen and sparkling with silver and polished glassware and groupings of votive candles, the flames flickering in the light evening breeze.

From up by the bar, the swimming pool and tables and the ring of torches looked like a huge brooch of turquoise surrounded by sapphires, with the gazebo as a blazing diamond. It was all set off by the black backdrop of Lake Tahoe at night.

The party was an intimate affair of 157 of Carston Kraytower's closest friends, business associates, and investors, mostly from the Bay Area, mostly in their late 40s or mid 50s. In addition to the guests were 16 members of the chamber orchestra playing Baroque classics up on the flagstone patio around the pool, 23 wait staff, 6 bartenders, a dozen house servants and car park valets, and 4 guards moonlighting from their day jobs as Placer County Sheriff's deputies, the county in which Kraytower's Tahoe home was located.

The high-elevation mountain air was cooling fast, and the women, most of whom wore evening gowns, had pulled on alpaca cardigans or draped their shoulders in elegant Nepalese shawls. The men, already wearing dress jackets, were less vulnerable to Tahoe's temperatures, which, despite the warm days of late July, plunged into the 30s at night.

Carston Kraytower had strolled down the lawn to the foot of the pier, where there was a second patio rimmed with heavy benches hewn from Redwood trees. A large knot of financial sycophants and groupies accompanied Kraytower, hoping to hear gems of wisdom from the founder of the West Coast's largest hedge fund.

Kraytower stood at one side of the patio, with his back to a group of huge old-growth Jeffrey Pine and California Red Fir. Like a practiced orator, Kraytower made grand gestures to emphasize his pronouncements. He was telling a funny golf story about his good buddy, the chair of the Federal Reserve. The joke's point was a slightly-veiled barb at the advancing age of the powerful government figure. Kraytower's friends laughed as if they were in the audience at a Saturday Night Live filming.

Off in the shadows of the giant trees, a person dressed in black approached, moving slowly and pausing behind each massive tree trunk. The intruder wore a black knit ski mask, black turtleneck above black pants, and black leather gloves, and was nearly invisible on the moonless night.

The intruder carried a tall black hiking staff with a leather wrist thong and fitted with rubber tips top and bottom. The person paused in a dense group of trees, pulled off the rubber tips and slipped them into a pocket. Without the tips, what remained was a simple 60-inch copper plumbing pipe that had been painted black. It was a blowgun, silent, deadly accurate at short range, and nearly invisible. Blowguns were illegal in California, one of those ironies in a state where firearms, although regulated, were legal. The intruder didn't care. Take off the ski mask and reinstall the rubber tips on the copper pipe, and the shooter would just appear to be an evening hiker using a walking stick to maintain footing in the growing darkness.

The intruder unzipped a small, black fanny pack and removed

a tranquilizer dart. The dart—also painted black—contained 25 milligrams of etorphine, a distant synthetic cousin of morphine but two thousand times as potent. The volume of 25 milligrams was the equivalent of one-half of a drop of water, a tiny quantity yet sufficient to immobilize an elephant or rhinoceros, which was its intended use in zoos. That much etorphine was also hundreds of times the fatal dose for humans. The drug was fast acting. Injected into a major muscle, it would stop a man's heart in one minute. The etorphine had been stolen years earlier from an animal pharmaceutical warehouse in Brooklyn, New York. The theft was never solved. The stolen drug would be identifiable in a sophisticated toxicology test but not traceable to its source.

The trespasser's intended victim was James Lightfoot, Kraytower's closest associate and a vice president in his company.

The dart was like a small syringe. It had a thin hollow needle for its point and there was a small plunger at the rear. The intruder pushed the plunger down, compressing a bubble of air. The plunger clicked into place like cocking a miniature gun. When the needle penetrated flesh, the impact would open a tiny valve, and the compressed air would drive the drug into the victim. At the back end of the dart was a miniature coil of micro-thin monofilament line that would unspool as the dart flew. The line was 20 feet long, sufficient for the distance a dart could be accurately fired.

The trespasser moved behind a closer tree, this one a young California Red Fir heavy with long branches that draped down and created good cover. The intruder leaned out to peer through the branches, eyes squinted to minimize the chance anyone saw reflected light in the eye openings of the ski mask.

The people around Kraytower were laughing and commenting with raised voices as they sipped their champagne and martinis. It was a raucous group, and their din was enough to drown out the music from the orchestra up by the pool.

The shooter slipped the dart into the end of the copper tube and hooked the monofilament line over a little nub of metal designed for that purpose. The shooter gently raised the copper tube, poked it through the dense branches, and stabilized it by holding it against the tree trunk.

Because Carston Kraytower had maneuvered himself so he could face all of his adoring fans at once, it was easy to identify his position. It was also easy to focus on Kraytower's right-hand man, James Lightfoot. Lightfoot was a mere twelve feet from where the shooter hid behind the tree.

The person in black took a deep breath, aimed the blowgun toward Lightfoot's back, and, while Kraytower spoke in a booming voice, gave a strong blow on the pipe.

The dart was a black streak in the night. Its trajectory went lower than intended. But it nevertheless stabbed Lightfoot in the left buttock sufficiently that the needle held the dart in place.

The shooter quickly gave a small tug on the trailing line, and the dart pulled out of Lightfoot's flesh and fell to the patio. It rolled to a dip between the stones as Lightfoot reached down and rubbed his butt.

The intruder pulled on the line. The dart seemed to jump. But when it landed, it caught on a large Jeffrey pinecone that lay at the edge of the patio, the monofilament line snagging on the cone's scales. As the shooter tugged, the pinecone began to come with the dart. Unlike the little black dart, the pinecone was huge and visible in the dim light from the gas torches.

Its movement would surely be spotted by the group.

The shooter needed a distraction. But there was nothing to do but wait.

Carston Kraytower was still orating.

Lightfoot reached down a second time as if trying to massage away the sting of a wasp.

A moment later, Lightfoot reached his right hand across his chest, grabbed his upper left arm, then crumpled to the patio.

Several people gasped. Two men kneeled down next to Lightfoot.

Someone shouted, "Call a doctor!"

Carston Kraytower bent over, then knelt on one knee. "Jim? Jim? Can you hear me?" He shook Lightfoot's shoulder. "Jim, what's wrong?! Are you okay? Speak to me, Jim."

"Virginia Clover is at this party somewhere," another man said. "VIRGINIA?!" the man called out toward the house. "Virginia, are you out on the lawn? We need a doctor down by the lake!"

Many people turned and scanned the lawn.

The trespasser reeled in the dart and its pinecone cargo. As the monofilament hoisted both dart and pinecone up through the branches of the fir tree, it snagged again. The shooter pulled and realized that the line was hopelessly snarled. The shooter reached out, took a strong grip on both the dart and pinecone, and jerked them apart, breaking the tiny line. But the pinecone and line were still snagged in the branches. Holding the dart, the intruder wiggled the line until the cone lowered to the ground, then backed away from the tree and slowly disappeared into the dark forest.

As the person in black walked slowly through the forest, holding one arm outstretched in front to protect against unseen branches, the other arm slipped the dart back into the fanny pack, removed the ski mask, and put on a baseball cap. The rubber tips were refitted on the copper pipe, making it once again appear to be a hiking staff.

The shooter came to a bicycle stashed in the trees near the West Shore Highway. Hanging on the bike was a bungee cord, perfect for attaching the hiking staff to the top bar of the bike frame. The killer pulled on reflector arm bands, climbed onto the bike, turned on the white front lamp and the red rear strobe, and rode south down the highway.

ONE

We were out on the deck of my little log cabin, 1000 feet above the East Shore of Lake Tahoe. Street Casey and I sat on my cheap folding chairs. Spot, my Harlequin Great Dane, lay at the edge of the deck. He stared down at what he probably thought were tiny white bugs that made very-slow-but-epic journeys across the giant lake. The bugs left white lines on the blue, like some kind of bug foam that spread into narrow V shapes. After a time, Spot lowered his jaw to his paws, shut his eyes, and appeared to sleep.

Blondie sat near Street, her eyes lovingly focused on Street's face like the storybook Yellow Lab rescue dog she was.

"Your hound's devotion to you could inspire a sonnet," I said. "My hound's lack of devotion to me would merely suggest doggerel."

"You mean, like a bawdy limerick?" she said. "There once was a Great Dane named Spot...?"

"Exactly," I said.

"You should write it."

"Maybe I will someday," I said.

The summer sun was as hot on our skin as an electric iron set to "linen." But the air in the shade at 7200 feet was cool enough by day and cold enough by night that I kept a case of beer outdoors under the shade of an overhanging pine. The beer was cool no matter the time of day you popped the top.

"Beer?" I asked.

"No thanks," Street said. There was something in her tone that made me want to respond.

"A late-morning brew shows that a person is not overly concerned with social decorum. It is the mark of an individualist who thinks for himself."

"An individualist who has to take a nap in the afternoon," she said.

"That, too," I said.

We'd been playing an imaginative charades-like game called What's That Squall. Street turned and pointed at an irregular wave pattern coloring the lake's surface about 12 miles away over by Tahoe City. She began acting out something like galloping on a horse. I couldn't figure it out. By the puzzled furrows on Blondie's brow, her dog couldn't figure it out, either.

"A knight errant!" Street finally shouted. "Don't you see it?"

I shook my head. I stared out at the lake "I don't. What would I look for? Shining armor? A sword?"

"No, honey. You're too literal. There is a vague shape of a horse and rider. But its boldness suggests a heroic figure. You know, skill and prowess. The chivalry of a knight. Stuff like that."

My phone rang. The portable extension was on the small deck table. I fumbled it up to my chin.

"Owen McKenna," I said vacantly. Then I covered the phone and said to Street, "So what is this metaphorical knight's name?" No way could she come up with a quick, believable answer to that unless it was King Arthur or some other medieval pop star.

"Don Quixote, of course," she immediately said.

Someone was talking on the phone. I brought it back to my ear. "I'm sorry, I didn't hear what you said." I didn't add that no matter who the caller was, they stood no chance of pulling my attention away from Street, a woman who was an unlikely combination of sharp intelligence and intense hunger for life. The long lean curves and a kind of severe beauty didn't hurt, a combo that raised my heart rate toward the red line. Especially when she pretended to ride a galloping horse.

"Sergeant Santiago here," the voice said. "It sounds like I'm interrupting a conversation about Cervantes?"

"Hey, sarge," I said. "What makes you think we're talking about Cervantes? And who was he, anyway?"

"He was a Spanish writer, way back. His great novel was Don Quixote. And I'm of Spanish heritage, of course."

"And your knowledge of Cervantes comes from…"

"I succumbed to a little college before I went to cop school," he said. "Took a literature class. I thought I should know some poetry when I'm about to bust someone's chops."

"You still surprise." I said.

"It sounds good, anyway, huh? You're always thinking about great paintings. You should expand your horizons and think about literature, too."

"We're trying. A limerick about my hound is in the offing. What's up?" I asked.

"Last night, over on my side of the lake, we had a little party-time upset in the form of a financial executive named James Lightfoot whose heart gave out on Carston Kraytower's lakeside patio."

"I don't know either name."

"I didn't either until dispatch called me. I got to Kraytower's house in time to see Lightfoot, who happens to be a VP in Kraytower's company, carted away on a gurney."

"What is Kraytower's company?"

"It's called the KGA Fund, which stands for Kraytower Growth Assets. It's a hedge fund."

"I've heard of those, but I don't know what they do."

"I didn't know either, until this morning," Santiago said. "I was told mutual funds mostly invest in stocks and bonds and the like, while hedge funds invest in anything. They're high risk but often generate high returns. Not for the faint of heart or anyone who isn't already rich, as they require a high buy-in and there's always the risk you'll lose it all."

"Is Kraytower's fund successful?"

"By the looks of his mansion on the lake, I'd say so."

"So why call me? I didn't even know Cervantes was Spanish."

"The sheriff said that everyone in San Francisco's financial district is Kraytower's buddy. And a smattering of people on Wall Street know him as well. And of course several of the former and a few of the latter have places in Tahoe. Which is why the sheriff is concerned we handle the situation thoroughly and delicately."

"What does this have to do with me? I don't think I've ever been accused of being delicate."

"Frankly, the sheriff feels that Kraytower deserves extra attention. I think, but don't know, that Kraytower must have told the sheriff that he doesn't think that Lightfoot had a heart attack. Or, at least, a normal heart attack. We already did the basic routine last night. Now it's time for followup. A quirk of the system makes it so our budget has a little room to bring in outside help."

"What would I do? Do you suspect foul play in the death of Lightfoot?" I asked.

"No, we don't. But the pathologist hasn't yet stated the cause of death. And what looks like a heart attack could be something else, right? And even if it is a heart attack, it could have been triggered by something beyond champagne. Am I wrong?"

"Like in a spy novel," I said. "The secret agent administers the chemical trigger and, voila, you have an Agatha Christie heart attack."

I was joking, but Santiago played it straight. He said, "So we'd like you to try your version of sniffing around while the scene is still fresh."

"My sniffer ain't very good."

"Right. Your hound's version is better," Santiago said.

"What would he sniff?" I asked.

"I don't know. That's what investigation is all about, right?"

"Figuring out what smells?" I said.

"Yeah," Santiago said. "We've nothing else to go on. After asking a lot of questions of people who were at the party, every single person seemed to like James Lightfoot. So we've got a death and not even a hint of motive. Having you investigate this is just a pro forma thing. Go through the motions, make the Placer County Sheriff's Office look thorough. If you could give me a couple of days, the sheriff will okay the expense."

"You may as well tell the truth. I'm cheap," I said.

"You should be, not knowing about Cervantes."

Santiago gave me the address of the Kraytower abode, and we agreed to meet there in the afternoon.

TWO

The address Sergeant Santiago gave me was south of Tahoe City near Sunnyside. If I had a telescope, I could have seen my destination across the lake from my deck.

Spot and I dropped Street and Blondie at her condo, and cruised north around the lake, through Incline Village, over the state border between Nevada and California, and through the smaller North Shore towns.

When I got to Tahoe City, I headed south on 89, found the address, and turned off. Because of endless tourist-traffic delays, it was two and a half hours after I'd said goodbye to Street before I drove between the stone columns of the Carston Kraytower residence. I could have paddled a kayak the 12 miles across the lake in the same time.

I followed a long curving drive made of old bricks that were shiny and steely black and laid in a herringbone pattern. It reminded me of what I'd seen in Rome.

I went past two tennis courts and a golf green, pulled in next to a sheriff's SUV, and parked on a broad area not much smaller than the Piazza Venezia. Appropriate to the Italian drive, there was a red Lamborghini and a tiny mustard-colored Fiat parked next to a fountain. Water tumbled from a chalice that was held up by a marble maiden with Bernini curves. The spread before me was made of cut stone, with grand, sweeping lines and huge roofs. It looked like a villa that belonged at the top of one of Rome's seven hills. The palace was L-shaped with a steep roof of slate. The roof was punctuated by seven stone chimneys as dramatic as exclamation points. On one part of the roof was a second-floor, rooftop sculpture garden, accessed through a second-story door.

There was a row of Greek-inspired fluted marble columns with Doric tops. Between each pair of columns were marble statues that showed the sculptor's skill in depicting bare flesh draped here and there with enough flowing robes to make the subjects seem important.

The columns didn't support any structure. Perhaps one just strolled among them, like Caesar and Brutus having a Socratic dialogue.

I got out and opened the back door for Spot.

Santiago was leaning against the Sheriff's SUV. He held an iPad. Maybe the sheriff's office was getting very modern and he was making notes about the case. Or maybe he was adding movies to his Netflix queue.

"Sergeant," I said. "Sorry for the delay in getting here. Lotta tourists in the basin in July."

He nodded and closed the bendy flap across the front of the iPad.

We shook hands. Santiago was a good 8 inches shorter than my 6-6, but he was as tough and strong as he was smart. If he ever wanted to bust my chops, I'd be hoping he was distracted by the poetry he referred to.

"Where should I start?" I asked.

Santiago shrugged. "This is cover-our-ass stuff for the sheriff's office."

"Do we need to let the Kraytower family know I'll be walking the grounds?"

"They already know I'm here. But I should introduce you."

I held Spot's collar as we walked past the fountain and around the lovely marble maiden to the front door of the palace. The double door was made of heavy planks and had cast-iron hinges.

I said, "This door is tall and wide enough that if both sides were opened, two riders on horseback could go through it side by side," I said.

"Don Quixote and Sancho Panza," Santiago said.

The man who answered the door was a thin, white-haired gentleman with a pencil moustache and Van Dyke beard. He leaned on a mahogany cane. His hand and cane shook with a tremor.

"Afternoon, Mr. Casteem," Santiago said. "I want you to meet Owen McKenna. McKenna is a former cop from San Francisco."

"Good afternoon, sergeant." The man was a pleasant-looking fellow who had a sweet angelic quality about him. He wore a white shirt and black pants that were ironed until they had a crease sharp enough to cleave Angel Food cake. The man turned from Santiago and looked at me and then at Spot. His eyes stayed on Spot. He didn't show any fear of Spot. But he telegraphed meekness or cautious reserve.

The man shifted his cane to his left hand, reached out his right hand and shook. "Good to meet you. I'm Gerard Casteem." Casteem's hand vibrated. He quickly transferred the cane back to that hand.

Casteem looked at Spot. "And your dog?"

"This is my sidekick Spot."

At the sound of his name, Spot glanced at me, wagged, then looked back at the old man.

"He won't bother the wildlife?" Casteem asked.

"He's a large, undisciplined fellow with a fondness for chasing Douglas Squirrels. But they just taunt him from above. So he won't cause any problems."

Gerard Casteem made the smallest of smiles. "I'm happy to have him chase the squirrels. Bears, too. We had one come through the kitchen window last week. Got into the ice box and ate the mint chocolate chip. I took it personally." He made another little grin.

"I would too," I said.

"Especially if you saw the window repair bill. In my next life, I'll be a window and glass guy."

Santiago seemed impatient. "I explained to McKenna that the sheriff has told me that Mr. Kraytower is unnerved by Mr. Lightfoot's death, and he wants an assessment of the situation. So we've brought Mr. McKenna in here in an effort to be as thorough as possible. We'd like permission to stroll the grounds with McKenna's patrol dog."

Casteem stared at Spot as he nodded and said, "I'm sure Mr.

Kraytower would like whatever is useful to the sheriff. May I ask, please, is this boy a Great Dane?"

"Yeah," I said.

"May I, um, pet him?"

"He would love it."

Casteem stepped forward. He reached out his shaky hand, approaching Spot as if he were approaching a tiger. "I believe you said his name is Spot."

"Yes. He also answers to His Largeness."

"He is large indeed," Casteem said. Casteem pet Spot between his ears, moving as gently as a little boy petting a kitten.

Perhaps Spot could feel it. His tail made the slowest of wags.

"Magnificent," Casteem said.

"Thank you, Mr. Casteem."

"Call me Gerard. Or Gary. Heck, the kids call me Gramps. So I pretty much answer to anything."

"Kids?" Santiago said. "Kraytower only has one, right?"

"Right. Joshua. Very quiet, very smart. He hangs out with a kid from down the highway. Mr Kraytower's new driver, Sky Kool, if you can believe that. He's the one who started calling me Gramps."

"Thanks, Gary," I said.

"You're welcome."

Casteem made an imperceptible nod and slowly shut the door.

Santiago led Spot and me through a gate in a stone wall, and we entered onto the back lawn. He pointed toward the lake and held his arms wide apart. "Kraytower held a grand party that spread all across the grounds. He was down at that far patio, regaling his associates with stories, when Lightfoot died."

"You learn regaling at cop school?" I asked.

"The meaning, not the skill. Anyway, that's where James Lightfoot had his heart attack. Let's walk down there."

The lawn flowed around trees and shrubs and flower gardens thick with blossoms, up to a terrace and pool, a long rectangle, formal yet modern. The terrace was dark gray flagstone. At its outer edges were yet more marble figures, regal young women, partially clothed, rendered at a smaller scale than real life. The figures reflected in the pool water, which was as calm and smooth as glass.

"You know art," said Santiago. "Any idea who did them?"

"Not sure. They look like Berninis."

"Heard the name," Santiago said.

"Italian dude. Probably the greatest sculptor who ever lived."

"And he wasn't even Spanish." Santiago kept a straight face.

"Did James Lightfoot live in Tahoe?" I asked as we walked down toward the lake.

"No. His main residence was in San Francisco, like Kraytower. I understand that Kraytower lives in the Pacific Heights neighborhood. He said where Lightfoot's house was. I forget the name. Begins with a P and maybe has a hill in it."

"Potrero Hill?" I said.

"Score," Santiago said.

"Do you know if he has family?"

"Other than his ex-wife, no."

"You got statements from Kraytower or his associates?"

"Sort of. The cause of death is not suspicious, so there is no criminal investigation. But I talked to several people who were there when Lightfoot died. They seemed especially sad about his demise."

"Hear anything intriguing about Lightfoot?" I asked.

"Nope."

"About anyone else?"

He shook his head.

"Do you know how it is that the sheriff knows Kraytower?"

"When Kraytower bought this place, he invited the sheriff and his family over for wine out by the pool. The sheriff holds him in high regard."

"Is high regard an accurate description? Or is it a euphemistic expression?"

Santiago replied with a question. "You learn euphemistic when you were on the SFPD?"

"The meaning, not the skill." I grinned.

Santiago paused. "I think high regard is accurate."

We came down to the pier. Santiago walked over to a round patio made of the same steely black bricks as the drive.

Santiago stood near some huge trees. "I was told that this is where James Lightfoot was standing when he had his heart attack." He looked at Spot. "So how do you get him to do his smell investigation?"

"I just make him comfortable and let him assess the territory."

"What's to assess?" the sergeant asked.

"Maybe nothing. But all creatures notice things that are unusual. People do that primarily with their eyes. Dogs do it with their nose."

"Give me an example?" Santiago asked.

"Let's say you're walking through a crowded farmer's market in Tahoe. Nothing remarkable or notable, right?"

"Right."

"Then you come to some vendor who's unloading strawberries from a shiny black Tesla. Maybe it's two guys speaking Russian."

"I get it," Santiago said. "When your dog is assessing the territory, it provides him the background to notice if inputs blend in or stand out."

"Couldn't have said it better myself. Practically poetry the way you cops speak."

"It was that literature class. You'd be surprised at what cops can do," Santiago said. "Oh, wait, you were a cop. So maybe you aren't surprised."

"Twenty years on the SFPD. Anyway, you start writing up your reports in iambic pentameter, I'll be surprised."

Spot had gone a few steps out on the pier and paused. He held his head high, nostrils flexing.

"Go ahead, boy," I said. "Explore. Look for buried bones."

Spot glanced at me for a moment. I couldn't think of when he'd ever been at such an elaborate private estate. He trotted down the pier. He paused and looked over the edge. Then walked to the end. He stared at a big cruiser going by. There was a small dog at the very tip of the bow, its nose parting the wind. A Jack Russell maybe. Spot's tail made a slow swish through the air. The dog on the boat made a single, high-pitched bark. Spot turned and came back toward the lawn.

Spot stepped off the pier onto the Roman bricks of the patio. He walked past Santiago, seemingly ignoring us. He began sniffing the edges of the patio, lifted his head and stared off through several giant, old-growth trees. Then Spot lowered his head again and sniffed his way off the patio, between the trees, and over to a large Jeffrey pinecone. He paused on it for a bit, then pawed it to roll it over. He sniffed for several more seconds than was typical for a pinecone.

Spot abandoned the cone and walked farther into the trees.

I saw a very faint glint of light at the cone. I walked over and squatted down. I didn't touch the cone.

"Check this out," I said to Santiago. "There's some kind of line tangled up in the pinecone."

THREE

Santiago came over and bent down, his hands on his knees. "Monofilament," he said. "You think it means something?"

"It's probably not the equivalent of two Russians selling fruit out of a Tesla," I said, "but it fits into the category of unusual items for this yard."

Santiago nodded. "Most pinecones don't have monofilament tangled in them. The cone isn't weathered. And the line looks shiny. So they are both recent." Santiago looked at me. "Can you think of a reason a line could get tangled in a pinecone?"

"Nothing obvious," I said. "The line is so thin, a good wind could have blown it here. And if it came into random contact with a pinecone, it would be hard for it not to get tangled. Jeffrey pinecone scales have sharp hooks on them."

"You think a pinecone could reveal fingerprints?" Santiago said.

"I doubt it. No smooth surfaces."

"Can you imagine any reason to bag it?"

"As evidence?" I said. "It would give you something to show your sheriff so he knows how thorough you're being. Then he can assure Kraytower that you are leaving nothing to chance."

"Then again," Santiago said, "he may think I'm wasting time and department resources. His first question would be, 'How could a pinecone have anything to do with Lightfoot's heart attack?'"

"Your call," I said. "Meanwhile, I should see where my dog went."

I stepped between the giant trees and looked into the forest. Spot was not in sight.

I whistled.

In time, Spot appeared, trotting through the trees. He stopped in front of me, wagging, stretching his nose toward the pocket where I keep treats. I gave him a pet instead.

"I could send my dog on a search."

"For what?"

"Something connected to the pinecone."

"How?"

"I scent him on the cone, tell him to search, and he wanders off and maybe finds something."

"Because he knows that even if he doesn't find anything, you'll still give him a treat."

"Exactly."

"Suit yourself," Santiago said.

So I put Spot through the motions as if it were a serious search. I had him sit so he was facing the forest where he'd wandered just after he first sniffed the pinecone. I used a tissue to pick up the cone and its tangled monofilament. I held it in front of his nose, trying to get it close but without poking him with the prickers.

"Sniff the cone, boy!" I said. "Do you have the scent? Sniff it again! Atta boy!" I used my other hand on his back to shake and vibrate him, giving him a sense of excitement. Then I pulled the cone away as I held my hand open, palm next to his head, and dropped my hand down and forward in a pointing maneuver.

"Find the suspect, boy!" I gave him a light smack on his rear as he ran off.

Spot loped at some speed into the woods. I left the cone on the ground and trotted after him.

Spot slowed to a trot almost immediately. But he kept his nose to the ground as if following a scent trail.

When the source of a scent is near, a dog will often air-scent, picking up whatever scent molecules are being currently lofted into the air. You can tell that approach because dogs hold their heads up. But when the scent source is gone and it's been more than a few hours, a dog has to follow a ground trail, if there is any. In that situation, the dog will run with its nose to the ground, finding the best scent source that matches or comes close to the scent they were originally given.

Spot had his nose to the ground. His trot slowed to a fast walk. Thirty yards into the forest, he stopped, turned around and came back some distance. He explored a patch of dirt that looked like it had been disturbed. Then he turned again and went farther into the woods, angling toward the West Shore Highway.

I followed Spot, and Santiago followed me. Spot approached the highway. He seemed to investigate an area about thirty feet off the asphalt. He turned and watched a convertible Mustang drive by. The car's top was down, and there were four young women in it, all four laughing.

"Find the scent, Spot," I said again. Spot looked at me. He showed no inclination to follow any scent. Then he looked back at the receding Mustang.

Santiago spoke from behind me. "Hound's got girls on the brain."

"Yeah. He's learned that young women gush over him like no other category of human." I took hold of his collar so he couldn't trot out into traffic.

"So he didn't find anything here," Santiago said, gesturing at the area.

"Nope. The soil is covered with pine needles. And what's not covered is fine and silty. Neither pick up footprints. Although these general marks here could be caused by people. And that curved shape could be from a bike. But I'm guessing. There's nothing definitive."

"The dog investigation is a bust."

"Maybe."

We turned and began walking back through the forest. As I pulled on Spot's collar, a faint distant shriek of laughing girls came down the highway. Spot turned to take a last look at the Mustang.

"You got a suggestion for other inquiries?" Santiago said.

"Did Lightfoot have family?"

"Just an ex-wife. Kraytower said she moved to Florida a decade ago. No kids. Apparently, this particular hedge fund has a bunch of childless executives. Except for Kraytower, that is. He has a son. Although I haven't met him."

"Maybe hedge fund types work a hundred hours a week and don't have time for family," I said.

"As likely an explanation as any, I suppose," Santiago said.

We came back to the yard and turned up the lawn toward the pool. The water was no longer calm. It had choppy waves that indicated someone had recently been swimming. There were two kids sitting in poolside lounge chairs, one of them a slight, skinny boy in his teens, who was dry and clothed, his knees pulled up to his chest. He hugged his knees as if for comfort more than warmth. The skinny kid had a plain black hardbound book on the lounge chair next to him. It looked like an artist's sketchbook.

The other, larger and muscular kid, was in his twenties. He was dripping wet. He sprawled back, one leg off the side of the chair and propped up on a small, low table. His black hair, in spite of being wet, was swept back like Elvis Presley's hair as if he'd just run his fingers through it after he got out of the pool. His white swim shorts emphasized his tan. On a low table next to his lounge chair was his phone. Next to the phone were small puddles of water. The kid watched us approach, his jaw floating left and right as if he were effecting a casual air to impress all the marble maidens.

I spoke softly to Santiago. "You know these kids?"

"Nope."

"Okay with you if I regale them a bit?" I said.

"Of course. I could listen and maybe pick up some euphemisms."

We walked up the grass and onto the terrace.

FOUR

"Hi guys," I said to the kids as Santiago and I got up to the pool. "I'm Owen McKenna and this is Sergeant Santiago. Mind if we pull up a chair?"

The wet kid spoke. "We're gonna be debriefed, huh?" He had an unusually husky baritone voice. If I'd only heard him and not seen him, I'd have thought he was much older.

"Interesting word choice," I said.

The kid looked from me to Santiago. "Well, you're with Mr. Police Officer in the uniform. So maybe you're Mr. Plainclothes Detective. And a rich guy just plonked over dead as a doornail last night. Makes sense you'd come around to ask questions."

Santiago and I each pulled an empty lounge chair closer and sat.

"Do you think the man's death was suspicious?" I asked.

"Not until you showed up. Now I do."

"May I ask your names?"

The wet kid answered, "I'm Happy and he's Harsh."

"Cute," I said.

His smile might have been embarrassment. "I'm happy being wild and he's harshly out of tune. It's our basic personalities."

I looked at the skinny kid hugging his knees. He was clearly introverted and tentative, the opposite of the older wet kid. He was maybe 16 years old, six or eight years younger than the wet kid. He looked to be just beginning puberty, a few large pimples marking a gawky face. His young brow had deep creases that looked like worry lines. He had no phone that I could see. He let go of his knees and straightened his legs as if to look a little less nervous. With his knees down, I could see that his T-shirt had a sketch portrait of a bearded man. Under the sketch it said John Muir.

"Muir is one of my favorites," I said.

He looked at me as if it were suspicious that I knew who John Muir was.

"So Harsh, what is your given name?"

"Joshua," he said in a small voice. "Joshua Kraytower." The worry seemed to ratchet up a notch.

"You're Carston Kraytower's son."

Joshua paused a moment. "So he says." It was a surprisingly bold statement despite the soft delivery.

"Do you doubt it?" I asked.

The kid went back to hugging his knees. "I don't doubt the genetics. I doubt the, you know, commitment."

"The basic requirements for a father-son relationship are in short supply, huh?"

He nodded. "I have, like, all the material stuff. I'm not going hungry. When I want a new computer, all I have to do is order it on Amazon. I don't even have to ask permission."

"What about your father? What does he do if he's not being a father?"

"He makes money. That's his reason for living."

"See, Mr. Plainclothes?" the wet kid said. "What'd I tell you. He's harsh. Every kid I know would trade places with him. Me included."

"What about you, Happy? What is your real name?"

"Sky Kool."

"Unusual name."

"Kool is spelled with a K. The original version had an E on the end. But that E got lost way back. Sky comes from Skiver," he said. "My step mom's maiden name. It's Dutch, like Koole, my step dad's surname. I was an orphan from the age of three when my parents died. Years in a concrete block building with no central heat. But it worked until I was adopted. And in answer to your next question, a skiver is someone whose job was to polish diamonds. Back in the old days. Unless they were English instead of Dutch. An English skiver was someone who stripped leather into shoelaces and such. Guess which side I identify with."

"Not very close to Happy, either way."

"Happy's just my personality."

"Sky Kool would be a good stage name. You could be a rock star," I said.

The wet kid made a huge grin. "That's my plan, man."

"What's your axe?"

"Aren't you hip. I just bought a used Jeff Beck Stratocaster. Like he said, 'with a Strat, I finally sound like me.'"

"You have a band?"

"'Course. We're currently a trio looking for a drummer. I'm on vocals and play rhythm guitar, Rock plays lead, and Water's on bass."

"Rock and Water are stage names to go with Sky, right?"

"Yeah. Like nature."

"You got a name for your future drummer?"

"Thunder. If we ever get a keyboard player, he'll be Fire. You should come hear us. We're at Trash Talk on the South Shore the next two nights. Nine to one. Though it could be we play late what with audience demand."

"Maybe I'll come. But how can I hear your music at home? You sell CDs?"

The kid frowned at me. "I guess you're older than you look. It's a performance world, old timer. You get the downloads for free. That's supposed to hook you. Then you come and buy a ticket to see us."

"Got it. What's your band's name?"

"First, it was Fools of Nature. But I changed it to Sky Kool and the Palpable Hits."

"Sweet," I said.

He grinned.

I noticed that Joshua Kraytower had picked up his black book and opened it where an old-fashioned pencil split the pages. He wrote something and then closed the book.

Spot came running across the lawn toward us. He leaped over a garden area near one of the marble maidens, landed on the stone terrace, and came to a stop at the edge of the pool.

"Whoa," Sky said in a shaky voice. "Is that bad boy safe?" He turned his legs to the far side of the lounge chair and put both feet on the terrace as if ready to run.

Joshua looked like he was getting ready to climb up into one of the marble maiden's arms.

"Meet Spot," I said. "Don't worry, he's friendly."

Spot walked over and drank out of the pool. Then he shook his head, water flying in a large arc from his flopping jowls.

"That's a Great Dane, right?" Sky asked. "Is he a police dog?"

"Kind of," I said.

"I always thought police dogs were German Shepherds. Or at least something way smaller. What's he do? Sniff out bad guys?"

"Yeah."

"Then what?"

"Depends. Sometimes he chews on them. Makes them admit their crimes."

"You're kidding, right?"

"No."

Spot was looking at the pool with great focus.

"What's the deal with his ear stud?" Sky asked. "It looks totally rad! All that glitters is not gold, it's diamond!"

"He's a rock star like you."

"He looks like he wants to swim," Sky said.

"He's not an eager swimmer. But he likes the splash of jumping into the water."

"Dude, that would be so cool if he jumped off the diving board!"

Joshua said something in a soft voice, a reservation perhaps. Sky responded at low volume as well. Joshua shook his head.

Sky nearly shouted at Joshua. "It's the midnight train, man!"

Josh seemed to grit his teeth.

"What's that mean, the midnight train?" I asked.

Sky grinned. "It's a metaphor. A new awesome life experience. Us songwriters think in metaphors. You've probably heard the song, Midnight Train to Georgia, by Jim Weatherly."

It sounded familiar. "Did Aretha sing it?" I said.

"Actually, she did record it, and it was great. But the best version was by Gladys Knight and the Pips. That's Joshua's favorite song, right, Josh?"

Joshua shrugged.

Sky turned to Santiago and me. He jerked his thumb toward Joshua as he spoke to us. "Joshua always feels like the character in the song. Like life is too much for him, so he wants to go back to a simpler place. A simpler time."

"It comes back to me now," Santiago said. He hummed a few notes. "'Goin' back to the world I left behind.'" He scrambled the words and music, but I recognized the classic song from his mangled rendition.

"Are you from Georgia, Joshua?"

Sky laughed and said, "He's a Bay Area rich kid. But he feels like he's a country boy from Georgia. Isn't that right, Josh?"

Joshua made another shrug.

I realized that Joshua would never talk when Sky was around. If I wanted Josh's view on anything, I'd have to get him alone.

Sky pulled out his phone. "Here, I've got it on my play list." He tapped a few times. Gladys Knight came on in her best, #1 hit form.

Sky stood up from the lounge chair and did a little dance next to the pool. It was a combination of a break dance with a wave that seemed to roll up from his hips to his shoulders and then down his arms. Then he straightened his index fingers and did a little soft shoe down along the pool, while he used his pointed fingers to gesture with the beat.

Spot walked along behind him, his tail on slow speed, his head tilted as if trying to understand the unusual kid.

Sky did a pirouette, gently pet Spot along the ridge of his neck, then leaped back as if he'd gotten an electric shock. "See that, Josh? The man with the plan pet the mane of the Dane."

Off to my side, Sergeant Santiago murmured to me in a near whisper. "I guess you nailed 'regaling.' They are rapt. Neither one is thinking about anything but your hound and the 'midnight train' metaphor possibilities. You can see the whites of the skinny kid's eyes."

I leaned toward Santiago and spoke equally softly. "I'll accept your regaling acknowledgment. Next, I'll hit you with a euphemism."

In my peripheral vision I saw Joshua watching Spot, then turning to watch us, then turning back to Spot.

Sky spoke over Gladys's wonderful voice.

"So what's it gonna be, Mr. Plainclothes? Your dog gonna take the Midnight Train to Georgia?" He pointed at the diving board.

"I'll make a deal with you guys," I said. "I'll get him to jump off the diving board if you agree to answer any questions Sergeant Santiago or I ask."

"How long is the time period?" Sky asked.

"Forever."

Joshua spoke in a soft voice. "Don't do it, Sky."

"Why not, man? You gotta learn to live. You can't turn down glorious opportunities just because you're sensibly cautious. That ain't livin', dude."

I watched Sky and Josh. Gladys was singing about how the man was dreaming he'd be a star, yet found out that such dreams don't usually come true. I spoke loudly. "But I should warn you, when he jumps in, it makes a serious splash." I leaned over toward Santiago. "That's the euphemism."

"A serious splash," Santiago said back.

I nodded.

Sky said, "What do you say, Josh?"

Josh hesitated. It was the standard childhood dilemma. The shy kid reluctant to agree with the extroverted kid, wondering what unforeseen trouble lurks. "No one cares what we do with the pool," Josh finally said. "Sometimes dad just sits here and reads his old-fashioned paper. But almost no one ever swims."

"Awesome, Josh!" Sky turned toward me. "That's a green light, Mr. Plainclothes! Let's swim with the dog!" He looked at Spot then back to me. "What do we do?"

I took Spot's collar and walked him to the deep end of the pool. I bent down and showed him the water, splashed my hand in it. "You can jump in, Largeness. Cool off." I pulled out a doggie biscuit and showed it to him. He tried to grab it, but I jerked my hand back. I tugged on his collar until he stepped up onto the diving board. I held my other hand palm out. "You stay here, and I'll say when to jump."

I walked back to the shallow end of the pool and held out the biscuit.

"Okay, Spot. Jump in and swim to me and get the treat."

Both Sky and Josh stared as if they were about to witness a circus animal perform a grand trick.

Spot stepped down off the board, trotted around the pool, and reached for the treat.

"No, you have to jump in the water and swim." I walked him back to the deep end, repeated my words and movements, making a bigger example of splashing in the water, got him back up on the board, went back to the shallow end, and gave him the command.

He trotted around yet again.

I pulled the treat away. We made a third attempt. As he started to step off the board, I stepped forward and held my hand out, said 'no,' and bent down and splashed at the water.

He hesitated and stayed up on the board. That told me that he definitely understood. But I didn't know if he'd do as requested.

I bent down and held the treat out just above the water.

He walked to the end of the board, lowered his head and looked at the water three feet below. It was one of the goofy Great Dane positions, the lowered head making his jowls flop open and rendering the huge carnivore with big fangs a bit cartoonish.

I called out again. And again. He took a step back as if to give up, then took a step forward and then hesitated yet again.

Then he leaped.

Sky shrieked with delight, then gasped with shock.

When a Great Dane leaps off a diving board into water, the result is the opposite of sleek and grace. All 170 pounds of the animal creates a chest and belly flop of Goliath proportions. The amount of ejected water is double the weight of the dog. It rises in a turquoise curtain that ascends just a few feet before it explodes outward.

I had already made three fast steps back before the soaking shock wave arced through the air and soaked Sky and Joshua.

And Santiago.

Santiago leaped out of his chair. He stood looking down at his body and drooping arms, all dripping water.

"I was warned," he said, shaking his head. "'A big splash' was a euphemism. You warned me. How stupid can I get."

I looked up to see Sky and Joshua off on the grass. Sky was shrieking with delight and dancing around in circles. Joshua had found a towel and was using it to dry off his sketch book.

"That was SO AWESOME!" Sky shouted. He grabbed Joshua and shook him by the shoulders. "We've never seen anything like that! Am I right?!"

Joshua pulled away from Sky's touch. "Yeah, you're right," Joshua said in a low voice.

Spot climbed the pool steps, up and out of the water. He shook himself. The spray went all the way to Sky and Joshua on one side and to Santiago and me on the other.

Spot walked over and put his nose on my treat pocket.

I pulled one out, and he nearly took off my fingers as he grabbed it.

"Good boy, Largeness. You done good."

The kids came back. Sky pet Spot. Joshua watched from a distance.

"Okay, dude," Sky said. "Ask away. Any question in the world. We owe you."

"I'll save my serious questions for later," I said. I was thinking about how to get Joshua Kraytower to talk. "Joshua, I'm curious about the song. Midnight Train to Georgia." I said.

He made a small nod.

"Is it just that you like the song, or is there anything in particular about the song that draws you?"

Joshua shrugged. "It's more about, like, stuff I've never experienced."

He paused.

I waited.

"I've never been on a train," he said. "I've never been to Georgia."

"Tell him the real reason," Sky said. Without waiting for

Joshua to answer, Sky said, "Joshua, here, is a nature writer."

"Reader, mostly," Joshua said in a small voice.

Sky continued. "Josh has a thing for trees. He's always writing in his black book."

Sky paused as if waiting for Joshua to join in. "So anyway," Sky said, "Josh writes about some kind of principles having to do with trees and such." Another pause.

"And that connects to trains?" I said. "Or Georgia?"

Sky looked at Joshua, waiting for him to answer. But Sky was too impatient to wait. "Joshua's favorite writer is some lady who writes books about nature and trees. Principles, too, right Josh? And this writer runs some kind of nature-writing center in Georgia."

"What's the writer's name?" I asked. "Have I heard of her?"

Sky looked at Joshua. "Tell him, dude."

"Roxanne Monales," Joshua said.

"And the Midnight Train?" I said.

Sky answered, "Josh has never gone anywhere, so I told him he should take the midnight train to Georgia and visit the nature place. Then his writing and his reading and the nature place would all come together with his favorite song. Perfect, right?"

I turned and looked at Joshua.

He finally spoke. "You can't just visit the place. It's like, for scholars. Big time naturalists. You have to get invited."

Sky was shaking his head. "Dude, that's just what they say on their website. Everybody knows you have to be the squeaky wheel. You gotta bug 'em before they notice you."

"But I'm a nobody. I'm just a kid. Maybe when I'm an adult."

"You're just afraid of traveling on a train." Sky looked at me. "He's never gone anywhere except on his daddy's jet. Or in the SUV limo. He's never even flown commercial." Sky turned toward Joshua. "Trust me, dude, someday you're gonna ride that midnight train. You're gonna conquer your fear of everything. The only way stuff gets to seem normal is if you try it."

I sensed that under Sky's abrasive style was a genuine affection for Joshua. But once again, Sky did all the talking. I tried another question direct to Joshua.

"Joshua, I'm wondering what are the kinds of things you've never done?"

Joshua just looked at me.

"We had a deal…" I said.

He glanced at Sky, then looked down at the ground.

"You gotta answer his question, Josh. There's a ton of normal stuff you've never done. Some because you're a rich kid. But most because you're just…" Sky hesitated as he looked at Joshua. "Because you're not sure if maybe you're too afraid."

Joshua's brow was more furrowed than before. It seemed like part worry and part sadness. He looked at Spot. "I've never walked a dog."

"What's that mean?" I asked.

"Just what I said. We've never had a dog. I've never had a friend with a dog. I've seen it done. But I've never experienced it. Do you think I could walk your dog?"

It was a heartbreaking question. The rich kid who had everything yet had never had the simple pleasure of walking a dog.

"Yes, of course. I think Spot would love it."

"How would I do it?"

"Let me show you. Step over here."

I took hold of Spot's collar. Joshua came near. I turned him so he was facing the same direction as Spot.

"Take hold of his collar like this." I showed him.

Joshua slowly slid his hand into Spot's collar. He kept his arm out from his side as if he held the collar of a man-eating dragon.

"Now step closer so you are right next to him. Closer still. You want his shoulder to brush your thigh."

Eventually, we got Joshua into position.

Joshua looked afraid and uncertain. For a kid who had no familiarity with pets, the prospect of holding a dog that outweighed him by 50 pounds was no doubt frightening.

"Now that you have his collar," I said, "you just walk. He'll come with you. He loves to walk. But hold on firmly." I let go of Spot.

"What does that mean, firmly?" Joshua's knuckles were white.

"As you witnessed when he jumped off the diving board, Spot can be enthusiastic. If he sees a squirrel or something, he will pull. If you were to let go, he might run. But if you keep a good grip on him, he'll stay at your side."

Joshua looked at me, then back at Spot, his eyes wider than normal. Joshua was rigid.

"How do I turn him when we, you know, get to the water or something?"

"You just turn yourself and give a little tug on his collar, and he will turn with you."

I rubbed Spot's back. "Go walk with Joshua, boy." I turned to the kid. "Go ahead, it's okay."

Joshua took a tentative step. Then another. Soon they were walking down the lawn toward the lake.

Walking a dog was the most normal thing in the world for most kids. For Joshua, it looked like it was the most dangerous thing he'd ever tried.

Joshua and Spot made a big circle around the spacious lawn, then repeated it. Then they walked through the stone gate toward the Piazza Venezia parking area and disappeared.

Santiago moved the lounge chairs onto the grass in a spot of sunshine. We were drying nicely when Joshua approached with Spot.

"Sergeant," I said in a soft voice as I turned toward Santiago. "You want to jump in here with questions?"

"My jurisdiction," he said. "But you're doing a good job at what we hired you to do."

As Joshua approached, the boy had a look on his face that I couldn't place. Like he was about to grin but didn't know how.

"Go okay?" I said.

"That was…" He looked at Spot, then brought him to a stop near us. "I've never had an experience like that."

FIVE

"How do I let go of him?" Joshua asked.

"You can just release your grip."

Joshua let go, consciously straightening his fingers.

Spot trotted away, exploring.

"More questions," I said.

"Part of the deal," Sky said.

"Sky, how do you know the Kraytowers?" I asked.

He shrugged. "I work for Josh's dad as a driver. But I'm mainly just a friend. Does that description suit you, Josh?"

It was Joshua's turn to shrug. "I s'pose."

"Do you live here in Tahoe, Sky?"

"One of my band mates and I rent a summer cabin down the road. A one-room place. The door to the bathroom is a curtain, and the shower is just a part of the bathroom floor with some waterproof paint on it and a drain in the middle. But the cabin's got this funky roof with a deck on it. You get to it by a ladder stairs like on a boat. From up there, we can see the lake in one direction and the top of Eagle Rock in the other. Way rad."

"I always wanted a roof like that," I said. "Like that Carole King song, Up On The Roof."

"We cover a couple of her songs. Those old songwriters really knew their gig."

"How did you meet Josh and his family?" I asked.

"I was a car park valet at the Beach Restaurant down the way. Met Josh there when his dad and Josh came for the triple B. Beach, Burgers, and Beer."

Sky said, "Since then, his old man has had me park cars here at the house when he has parties. And I've been driving him to and from his jet."

"Were you parking cars here the night James Lightfoot

died?"

He made a solemn nod.

"Did you know Lightfoot?"

"No."

"Did you know of him?"

"No."

"Just for the record, is there anyone who can say where you were when the man died?"

Sky Kool smiled. "This is neat. Like a TV show. You're asking if I have an alibi, right?"

"Yeah." In the corner of my peripheral vision I saw Santiago grin.

"No," Sky said. "I have no alibi. I was running back and forth all evening, doing the hustle. I heard he just—you know—died. A heart attack or something. But if someone made him croak, I definitely could have done it."

That was a first, a potential suspect volunteering his access and lack of alibi. Which, I realized, meant nothing if Lightfoot didn't die of an Agatha Christie heart attack.

"How did it work?" I asked. "Where did you park the cars?"

"There's the main lot around the sculpture fountain, which will fit a dozen cars. Take the drive up toward the highway, there's space in the trees where we can fit about twenty cars. The rest go out on the West Shore Highway. Eighty-nine."

"That's a long way," I said. "You walk back and forth to the highway."

That made Sky laugh. "Try running. Sprinting. If some old dude and his wife are gasping for breath in the high-altitude air and they've obviously got knee or back problems or whatever, and they're leaning against the fountain sculpture, and he shoves a Ben Franklin in your hand and says he'd appreciate it if you could fetch his Jaguar on the fly, you do your Superman imitation through the trees, out to the highway. We keep some mountain bikes nearby for the fastest retrievals. They get us out to the cars fast. We leave the bikes in the dirt and drive back. Then, when we have a break, we walk out and bring the bikes back. Car park science. So I could have done it," Sky reiterated. "Whatever it is. Scare the guy to death. Book me. Drag me in and stick me in a lineup. They'll put me in prison, and before they know it, I'll have those inmates singing Palpable Hit songs."

"Joshua, did you know James Lightfoot?"

Joshua took his time. "I'd met him but I didn't know him. He was kind of a sycophant around my dad."

"You're out of my league on that," I said. "What's a sycophant?"

"It's a word my dad uses. Like, the guy always sucked up to my dad. Acted sort of groveling at my dad's feet. I don't think he was stupid. But he acted like my dad was God. It was embarrassing."

"Can either of you think of anyone who didn't like Lightfoot?"

Sky shrugged. "Josh?" he said.

"No."

"So if I toss out the idea that someone might have killed him, what is your response to that?"

Joshua looked at Sky.

"It was a hit," Sky said. "It only makes sense."

"Why do you think it was a hit?"

"Your bud, there, is a cop. And you look like a cop. Giant hound sniffing around. I saw you do that wild goose chase searching thing down on the patio. Gotta be a hit. It's the only reason you'd be here. A palpable hit, for sure."

"Palpable Hits is the name of your band," I said. "Where'd you get the idea for those words?"

Sky shrugged. "I dunno. Heard it somewhere, I guess."

"Joshua, is your dad home?"

"No. He left early to go to San Francisco."

"When will he be back?"

"I don't know. He's always flying someplace."

I asked, "Can either of you think of any reason why someone would want to hurt Lightfoot?"

They both shook their heads.

"Has either of you heard anyone say anything negative about Lightfoot? Anything that would suggest bad feelings or resentment?"

Joshua shook his head.

"Nope," Sky said.

"Has anything unusual happened recently."

"What qualifies as unusual?" Sky asked.

"Something that didn't happen a year or two ago."

Sky looked at Joshua. "Tell him about the hang ups, man."

Joshua looked uncomfortable.

"We made a deal with Plainclothes, here," Sky said.

Joshua didn't speak.

"Okay, I'll tell him," Sky said. "Nature man's been getting hang-up phone calls."

"Not just me," Joshua said.

"Do you mean, the phone rings, you answer, and the person on the other end of the line doesn't speak?"

"Pretty much," Joshua said. "I think it's only happened three times to me. A couple of times to the nanny and the housekeeper."

"Mr. Casteem?"

"No, the housekeeper in San Francisco. Aria."

"Who is the nanny?" I asked.

"Maya. She's not really a nanny anymore since I got older. But dad keeps her on as part of the house staff."

"Do any of these calls come to your cell phone?"

"No. They come to the land line at the San Francisco house."

"Does it show the caller's number?"

"Normally, yeah. But these calls say 'no caller ID.'"

"How do you answer such calls?" I asked.

"What do you mean?"

"Do you say hello? Or state your name?"

"I just say hello. Aria and Maya say, 'Kraytower residence. Aria speaking.' Like that."

"When do the calls come?"

"Usually right after dad leaves for work. Sometimes after Aria or Maya leave."

"And the caller says nothing."

"Right. No words. No breathing."

"Could it be one of the quirks of the phone system? A ring followed by a dead line?"

Joshua shook his head. "I don't think so. I can hear the caller hang up."

Sky said, "It's like the caller is trying to find out if anyone is home. Like he's scoping out the house for a burglary."

Sky looked at his phone. "Gotta go, dude," he said to Joshua.

I thanked Sky and Joshua for talking to us and stood to leave. Joshua walked over to Spot and pet him. Then he turned and headed for the house. I took Spot's collar, and Santiago led us back up to the Piazza Venezia parking area. Sky was in a hurry as he road a mountain bike out the driveway toward the highway. He was still wearing just his swim short.

I stopped at Santiago's patrol vehicle. "Any thoughts?" I asked.

"About what?"

I glanced back toward the lawn and pool. "Talking to those two kids. And the houseman earlier. What's his name? Casteem."

"Sometimes," Santiago said, "when I'm around a group of people, I get the sense that someone is in danger. It's like a sixth sense thing."

I nodded. "And that happened now?"

Santiago nodded. "Kraytower's kid. I think there's something he's not telling us."

"That's what I thought. I'm not sure what the danger is, though. Physical? Emotional?"

"Probably all of the above," Santiago said.

"Does the threat come from his dad? Or his friend Sky? Or the rest of the world?"

"Maybe all of the above." He looked off toward the lake. "You'll look into this some more?"

"Yeah."

Spot and I got into the Jeep and drove out to the highway. Santiago followed us out. We turned left toward Emerald Bay. He turned north toward Tahoe City.

SIX

I drove around the south side of the lake, through the throngs of tourists at Emerald Bay and Camp Richardson. I had no need to stop at my office, but I turned up Kingsbury Grade to visit Street Casey at her entomology lab nearby.

When I let Spot out of the Jeep, he ran to her door, partly to see Street, mostly to see Blondie. The door opened and Blondie came out as if shot out of a cannon, and she and Spot disappeared into the woods focused on nothing but play.

"It's possibly the singular characteristic of the species," Street said, pointing at the dogs as Spot raced after Blondie.

"Play?" I said, as I bent down to give Street a kiss and a hug.

"Many other species play, as well," she said, returning the hug. "Otters slide on snow. Dolphins leap in the bow waves of ships, birds perform what looks like synchronized aerobatics, young horses and deer and kittens and lion cubs all run and play. But canines seem to have a particular focus on fun."

"More than any other creature, I agree. Maybe we should do our version of chase and tumble." I ran my hands down the curves of her back. "We could unstack the boxes from the cot in your back room."

"I'm not sure I would call that play," she said. "But the allure is…" she turned her head as a vehicle pulled into the parking lot.

It was Sergeant Diamond Martinez in his patrol vehicle.

He got out. "I see I'm interrupting your embrace. I hope nothing more."

"Why would you think that?" I said. Maybe my voice sounded a bit sarcastic.

He turned to get back into his SUV.

"We were just going to have a snack, Diamond," Street said,

ever gracious. "Would you care to join us?"

Diamond regarded us. "I'll make it fast. I realize we all have lots on our schedule."

He came over and we went inside Street's lab.

Street reached into her mini fridge. She pulled out a glass of celery sticks and held the glass toward us.

"There's probably no chance you've got donuts in there," I said.

She scowled at me.

Diamond reached into his shirt pocket and pulled out a bar in a plastic wrapper. "I've got granola. That's healthier than donuts."

"May I?" Street asked. She took the bar and looked at the fine print on the side. "This has as much sugar as a Snicker's bar. More, even, than donuts."

Diamond looked at me, no doubt hoping for guidance.

I raised my eyebrows.

"Probably why it tastes so good," Diamond said. Chastened, he put the granola bar back in his shirt pocket.

Diamond and I each took one piece of celery and nibbled like introverted rabbits.

I told them about Sergeant Santiago and Spot, and our visit to hedge fund boss Carston Kraytower's palace, and the man named James Lightfoot who died of a heart attack.

"I just talked to Sergeant Santiago," Diamond said, "trading work gossip. He mentioned something about an Agatha Christie heart attack last night."

I chewed some celery. "James Lightfoot was supposedly in good health. So his boss, the hedge fund guy, is really stressed by his employee's death. We don't yet know that his death was a heart attack. But Dame Agatha might be able to dream up how it could be possible."

"Had a death like that last week on this side of the lake. Near Genoa Peak up above your cabin. Guy rode his mountain bike off a cliff on the Tahoe Rim Trail."

"So the cause of death was an accident," I said.

"Looks like it."

"Any witnesses?"

"I spoke to the two witnesses who called it in. They said the victim was up ahead of them on the trail, riding fast in the same direction. They said another biker went past them going fast and then nearly rear-ended the victim as he passed him. The victim suddenly swerved and shot off the trail. There was a steep drop off. The man landed on the rocks about eighty feet below. The witnesses hiked down and found the guy's head mashed. There was no pulse. Maybe we'll learn more when the toxicology test results come back. Should be any day now."

"What was the victim's name?"

"Sebastian Perry. A Bay Area guy."

We nibbled more celery.

"Did you find anything at the Kraytower house?" Street asked.

"I had Spot look around. He found nothing but a pinecone and some monofilament. But there was lots of play, which is maybe why Spot didn't find anything else. Spot jumped off the pool's diving board and splashed much of the water over the hedge fund owner's son and his friend and Santiago too."

"Uh, oh," Diamond said.

There was a small bark at the door. I opened it, and Blondie and Spot trotted in. Spot had a long stick in his mouth. When he tried to come through the door, the stick hit on both sides of the door frame. He backed up, then came forward again. The stick hit a second time.

Spot bit down on the stick, pulverizing it into pieces. Now it was easy to walk through the door. He still had one chunk of wood in his mouth.

When Blondie lay down on her bed, Spot got down on the hard cool floor, elbows spread like outriggers. He gripped the remaining stick between his paws and proceeded to chew the stick into little pieces.

"I'm so sorry for the mess," I said, standing up. "I'll grab your broom."

"I'll get it later," Street said. "I wouldn't want you to interrupt your celery snack."

"No," Diamond said, "we wouldn't want that." He took another bite of his celery, holding it up near mine to show that he was nearly half done while I was barely getting started.

I took another nibble. "You ever notice, one piece of celery lasts a lot longer than a donut," I said.

He nodded, chewing his celery carefully.

"Why did you stop by?" I asked Diamond.

"Finished lunch early. I knew Street would have some dessert in her fridge. Social hour with celery is always a favorite."

Street's eyes narrowed. I grinned.

Five minutes later, we left. As Diamond got into his sheriff's vehicle, I noticed one of his shirts on the passenger seat. The fabric had a large tear in it.

I pointed. "Tear your shirt?"

"Sí. I was closing a file cabinet door and pinched the fabric. Then I turned and tore it almost in half. Lucky I had another shirt at the sheriff's office."

Spot walked up next to me and stuck his head in Diamond's window. Diamond leaned to the right and held up his left hand to block Spot's nose.

"This boy gives me an idea," he said. Diamond reached over, picked up the shirt, spread out the fabric, and found the tear. With a vigorous jerk, he tore it further until the shirt was in two pieces. He gathered up the two pieces and handed the fabric ball to me. "You can use this for scent training. One piece to scent him on, another piece to hide and let him find it."

"You could be a dog trainer," I said. "Such an immediate grasp of the complexities of dog training."

"I hope the shirt doesn't smell too bad."

I gave the shirt a quick sniff. "No. You smell like a rose." I jerked my head toward Spot. "This guy will love it."

"He likes roses?"

"I don't think so in general. But a Mexican rose like you, it might be just the ticket."

Diamond frowned. "Never took you for an anthophile."

"What's that?"

"An organism that likes flowers."

"Like bugs?"

"Or people," Diamond said.

Spot tried to sniff the pieces of shirt as I held them above the roof of the patrol vehicle.

"Perfect," I said.

"What will be his reward if he can find this Mexican rose?" Diamond had put his hand back up as a barrier between him and Spot.

"A doggie biscuit?"

Diamond raised one eyebrow. "Does that really work?"

"Sometimes. He likes the biscuits, but I couldn't say he loves them."

Diamond pulled the granola bar out of his shirt pocket and held it up. "Use one of these as a treat instead. I bet he'll love it."

Spot pushed his head farther into the vehicle, his nostrils flexing.

I said, "You heard Street say they're no better than donuts. Too much sugar to be healthy."

"Isn't that the point of a treat?" Diamond said. "When was the last time you drove around town looking for a good place to buy a perfect piece of celery?"

"Good point," I said. I took the granola bar and stuffed it into the pants pocket that was on the other side from Spot. "Thanks," I said as I patted the roof of his vehicle. Diamond drove away.

Back at my cabin, I went out on the deck with Spot. I waited until he wasn't paying me any attention. Very casually, I went back inside. I shut the slider behind me. Spot stayed where he lay, looking out across the lake.

I got a paper grocery bag out of my kitchen nook, tiptoed into the bedroom and opened the closet door. I found a shirt and one of my socks in my laundry basket. I looked on the closet rod. Usually there are a few articles of Street's clothing. I flipped through hangers. I found a hooded sweatshirt that I knew she'd recently worn. Hanging on a hook was one of her scarfs, also something that I remembered her wearing out on my deck a few evenings before.

I put the items of clothing into the paper bag and folded over the top. I now had two items from each person in the paper bag.

When I came out of the bedroom, Spot was standing on the deck, nose to the slider window, trying to see me through the glass. In the same way that dogs can tell you're about to go for a walk no matter how carefully you hide your intentions, Spot could tell I was up to something unusual.

I let him inside and gave him a pet. He walked around looking for things out of place, like a mother suspicious of what her teenage son had been up to when she wasn't looking.

I picked up the bag with the clothing, and went outside, shutting Spot inside. He was no doubt confused, but he would be let out shortly.

To stay out of Spot's view from the windows, I walked around the cabin toward the private road that I share with my vacation-home neighbors. Like most times of the year, few of them were around despite Tahoe's world's-best summertime weather. Mrs. Duchamp and her poodle Treasure were the only neighbors I'd seen in days. But despite being in residence, they rarely made an appearance outside. Mrs. Duchamp seemed to prefer looking at the lake through her large windows rather than going outside and having to physically confront the broiling high-altitude sun.

I walked across the road to the edge of the forest. I stuffed Street's scarf into a Manzanita bush. Next, I went over to my Jeep, reached up into the wheel well and balanced my sock on top of the right front tire. Third, I took one of the torn pieces of Diamond's shirt over to the entrance of my parking pad and put it under a large rock, with just enough fabric sticking out to be visible. Or smellable as the case might be.

When I went back inside, Spot sniffed me, curious about where I'd been and what I'd been doing.

"Ready for some scent training?" I said with enthusiasm.

Spot moved his head toward my pocket, the one with Diamond's granola bar.

"Let's go outside and have some fun!"

Spot saw that I wasn't going to pull out Diamond's treat. He walked over to his bed, turned once, then lay down, crossed his front paws, and looked at me with droopy eyes.

Like all Great Dane owners, I knew that, of all the working breeds, Great Danes have the least work ethic. They just want to lounge on your couch and eat popcorn with you. But I was certain that Spot would want a biscuit or a granola bar. And the fact that I didn't own a couch made the choices easier for a dog.

I pulled a dog biscuit out of the cargo pants pocket where I routinely keep several.

He looked at it but didn't get up.

"Fat free," I said with enthusiasm, giving the biscuit a little wave. "Low calorie and low salt and low sugar. It could even be high fiber, but I haven't verified that."

Spot lay his head down on his crossed paws.

"Okay, boy, what about granola?" I pulled Diamond's plastic-wrapped granola bar out of my other pocket. I removed the wrap and waved the bar through the air.

Spot lifted his head, flexed his nostrils, and jumped to his feet.

I moved to the door, opened it, and stepped out, still holding the granola bar where Spot could see it.

Spot came outside after me.

"Good boy! Here's a treat!" I broke off a small piece, and fed it to him.

He inhaled it with an unnecessary excess of saliva dripping off his jowls.

I put the rest of the bar in my pocket. "Want more? Then sit."

Spot sniffed at my pocket.

"Gotta earn it, boy. Sit." I pushed down on his rear and got him to sit.

"Remember the game, Find the Suspect? Sure you do."

He was still looking at my pocket.

I pulled Street's sweatshirt out of the paper bag. I put the sweatshirt on his nose. "Smell this, boy? Take a whiff."

He turned his head. Maybe I was suffocating him with the

sweatshirt. I put it back over his nose.

"Do you have the scent?" I gave his chest a shake to communicate excitement. "Okay, Spot, find the suspect!" I dropped my hand next to his head, pointing across the road. I gave him a push and patted his rear as he jumped to his feet.

Spot loped off toward the street. He made a straight line toward Diamond's partial torn shirt that I'd hidden under the rock near the road. He grabbed the shirt, pulled it out from under the rock, and ran back to me, chomping on the fabric.

"Good job, Spot! But this is the wrong suspect. This is Diamond's shirt, not Street's scarf. Her scarf is across the road in the Manzanita bush."

Spot wagged. He again looked at my pocket.

With some effort, I removed the shirt from his mouth as I said, "You'll get your treat when you bring back the correct clothing." The fabric was soggy with dog slobber. When I headed back out to replace it under the rock, I felt something in the shirt. There was a lump inside the fabric where there was the most dog moisture.

I spread the piece of shirt open. The fabric included the shirt portion that had the shirt pocket. I felt the pocket.

The lump.

I slid my fingers into the pocket and pulled out a bit of granola bar.

I carried the bit of shirt and granola bar back and stood in front of Spot. "Would a German Shepherd ignore his training just because of a sugar treat?" I said. "That would be like me shirking my work responsibilities to focus on a donut." As soon as I said it, I realized that I'd probably done just that on more than one occasion.

I tossed Spot the soggy bit of granola. He caught it, teeth clicking.

"Did you even swallow?"

Spot looked at me and then looked at my pocket.

I opened the cabin door and tossed the soggy shirt fabric inside. Then I put Spot through the scent-and-search motions several more times. Without sugary granola calling to him from the forest, he did much better, eventually finding and retrieving the correct pieces of clothing—Street's scarf and my sock—when I scented him on the ones in the paper bag.

I rewarded him with lavish praise. He ignored my comments and stared at my pocket until I gave him a treat and then a headlock hug of praise.

The rest of the day was routine. That evening, I sweet-talked with Street on the phone and went to bed early.

SEVEN

The next morning, my phone rang early. I pushed myself up. Struggled to figure out where I was.

The phone rang again. I grabbed it and pressed the answer button.

I lifted the phone to my head. "Owen McKenna," I said.

"Hello. My name is Carston Kraytower," a voice said. "I'm calling because I have a house in Tahoe, and the Placer County Sheriff recommended you," the man said.

"It's very early." I looked at the clock. The numbers said 7:00 a.m. What kind of a person calls at 7 a.m.? Then I remembered who Kraytower was. The kind of person who creates a hugely successful business. "Is this an emergency?"

"Oh, sorry. The sheriff said he thought you were an early riser."

It was a ridiculous idea even though I did it now and then.

"What can I help you with?" I asked.

"You're the private investigator, right? I think you've already been out to my house."

"Yes, I'm an investigator. The sheriff and Sergeant Santiago had me come over to your house yesterday to check around. When someone dies, they like to make certain that everything is okay."

"There wasn't just one death. Two employes of mine have died. One was at my house. The other was also in Tahoe, but in a different county. Across the lake. They both look like natural deaths. They probably are natural deaths. One was a bicycle crash. The other looked like a heart attack. I'm hoping you can investigate. For me. Like you did for the sheriff." He paused.

"Yeah," I said, still trying to wake up.

"Having you investigate is okay, right?" he said. "I don't want to cause some kind of problem with the sheriff."

"Yeah, it's okay." I was wondering if I could still sound lucid if I went into the kitchen nook and got the coffee going while I talked. Probably not.

He asked, "Is that common, cops hiring private investigators?"

"Sometimes," I said again. It was just two syllables, but my enunciation seemed good for sleep talking. I didn't want to tell Kraytower that it wasn't the brilliance of private investigators the cops were after but our willingness to do crappy work they didn't want to do.

"The sheriff told me you didn't find anything."

I was trying to remember what I'd found, but my brain fog was too thick. Maybe I could call him back after I'd had coffee.

"Who else died besides Lightfoot?"

"Sebastian Perry. He was mountain biking on the Tahoe Rim Trail last week. He went off a cliff. Near some mountain called Genoa Peak."

The mountain biker Diamond told me about.

"Was he biking with anyone?" I asked.

"Not in the sense of going out with a group. Perry was a solo-type guy in most things."

"Thus it was an accident," I said.

"So it seems. But I have a hard time accepting that two of my business associates have died within days of each other."

"Yet it happens nevertheless, right?" I said.

"There's something else," he said. "I've gotten strange emails. From an anonymous sender. And Jim Lightfoot—the colleague who just died from a heart attack—he also got the same emails."

"What do the emails say?"

"I don't have them in front of me, but one was about freezing blood. And the other was about poison."

That woke me up. "Did you tell the sheriff about the emails?"

"No. They came to a household email account that I don't use very much. I log on maybe once a week. I first saw them yesterday, the day after Jim died."

"You just said that Lightfoot told you about the same emails, so you knew about them before he died."

"I knew about them, yes. But I didn't know they were also sent to me. To look at them, you'd think they were spam emails. You know, spurious messages designed to get you to click on a link so you end up downloading malware. This morning, I looked at the emails again, and I realized there was no link to click on. Jim had missed it, too. That's when I became concerned. So I'm calling you."

"Did Perry get these emails?"

"I don't know."

"Why call me and not the sheriff?" I said.

"Maybe I should call the sheriff," Kraytower said. "But, frankly, I think I already wore him out with my stress. When Jim Lightfoot died, I was kind of a pain in the ass to the sheriff and his officers. I wanted them to check every little thing because Lightfoot's death was high profile. And of course, the sheriff wanted to be certain that there's nothing out of the ordinary."

"Like freezing blood and poison," I said.

"Right. So I'm hoping you can give things an extra look. Kind of like insurance, so to speak."

"I'm not a show detective."

"What does that mean?" Kraytower sounded irritated.

"I don't work to create an image. I don't talk to the press. I won't go on TV and say that you or your company is squeaky clean."

Kraytower didn't respond. Maybe he was about to fire me before he'd even hired me.

"We should get together and discuss terms," I said.

"You mean pay? Not necessary. I'll pay your going rate. If the sheriff is willing to hire you, you must be fair. I can pay in advance, if you want. Email me a Paypal invoice."

"I still need to meet you and discuss the case. I'll need your input on the men who died, the circumstances. I should come to your house."

"But you were already there." Kraytower sounded frustrated.

"I didn't speak to you. I'll need to talk to you, in person, at your house."

"Really? Is this like me sizing up a potential investor?"

"If you want to think of it that way, sure."

"My schedule is packed. I'm in San Francisco right now, and I leave tomorrow for New York. I suppose you could come down to The City and we could talk this evening."

I got the sense that Kraytower was used to solving problems by picking up the phone. Make a demand, and pay whatever it cost to make the problem go away.

"Your employees died in Tahoe. I'll want to talk to you here."

"But I'm not the focus of the problem. I'm more like, I don't know, the victim."

"I'll wait until you get to Tahoe," I said.

I heard Kraytower breathing, his frustration obvious.

"I suppose I can leave earlier than I planned tomorrow and have my pilot stop in Truckee. My Tahoe driver could take me to the house to meet with you for an hour or so."

"Good," I said. "Name a time, and I'll meet you at your house."

"Eight a.m. tomorrow?" he said.

"I'll be there. Bring the emails."

EIGHT

A n hour later, Spot and I were at my office.
Spot's main office work was testing new positions on his Harlequin Great Dane camo bed. This morning he was trying out a reverse S curve, front legs and head to the left, rear legs to the right. It looked like performance art. If his black-and-white fur on his black-and-white bed could have been moved to the San Francisco Museum of Modern Art, it would draw record attendance.

My office work was making a pot of coffee and then eating a donut while I drank the coffee. Sometimes I expanded Spot's work by giving him a bite of donut. Spot and I both excelled at our jobs.

I called Diamond's cell.

"Early for you to call," he answered, no doubt seeing my name on his caller ID.

"I've been hard at work for over an hour already. Are you in the area?"

"Sí. You got coffee?"

"Coffee and donuts both," I said. "If we need celery, Street will probably be at her lab in twenty minutes. Or we could just suffer our nutritional deficiencies and see if we survive anyway."

"Cop life always entails a risk," he said. "Be there in five."

A few minutes later, Spot lifted his head and stared at the door. I don't know how he does it. I heard nothing beyond the heat clicks of the coffee pot. I don't have a good nose, but how would a nose help identify a sheriff's patrol vehicle approaching on Kingsbury Grade when there are multiple walls separating us?

Spot stood up and put his nose to the doorknob. His tail

made a kind of gentle circular motion, vaguely reminiscent of the agitator in a washing machine set on the slow, delicate setting.

Still no sound.

Yet another minute passed before his tail agitation moved to normal load. Apparently, his wag speed was proportional to the distance between him and the source of the wag motivation. Closer, faster. In another minute, I heard the telltale creaking on the office stairs. His tail got vigorous. The heavy soil setting.

The door opened.

Diamond stepped through, and Spot stuck his nose in Diamond's abdomen. Diamond proceeded to give him the full head massage, ears, neck, jaw muscles.

"I dibs the next head rub," I said.

"Hate to usurp Street Casey's role," Diamond said. He finished his rub by pulling Spot's jowls out, waving them like a plane's wings in a series of steep banks, left and right, while Diamond made dive-bombing and machine-gun sounds.

Spot's tail stayed on high speed.

"Now I'm glad you're not rubbing my head," I said.

I refilled my coffee mug and poured one for Diamond. He took it and sat in one of my visitor's chairs. He leaned back, the chair squeaking loudly, and put his feet on the front edge of my desk. I handed him a donut.

Spot looked at Diamond longingly as if to judge the likelihood that he might go for round two. Or maybe wondering if Diamond really needed all of the donut. He must have decided neither was likely because he went back to his camo mattress, turned a half circle, then lay down, this time in a C shape.

I looked at Diamond's shoes. "Few visitors dare to desecrate my thinking furniture with their footwear."

"I didn't know you were a thinker." He gestured at me. "What about your hiking boot heels hooked on the edge of your desk?"

"Good point," I said. I sipped coffee. "I was awakened this morning by a phone call from Carston Kraytower, the hedge fund guy whose employee died of a heart attack on the West Shore. He mentioned the guy you told me about, Sebastian Perry, who rode off the Tahoe Rim Trail. Perry was another one of Kraytower's employees."

"I didn't know that guy worked for your guy. It appeared the victim was one of those wild-man tourists who think they can take their mountain bike from sea level to nine thousand feet and still kick butt. Witnesses said he was riding fast and maybe a bit reckless. Probably, he got light headed from high altitude, and rode off the trail. This Kraytower say anything enlightening about Perry?"

I shook my head. "Not much. Kraytower and Lightfoot, the heart attack victim, received some emails that were quirky weird at best, threatening at worst. Maybe Perry did as well. What do you know about the mountain biking victim?" I asked.

"The guy lives in a town called Woodside, which is in San Mateo County."

"Sounds familiar," I said as I tried to remember Bay Area geography from back in my days on the San Francisco PD. "Down on the peninsula."

"South of your old stomping grounds," Diamond filled in without me asking. "In the hills west of Palo Alto and Stanford. Woodside is a pricey hangout, good for finance types who want to hang with rock stars and movie actors. These emails Kraytower got... What do they say?"

"Something about freezing blood and poison."

"Those words sound familiar," Diamond said. "But I can't place them."

"I'll get the exact wording when I meet him tomorrow morning."

NINE

At five before 8 a.m. the next day, I turned in between the stone columns on the West Shore and headed down the shiny Roman black-brick road. Spot had his head out the window, sniffing the air with enthusiasm, maybe thinking about another play session on the swimming pool diving board.

I pulled up near the fountain in the large parking area and parked next to a black Chevy stretch-limo Suburban. The vehicle had dark smoked windows and was polished as if for a photo shoot. Standing next to the Suburban at its right side, wearing black Dockers, white shirt, black jacket, and black shoes, was Joshua Kraytower's friend, Sky Kool.

He saw Spot, made a huge grin.

I rolled down the Jeep's windows. "Hey Sky, I believe you remember His Largeness and his skills on the high dive," I said.

Sky walked over, pet Spot, held his head lovingly, and started singing a Bob Hope song I'd heard in an old movie. 'Thanks for the memories...'"

Spot's tale thumped the inside of the Jeep.

"How do you know an ancient song like that?"

"A specialty of Sky Kool and The Palpable Hits. Sometimes we do covers of old songs. Old people love it."

"Old, like Boomer old?"

He nodded. "We had one audience—it must have been somebody's birthday—and practically everyone in the room was over fifty, even sixty."

"Imagine that."

"It was like we were on a cruise ship or something. So we played Beatles and Rolling Stones and Beach Boys. You shoulda seen it. Nothing but oldies, and everybody knew all the lyrics. And they danced. People in their sixties rocking out to sixties music."

I glanced at the limo. "You're doing lots of driving for Kraytower?" I said.

"At first he only used me in emergencies when his other driver was sick. But now he uses me more and more. I guess the guy recognizes inimitable style when he sees it." Sky did a little celebratory arm shake, clicked his fingers, and danced a snappy one-two footstep that made the hard heels of his black leather shoes click on the Roman bricks.

"How does he know if you're available? Does he call you when he wants a ride?"

Sky made a little head shake. "No, mostly gramps… I mean, Mr. Casteem, does the scheduling. He has this schedule for who's available for driving each day. He charts that thing out two weeks in advance." Sky glanced toward the front door of the palace, then spoke in a low voice. "The old guy looks like he would have his hands full just ordering the wine delivery and hiring the gardener. But that brain is juggling algorithms like a computer. He shoulda been an accountant or something."

"I better go before I'm late for my appointment."

Sky turned, pet Spot again, and said, "Your job, Largeness, is to keep an eye on the marble maidens." Sky put one hand on Spot's head, pointed at the sculptures with his other hand, and winked. Then he went back to the limo and resumed standing near the right, rear passenger door.

I walked up to the grand front door and was raising my hand to press the bell when the door opened.

As with the first time I'd been there, Mr. Casteem, the houseman, wore the same colors, black pants, white shirt, black jacket, and he leaned on his cane. Despite the man's lack of a smile, he had a pleasant look on his face. His white moustache and Van Dyke beard were freshly trimmed, as evenly mowed as a putting green.

"Mr. Casteem," I said. "Good to see you again."

"You're here to meet with Mr. Kraytower," he said. "His driver just dropped him off. I'll let him know you've arrived."

Casteem turned, his cane tightly gripped at his thigh as if that leg had a bad knee and his tight grip would steady his tremor. Casteem walked back inside the front door and lifted a telephone handset off the wall. He pressed a few buttons, then said a few words in a low voice, and hung up.

"Mr. Kraytower will be down shortly."

We stood in silence for a moment.

As if uncomfortable just standing near me, the man said, "Mr. Kraytower always presents me as Mr. Gerard Casteem. I was introduced to the sheriff that way, too." Casteem lowered his voice. "The household help call me Mr. Casteem. But most other people call me Gary." He glanced behind him as if worried that Kraytower might be near.

"Or Gramps, if I remember correctly." I made a small smile.

Casteem looked embarrassed. He looked out toward where Sky stood next to the Suburban. "That friend of Joshua's is quite impertinent. He says his name is Sky Kool, and he thinks he's being cute. He's a musician, so I suspect it's a stage name. I think he feels that, because the Sky Kool name sounds so casual, it gives him permission to be casual in his dealings with others. I was going to scold him for not showing respect for elders. But I didn't want to make Joshua feel bad. That poor boy has enough stress to deal with. So I decided that if those boys kept their gramps jokes behind my back, I would ignore it. Whether those boys believe it or not, I was a boy once, myself."

"He told me you schedule the driving for Mr. Kraytower."

Casteem nodded. "Mr. Kraytower's other driver is older like me and wants to reduce his hours. So I called Sky last night and asked him to pick up Mr. Kraytower this morning at the Truckee airport. And when you're done with your appointment, he will drive Mr. Kraytower back to his plane."

We were silent once again. "Does Sky have another job when he's not working as a chauffeur?" I asked. "Or is it just music?"

"I believe that's his main activity when he's not driving. I heard he has a band. But sometimes, Mr. Kraytower has me put the boy on call for several days at a time. At those times, he has to stay within a few minutes of the house. And he's sworn to not drink or do any drugs when he's on call. Because when he gets the call, he has to be able to dash off in a moment and be in good shape. I worry about that. You know how kids are. They're inclined to think, 'what would it matter if I just have a couple of beers? I could sober up with a quick cup of coffee.'"

"I see what you mean," I said. "And hanging around musicians would tempt one. The musicians I know are fond of their mood enhancers."

Casteem made an exaggerated nod. "Of course, Sky can't have a music performance when he's on call. So that's part of the scheduling difficulty. Any time he books performances, he has to give me the dates and times well in advance."

"Is being on call just for driving Kraytower? Or does he do other work around here?"

"Sometimes, Mr. Kraytower has friends who show up unannounced. It's even happened when he's nowhere nearby. A VIP will fly in and expect to stay. That's unconscionable, in my opinion. But Mr. Kraytower is always gracious. At those times, I call him on the phone, and he tells me to put them in the southeast bedroom with the best view of the lake. I try to be helpful directing them to local activities. Sometimes that includes dinner at a restaurant. In that case Sky will often drive them so they can enjoy their wine without worry. And Sky has recently been through boat captain training, as well. He doesn't yet have enough experience to get his license. But Mr. Kraytower has had him takes guests by boat to the various lake side restaurants."

"Sounds like being Kraytower's driver is a great job."

Casteem leaned closer to me. "The boy likes to say, 'Another cool job for Sky Kool.'" Casteem straightened up. "The kid's got personality, I'll give him that."

"When I was here before, I didn't see any boat. Maybe it was in the boat house?"

"There are two of them. There's the regular Chris Craft. It's nice. I've even been out on it. But the showpiece is the woodie, a Baby Gar, with the three cockpits."

"And probably kept in perfect shape, right?"

"Oh, my. You have to see it to believe how beautiful it is. Mr. Kraytower has it refinished every year."

I nodded. After an awkward silence, I said, "It's good to see that you can keep your sense of perspective when you hear them calling you gramps behind your back," I said.

"Of course, a kid like that can get in trouble if he pushes it too far," Casteem said. "In a previous lifetime, I was a track-and-field coach and Phys-Ed teacher in a public school in Arizona. So I know about kids who push boundaries. But sometimes they are more engaged than the other students who are better behaved."

"When I met Sky and Joshua," I said, "Sky clearly was the dominant one of the two. It seemed he made Joshua uncomfortable."

"He intimidates Joshua. But he also helps draw Joshua out."

"Kraytower doesn't want you to be stern with the kids?"

Casteem nodded. "When Mr. Kraytower heard Sky call me gramps, not only did he not take offense, he laughed. I tried hard not to mind. But mind or not, my job is to keep Mr. Kraytower happy. I just hope his son Joshua doesn't pick it up as well. Joshua doesn't have the chutzpah to get away with impertinence. He could end up in trouble."

Casteem turned around and looked into the house as if wondering where Kraytower was.

I said, "How'd you get from coaching track to being Mr. Kraytower's houseman?"

"I broke my ankle in a gopher hole near the track. It took a long time healing, and my coaching suffered. Kids had a hard time accepting a coach who was hobbling across the field. Then the school district shifted their focus. They cut funding for physical education for all students even as they doubled funding for football, which of course was just for a few students. They got an opportunity to hire a new football coach, a young guy who'd played one season with the Cardinals. So they offered me a small settlement to retire early. That way they could cancel track and field. I was fifty-five at that point and had sixteen years in. So it made sense for me to leave. I decided I'd never again work for a big bureaucracy, whether public or private. I cast about for several years, knocking around L.A. and then the Bay Area. Of course, that helped me burn through my little kitty. So I needed to find some employment. A friend who had a cabin in Tahoe had heard about Mr. Kraytower's company and knew he'd bought a place in Tahoe. So I wrote a letter to Kraytower explaining that my coaching skills were essentially about organizing small-to-medium groups of people and that I believed those skills would transfer to a domestic position. I was long divorced with no children and didn't need more than a modest room to live in. He called me in for an interview, and he hired me to run the household. I've been here now for eight years." He turned around as if wondering again when Kraytower would appear.

I said, "Does Mr. Kraytower fly a lot?"

Casteem widened his eyes, raised his eyebrows, and made a single nod. "I would've thought that running an investment business was done with a computer and a telephone. But I've learned that it's as much a people business as anything. He's often in New York or D.C. or Europe. Increasingly, he's got business in Singapore, which drives him crazy because it's nearly impossible to get across the Pacific in his Citation. It's got less than a four thousand-mile range. He did it once. I think he went from San Francisco to Anchorage to Tokyo to Hong Kong to Singapore. Imagine that. Since then he started chartering a Gulf Stream Six Fifty. That can fly nonstop from San Francisco to Tokyo, and nonstop Tokyo to Singapore."

Behind Casteem, a man came down the large stairway at the rear of the entry hall. He was almost as tall as I am but was clearly out of shape, his stomach girth larger than his chest. He wore a beige cardigan sweater with the buttons fastened, all of which pulled at their buttonholes. His thick black hair was combed up and back. He had black eyebrows to match. His pale blue eyes were visible from a distance. He looked very stressed, his brow crisscrossed with lines.

"Mr. McKenna, I presume," he said as he approached. He held out his hand, and we shook. "Carston Kraytower."

"Good to meet you," I said. "Please call me Owen."

"I go by Carston as well."

Kraytower appeared to be in his early forties, younger than I am by a few years. He telegraphed the authority that I imagined was critical to convincing wealthy people to hand over millions for investment.

"Where shall we talk?" Kraytower asked.

I looked around at the grand entrance hall. "How much of your house was open to the guests at your party the night that James Lightfoot died?"

"Everything. I like people to be able to roam free."

"Then I'd like a quick tour if I may. That's always helpful to get a sense of the territory."

"Of course," he said.

Kraytower took me through the entry, into many large rooms with high coffered ceilings, a kitchen that was too big for many restaurants, a dining room that could serve heads of state, a living room with a huge portrait above the fireplace, a man in business clothes. I didn't know the subject, but it looked like a John Singer Sargent painting. Upstairs were more bedrooms than I could count, each with an en suite bathroom. There was a study with two fireplaces and enough furniture for the San Francisco yacht club lobby, and the bookshelves held sufficient books to stock a small-town public library. Outside the study was a door that led to the roof-top sculpture garden.

On the third floor was a game room with two pool tables and three table-tennis tables and a rack of pinball machines. There was a lounge with leather chairs and a mirrored-back bar that had dozens of bottles. Off the bar was a solarium with ten-foot-high windows that overlooked the lake and the sculpture garden one floor below.

"Shall we visit the lower level?" Kraytower said. "There is a conversation pit in the wine cellar where we can talk."

I nodded.

I followed Kraytower down three flights to the ground floor. While the north and west sides appeared to be below grade, the south and east sides were floor-to-ceiling windows. The views of the lake were spectacular, and they included the Carson Range mountains of the East Shore, twelve miles across the water. Hidden somewhere on the forested slope was my cabin.

The lower level had a small indoor pool, jacuzzi, steam room, and showers. There was an indoor garden patio that seemed to blend through the glass doors with the outdoor patio.

"Over here is the wine cellar," Kraytower said. He opened a wide door that was made of heavy wood. With its stout metal hinges and rounded top, it looked like something in a medieval castle.

We walked through into a room with stone walls and no windows. It was lined with floor-to-ceiling wine racks. Recessed spotlights shone on the wine bottles, making them sparkle.

"Feels like a wine cave in one of the old Napa wineries," I said.

"Precisely. The builder even excavated his own cave." Kraytower pointed toward the west wall away from the lake. "You may have noticed outside that the ground on this corner of the house slopes up toward the West Shore Highway." He waved his arm. "This whole part of the wine cellar is under that ground."

I walked toward the area. "It feels cool like a cave."

He nodded. "Climate controlled for the best wine storage. The cool comes from being underground." He turned. "Step through this other door and we go into the conversation pit." He opened another door with a rounded top. "It's warmer in here, better for conversation."

As I approached the door, I saw a wooden box on a high counter. It was illuminated by a spotlight from above. The box had a hinged lid and a brass lock. The wood had been broken and splintered, and the lock was bent.

"Someone had an accident?" I asked.

"Not an accident, I fear," Kraytower said. "Theft."

"Did this happen the night of the party?"

"Either that night or the day before."

"What was stolen?" I asked.

"My precious bottle of Chateau Lafite, a bordeaux from seventeen eighty-seven."

"Certainly sounds precious," I said.

"Oh, I can't properly describe how much I treasured it," Kraytower said. "It was a bottle once owned by Thomas Jefferson."

TEN

My phone rang.
"Sorry, I forgot to mute this," I said to Kraytower as I pulled it out. The call was from Diamond.

"I'm not the only person who has a busy schedule," Kraytower said. He pulled out his own phone as if to make me feel comfortable about taking the call. I stood several steps away as I answered.

"Diamond," I said.

"You remember Sebastian Perry," Diamond said.

"I think," I said, trying to be vague in case Kraytower could hear me.

"Guy who rode his bike off the Tahoe Rim Trail a thousand feet above your cabin."

"Got it," I said.

"The pathologist who performed the autopsy thought something was funny about an accidental mountain biking death. He said a man who earns a high-powered living as a financial analyst wouldn't be so sloppy as to ride a bike off a cliff."

"So…" I said.

"You have an audience," Diamond said.

"Yeah."

"So the pathologist ordered a toxicology report. We just got the results."

"Uh huh."

"His blood had traces of etorphine in it."

"What's that?"

"Some kind of tranquilizer that vets use on rhinoceroses and elephants."

"Not friendly to your average Joe, right?"

"Sí. Turns out you only need a trace of etorphine to stop a

person's heart."

"Interesting," I said as I glanced at Kraytower. He was tapping out a text on his phone.

"The Agatha Christie heart attack is no longer speculation," Diamond said.

"Good to know," I said. "Stay in touch."

We hung up.

It was now clear that at least one person in Kraytower's world had been murdered. That made for high odds that Lightfoot's death was murder as well.

I'd thought I'd keep this new information to myself as I walked back toward Kraytower.

He put his phone in his pocket. "Where were we?" he asked.

ELEVEN

I picked up the broken wood box. Kraytower watched me as I turned it over.

Whoever broke it open must have been in a hurry. It appeared that someone had forced a pry bar between the lid and the box and levered it until the wood and lock shattered. The inside of the box was lined with red fabric.

"I'm guessing that a bottle owned by Jefferson was valuable," I said.

"Yes, I paid a hundred and seventy thousand for it. But the price is not the point. It's being able to hold something that Jefferson held. I studied history at Yale, and I developed a serious appreciation for our founding fathers. To feel a connection like that to one of our greatest presidents, well, you can't imagine what a thrill it is."

"You think someone at your party stole it?"

"Yes. It's astonishing to think that someone I know would do such a thing. But there it is." He reached out his arm and touched the broken box.

"Why would someone steal it?"

"It certainly wasn't to drink it. Any wine older than forty or fifty years has long since turned to vinegar. It can only be that someone wanted the same thrill it gave me. To hold and gaze upon one of Jefferson's wines."

"Why wasn't it in a safe?"

Kraytower seemed taken aback. "Well, first of all, it needed to be kept in a cool environment like the wine cellar. My wine consultant told me that even if the wine has gone bad, the cool temps help keep the cork from drying out and the wine from evaporating. Anyway, it's not like I have a safe in the wine cellar. Also, my house has many valuable items. I have an early American cut glass collection that is valuable. My paintings are worth a great deal. The Sargent portrait in the living room is worth millions. I wouldn't very well keep that in a safe. The pleasure in all these things is being able to look at them. Hold them."

"Good point." I set the broken box back where I'd found it.

Kraytower turned and walked through a doorway in the side wall of the cellar. We went from the dark, cold cellar into a room that faced the lake and had a wall of windows that provided a view of lawn and sculptures and sparkling water.

There was a section of the floor that was defined by a step down. There was a circular fireplace filled with pebbles. Above it was a conical metal hood. There were no ashes on the pebbles.

Kraytower adjusted a thermostat on the wall, and a yellow-blue flame grew among the pebbles in the center of the fireplace.

"I'll just keep it low. The heat is nice because the ground floor is always cool even on the warmest summer day. But the ambiance is nice as well."

"A nice place to sit where you can see the lake," I said.

Kraytower nodded. "I could live in this part of the house alone. Over behind you, that door goes to living quarters that are attached to the wine cellar. What they sometimes call a mother-in-law apartment. But of course you'd want to make sure your mother-in-law didn't have too much of a wine habit." Kraytower smiled, then looked at his watch, a thin, modern dial that looked like it was made of platinum.

"It is still morning, a time for coffee," he said. "I'm happy to have the kitchen help bring us a cup. But if you'd like a glass of wine to go with the setting, I'd open a vintage you probably haven't had."

"Thanks. I don't need either. You called me because you suspect the deaths of your colleagues might not be accidents," I said.

Kraytower nodded. "It seems they could only be accidents. But someone could push a bike rider, right? And there might be a way to trigger a heart attack. It was the peculiar emails that got me thinking this way."

"You printed them out?"

"Yes." He reached under his cardigan and into his front shirt pocket, pulled out a folded paper, and handed it to me. "There were three emails that came over the space of three days. I put them on one piece of paper. Each number is for a separate email. There was no salutation and no sign off."

I unfolded it. There were three lines with numbers in front of them.

1 The story would freeze your blood.

2 It was no accident. He poured in the poison.

3 The killer now wears the victim's garlands.

"Do you have any ideas about their meaning?" I asked.

"None other than the thought that someone is trying to unnerve me. Jim Lightfoot, too."

"And maybe the other person who died bicycling off the cliff," I said, "Sebastian Perry."

"Right," Kraytower said.

"The word choices are unusual," I said.

Kraytower nodded. "I even Googled the words. For example, if you type in 'Freeze your blood,' you get medical websites about preserving blood and how freezing destroys the cells. Same with the other words. How to work with poison without getting contaminated. The line about a killer and a victim's garlands is even more inscrutable. Nothing makes sense."

We sat in silence for a moment.

I asked, "Can you think of any reason why someone might want to arrange an accident for Lightfoot or Perry?"

"No. Not at all. They were successful investors. People liked them both. They had no enemies that I'm aware of."

"I heard Perry lived in Woodside. Where did Lightfoot live?"

"San Francisco. Lightfoot's house is in the Potrero Hill neighborhood."

"Families?" I asked.

"Perry was a bachelor, although he didn't date much. He was too focused on his work. Lightfoot had an ex-wife, no kids. He too was obsessed with his work."

"His ex-wife's name?"

"Olivia. A nice woman. Very high strung, very intense. But nice. She moved to Florida after their divorce. Ten or twelve years ago."

"Who stands to benefit from Lightfoot's and Perry's deaths?"

"No one that I know of. I'm somewhat familiar with their estates because we try to practice what we preach. Invest thoughtfully, construct your estate to benefit the things and people you care about. We talked about those things enough that I believe Perry's entire estate goes to UC Berkeley, where he got his MBA. Lightfoot's goes to the Wharton School of Business where he got his MBA."

"What about you?"

"You mean, do I benefit? God, no. Their deaths are a huge blow to me. Psychologically, emotionally, financially. My hedge fund will suffer a big loss as Lightfoot's and Perry's investors re-evaluate their portfolios. We'll hang onto some of the investors, of course. But I imagine we'll still lose several hundred million in investor assets."

"Do you have family?"

"Only my son Joshua."

"Tell me about him."

Kraytower stood up and walked over to the windows.

"Joshua is an enigma. I don't really know him. A very bright boy, but very shy and awkward. He's been raised with everything any boy could want, yet he doesn't appear to want any of it. He just reads books and writes in his journal."

"What kind of books? What kind of writing?"

"Frankly, I don't know very much. He keeps it from me. He's got a thing for nature. Trees, mostly. He says nature has a divide between good and bad."

"What does that mean?"

"I'm not sure. But he once said that trees help the world while people harm the world. So he does this nature writing about the goodness of trees, I guess."

"Joshua's mother?"

"Isabel died during Joshua's birth."

"I'm sorry," I said.

"Thanks. Sixteen years later, I still can't quite accept it. There was an accident on the Bay Bridge, two trucks, with one rolled on its side. They blocked all the lanes. We were stuck in the terrible traffic jam for three hours when Isabel went into labor. I called nine-one-one and reported it. Then I called Isabel's doctor. She didn't pick up. So I got out of the car and started yelling for help. A woman came from many cars back. She was a trained midwife, so I thought we'd be okay. But there were complications. Isabel hemorrhaged. The midwife took care of Joshua when he was born. He survived. But Isabel died on the bridge."

"I'm so sorry," I said again.

Kraytower was breathing hard, the memory still difficult.

"I've always blamed myself. She was eight months and one week pregnant. There were no advance warnings. The doctor said she was healthy and she should do most everything she always did. She wanted to see a play at the Berkeley Rep. So we headed out for an early dinner in Oakland before the theater. But I should have never driven with her in traffic. I was stupid."

"How does Joshua deal with it?"

"I don't think it's been too terrible. Of course, he never knew his mother, so there wasn't anyone for him to miss. But it still represents a hole in his life. Most of his friends and acquaintances have mothers. He doesn't."

"You raised him yourself?"

"Yes and no. He's had three or four nannies over the years. I tried to be there for him. But running a hedge fund... Well, it's an eighty- or a hundred-hour-a-week job." His phone rang. He pulled it out of his pocket, looked at the screen, then pressed the button. "Yes, Randall?" He listened for several seconds, then spoke. "We had a large-cap focus on that portfolio, right? I'd default toward the ones with a lower P/E ratio, so that narrows the group." Pause. "I know. He's the most risk-averse client." Pause. "I'll be on the plane in another hour. I'll call when we're airborne." He clicked off and turned to me. "Sorry about that."

"Nothing to be sorry about. Back to Joshua... Are there any relatives who have been able to help raise him? Someone to be a stable presence in his life?"

"Not really. I was an only child like him. My career has kept me from forming close friendships." Kraytower paused and looked at me hard. "People look at me and see my accomplishments and think I'm so successful. But the truth is that I'm a failure at the personal side of my life."

"Any women friends since Isabel died?"

He shook his head. "The only woman who I would consider as a friend of the family is Nettie Moon Water."

"Interesting name."

"Moon Water is Native American. Not her name, her ancestry. Washoe, I think. She's some kind of shaman. Jim Lightfoot went to her for advice. But I don't know more than that. Isabel met her at a fundraiser in Reno, where Nettie lives. They became good friends. Nettie even came down to San Francisco to do things with Isabel. After Joshua was born, Nettie tried to fill in here and there. She took care of Joshua several times, and she showed up for birthday parties. Actually, it would be more accurate to say that she arranged those birthday parties because I was often gone on business. So Nettie Moon Water has known Joshua all his life. But she's a little removed."

"How do you mean?"

"She comes to certain functions, for example when Joshua graduated from high school. She's very nice to Joshua. She even agreed to be named as Joshua's guardian if anything should happen to me. But she keeps her distance. I don't know why. I think it simply comes down to the fact that something about me puts her off. She doesn't want to be near me."

"Why do you think that?"

He shrugged. "She's very warm and kind with everyone including Joshua. But not with me. You're probably a good judge of character. Maybe you could guess why."

"Did you ever come on to her after Isabel died?"

"No. I'm not that kind of guy. In fact, I think that's where Joshua gets his awkwardness. I'm awkward too. I don't know how to date. I don't know how to be pals with someone. I just know how to make money. It's quite lonely, if you want to know the truth."

"Did Isabel have problems with you? Problems she may have related to Moon Water?"

"Not that I know of."

"Did Nettie Moon Water ever witness you mistreating Joshua?"

"You are perceptive to think of such things. But I believe the answer is no. I've never hit him or even yelled at him in any major way. If Nettie is standoffish because of some way I've been with Joshua, it would probably be that she thinks my focus on work is misplaced. She would logically think that if you have a child, that child should be the central focus of your life. I can't say that the viewpoint is wrong. And I'm the first to admit that I'm probably too wrapped up in my work."

"Did Nettie Moon Water come to your party the night James Lightfoot died?"

"I invited her, but I never saw that she came. She lives in a cabin at Fallen Leaf Lake during the summer."

"Can you give me her contact info?"

"Yes, of course." He found a business card, wrote on it, and handed it to me.

"I'd also like to go to your workplace. Speak to your colleagues."

A sudden look of anger colored Kraytower's face. "What for? If you're going to ask them about my parenting, they will tell you what I've already told you, that I'm too focused on work. I've already established that I'm not the perfect father. And how does this have anything to do with Lightfoot and Perry dying in accidents?"

"I don't have an answer for you other than to say that this is what investigators do. We go around turning over rocks to see what might crawl out."

Kraytower's booming voice was loud. "So this is turning into an investigation of me? I thought you'd look into Lightfoot and Perry's lives."

"Please take a breath, Carston. Imagine that someone wants to cause problems for you. I don't know why. Maybe they invested with your company and lost a lot of money. If they arranged for

Lightfoot and Perry to die in accidents, that would succeed in making your life difficult, right?"

Kraytower took several breaths and then spoke in a calmer voice. "I see what you mean. The deaths could be a kind of revenge against me. I'm sorry. I feel under siege right now. When two of your closet associates die, it screws you up pretty bad." He reached under his cardigan sweater and into his shirt pocket. He pulled out another card, turned it over, and wrote on the back. "Kraytower Growth Assets is in the Transamerica Pyramid."

He handed the card to me. "If you call this number and speak to Wendell Merchant, our investor liaison, he'll escort you past the guard and up to our offices. I'll tell him to give you full access to any employee and any office. All I ask is that you avoid those advisors who may be in conference with investors."

"What about your other friends? Non-work pals."

Kraytower looked embarrassed. "I don't have any pals."

"Is that because you don't engage with friends? Or is it like Nettie Moon Water in that they stay away from you because you put them off?"

Kraytower was shaking his head. "These are uncomfortable questions. They get to the heart of my failures as a person. I'm sorry. I'm not a buddy to anyone. I don't hang out with people. I don't have breakfast or lunch with anyone but occasional clients and business associates. I'm an introvert who has trained himself to reach out to others in order to run my business. I do lots of dinners with associates and investors. I have extravagant parties. But that's just more business."

"Your Tahoe party was business?"

He nodded slowly. "It's a performance. Like stage acting. You invite your business acquaintances—colleagues, employees, investors—out to a restaurant or up to Tahoe to have a mountain getaway. It's morale building, team building, confidence building. You tell some stories to make people comfortable. You serve expensive food and liquor. You lavish attention on everyone. And through it all, you make certain that your main colleagues stay close so potential investors can see that you've got a cohesive team." Kraytower took a deep breath. "It's the same as in any other field. The personal relationships you develop are what produces your business success."

"What drives your desire for this?"

"I'm not sure I understand what you mean. I work hard. There is value in working hard. It's good to be productive, right?"

"What I mean is, what is your prime motivation? Is it money? Is it like a game that you want to win? Is it the celebrity of being known and talked about and written up in the financial press?"

Kraytower seemed to think about it. "I grew up poor in a small town in Oklahoma. Very poor. My dad was a school janitor who died of lung cancer when I was twelve. My mother was a substitute English teacher who struggled with scoliosis and congenital kidney problems. Her health problems made her walk very slowly and made her tired and weak. She never received a full-time position. She was intellectually qualified, but the school district kept passing her over when a position became available. We were poor enough that the school lunch program was the best meal of the day for me. From a very young age, I was determined to be financially successful. That drove me to excel in school. I went to Yale on a scholarship. I did well there, got my MBA at Harvard, then moved west to start my company. After a few years, I'd made enough to buy my mother a nice house. But she died of kidney failure during the days she was moving into it." He bent his head forward. His breath wheezed as if he had trouble breathing.

"Does Joshua come to your parties or dinners out? Does he get to know your team? Is he part of that life?"

"Why all these questions about Joshua?"

"Two people close to you have died. They could be random deaths. But your concerns and these emails suggest otherwise. If the deaths aren't random, then the fact that you also got the emails means that you are connected. So I need to know about you, and Joshua is a big part of that. And if someone wanted to get at you by harming your work colleagues, they might also want to harm Joshua."

Kraytower looked horrified. "Oh God, what a horrible thought."

TWELVE

"Is Joshua around?"

"Somewhere. Probably up in his room writing. What he calls nature writing."

"I heard about that when I came by at the sheriff's request," I said. "I got the idea he wants to be a naturalist." I didn't tell Kraytower about Joshua walking Spot and Spot jumping into the pool. I figure the boys hadn't told him, either.

Kraytower was shaking his head. "What's the point of him being a naturalist? Imagine pursuing a career that has no benefit. Not to him. Not to others."

"What else can you tell me about him?"

Kraytower shook his head as if to clear it. "I'm embarrassed to say that Joshua's almost a stranger to me. I think he's a stranger to all people. And he's weird around other people."

"In what way?"

"For example, he won't touch. You can go to shake his hand, but he won't reach out to shake yours. If you try to hug him, he'll squirm away. I once hugged him hard, and he yelled and ran from me. Like he was allergic to his own father."

Kraytower looked out the windows. "There's a local kid whose name is Sky Kool. It's an unusual name to say the least. My Tahoe houseman, Gary Casteem, has hired him to be my driver when my other driver is away. Sky is my driver today. You no doubt saw him out in the drive."

"I met him. Quite charming."

"He spells Kool with a K. Whoever heard of such a name? But I guess it's like rappers. It's popular these days to adopt a name even if you're not a performer, which I gather Sky is in some capacity. He told me he plays guitar in his own band. Anyway, Joshua has taken to Sky. They seem like friends. I'm very glad for that. I hope being one of my drivers will keep him around so Joshua will have a friend when we're up here at the lake."

"That sounds smart," I said. "How often are you up here?"

Kraytower shrugged. "It varies. I bought this place twelve years ago. Joshua was a little boy. Since then, we've come to Tahoe many times in the summer. This place works very well for my business presentations. But we rarely come in the winter. The snow is too brutal. Anyway, I think the Tahoe visits have been good for Joshua. He loves the trees. And now he likes seeing Sky. My houseman Casteem has been nice to Joshua as well. I won't say they have a great bond or anything. That doesn't happen with Joshua. But they are friendly. The other help have been nice as well. I like to think that Tahoe has been good for Joshua. Of course, it's good for everyone to get out of the hustle of a big city and breathe the clean mountain air."

"Who is the other help?"

"There is my older driver, David Wrenshaw. He wants to reduce his schedule, which is why Sky Kool is doing more of the driving these days. There's our gardener lady, Mary Mason. She doesn't talk very much, but she's nice to Joshua. Mary goes back and forth between this house and my house in San Francisco. In the summer, she's here in Tahoe three or four days most weeks and in The City one day. In the winter, she's in The City five days a week. I don't know if the pattern is necessary for the gardens. But it seems good for Joshua to see familiar faces in both places."

"Where do you live in San Francisco?"

"Pacific Heights." He reached back into his pants pocket and fished around. He handed me a third card. "Here's the address and phone. My house woman there is Aria Ibarra. She's Basque by way of Mexico. Very nice. And my driver there is Jorge Medina… something." Kraytower used the Mexican pronunciation, HorHey. "He's got two last names. I guess that's normal. There is also my Nigerian chef, Abeo. Aria schedules him based on my schedule. The man is a wizard with food. The best I've ever had. But it's Aria and Jorge in San Francisco and Casteem here in Tahoe who keep my world together."

Kraytower looked out at the lake.

He said, "If I had an ordinary job, I wouldn't even need them. I could drive myself and eat takeout and have a cleaning service come in every now and then. It's dealing with deep-pocket investors that requires the grand presentation."

"Do you mean their decisions to invest with you are influenced by your houses?"

"Absolutely. I think of the houses like stage sets in a play. Everything is designed to communicate luxury, financial stability, business optimism. And my staff is trained in how to behave. We even bring in an etiquette consultant."

"How to address guests and serve them meals?"

"That and more. The same company works with my investment counselors at the office."

Kraytower turned and looked at the yellow-blue flame coming from the pebble bed under the fireplace hood.

"James Lightfoot and Sebastian Perry both died here in Tahoe," I said. "If their deaths were arranged, why Tahoe? Why didn't they die in San Francisco or someplace else?"

"I don't know. It may simply be that they spend a lot of time here."

"That's curious," I said. "Did they come here because you had a place here?"

"No. It goes way back to college. Both of them went to Yale with me. We took a couple of ski vacations to Tahoe, and we all fell in love with the place."

I said, "From the East Coast, you would fly over all the ski resorts in Colorado and Wyoming and Utah and come to Tahoe instead. Why?"

"I think it traces back to another student at Yale, a girl named Julie. She was kind of a Tahoe nut."

"Why? Did she have family here?"

"No. She was an artistic person. Dance and painting. Apparently, her family once took a vacation to Tahoe, and she fell in love with the color of the lake. Something about the blue color. Julie was also quite charismatic. So when she wanted to go on a ski trip to Tahoe, everyone said, 'Sure, let's do it.'"

We were quiet for a moment.

"When you started Kraytower Growth Assets, you hired your college buddies?" I said.

"Yeah. I knew I could be comfortable working with them. I knew I could trust them."

"When you finished Yale, what made you come west for business?"

"Partly, it was my love for Tahoe. I wanted to be close to the lake. And from that first ski trip, I had an idea that one day I'd buy a place here. But mostly, it was San Francisco and Silicon Valley. There is no other place in the world that produces such a plethora of new, profitable companies. Hundreds of significant startups each year. Every single year, this one small spot on the planet has tens of thousands of new job openings with starting pay of a hundred thousand plus. So I started my company there and have done well."

"I'd like to ask you about your staff who were on duty the night Lightfoot died."

Kraytower seemed irritated. "Why? They could have no reason to dislike my colleagues. Most of my staff has never even met my workmates."

"It's what I do. I try to talk to everyone who knows you. Maybe one of them saw or heard something that would seem meaningless to them or you. You said that Jim Lightfoot's death was high profile?"

"Oh, maybe that was an inappropriate thing to say. Let's just say that when a wealthy person dies, sometimes the vultures circle around looking for scraps. If someone later files a lawsuit or makes some kind of claim against the estate or questions how the death was handled, the police want it obvious that the death was thoroughly investigated. I want it obvious as well."

"What kind of wealth scale are we talking about?" I asked.

"Well, I don't know exactly. But Lightfoot's assets were probably north of five hundred million. Perry's weren't far behind."

"That's some scale."

"Sure. But it's nothing like those guys over on Billionaire's Row in Incline Village."

"I presume you are in the same category?"

"Similar to Lightfoot and Perry? Yes. I have the largest stake in our company. But again, my money is pocket change to guys like my new neighbor, the Facebook guy." He looked to the side as if he could see through the forest to the person he was talking about.

"Has anything else happened that makes you feel threatened?"

Kraytower shook his head. "No. Just those emails."

"You said Sebastian Perry didn't get the emails. Or at least he didn't mention them."

"Jim and I got the emails the day before Perry died. So he may have gotten them, but we would never know. Jim and I were always in contact. Little went on in his life that I didn't know about. But I didn't talk to Perry as often." Kraytower paused. "What do you think about this freezing blood and poison thing?"

"I have no idea." I said.

"I'm not embarrassed to say this scares me. I'm just a regular businessman. I concentrate on my job. To get these emails and then have two employees die is... Well, I already said it. It's frightening. And it's a distraction. I don't have time for psycho emails."

"I understand that."

"I want to do whatever is necessary to resolve this situation." Kraytower changed his voice as if giving an order rather than discussing. "If those emails contributed to Jim's stress and made him have a heart attack, that's murder in my book. Maybe the same thing happened to Sebastian Perry. I can imagine riding along the Tahoe Rim Trail and not even being able to enjoy it because of something a nutcase emailed you. That stress might cause you to make a mistake on a mountain bike. I want you to find out who sent those emails."

"That's not always easy."

"You can get a search warrant and serve it on the email company." He sounded irritated.

"If we can show probable cause, yes. But a crazy email isn't probable cause. And even if we could get a warrant, often all that does is give us the information on file for the person who obtained the sender's email address. If that person signed up anonymously or with a pseudonym or other false information, it does us no good. And if the sender uses different computers to send emails, like public computers at libraries, that makes it extremely difficult to track. There is also the TOR network, which is designed to make senders anonymous. Anyone who uses that is effectively out of reach. We have more success searching the old fashioned way."

"What's that?"

"Gumshoe work. Talk to the victim's friends, enemies, acquaintances. Interview any witnesses to the death. Try to find out why someone would want to harm the victim."

"That sounds very slow." Kraytower was clearly disappointed.

"It is. Sorry. And we have to remember that both deaths could be natural," I said, even though Diamond's phone call explained that Perry's was murder by etorphine.

"Right. But I still want to run down every possibility. Will you do that?"

"Yes."

We discussed my terms. Kraytower seemed puzzled at my fee. It was as if he wondered if I could be any good when I charged so little. But he didn't protest.

"I should go now," he said. "My driver is waiting to take me to the Truckee airport right now."

"What do you fly?"

"We have a Citation Ten."

"A serious business jet," I said.

"You know your aircraft. Our monthly tab flying commercial to New York and London didn't make sense," he said, excessively serious. "The Citation has cut expenses and increased our schedule flexibility. And the Truckee airport has enough tarmac to get us airborne even though it's a high elevation strip."

Should've been a financier, I thought. "Truckee Airport to SFO is less than an hour, right? Same time it takes to drive from the West Shore to Truckee."

"That's true. Makes me wonder if owning this Tahoe spread is worth it. The plane is fast. But the connections to and from the airports are slow."

"When will you be back in Tahoe?"

"Let me check my calendar." He pulled out his large phone and tapped on it.

I waited.

"I could be back day after next," Kraytower said. "But I have some tentative items on my schedule. I have to be in New York tonight to meet one of the Federal Reserve Board members for dinner. I may head on from there to London. But I won't know until later today."

"Does Joshua stay here when you travel?"

"Not usually. He's more comfortable in San Francisco. He's known Aria, the housekeeper, and Maya, his nanny, for most of his life. Even my city driver Jorge has been around for years. I think Joshua also likes his room at the Pacific Heights house. But things are changing. Now that he's met Sky here in Tahoe, he's getting more comfortable staying here. And, of course, Tahoe's got more of his beloved trees. So our plan had been that he'd stay here today and tonight when I'm gone. Then I'll pick him up at the Truckee airport when I come back. He'll fly back to The City with me."

Kraytower looked at his watch. "I've got to go. I have a dinner I have to attend." He stood up.

"Do you often fly to New York to go to dinner?"

"It's one of those Wall Street things. They've asked me to give the keynote speech. So you go and eat and press the flesh and talk the talk. If you're lucky, maybe the pesky financial writers adjust their ratings in your favor. Maybe you get another big investor or find a new analyst who might like to trade the New York hustle for work on the West Coast."

He accompanied me back up the stairs and out the giant door.

Sky Kool was waiting. He opened the back door of the polished limo, and they left.

Casteem, the houseman, was still standing in the open doorway.

"A quick question?" I said.

Casteem nodded.

"Mr. Kraytower has asked me to investigate all aspects of James Lightfoot's death. I believe he wants to find some closure, to know that everything in his world is okay."

"I understand."

"I may want to talk to everyone who was here during the party. Can you tell who was here by looking in your schedule book?"

"Of course," Casteem said with a touch of pride. He stepped over to the table and picked up the book. He opened it to the page that showed the schedule on the party night and handed the book to me.

"Lots of people," I said. "Maybe I should just ask if any of the household help were not here."

Casteem scanned the book. "No, we pretty much have all hands on deck for a big event like that party." He went to close the book, then reopened it. Ran his finger down the list of names. "Except the gardener. Mary Mason. She wasn't here. But of course, there isn't any need for a gardener during an evening party." He looked again at the page. "Now that I think of it, she had left the day before to go down to San Francisco. They were getting a shipment of plants at the Pacific Heights house, and she had to be there to receive it."

"Thanks. I appreciate the help."

He and I said goodbye. Spot and I drove out to the West Shore highway, where I stopped.

I'd been meaning to call Doc Lee. No better time than now.

I dialed his personal number and got his voicemail.

His greeting sounded cheerful and said, "I'm either in the ER or on my way to or from the ER or trying to take a nap on the narrow hard cot we keep in the little ER utility closet, although the lingering scents of antiseptic are cause for disturbing dreams should I ever actually drop off. If you feel the need to interrupt my nap, leave a message and I'll consider returning your call."

The phone beeped.

"Wow," I said, leaving a responding message. "As a trained investigator, I'm detecting a hint of curmudgeon creeping into your attitude. Way to go. A nap in a closet. That sounds great. You docs work too hard to only have sports cars as a reward. Anyway, I just wanted to see if I could entice you to share a beer on a gorgeous summer day in Tahoe. I know about your pledge. So I'm taking 'First, do no harm' and amending 'Second, indulge in a summertime beer.'"

I clicked off and turned right to drive to Tahoe City.

I found a dog-friendly restaurant with an outdoor patio. Spot and I had grilled chicken sandwiches. I knew that the few local beaches that allow dogs would be overrun in the summer, so we walked a trail through Paige Meadows, then drove back to the Kraytower place. The black Suburban was back in the drive.

I rang the bell, and Gerard Casteem answered the door. I asked to visit with Joshua.

He seemed taken aback but recovered quickly. "It makes sense," he said. "The boy doesn't talk freely with his father nearby. He's with Sky Kool, out in the gazebo at the end of the pier. Shall I announce you? Or do you feel comfortable just walking down there?"

"I think I'll be fine, thanks."

THIRTEEN

Casteem nodded and slowly shut the door.
I fetched Spot from the Jeep, and we walked to the gate in the stone wall, and then strolled through the sculpture gardens down to the pier.

The two kids were sitting on built-in benches. They appeared deep in thought.

"I'm interrupting something important?" I said.

Joshua looked depressed. Sky looked resigned to Joshua's depression.

Sky said, "The problem, Mr. Plainclothes, is that Joshua here has never done anything fun in his life."

"I don't do much fun stuff either," I said.

"No," Sky corrected, "I mean, this young man has never done anything fun." He turned to Joshua. "Am I right, nature man?"

Joshua shrugged.

Spot walked over next to Joshua and stood so that his head was over the kid's lap. Joshua pet the side of Spot's neck.

"Hey, don't back away from me now," Sky said. "You've told me several times. 'Fess up, and tell the truth. You've never done anything fun."

"Pretty much," Joshua said.

"We should fix that," I said.

"That's what I say," Sky said. "But nature man won't put a preference into words. I'll say, let's go mountain biking on the Tahoe Rim Trail. Or let's take the Baby Gar out and go wave jumping. Or, I'll come into The City and we'll go to a club in North Beach and chat up some girls. But he just shrugs." Sky suddenly pointed at Joshua. "See, he's doing it now. You can't get him to commit to a preference. All he does is write about trees and stuff."

I turned to Joshua. "Maybe you just haven't thought much about the concept. For example, let me ask you a question. From the time you were very young, what seemed like it would be fun?"

"Nothing."

"Think of movies. You've seen lots of fun stuff in movies, right? What made you think, 'I'd like to try that?'"

Another shrug.

Sky said, "He's more shrug man than nature man."

I kept talking. "Race car driving? Skiing? Snowboarding? Flying airplanes? Riding zip lines? Paragliding?" I paused, realizing I was thinking of typical action-focused stuff. Think atypical, McKenna. Less action. "Scientific discoveries? A great novel about nature?"

Did Joshua's eyebrows twitch?

I waited.

"Name a great novel about nature," he asked.

"Not my area of expertise," I said. "Moby Dick?"

Joshua spoke in a bored voice that sounded robotic. "Captain Ahab sails around the world in search of the whale that bit his leg off. I read it two years ago. Not much fun."

"How old were you two years ago?"

"Fourteen. Plenty old enough for Moby Dick."

"No doubt," I said. "How about Twenty Thousand Leagues Under The Sea?"

"Jules Verne. Read it, too." Joshua looked down. For a brief moment, he glanced at Spot.

I waited. Sky didn't speak. Maybe he sensed something.

"I once saw a show about the Iditarod dogsled race," Joshua said. "Up in Alaska. The mushers and their dogs were pretty interesting. I've always wondered what it would be like to ride on a dogsled."

"Yeah, me too," I said. "You want to try it?"

He shrugged. "Maybe sometime I'll go to Alaska."

Sky said, "A long distance between here and fun."

"Yeah." I turned to Sky, "You got Mr. Kraytower to his plane in Truckee?"

"Yep. I watched as that baby shot into the sky. Like a rocket dream for a poor kid like me." He looked off at the lake. "So what now, Mr. Plainclothes?"

"I'm gonna think about something not so far away. I'll let you know if anything comes to mind."

Spot and I left.

FOURTEEN

That night during dinner, I told Street about talking to Joshua and Sky. Spot and I were at her condo. Blondie and Spot were snoozing on Street's kitchen floor. Probably the hard surface felt cool. Street had to step over them to cook dinner. I had to step over them to fetch a beer.

Street had lit the candles, poured a pinot noir, and served up salmon and red potatoes. She pulled asparagus out of the little steamer pan and was dishing it up last so it would stay warm.

"You could do that," she said, turning slightly away to reach for the pepper.

I took one of the green spears, folded it in thirds, and stuffed it into my mouth. She turned back having never seen me eat it without cutting it first. It was still slightly crisp. Delicious.

"Do what?" I said, minimizing my chewing motions.

"Dog sledding. Or at least a variation on the theme."

"How? I don't know of any dog sledders in the Tahoe Basin. And it's summer."

"There's still lots of snow up on the Crystal Range." She took a delicate bite of a quarter piece of a small red potato. "And remember when we went sledding? After a few runs, you hooked the sled up to His Largeness, and he pulled it across the snow."

"Ah." I was trying not to eat my salmon too fast. Even if Street didn't care about such decorum, it was embarrassing to finish my meal before she'd even tasted all of the components.

"A good idea, no?" Street said. She sipped a drop of pinot.

"You think if I hook a sled up to my hound, Joshua would sit on the sled and feel like that was dog sledding?"

"Maybe not. But if you could get him to try it, it would be fun."

"And Joshua is probably my best avenue for learning more

about what's wrong in the Kraytower universe," I said.

After dinner, I found the Sky Kool and The Palpable Hits business card Sky had given me. I figured that if I could enlist him in my activity, I'd have a better chance of getting Joshua to give it a try.

I dialed the number.

"Sky Kool," his voice answered.

"Hey, Sky, Owen McKenna. Remember earlier today when we were talking about getting Joshua to do something fun? I thought I'd come by tomorrow with an idea. I wondered if you'd be around."

"Gramps doesn't have me on the driving schedule tomorrow," he said. "But I could head over to Kraytower country and see if Joshua can come out to play. What did you have in mind?"

I told him.

"Great idea. But it's best not to give him advance notice," Sky said. "We'll just wing it. But I'll be waiting with bated breath."

We chose to meet at the Kraytower palace at 7:30 a.m.

After I disconnected, I said to Street, "Maybe you'd like to come along."

Street seemed surprised by the idea. "Let me think. My schedule is all errands, no appointments. So I could probably get away. Do you think they wouldn't mind my presence?"

"On the contrary, Sky would be delighted to have you join us. And Joshua would warm to you far more than to me."

"Should you contact his father and see if he's okay with us going over to his house?"

"If we can convince Joshua to come along with us, I'll ask his permission. But I don't want to call him in advance. He might torpedo the idea."

The next morning, we pulled into the Roman-brick drive. The dogs were crammed into the back seat, our packs with clothes and food were in the rear along with an extra empty pack. I had the short wooden toboggan strapped to the roof rack. Sky was already at the Kraytower house. The Suburban limo was not in view, no doubt parked in one of the garages. Sky leaned back against the tailgate of an old blue station wagon.

We got out of the Jeep. "Hi Sky, I'd like you to meet Street Casey."

He stood up, grinned, and reached out both of his hands to shake hers. "Sky Kool. It is a pleasure, Ms. Casey. I've been waiting all morning to meet you. I can't believe that Sherlock, here, hasn't told me about you."

Street grinned. "You live up to your charismatic billing as well as your name, Mr. Kool."

Sky looked over at the big house. "I've already called Joshua and told him I'm here for a visit."

At that moment, the front door opened and Joshua came out. He turned around and gently shut the door, then walked toward us with slow, soft footsteps. He looked more worried than normal. No doubt he hadn't anticipated a group.

I made the introductions. Street smiled and spoke to Joshua in a low voice. Remembering what I'd said about his reluctance to touch, she did not reach to shake his hand. She gestured at the sculptures and, as if using an invisible push, slightly steered Joshua away from us. I took the hint and turned to Sky.

"This is a Chevy Nova, right?" I ran my fingers along the roof of his car. "I didn't realize the Nova was made in a station wagon model."

"This baby's one sweet ride," Sky said. "A sixty-nine wagon. I call these M and Ms, the musician's model. I can haul all four band members and still fit our amps in back."

"Goes pretty good?"

He nodded. "It's got the inline six. One hundred ninety-four cubic inches of pure smooth power." He grinned. "Except when it backfires. That's not real smooth." He glanced over at Joshua and Street who were looking at one of the sculptures. "You just gonna spring this snow thing on Joshua?"

"Maybe you could introduce the concept."

He seemed to think about it. "Why not?" He turned and called out.

"Hey nature man, come check out this sled."

Joshua looked at us. Sky waved his arm and pointed at the roof of the Jeep.

Street walked toward us. Joshua followed.

"Sherlock and Ms. Casey got a sled," Sky said. "And they've got a big dog to pull it."

I said, "Joshua, remember when you said you'd never done anything fun and you were interested in dog sledding?"

Joshua looked very skeptical. "Are you serious?"

I said, "I have a harness that Spot uses to pull the sled. He can pull me at a good rate, and I'm a big guy. He'd pull you even..." I was about to say, 'faster,' but realized that might not be desired. "Better," I said.

"It sounds contrived, having one dog pull me on a sled."

"Yes, it's contrived. The pirate ride at Disneyland is contrived, too. But it's still fun."

"Joshua's been to Disneyland," Sky said. "But he never went on any rides."

I tried not to look surprised. I thought the whole point of Disneyland was the rides.

"Anyway, it's the middle of summer," Joshua said. "I'd have to wait until winter."

"No, you wouldn't. We could go up to Lake Aloha in Desolation Wilderness. That's still buried in snow from last winter."

"What elevation is that?"

"Lake Aloha is at eighty-four hundred feet. It's still frozen. And the snowfields go up from there."

Joshua shook his head. "I doubt that." He pointed across the lake toward Heavenly resort. "The mountain to the right of Heavenly is almost eleven thousand feet. You can see from here that the snow is mostly all melted."

"True. But Lake Aloha sits just below the Crystal Range on the Sierra Crest. It gets far more snow than Heavenly and Freel Peak. If you go up Kingsbury Grade and look across at the Crystal Range, you'll see there are still a thousand vertical feet of snowfields above Lake Aloha."

"I've never even heard of it."

"If you've driven Highway Fifty over Echo Summit, you've seen its water."

"We've driven that way a few times. I never saw a lake."

"Not the lake, the water. Remember the big curves up above Lovers Leap? Horsetail Falls is just to the north and it gushes most of the year. I'm sure you've seen it. That water comes from the melting snow at Lake Aloha."

Joshua made a single slow nod.

"How do you get to Lake Aloha?" Sky asked.

"It's an easy hike. From Echo Summit, it's only a mile out to Echo Lakes. We'd park there. Then the boat taxi takes us the length of the lakes."

Joshua looked very uncomfortable.

"From the west end of Echo Lakes, it's a nice hike of two or three miles up to Lake Aloha. The climb is only a thousand vertical feet. There's great views and you'll come to lots of snow. We could do some dog-sledding there."

Joshua looked at Street as if for reassurance and then turned back to me.

"Why would your dog pull me?"

"When a person is on the sled it becomes a game to him."

"That sounds weird. He only likes it if a person is involved?"

Sky said, "You know that's how dogs are. You're the nature man. Dogs are, like, all about doing fun stuff and helping people. Everything is a game."

I nodded. "Dog games need someone else involved. A person or another dog."

"Like throwing a frisbee or chasing another dog," Sky said.

I said, "Let's call your dad and ask if he's okay with you going up there. We could go up today." It was a bit shifty psychologically to redirect attention from whether Joshua wanted to go to whether his dad would allow it. But it seemed harmless and possibly effective.

Joshua thought about it. He pulled out his phone, walked 20 feet away, and dialed. We heard him speaking in low tones. He walked back to us and handed me his phone.

"Owen McKenna here," I said. I too walked a short distance

away from Street and the boys so that my conversation was less obvious.

"This is Carston. What's this about taking Joshua someplace?"

"My girlfriend and I are at your Tahoe house, and we've been speaking to both Joshua and Sky," I said. "We'd like to take them up to Lake Aloha. There's still snow up there. I'd like to show him how to go snow sledding. He's never done that before. So I'm calling to ask your permission."

Kraytower didn't immediately respond. "How does this connect to your investigation?"

"It doesn't in any significant sense. But like you said about your KGA company, your work is all about developing relationships. Same thing for me."

"I don't understand why you would go snow sledding. That's just playing. Not productive in any way."

"Joshua seems to lead a serious life without a lot of fun. I thought it would be a good experience for him." I saw Joshua staring at me. I added, "Me too, for that matter."

"Joshua's a kid, so I understand that. But why would you go?"

"I like sledding, too."

Kraytower was silent.

I said, "My girlfriend and her dog will come along. It'll be a summer snow party."

"Your girlfriend likes sledding, too?"

"Sure. If you've never tried it, you should. You go fast, and you fall off, and get snow down the back of your neck, and sometimes in your mouth. And then the dogs come and jump all over you." Joshua's eyes widened a bit.

More silence. "And that's fun," Kraytower said in my ear, his voice very somber. No wonder Joshua was excessively serious.

"It's a riot. What say you, sir? Is it okay? I'll have Joshua home before dark."

"It sounds like you're going on a date."

"We are. A snow date."

I heard Kraytower sigh. "Hold on. I'm going to call Casteem

on another line."

I held on. After it became obvious that Kraytower wasn't talking to me, Joshua frowned.

"He asked me to hold while he calls Mr. Casteem," I said.

Joshua looked up at the trees.

"Whooeee!" Sky said, his voice rising high. "Let's make sure Gramps is onboard cuz you know how much he's into dog sledding!"

Joshua grinned, the first I'd seen since we met.

Kraytower came back in my ear. "I gave Gerard Casteem my local number in case my cell voicemail is jammed up with calls."

"Should I have it, too?"

"Joshua has it. Make sure he gets home safely. Just because I'm gone a lot, doesn't mean I don't care. I'm holding you responsible."

"Got it," I said. "Thanks. By the way, where are you?"

"London. KGA keeps a flat here. That's why I sound a bit short. It's midnight here. Long past my bedtime. Stay in touch."

I thanked him and hung up.

Without ever asking Joshua if he wanted to go, I said, "We're on. Aloha, Lake Aloha."

FIFTEEN

I spoke to Joshua and Sky. "There are a few things you should bring." I waited, thinking that someone would take notes. Joshua pulled out his phone. He did the thumb dance as I listed off items to bring: hiking boots, heavy pants, lunch, water, sunscreen, gloves, dark sunglasses, sun hat or baseball cap with visor, jacket, daypack to carry it all.

I turned to Sky. "Can you and Joshua ride in your wheels?"

He spoke with pride. "The true blue, very blue, classic sixty-nine Chevy Nova SS Coupe M and M wagon awaits. We'll gather our stuff and follow you."

Fifteen minutes later, we left the Kraytower estate and drove down the West Shore. An hour later, we were driving up Echo Summit. We turned off on the narrow road to Echo Lakes and parked at the end.

Echo Lakes are two of the prettiest lakes in the Sierra. Sitting at 7400 feet, they are often frozen six months of the year. There are many summer cabins along the shore, but no road access to the cabins. There is only a hiking trail and a boat taxi, a handy aid to hikers who want to get into the high country fast. I parked at the upper lot.

I unstrapped the sled and pulled out our packs and strapped on Spot's saddle bags with the dog food.

"His Largeness carries a pack!" Sky shouted. He pulled out his phone and took a picture, taking out-sized delight in the concept. "A dog with a pack and a diamond stud, too!"

"Everybody's gonna want lunch," I said. "Dogs, too."

We walked down to the boat taxi. Street stared at the water, clearly transfixed by the beauty. As always, the lake was a picture out of a tourist brochure, a narrow stripe of blue water, flanked by mountains, sparkling and gorgeous.

Sky and Joshua hung back a moment, close together as they faced away from us, conferring about something. Maybe Joshua was hesitant and Sky was giving him a pep talk.

I walked down, went into the general store, and bought six tickets for the boat taxi. I didn't tell them that two of my companions were dogs.

When we got to the docks, I handed the tickets to the boat driver.

He was a young man about Sky's age. He looked apprehensive as Spot approached. "Is that, um, dog going to come in the boat?"

Sky swung his arm out like a practiced orator, put the other arm behind his back as he bent forward in a sweeping bow. "Allow me to introduce His Largeness, the diving-board wonder fresh from his recent West Shore performance."

The boat driver stepped back, whether from apprehension about Spot or about Sky, I couldn't tell. With Sky's encouragement, Spot put his front paws up on the boat gunnel, then jumped in. In addition to our party of four, two dogs, a sled, and backpacks, there were three other passengers. The people all put on flotation vests.

We were underway a minute later. Joshua sat on one of the seats. Spot stood nearby. Joshua put his hand around Spot's collar, although whether for companionship or stability on a rocking boat, I didn't know. Unlike Joshua, Spot was happy for any touch he could get.

I spoke to Joshua. "I heard from your father that a family friend, Nettie Moon Water, has a cabin on Fallen Leaf Lake. Have you been there?" I didn't mention that he'd told me that Moon Water was Joshua's designated guardian should Carston Kraytower die.

"No. I know Nettie. But I have no idea where Fallen Leaf Lake is." Joshua nearly had to shout to be heard over the roar of the outboard motor. I think our understanding came from reading lips more than hearing our voices.

I pointed toward Pyramid Peak in the distance to the west.

"From where we're going at Lake Aloha, if you climb up toward Pyramid Peak, you can look down and see Fallen Leaf. It's as pretty as lakes get. You should go there sometime. Maybe meet Nettie Moon Water at her cabin."

Josh didn't respond, but he seemed to think about it.

After several minutes, the boat slowed to go through the narrow passage between lower and upper Echo Lakes, then resumed speed. We came to the dock at the end a few minutes later.

Street carried one of our packs, while I put the other on my front side. I carried the sled on my back. Sky swung the third one onto his back.

"If you want, I can carry the sled, too," he said.

"We'll trade off," I said.

We headed up the trail, the dogs running ahead, followed by Street and Joshua and Sky. I took up the rear.

The trail snaked through the forest, curving around rocky outcroppings. Sometimes the trail was close to level. Other times it climbed up at a good angle. There were creeks and, increasingly, areas of snow in the shady parts of the forest. Ralston Peak loomed above us to the south. And the taller Pyramid Peak towered to the west. Despite the warm days of late July, waves of spring flowers bloomed in the moist ground at the edge of the snow patches. When the snow melts, plants see sunshine and think it must be spring, regardless of the month.

We'd only been hiking for a half hour or less when the terrain became largely snow-covered and the nearby creek became snow covered. The snow, though slippery, was relatively firm, a quality called corn snow that makes for great skiing and boarding. As long as the surface wasn't too steep, it was easy to walk on.

The dogs ran off across the snow fields, excited at the sudden return of the winter sensation beneath their toes.

In another half hour, we arrived at Lake Aloha. Despite the sounds of flowing water beneath the snow, there was no blue water to be seen. The lake was covered with ice and buried in snow. The only indication of a lake was the lay of the land, a large, treeless basin of snow with the jagged peaks of the Crystal

Range to the west.

When we got to a level area, I called out. "This is a good lunch spot."

We took off our packs and set them in the snow. I turned the sled over so its smooth wooden bottom faced up. I found the red-checkered cloth and spread it out over the surface. Street helped me put out the food: Bread and crackers and cheddar and swiss cheese. A salad of spinach and tomatoes and carrots. Baggies of grapes and orange slices.

Sky put out the lunch he and Joshua brought. Corn chips, salsa, and energy drinks.

Joshua had been wearing a new pair of buckskin gloves with sheepskin linings. He took them off and lay them on top of one of the packs.

While we ate, I unfolded the camping dog food bowls and gave Spot and Blondie just a little food from out of Spot's pack.

Sky watched with interest.

"Do you have to carry water for them, too?"

"No. Unlike humans, the dogs drink water from the creeks and they sometimes eat snow."

"Aren't there, you know, germs that affect dogs the same as people?"

"Maybe. But the problem is, you can't keep them from drinking out of lakes and creeks. Even if you bring water, they'll drink from natural sources when you're not looking. So eventually you give in and hope for the best. They don't seem to get sick." I turned and looked around at the landscape. "There's an open area of water over there, part of a little creek that flows into Lake Aloha. When they're done eating, they'll probably head over there to drink."

Sure enough, Blondie went there first, lowered her head and drank from a pool of water. Spot joined in. But it wasn't enough of a hole, so he dug in the snow for awhile, made the hole bigger, and lapped up water.

A minute later, the dogs were lying in the snow, soaking up the sunshine.

"Nature man," Sky called out. "The dog's got your glove."

We all looked up and saw that Spot had grabbed one of Joshua's new gloves and was chewing it.

I ran over to get it. Spot realized what I was after and took off running. We did the requisite figure 8 with Spot dodging this way and that as if trying to make me look like a stodgy human. Eventually I got it out of his mouth. It was soggy with dog slobber, but it hadn't yet been destroyed. I wiped it off on the snow.

As I walked back toward our lunch area, I saw that Sky and Joshua were in another huddle, heads together, facing away from us again. Then they turned and walked toward us.

Sky said, "I think I've finally got nature man convinced that this sledding is a good idea. Right, Josh?"

Josh shrugged.

"Sorry about your glove, Joshua," I said. "I'll get you a new pair."

He looked at the chewed glove and didn't react.

"Okay, who's up for a sled ride?"

Everyone looked at me.

"Joshua? Ready to give it a go?"

He didn't move, frozen with fear or unable to visualize a fun experience.

"I'll go first," Sky said. "What do I do?"

"Okay, Sky is our first rocket man. Step right up and help me put this harness on Spot."

Together we got the straps buckled around Spot's chest and hooked a tow line from Spot's harness to the sled. Joshua watched all this with what looked like a mixture of interest and horror.

"Now what?" Sky asked.

"Now you sit on the sled. I walk with Spot until the tow line is tight. Then Street and Blondie walk out to the finish line."

"Where's that?"

"Watch and you'll see."

I pulled out a dog biscuit and handed it to Street. "If you would, my dear, show this to His Largeness so he knows you've got it. Then take Blondie and walk over to that big boulder. When you're ready, hold the biscuit high, call him, and pat your thighs. I'll let go and give him a little encouragement, and with luck he'll run to you and Blondie and the biscuit and not off through Desolation Wilderness."

She nodded, took Blondie, and began walking.

I turned to Sky and Joshua. "A few rules," I said.

They looked very focused. "You sit on the sled. Don't get up on your knees or try to turn it by leaning or dragging your hand. Don't get fancy or the sled will likely tip over and Spot will get an uncomfortable jerk as the sled digs into the snow and stops."

"How fast will he go?" Sky asked.

"He can run fast. But it depends on how firm the snow surface is. It won't be any faster than riding a sled down a good hill." I looked at Sky. "Ready?"

Sky nodded. He sat down on the sled, shifted a bit until he was comfortable. I handed him the short line that was attached to the front curve of the sled.

"What do I do with this?"

"Just hang on."

He nodded, held the line and moved it back and forth. Joshua was very focused as if studying Sky to learn the moves to a complicated dance.

Street stopped walking and turned around. I heard her call out. "Ready?"

"Ready," I shouted back.

Street held up the biscuit with her right hand and kept hold of Blondie's leash with her left.

She shouted. "SPOT! COME!"

I dropped my hand next to Spot's head, and he ran forward. It wasn't a quick start like when he has no load to pull. But he accelerated well and soon was moving across the snowfield at a good rate of speed. Sky raised a clenched fist skyward and began cheering woo, woo! Snow flew up from Spot's feet and a rooster tale of snow came off the rear end of the sled.

I turned away for a moment to look at Joshua, and he appeared mesmerized, his eyes wide and his mouth open. His hands were clenched in fists at his side.

Spot got to Street and jerked to a stop as he grabbed the biscuit from her hand. The tow line slackened as the sled careened past Spot and Street. The tow line retightened from the far side, and Spot was jerked around. Sky came off the sled, made two complete rolls, and then got to his feet and started jumping around. Spot and Blondie and Street all joined in a free-for-all jumble.

"That was great," I said to Joshua.

He nodded but didn't speak.

"Let's join them. Then we can get Spot to do a return trip coming back to this point."

Joshua and I walked to the others. I pet Spot. "Good boy, Largeness! Want to do it again?" I held up another biscuit. He looked at my hand and wagged. I could tell he was wondering if he could snatch it away from me.

I handed the biscuit to Street, making sure that Spot saw me. Then Street walked with Blondie back to our original starting position.

"Good ride, Sky?"

"Yeah, that was awesome! I didn't know a dog could run that fast. I'm not a lightweight, but His Largeness was burning rubber!" He turned to Joshua. "You're gonna love it, nature man!"

I positioned the sled, got Spot lined up, the tow line taut. Sky helped Joshua get comfortable and handed him the reins.

"Just a reminder," I said. "The key to a good ride is to stay stable. Just sit in one place so your weight doesn't shift. And don't lean side to side."

"Ready, Josh?" Sky shouted. "Get cranked, get stoked! You're gonna be the rocket man!" Sky reached down and shook Joshua by his shoulders the same way I shake Spot when I want to send him on a suspect search. Unlike with other humans touching him, Joshua didn't seem to be upset.

Joshua nodded.

I called out to Street. "Ready?"

"Ready!" came the response. She held up the biscuit and shouted. "SPOT COME! Come get your treat!"

I dropped my hand next to Spot's head, gave him a little pat on his rear, and they were off.

I thought Spot would be more tired this second trip hauling

the sled across the snow. But he seemed to have even more energy and enthusiasm. And his load with Joshua was much lighter than it had been with Sky. It might have even been a touch downhill compared to a slightly uphill ride with Sky.

Spot accelerated faster than before. The sled seemed to bounce on the snow. The rooster tale shot into a higher arc than it had with Sky. Joshua started yelling with joy. He called out over and over, like war whoops.

"He loves it!" Sky shouted. "I've never seen him like this! He's flying, man! Flying!" Then Sky lowered his voice. "Oh, oh. Not good, dude."

I didn't understand at first. Then it was obvious. Joshua was changing his position. He stood up on the sled. He held the reins and leaned back as if he were waterskiing.

"Sit down, nature man!" Sky called out. "Sit down!"

But Joshua didn't hear him. He leaned a little to the left, which made the sled turn to the left. Then he leaned to the right. The sled carved a right turn. Spot was running faster than ever.

I saw Street running toward Spot and Joshua.

Sky and I started running as well.

Street waved her arms. If Joshua saw her warning, he didn't care. He was having too much fun. He was screaming with joy, an ecstatic yell. He leaned back to the left. The sled made a tighter turn than before. A bump in the snow lifted the outer edge of the sled. It went into the air, doing a slow barrel roll.

Joshua arced through the air. He landed head first in the snow. But he went in farther than I would have expected. I was sprinting as fast as was possible in the snow. Sky was right behind me. As I got closer, I realized what happened.

Joshua had landed near the hole where Blondie and Spot had drunk water. He had punched a new hole. His feet were visible. He was head down, the upper half of his body submerged in ice water.

He wasn't moving.

SIXTEEN

We all got to Joshua at the same time. I pulled Joshua out of the water, seeing a flash of silver as his phone fell out of his pants pocket and disappeared into the water. He was soaked in ice water. I lay him down on the snow. He wasn't breathing.

"Oh, God," Sky said. "Josh, wake up! Breathe!" Sky grabbed Joshua's shoulder and shook him.

I turned Josh on his stomach, put my palms against his back and gave a strong push.

Josh coughed out water. He took a weak choking breath. He was breathing. I felt a little less panicked. But then I realized his breaths were sporadic and shallow. He was shivering violently, and his skin was turning blue.

"Street, we need to call an air ambulance. Josh is becoming hypothermic."

I glanced behind me. Street was already on her phone. I heard her talking.

"...the north side of Lake Aloha in Desolation Wilderness," she said. "On the snow. He's hypothermic. He fell into ice water. What? The victim is male, sixteen years old. At first, he wasn't breathing. Now he is, but just barely. We need a warm chopper. Warm with blankets. The landing area is snow, for what that's worth."

Sky helped me get Josh's wet jacket, shirt, and undershirt off. Sky took off his own jacket and shirt, and we began to put the shirt on Josh. Josh was mumbling and shivering so hard that we had a difficult time getting his wet, clammy arms into the sleeves of Sky's shirt.

"Wait, Sky," Street said. "You can't go all the way back to your car without any clothes. I have an extra jacket in my pack.

It's too small for you, but not for Joshua. He can wear that." She pulled it out, and we got it on Josh.

"We'll drape your jacket around him until the chopper gets here."

We put my pack on the ground. We got Joshua sitting on it. I sat behind him. With Sky's jacket wrapped over Joshua from the front and my own jacket open to release heat and my arms wrapped around Joshua from behind, we made a cocoon of sorts. While I held Josh, Street got his gloves on.

But Joshua was now unconscious, and his skin stayed blue. His shivering decreased even though he hadn't seemed to warm up. I knew how hypothermia works. With substantial cooling of the body, you begin shivering violently. But more cooling brings you past the point of the shivering reflex. If that was the case, it meant that we were in danger of losing him. I hugged him hard, trying to think of how else to warm him. But we had no thermos of hot water and no cook stove. All we had was our own heat and the summer sun, which, though bright, was diminished by a haze in the sky. It didn't feel very warm while we sat in the snow at 8400 feet. I knew that taking most clothes off a warm person and getting them into a sleeping bag with the hypothermia victim could help. But we had no sleeping bag.

In ten minutes we heard the thwap, thwap of an approaching helicopter. An orange chopper appeared over Cracked Craig, the mountain directly to the east of us.

The chopper had broad ski-type landing skids. The pilot circled in a manner that suggested an assessment of local breeze and set down gently in a place where the downdraft wouldn't immediately blow over us and blind the operation. Because the snow-covered ground was potentially unstable, the pilot held the position, the roar of the chopper's turbine overwhelming. Two EMTs, a man and a woman, came out of the side door carrying a litter basket. They ran toward us, set the litter down, and began strapping Joshua in. I tried to help. As I positioned Joshua's head, he became responsive to some degree and slapped at my hands.

Joshua shouted at me, words I only heard over the chopper because his lips were next to my ears. "Don't touch me!" His words blurred with cold. "Take your hands off me!"

His anger was pronounced. But I recalled that patients under stress are often irritable. Add to that Joshua's desire not to be touched at any time, and it made sense he would be upset.

I shouted at the EMTs. "He's hypothermic. His shivering reflex has disappeared."

"We'll try to warm him in the chopper."

I helped the EMTs carry the litter back to the chopper. As they were closing themselves inside, Joshua appeared to have become completely non-responsive.

I hustled away from the chopper to get out of the downdraft, and the machine rose into the sky.

SEVENTEEN

Street and Sky and I were subdued as we hiked back down toward Echo Lake. Even the dogs walked without energy.

"We really screwed up, right?" Sky said. His voice wavered. It seemed he'd never before experienced that kind of trauma.

"Yes and no," I said. "Yes, the accident was horrible. But it was an accident. If you wanted to prepare for every possible accident, you'd have to live in a padded cell."

"But we put Joshua in serious danger. He could die, right?"

"He could," I said. "But I'm hoping that he got medical help soon enough."

"Where will they take him?"

"As the chopper flew away from us, it was heading to the South Shore, which is where the closest hospital is. But sometimes they get certain situations that cause them to take patients to Reno. And once in a while, to Sacramento or UC Davis."

"How will we find out?"

Street had been quiet. She spoke up. "The dispatcher has my contact info. And Owen, you know who to call on these things, right?"

"Yeah. We'll have an answer on his condition by the time we get back down to town."

I knew I had to call Carston Kraytower to tell him his son had suffered an accident and was in the hospital. I've always subscribed to the notion of a person's right to know information central to their lives. This was tempered, however, by the fact that calling him would wake him up in the middle of the London night with frightening news. If, when I woke him, I could say that Joshua was going to be okay, it would be much better. So I delayed the call.

After we got down to Echo Lakes, we had to wait 40 minutes for the boat taxi to arrive. It was another 20 minutes to the parking area. When we got to our vehicles, I had a decent cell signal. I called the South Shore hospital and spoke to the receptionist.

"My name's Owen McKenna. Our hiking companion, Joshua Kraytower, suffered hypothermia and was air-evacuated from Desolation Wilderness. I believe he was brought to your hospital. I'm hoping you can give me some word of his condition. If you want authorization to speak to me, Doc Lee in the ER will give it to you."

She put me on hold. A minute later she came back on the line. "Joshua Kraytower is doing fine. The doctor says we expect to hold him overnight for observation and will likely release him tomorrow morning."

"Thank you."

Before I'd even disconnected, the relief for Sky and Street was obvious on their faces.

"He's going to be okay," I said.

Street hugged me, then Sky.

I said, "Sky, it would be good if you visited Joshua in the hospital. When Joshua is released tomorrow, I'll drive him back to Kraytower's house and you can see him there, too."

Sky nodded. He was, of course, distressed about Joshua. But there seemed to be some other source of concern. I assumed it was his first brush with a potentially deadly accident. He got into his vehicle and left.

EIGHTEEN

After Sky drove away, Street stayed with the dogs while I walked up to a high spot where I could get good cell reception. I called Kraytower.

"How did your snow play date go?" he said in a voice that sounded condescending. "You woke me up."

"I'm sorry for waking you." I told him what had happened.

"My boy fell into ice water and is now in the hospital?!" The strain of his shouted voice seemed like it came from a block away rather than 6000 miles away in London.

"I'm very sorry," I said again. I gave him more details and explained that I'd just spoken to the hospital and that Joshua was okay. I told him that I'd pick up Joshua the next day and take him home. He'd be at their Tahoe house when Kraytower came home.

"This is malfeasance, McKenna," Kraytower said. "I hired you to provide a safer world for me and my boy. Instead, you nearly killed him. I've a mind to have you charged with reckless endangerment of a minor. And I may pursue civil action against you. You shouldn't be allowed to be an investigator when you have such poor judgment."

I assured Kraytower that Joshua would be safely home the next day.

Street and I put the dogs in the back of my Jeep, and I drove them to Street's lab on Kingsbury Grade. When we walked through her door, Street turned and looked up at me, her eyes searching my face.

"You wanted Joshua to go sledding as part of a way to make his life better," she said, her eyes showing worry and sadness.

"Yeah. I'm concerned about him. There's something important in his life that's missing. I think he'll recover from the hypothermia. But I don't know about the larger picture."

I thanked Street for her efforts and kissed her goodbye.

Back at my office, I remembered that Kraytower had mentioned his closest woman friend, Nettie Moon Water, the person he'd designated as Joshua's guardian, should he die. Kraytower also said that Moon Water had known James Lightfoot. He'd written down her number. I dialed.

I left a voicemail mentioning James Lightfoot. My phone rang an hour later.

"This is Nettie Moon Water returning your call." The woman's voice was a contralto and smooth, a naturally soothing combination.

I explained to Moon Water that I was a private investigator working for both the Placer County Sheriff's office and Carston Kraytower. "I understand that you are familiar with James Lightfoot," I said.

"Yes…" She seemed to hesitate.

"Perhaps you heard that Lightfoot died," I said.

"I did hear that. Carston called to tell me. What a tragedy. He was so young to have a heart attack."

"Kraytower told me that you're a Washoe shaman and that James consulted you."

"James talked to me. But I'm no shaman. I was just a friend to him."

"Since Lightfoot's death," I said, "some questions have come up. I'd like to talk to you, please."

"I'm happy to talk. I'm currently staying at my summer cabin at Fallen Leaf Lake. Can you come here?"

"Yes, of course. What is the address?"

"My place is on the West Shore of Fallen Leaf. Unfortunately, you can't drive here in the next few days because an old-growth Red Fir fell across the road. We've got a crew out here, and they have the large-sized chain saws, but a three-foot chain saw blade is slow-going against a trunk that's eight feet in diameter."

"Do they have an estimate on how many days it'll be until they clear the road?" I asked.

"The guy in charge guessed three days. So we can talk again in a few days and see how they're coming along. Otherwise, I have to go to the marina store at the south end of the lake for some supplies tomorrow. If you're willing to ride in a canoe, I can give you a ride."

"I would like that. However, I have a Great Dane. Would he fit as well? Or should I leave him at home?"

"Oh." She paused. "Well, it's a sixteen-foot Old Towne, with the center thwart. But there's a compartment between the thwart and the bow seat, so he might be able to fit there if he's good at squeezing into small spaces. I could put my groceries by the stern seat. Has your dog ever ridden in a canoe?"

"Yeah. He once rode with another dog in a canoe that my girlfriend and I paddled from Baldwin Beach out to Fannette Island in Emerald Bay. So I think it would work."

"Then let's do it." Moon Water telegraphed confidence, something one might expect from a woman who carried her supplies by canoe and was inviting a Great Dane she'd never met to take a canoe ride. We chose a time in the afternoon that allowed for me to pick up Joshua in the morning, take him home, then get back to Fallen Leaf Lake in the afternoon.

"Look for me at the marina dock," Nettie said. "I'll have a red canoe."

NINETEEN

The next morning, I arrived at the South Shore hospital. I went to the reception counter and explained that I was temporarily in charge of Joshua Kraytower because his father was in London. A receptionist made a call, verified the details, and then told me to go up to the second floor. She said the nurse in charge would meet me.

I skipped the elevator and went up the stairs two at a time. I gave my name at the information counter.

After a short wait, a nurse approached. "Hello, Mr. McKenna, I'm Shirley Fortier. Joshua Kraytower is ready to be discharged. He had a close call with the hypothermia, but he's fine, and there should be no lasting effects."

"Good to know. Thank you for taking care of him."

"There is one thing you might want to know," she said.

I raised my eyebrows.

"When the boy was admitted, he had a substantial level of blood alcohol in his system. Point oh eight percent, which is legally drunk."

The information was a jolt, but I managed not to have a big reaction. I thought about the times I'd seen Sky Kool and Joshua Kraytower huddling together. I had thought that Sky was verbally bucking up Joshua, trying to give him confidence to take the sled ride across the snow.

"Thank you for telling me," I said. "I didn't know he'd been drinking. I'll have to pay closer attention."

"The doctor will stop at Joshua's room in a few minutes. You can go there now."

The door was open to Joshua's room, so I walked in. Joshua was dressed and sitting up in the bed, which was raised up into a sitting position. The hospital must have dried his clothes.

"Hi, Joshua. How do you feel?"

He didn't immediately answer. "I feel tired. Like my body has been drained of blood or something."

"You had a close call. You stopped breathing. I'm glad you made it."

"What exactly happened? I don't remember."

"First, Sky rode on the sled while Spot pulled him."

"I remember him yelling with excitement, but I don't remember anything after that."

"You took the sled ride after Sky. When you were going fast, you stood up. I was worried, but you were dramatic and impressive."

"I could never be impressive," Joshua said.

"Unfortunately, the sled flipped over, and you went head first into a snow-covered stream. By the time we got you pulled out, you weren't breathing. And you were hypothermic, too cold to shiver. The medical helicopter came and took you here to the hospital."

"I sort of remember standing up. Your dog was running very fast. It made me feel like I could have a different kind of life."

"How would it be different?"

"I don't know. A life that isn't heavy with family secrets."

"Secrets?" I hoped he would elaborate.

"Sometimes."

"But your family is just you and your father."

"Right." He turned his head and looked out the window.

"Do you know what the secrets are?"

Joshua shook his head. "No. But I can tell they exist."

A doctor in a white coat came in through the doorway. He held a clipboard and looked at the pages on it. "Everything is looking good, Joshua. We're discharging you. Do you have any questions?"

"No."

"Please give a call if you feel light headed or short of breath or have any nausea or other discomfort."

Joshua nodded.

The doctor lowered the clipboard to his side. "Stay out of ice water, okay? And be a little more thoughtful about how you stay hydrated." The doctor glanced at me.

I appreciated his discretion. He knew I wasn't family.

"Yeah," Joshua said.

The doctor left.

"Would you like me to drive you home? Your father is still on his way back from London."

Joshua nodded again.

We were in the Jeep fifteen minutes later. Spot leaned over from the back seat and sniffed Joshua. Joshua didn't try to block him as I'd expected. He just reached his hand up above his shoulder and held Spot's collar.

As I drove toward Emerald Bay, I asked a few questions. Joshua gave the shortest answers possible, often just one word here and there.

"The nurse told me that your blood alcohol level was pretty high when they brought you to the hospital."

Joshua didn't respond.

"I'm not judging you," I said. "But if you have questions, I can answer them."

We'd come around the end of the bay and were approaching D.L. Bliss State Park when Joshua spoke.

"Sky told me that whiskey would make the sled ride less scary and more fun."

"Did it?"

"I guess so. I wouldn't have gone otherwise. Is it really bad what I did?"

"If you'd died, a bunch of us would have thought it really bad. The reality is that alcohol can make lots of things more fun. But you're pretty young for it. One trick to remember is to stop drinking before you want to and then wait for what's in your stomach to be absorbed."

"There's another trick?"

"You've heard the phrase, 'don't drink and drive.'"

"Meaning cars and sleds, too," Joshua said.

We came to a high place in the road with a dramatic view

of the lake. Joshua stared out at the water. He kept his grip on Spot's collar, and when Joshua turned his head to face the lake, Spot did as well.

"Your father told me he'll have his plane stop in Truckee on the way home, and his driver will bring you there to fly back to San Francisco. I assume that means Sky."

"Yeah," Joshua said.

"I was thinking I'd go to San Francisco," I said. "Your father suggested that I stop there."

"Why? What does he want you to do?"

"As you know, he has two work colleagues who have recently died."

"I knew about James Lightfoot. I was there the night he died. But I didn't know there was someone else."

That was revealing.

I said, "In addition to James Lightfoot, there was Sebastian Perry. Do you know him?"

"No. I don't think I've ever heard of him."

"He didn't tell you about Perry?" I said. "I wonder why."

"More secrets," Joshua said.

We drove in silence for awhile.

"In the hospital," I said, "you referred to family secrets. Can you tell me any more about that?"

Joshua didn't answer. He shrugged.

"Are you not answering because you don't know what the secrets are? Or is it that you just don't want to talk about it?"

"Both."

I got the sense that he regretted saying anything about it. But I couldn't tell why.

TWENTY

During the tourist seasons, Tahoe has rush hours not unlike cities. The summer traffic jam of tourists is heavy in the morning as people head to the beaches, boats, and trails. During the midday when people are occupied, the traffic thins a bit. But come 4 p.m. it gets even heavier as tourists head back to their lodging to shower and prepare for dinner.

After I dropped Joshua off and said a few words to Gerard Casteem about checking on the boy now and then, I left.

Fallen Leaf Lake is a twin to Emerald Bay. They're both long, broad, parallel fingers of water where massive glaciers gouged out depressions during the last ice age. The Emerald Bay glacier made it all the way to Lake Tahoe, thus becoming a future bay. The Fallen Leaf glacier didn't make it as far, thus becoming a future lake.

The parking lots near the Fallen Leaf Lake marina store were all full, so I did what the Forest Service hates and looked for an off-road place to leave my wheels. I drove over to Glen Alpine Falls, which was still roaring with snowmelt rushing down from Dick's and Jack's Peaks, the mountains up near Lake Aloha where we'd been the day before. I put the Jeep in 4-wheel-low, and ran the left front wheel up a slanted boulder that was three feet high. That got the Jeep off the road and left it at a 40-degree angle. The left front and right rear suspension were compressed all the way. When I crawled out, slid down the boulder, and opened the rear door for Spot to get out, he jumped out, then turned and looked at the Jeep as if he wondered why I'd parked in such a strange way. The opposing wheels—right front and left rear—were basically unweighted. Their tread touched the ground, but it was only a touch. I pushed on the Jeep, and it rocked back and forth on the diagonal. The ground was mostly rock, so I didn't think my off-road parking would cause erosion on a storm-free summer day.

Spot and I walked back to the marina store and went around to the lake side.

The water was deep blue, and the waves sparkled in the brilliant sunlight. The lake is a mile wide and three miles long. On the west side of the lake is the face of Mt. Tallac, a wall of cliffs that reach 3400 feet above. Like Lake Aloha, the high slopes of Tallac still had snow fields left over from the previous winter.

After a few minutes, I noticed that a woman was down on the dock, and she held a line that went to a red canoe. We walked to the dock.

"Sorry to keep you waiting," I said. "I'm Owen McKenna. You must be Nettie Moon Water."

Moon Water was striking. She had rich red-brown skin that looked like oiled cherry. Her large black eyes were set off by long shiny hair mostly black but with many strands of silver. Her hair was gathered in a thick pony tail. She was thin and seemed to stand so lightly that if she took three running steps she might fly away. Although her skin was smooth like that of someone in her 40s, the gray strands and her aura of wisdom made me think she was in her 60s.

As we got closer, I said, "And this is my dog Spot."

I held Spot back with my left hand as Nettie and I shook hands. She took my hand in both of hers and made an almost imperceptible bow as she grasped mine.

"I'm Nettie Moon Water. Very pleased to meet you," she said and gave me a brief smile that showed straight white teeth.

She wore slim black pants and a fitted shirt, and over it a light, open coat that hung down to her knees. The coat was woven and had red and maroon stripes on a light yellow background. The fabric looked similar to a handwoven, wool blanket. The look was a mix of functional outdoor clothing with the addition of a certain elegance. The elegance was interrupted by a pair of purple Nikes with thick wide soles, no doubt perfect for climbing over the rocks and uneven terrain.

She turned to Spot. "And does this boy shake hands?"

"Yes, when he's motivated." I turned to Spot and gave a little tug back on his collar. "Spot, sit." He glanced up at me, then turned back to Moon Water. "Go on, sit."

He sat slowly.

"Shake hands with Ms. Moon Water."

He lifted his paw and swiped hard at the air. I thought that Moon Water would miss it like most people. But she was fast and strong. She caught his paw with both hands and pumped it.

"He's a charmer, isn't he? Wow, his paw is so much bigger than my wrist and hand." She beamed and rubbed the sides of his head, and he started panting. "You said his name is Spot?"

"Yes. AKA His Largeness."

Moon Water rotated so that she was next to him and ran her hand along the side of his neck.

He leaned against her.

"Oh, my," she said as she had to step sideways to counteract the pressure of his lean. "He leans hard."

"It's a trait of the breed. Lazy dogs who like to take a bit of load off by leaning on the nearest person."

"How do we put him in the canoe? I already loaded my groceries, so we're ready to go."

"He's pretty good at getting into boats. It works best if you get in first."

Nettie took the mooring line from her pocket and tossed it into the canoe. She stepped down into the stern of the canoe, sat on the seat, and picked up her paddle. She braced the paddle across the canoe's gunnels and onto the dock, taking the tippiness out of the process.

I sat on the dock with my feet down in the canoe's bow section. I picked up a paddle that Moon Water had positioned near the bow seat. I pointed at the cargo area behind the bow seat where Nettie had put a rug on the floor of the canoe. "Into the boat, Spot. You know the routine. Our host has even made a comfy bed for you." I tugged on his collar.

He lowered his front legs so that his chest was down near the dock and his back was arched. He stepped into the canoe, one paw at a time. Despite Nettie's canoe paddle braced against the dock and me gripping the gunnels, the canoe still tipped dramatically. I heard Nettie inhale in surprise.

In my peripheral vision, I saw a group of people with their phones out, taking pictures of the Great Dane in a canoe.

Spot managed to compress himself into an arc small enough that he could lie in the cargo area with his front legs protruding under the bow seat and his hips under the center thwart and pushing up against Nettie's groceries.

"Perfect," Nettie said. "Are we ready to paddle?"

"Indeed, I think he's settled."

I got into the bow seat.

"I take it you are an experienced canoeist, having paddled to Fannette Island."

"Not very experienced." I began paddling at a steady rate, knowing that the bow paddler traditionally sets the pace while the stern paddler matches the pace and does the steering.

Spot had his head projecting over the side of the bow seat so that his jaw was against the side of my hip.

Because I was in the front of the canoe and facing forward, I spoke loudly. "Don't be surprised when my hound periodically shifts position. Even if he only moves his head, the canoe will rock. But we most likely won't capsize."

"That would be good because this water is deadly cold."

"A smaller lake than Tahoe should warm up a little more in the summer sun?" I said.

"You'd think so, but it's countered by the large inflow of water that just melted a few hours ago. Tahoe has cold inflow as well, but it's a smaller portion relative to lake size."

"We'll be careful. We don't want our afternoon spoiled by hypothermia. That happened to Joshua Kraytower yesterday."

"Joshua fell in the water?!"

"We were sledding up at Lake Aloha. He went through the snow into the water. But he came out okay."

"Was he soaked? How did you warm him?" Nettie sounded very concerned.

"Yeah, he got a bad soaking. They evacuated him by helicopter, warmed him up at the hospital and made sure he was okay. I drove him home this morning." I didn't tell her that he'd stopped breathing, that we came close to losing him.

"What motivated sledding at Lake Aloha?" she asked.

"Joshua has a friend named Sky Kool. Sky said that Joshua had never done anything fun. Joshua more or less agreed. So my girlfriend and I suggested sledding."

We paddled ahead. The canoe traveled northwest in a very straight line, aiming toward the shore a mile or two away. Moon Water was obviously an experienced canoeist.

We came to a cabin with a green metal roof that was more complicated than a standard gable. It had unusual angles and several skylights. From behind the cabin came the whine of two or three chain saws, no doubt working on the fallen fir that blocked the road.

Nettie steered up alongside of a dock. I grabbed a dock post and held the canoe steady as Spot stood up and hopped onto the dock. Looking down into the water, it was crystal clear. Nettie and I got out. She tied the line, and I helped her carry groceries into a small, light-filled cabin.

She put away some things, left others on the counter, and then walked back outside.

"Come. We'll talk over here." She turned and walked up and over a huge flat slab of granite on the east side of her cabin.

There was a pair of old wooden chairs with thick cushions. Between the chairs was a small wooden table. The table and chairs sat in the shade of two large fir trees that had been trimmed of branches up to a good height and away from the cabin, something Tahoe locals have come to learn is an important fire safety procedure to help provide defensible space around houses.

"You sit," she said. "I'll get us some water."

"Is it okay if my hound explores?"

"Yes, as long as he doesn't run and scare approaching hikers coming down the road."

"He won't."

She went into the cabin and came back out with a jar of peanuts and two cans of seltzer water tucked under one arm. In her other hand, she carried a thin vase that contained a single yellow flower, something I didn't recognize, wild and delicate.

She set them all on the table. "Most of us get our water from the lake. But I upgrade to seltzer for guests."

"No small thing when some of your supplies come by boat."

She nodded. "Even when the road is open, I paddle my canoe to the store twice a week. It's good exercise. And it's faster than driving around the lake."

"I imagine you live someplace else in the winter?" I said.

She nodded. "Like my Washoe ancestors, I head down the mountain in winter. But unlike their huts in Carson Valley, I go to my apartment in Reno come the end of October. Then I come back up when the ice melts. Usually, that's the latter part of June."

"Sounds great," I said, looking around. "Nice cabin, great lake, and a view straight up at Mt. Tallac. I love it."

She nodded and glanced up at the mountain above us.

Moon Water turned back to me. "Is Owen McKenna an Irish name? Or Scottish?"

"McKenna is both, I think. And Owen is Welsh. What about Moon Water? Is that a translation from Washoe?"

"No. Like so many of my people, I didn't learn much of the Washoe language as a child. I still feel guilty because Washoe is considered by some to be a language isolate, no similarities to any other language on Earth, including our Native neighbors, the Paiute, Miwok, and Maidu. Others think Washoe is a Hokan language, distantly related to a few others. Either way, there are only a few dozen people left who speak Washoe. Unless they are very focused on teaching the language to their kids, it will die out."

"How did you get the name Nettie Moon Water?"

"Nettie was what I was called as a small child. A version of Annette, I suppose, although I never knew. The little bit of attention from the adults at the orphanage was split among fourteen girls. Moon Water is a name of my own choosing. When I was a little girl, I went to a small Indian Residential School called the Desert Sunset Academy, a fancy name for a one-room school just west of Reno near Verdi. It's gone now. Do you know about the Indian Residential Schools?"

"I'm sorry to say that I don't."

She nodded as if she expected that answer. "The U.S. government paid religious groups to take Indian kids off the reservations and try to help them assimilate into early twentieth century society. The schools were supposed to force us to adopt European/American culture, turn us pagan babies into Christians, as well as teach us to read and write English. It was in some respects a positive outreach effort that tried to mitigate the ongoing effects from the earlier Indian Removal Program that forced us onto the reservations in the first place."

Moon Water sipped seltzer, then continued.

"Most of us in the Desert Sunset school were orphans. It was a relief to the community elders to think that someone was going to feed and care for us. My school had two Washoe kids, four Paiute kids, and one Shoshone. We also had five white kids who had no other school to go to. One day, our teacher thought it would be fun if every child, native and white, took symbolic names. Because all Native American tribes consider the elements of nature to be special or even sacred, we all chose our names based on nature."

"Moon Water was an inspired choice," I said.

"Yes. Because I began to use it as my last name, it ended up on school forms and government forms, as well. The school even created a proxy form for our non-existent birth certificates and filled out Social Security forms for us. I don't remember my earlier surname. From the age of six I was Nettie Moon Water."

Spot came back from exploring and sat on the rock next to her. He walked his front feet out until his chest rested on the rock. Immediately, he realized that the rock was too hard on his elbows, so he flopped over on his side, his panting tongue flopping out on the granite.

Moon Water reached down and ran her hand along his neck. "You said on the phone that you had questions about James Lightfoot."

"Yes." I watched Moon Water carefully as I said the next sentence. "It looks like he was murdered."

Nettie Moon Water gasped. "Murdered?!"

TWENTY-ONE

Nettie Moon Water seemed genuinely surprised to learn of Lightfoot's murder. "I don't understand," she said. "I heard he had a heart attack."

"It appears he was poisoned. He had a colleague who died as well. That death was a bicycle accident. But that man's toxicology test revealed poison. We're reasonably sure Lightfoot succumbed to the same poison."

"It's incredible. James Lightfoot was a nice guy." Moon Water looked astonished and then worried. "I feel so bad for Carston and all of Lightfoot's friends."

"Yes, it's hard. What makes it worse is that James was apparently being targeted by the killer well in advance of his murder."

"I don't understand."

"Before James was killed, he received anonymous email messages that were a bit obscure but that were threatening. Carston received similar threats."

"No! That's so vile!" She was shaking her head, her disbelief obvious. "May I ask what the emails said?"

"I don't remember the specifics. There were a few, sent a few days apart. One talked about pouring in poison. Another talked about freezing blood."

"My God."

"The second man who died was Sebastian Perry, and he also worked for Kraytower. Perry died a week before Lightfoot. Did you know him?"

Moon Water looked sick. She shook her head.

"We don't know if he got the same emails. I'm talking to people who knew them, especially people in the Tahoe area because they both died here."

Moon Water looked shaken. Her hands gripped each other in her lap. "How can I help?"

"First, did James or Carston ever tell you that they felt under threat?"

"Not that I recall." She paused, thinking. "Certainly, Carston didn't. We don't have that close of a relationship. I knew Lightfoot better. But I don't think he ever said anything like that. It would have stood out."

"Did he ever talk about subjects that would suggest that someone was angry with him?"

"No. Not at all. He seemed to be an ethical person, someone sensitive to the concerns of others. That's not the kind of person who makes many enemies."

"Do you know anything about James's past?"

Moon Water shook her head. "Not really. I think he went to Yale. I believe he had a finance-related major, like economics. After grad school, he moved to the West Coast. That was about the same time that Carston started his hedge fund. That's all I can think of."

"How did James come to know you? And what did you two talk about?"

"I believe it was actually Carston's wife Isabel who told him about me. Many years ago, I lived for a time in San Francisco. I met Isabel at a book club before she and Carston got married. Although I never cultivated it, I had a bit of a reputation for being able to find common sense ways through conundrums."

"The shaman reputation?"

Moon Water paused. "I suppose."

She seemed hesitant.

"But…" I said, trying to keep her talking.

"The Washoe, or Wa She Shu, meaning The People, don't have shamans so much as healers," Moon Water said. "Certainly, the healer description is my preference."

"What's the difference between a shaman and a healer?"

"Shamanism implies a religious or spiritual connection. A shaman can communicate with the spirits. A shaman is more engaged with the kind of medicines and rituals that can lead to altered states of consciousness."

"You mean, hallucinations from drugs like peyote?"

"That would be part of it. But the larger portion would be the shaman's ability to use a kind of hypnotic power to bring people along a journey that leads to healing and transformation."

"Could some of those journeys actually work by the placebo effect?" I asked.

"Many in western medicine would think of it that way."

"Okay. So you are a healer, not a shaman."

"Yeah, but calling myself a healer also seems overstated."

"But others have," I said.

"I think that the main thing I have to offer is my ability to be a good listener. People who think that no one cares about them might find that I can give them what they're missing."

"That you care about them."

"Yes. A person can do enormous amounts of self-healing, physical and psychic, mental and emotional, if they just think that someone out there understands and supports them. That they're not completely alone."

"How did your healing reputation start?"

Moon Water took a deep breath as if the answer required a long story. "Years ago my niece had problems with her husband and her father. The two men both thought she should be a stay-at-home mom in Carson City. Nothing wrong with that, of course. But she chafed at their decision because they gave her no choice in the matter. The men had the ancient prejudice against women working a job outside the home. She often talked to me about it. I suggested a compromise. Instead of getting an ordinary job, why not go to the library and research how to start a business that could largely be run from home. She had no idea how that would work, and, frankly, neither did I. But I believed she could do it. I knew that she was smart enough and motivated enough to succeed.

"In the end, it was a Carson City librarian who pointed her toward the right resources. So my niece started a job placement service for other women like her, young women who, though smart, didn't have much formal education. Her company matches workers' skills and preferences with individuals and small employers who need help. She created a Kickstarter campaign to raise money and ended up with some capital." Moon Water leaned over and pet Spot, who seemed to be asleep.

"The women do everything you can think of, from sewing to gardening to clerical computer work to house cleaning to teaching. Her job placement company requires the employer companies to pay a good per-hour rate so that the workers don't undermine their efforts by selling their services too cheap. My niece's business charges the employers a small fee for each job placed. Her company provides worker's comp and liability insurance protecting all parties. While any woman is eligible to register in the system, it has been especially well received by Native American and other minority workers who might otherwise face struggles finding work. And many of the workers have kids and work from home. It's a system that honors what you know how to do, not what degrees you have after your name. The company even has teaching programs to help women develop skills in the areas where there is the most demand."

"Sounds very smart."

"Ten years in, her company is grossing seven million a year."

"Let me guess where this is going," I said. "Your niece credits you with the inspiration."

Moon Water made a small smile. "In her company literature, she tells the story of how her aunt's brainstorming was the genesis of her company. She wrote that I work like a shaman, applying timeless insights and common sense that cut through analysis and fancy thinking." Moon Water looked embarrassed. "I've been asked about it enough that I can quote it verbatim. Anyway, some time back, a reporter for one of the big business magazines wrote a profile of my niece and her company and included the story of the Washoe shaman named Nettie Moon Water."

Moon Water took a sip of water and shook her head. "No matter how hard I've tried to dispel the image, I can't shake it."

"How about you? Were you able to get a formal education?"

Another embarrassed grin. "I was very fortunate. After I left the Indian Residence school, I moved to Sacramento and waited tables at a Midtown Sac restaurant while I went to Sac State. I had a very good professor who took me under her wing and showed me how the system works. She wrote letters of recommendation and helped me get into grad school at the University of North Carolina, Chapel Hill, where I eventually received a Ph.D. in Clinical Psychology."

"That's a high-powered school. Are you currently practicing?"

"I did for thirty years. Now, I'm mostly retired. Although I still do a little teaching at the University of Nevada Reno, and I volunteer at a clinic in Reno during the winter."

"Did James Lightfoot contact you because of your psychology knowledge or because of your rep as a healer?"

"I think neither. Isabel knew that James had some questions about moral values, and he thought a shaman could give him some guidance. So Isabel directed him to me."

"Can you tell me about his questions?"

"Yes, as far as I remember them. There is not very much client doctor privilege after the client dies. Not that any of what we talked about is sensitive."

I nodded.

Moon Water continued, "James was interested in everything. He talked about history. He was interested in mysticism and religion and science. And he was one of the first people I'd ever met who was interested in anthropocentrism."

"Anthro refers to humans, right? So that would be something about humans being the center of things?"

"Right. He questioned the notion. He was also interested in what is now being called ecocentrism."

"Ecology being at the center of things?"

Moon Water made a single slow nod. "Anthropocentrism is about humans being the primary focus of the world. Ecocentrism is about nature being the focus. Nature, of course, includes humans. But humans are only a portion of the natural world."

"I understand the intellectual interest. It seems fascinating. But do you have any idea of why he pursued it to such an extent that he wanted to talk to you about it?"

"I'm not sure. I think he was trying to sort out humanity's place in the universe. And I think it dovetailed with mistakes that he had made in the past. Mistakes that he may have kept secret."

I thought of Joshua's comment about secrets. I drank some of the seltzer water Nettie had brought.

"Any idea what those mistakes were?"

She shook her head. "Sorry, nothing comes to mind."

"Then how about a random guess or thought."

"Even a guess would be too strong of a word."

"Understood," I said. "Then do like the blind man searching in the dark cellar for the black cat that isn't there."

"You know your philosophical puzzles."

"Just something I heard," I said.

Moon Water said, "James often seemed focused on animals. He mentioned finding homes for rescue dogs and cats. He was interested in working with endangered species. He talked about how people have caused so much habitat destruction that tens of thousands of animal species are at risk. Billions of small animals like birds have died. He was especially upset about the estimates that in one hundred years, we may see the extinction of most of the big cats, polar bears, elephants, rhinos, gorillas, sea turtles, and others. All because we've taken away their land or polluted it."

"It wasn't just James's concern," I said. "You also have passion when you talk about animals."

"More people should. There are billions of people taking over the planet. But we're down to just a few thousand of many animals. In some cases a few hundred. It just makes sense. Like James, I'm not as anthropocentric as most people."

"Meaning you don't value people as much as other people do?"

"Let's change the word from value. Many people think that people as a species are sacred and that animals are just resources for the taking. But like many Washoe, I think all of the Earth's creatures are sacred. This is something that James Lightfoot and I talked about a fair amount."

"What did he think?"

"He thought that all species are equally sacred. He wanted to know how Washoe people view these thoughts. He had a particular question that he felt split people into groups. Groups with passionate and opposite beliefs. The question makes some people mad as can be, and it makes others quiet and contemplative. But regardless of how people respond, all find the question provocative."

"What was it?"

"The question is, 'Is the life of a really bad man automatically more important than the life of a really good dog?'"

I thought about it. "Can you elaborate?"

"Here's a clichéd illustration. A mean man who is a relentless wife beater and who even beats his children is walking next to an icy river. Not far away is a dog that came from another family. For years the dog has played with and entertained and protected several children and even the cat in the family where it lives. A gust of wind blows both the man and the dog into the river. You only have time to save one. Which one do you pick to save?"

"That is a painful moral dilemma," I said. "Which would James have saved?"

"The dog. James was unapologetic about it. He thought that all species have equal rights. So preference should go to the better creature, whether it is human or not."

"If James was vocal about his opinion, that could certainly cause some people to think of him as their enemy."

"Yes. Some people are very intolerant of others who don't agree with them. Maybe he was killed for his lack of anthropocentrism."

"Can I ask which would you save, man or dog? Of course, you don't have to answer. It's none of my business."

"That's a very hard question for me to answer. Part of me would like to save the finest character, regardless of the species it belonged to. In principle, I think a good dog has more right to life than a bad man. But, of course, we often can't know the character of the person or the animal at stake. Yet the question reveals how people think. What matters is whether we automatically assume that our own kind always comes first, that our own kind has more right to exist than others."

"Maybe this next question is irrelevant. But does that mean you are a vegetarian?"

"No. I don't eat a lot of meat. But I eat some meat. I think it's important to realize that James's question isn't about whether or not you can kill an animal for food. Native people all believe that there is a natural order. People hunt and fish for food. Other animals hunt and fish for food, as well. Even fish hunt for food. When a pack of wolves kills an elk, or an eagle kills a marmot, that is natural. Native people think that the animals they eat are sacred. We always pray for forgiveness before a hunt. We never kill more than we need to eat. And we never kill animals for fun." She paused.

"So I don't assume that a bad man automatically has more right to life than a good dog," she said. Moon Water leaned over and pet my sleeping dog again. She caressed him and rubbed his neck. As she turned, I saw reflected light from tears in her eyes.

"Is it possible," I said, "that James Lightfoot had killed animals in the past and was trying to reconcile his feelings about it? Could that be one of his mistakes?"

"Maybe." Nettie Moon Water looked out at the lake.

I looked at the time. "Nettie, you've been very generous with your time and with providing canoe ride service," I said. "And your comments have been illuminating. Thank you very much."

Nettie nodded. "You're welcome. The temperature is dropping, and the breeze is kicking up. So it's a good time to return you and Spot to your car."

At the sound of his name, Spot opened one eye. He looked very drowsy.

Nettie stood, went inside, and came back wearing a jacket and carrying her daypack.

We got back in the canoe and paddled back to the marina.

After Spot and I had gotten out of her canoe, Nettie said, "Good luck," and paddled away.

TWENTY-TWO

I called Carston Kraytower and asked if I could come to San Francisco and visit his offices and his house. He said he was just landing in Truckee and that he and Joshua would be home in San Francisco by evening. I was welcome to stop by anytime after six in the morning.

Kraytower's apparent comfort with me contrasted with his earlier anger when he accused me of malfeasance after Joshua fell in the ice water. I wondered about his dramatic personality swings.

That night, after dinner with Street, I went to bed thinking about Lightfoot's questions and concerns about the rights of species and how human presence had altered the world so much that the future existence of other species was at risk. Was his concern connected to a motive for killing him? There was no obvious answer.

I drove into the Bay Area very early the next morning, beating most of the rush hour. I went north around the bay, dropped down across the Golden Gate, pulled off Lombard just past the Presidio, and headed up the steep hill. I found a place to park not far from Alta Plaza park. I squeezed the Jeep in between a navy blue Smart car and a black Mercedes. A young woman was just getting into the Smart car. I told Spot to be good, but he was more interested in the Smart car woman than anything I had to say. I walked over to Pacific Avenue, which runs the high ridge the Pacific Heights neighborhood is named for.

When I came to Carston Kraytower's house and crossed the street in front of it, I could see all the way to the Transamerica Pyramid building where Kraytower Growth Assets was located.

The Kraytower place was a dramatic Victorian with yellow siding, lilac window trim, and green eaves the color of Golden

Delicious apples. There were metallic gold decorative designs above and below each window, above the door, and along the top of the third-story wall. If someone had described the paint design to me, I would have thought it ridiculously over-designed. But seeing it up close, surrounded by a profusion of gardens with flowers in all colors, the paint looked merely appropriate to the dramatic Victorian architecture.

Although not as large as Kraytower's Tahoe palace, the house was nevertheless huge. I guessed it had 15 rooms over its four floors, plus a basement. From a couple of unusually-placed small windows, I figured it had both front and back stairways. The ground floor and second floor rooms had bay windows. The third floor had a turret room that projected out of one corner and rose up higher than the floor above it. The turret had large windows of curved glass.

A narrow concrete drive led back along the side of the house. Visible in the back was a carriage house large enough for four or five horse-drawn buggies and a second floor coachman's apartment. Parked in front of the carriage house was a silver Maserati. Might as well stay with the Italian theme established by the cars at the Tahoe palace. I could see from the front street that a young man was polishing the Maserati.

There was a woman working in the gardens at the front of the house. She was down on hands and knees. She wore heavy work gloves and had knee pads over her jeans. In one hand was a succulent plant with yellow flowers. In the other hand was a garden trowel, and she was using it to make a hole for the plant. Next to her were two plastic bags with the tops torn open. It looked like one was black dirt and the other was redwood bark chips.

The woman looked up at me as I came up the first of multiple flights of steps that cascaded down from the yellow, lilac, and green front door.

"Hi, I'm Owen McKenna from Tahoe. I'm guessing you're the gardener who works at Carston's Tahoe house as well as this house."

She nodded and looked up at me. "My name's Mary Mason,"

she said without getting up off her knees. She was a thin woman in her sixties with a prominent nose, a small chin, and skin that showed the weathering from years of working outdoors. She looked a bit like a beautiful bird, with fine bone structure and pretty eyes beneath short white hair. Her small size reminded me of a lighter version of Nettie Moon Water, although she didn't telegraph the same aura of wisdom.

She said, "I heard about you from Mr. Kraytower's houseman in Tahoe. Investigating the deaths of Mr. Kraytower's investment guys. He said you might want to talk to all of the household help."

"I appreciate it. I don't have many questions, but I'll ask when they come up." I gestured toward the jumble of flowers. "Gorgeous work you do. It must be hard to juggle two sets of gardens, two hundred miles apart, two different climates."

"Not too bad. I like the contrast. And both Tahoe and San Francisco share some aspects of the Mediterranean climate. Warm summer days, cold wet winters. Although Tahoe is way more extreme. Warmer days in the summer. But colder nights. Much colder nights. And of course everything is much colder in the winter."

"I'm surprised," I said. "I don't think of San Francisco as being anything like the mountains."

Mary Mason got the yellow flowers firmly set into the dirt. She tamped down the ground around it. "It's the Csb Koppen Climate Classification that labels them similarly. And it's pretty much true. For example, did you know that the ground at lake level in Tahoe doesn't really freeze much in the winter? All that snow makes it seem otherwise. Of course, when you go up on the mountains high above Lake Tahoe, it's completely different."

"Good to know," I said. "You'll be my go-to climate specialist when I have a question."

She nodded and pointed up toward the front door, which was another flight of steps above the garden level. "Knock on the door. Aria's the housewoman. She will talk to you."

I walked up the next set of steps to a covered front porch that was bigger than my log cabin. I pressed the bell.

The door opened a minute later. The petite Hispanic woman standing there had a pleasant half smile like the Mona Lisa. She wore a blue work dress, white shoes, a white apron, and a white head piece that was vaguely like a nurse's cap. Her long, thick brown hair was pulled back into a bun.

"Good afternoon. My name is Owen McKenna." I handed her my card. "Carston Kraytower asked me to stop by."

She looked at the card. "Mr. Kraytower said you'd be coming to talk. I am to answer your questions. Please come in." She turned and led me into an entry that had two wall-mounted vases on the left wall. In each vase was a small bouquet of green leaves with little sprigs of tiny white flowers.

The right wall had French doors, both open. The woman walked through them and into a small sitting room. There was an upholstered love seat that would fit two people. Across from it were two coordinating chairs. All three pieces had velvet fabric the color of light celery, and all had carved wooden legs that bowed out in that strange style that was named for Queen Victoria, who lorded over Britain's 19th century in a way no dozen U.S. presidents could have done. To sit in a Victorian house built 6000 miles away from Britain and many years after her death suggested I needed to revisit how she achieved such influence. I couldn't even influence my dog.

There was a low, antique rosewood table in the center of the furniture arrangement. On the table was a vase with a large bouquet of white gladioli flowers. Mixed in were little wispy sprigs that were light green, the same tone as the green furniture. The floral color scheme was the reverse of the vases in the entry.

The woman gestured to the love seat. "Have a seat."

I sat, and she sat across from me. She crossed her ankles and rested her hands in her lap. She looked again at the card I'd given her. She read, "Owen McKenna, Private Investigation. Lake Tahoe."

"Yes, that's me."

"My name is Aria Ibarra," she said. She had a slight accent as if she'd immigrated when she was a young adult. "I can possibly answer some of your questions." After a moment, she added,

"If they are not too difficult." She made a little grin like a shy schoolgirl.

"Good to meet you, Aria." I pointed to the vase of flowers. "Are you in charge of the flowers?"

She nodded. "Mrs. Mason helps. She's a magician at growing them. Look at her gardens. You just want to look at them all the day long."

"Yet you have a flair for floral design." I pointed at the vase. "It's like you paint with flowers. Frida Kahlo couldn't have been more effective."

"Kahlo was a Mexican painter, no?"

"Yes. She did many spectacular paintings, some of which were of flowers."

"You are trying to flatter me with mention of a famous painter."

"It's a sincere comment. If it flatters you, is that bad?"

She shook her head, her smile growing. "No. In my world, there is a lot of—what is the word—the opposite of flattery."

"Maybe those people should see your floral art. Unless, of course, those people are here in this house where they already experience your art."

"Now you embarrass me. First I have a flair. Then I am an artist. Anyway, those people are not here. They are at my home. Or not at home. Depending on how much they are unflattering me. The daughter likes to hate me. The husband thinks I waste my time with flowers. I tell him I have flower desire. That is less than a flair, no? But the only thing he wants me to have a flair about is to make him dinner and bring him beer."

The woman suddenly seemed more embarrassed. "Now I am at work talking about the… What's the word for things that are not work?"

"Non-work stuff?"

"Yes. So you need to ask me the work questions. And I will avoid answering the non-work questions."

"Who all lives in this house?"

"Mr. Kraytower, of course. And his son Joshua. We also have Jorge, the car boy. The gardener, Mrs. Mason, is often here, but she doesn't live here. And there is the nanny, Maya Floros. She is becoming an actress in her spare time. We are very proud of her. She has a stage name. Ophelia English. She works here in the day. In the evening, she is at a theater called American… something."

There was a noise toward the back of the house. A door closed. Another opened. A young woman carrying a laundry basket of folded linen towels walked out.

"Here she is now," Aria said. "Maya, I was just telling Mr. McKenna about your acting."

The young woman made a sheepish smile.

"Aria is obviously proud of your acting accomplishments," I said.

"Thank you. I'm really just learning." Maya made a little bow with her head, turned and lifted some folded napkins out of the basket and put them in a drawer, and then left, carrying the basket with the remaining laundry.

Aria looked back at my business card. "Tell me why you are here?"

"Two of Mr. Kraytower's colleagues have recently died. James Lightfoot and Sebastian Perry. Mr. Kraytower wants me to learn more about them."

Aria's eyes got very wide. "I don't know Mr. Perry. But I know Mr. Lightfoot. He's the man who died at Mr. Kraytower's Tahoe party." She lowered her voice. "One of the staff at Tahoe called me and told me a party guest died."

"Who was it that gave you the news?"

"It was Mr. Casteem. He is the houseman. Kind of like me at this house. He wanted me to be prepared that Mr. Kraytower was upset. So I should be—what are the words—polite and considerate."

"How long have you known Mr. Casteem?"

"A long time. Eight years. Ten years maybe."

Footsteps came from the entry hall. A young man looked in.

"Yes, Jorge?" Aria asked.

"I've finished with Mr. Kraytower's car. Can I put it in the garage?"

"Yes. But if you dent it, you know you will spend eternity in purgatory with a car parked on your head."

"Great!" He ran back through the house.

Aria turned back to me. "The garage boy lives for the weather to blow dirt and rain on whatever car Mr. Kraytower is driving. Then Jorge can wash and polish the car and then drive it twenty feet into the garage. If Mr. Kraytower drives his other car, it's the same thing. Before Jorge gets out of either car, he... What is spending extra time just sitting in the driver's seat? Listening to his rap music."

"Lingering?"

"Yes. He lingers in the car. He likes the cars more than girls. This is a thing I don't understand about boys. Especially Jorge, who is a little bit girl crazy."

"I saw the Maserati behind the house. What are the other cars Mr. Kraytower drives?"

Aria shook her head. "There is an orange one and another that is red like dark cherries." She held out her hand, palm down. "Very low to the ground. It growls like a jungle Jaguar. I think those cars might be in Tahoe. Sometimes he drives a car just one way. To Tahoe in the summer. To San Francisco in the winter."

"Did you know James Lightfoot?"

"A little. He worked for Mr. Kraytower many years. He comes to the house when Mr. Kraytower has a… A fiesta. But I didn't know him well."

"What was your sense of him?"

"He was very kind. Good with the help. He talked to all of us, not just the family. He had a... A good style."

"Did anyone not like him?"

She shook her head. "No. I think everyone liked him."

"Can you think of anyone who might want to hurt him?"

She frowned. "Pardon me, but I don't understand. I thought he died because of a heartbeat problem."

"He did. But it may be that someone made the problem worse."

She thought about that. It was obvious she didn't like the

thought.

She said, "If everyone liked him, then how could someone want to hurt him?"

"It could be a reason separate from his personality. Imagine that someone likes James Lightfoot very much. But Lightfoot's nephew is married to that someone's daughter. And the young couple have a child with cancer and they are broke. Their child will die. But if Lightfoot dies, the young couple will inherit millions. Their child might live."

Aria made a big nod. "Now I understand. This is not how I would think. You have the job to think this way."

"Yes."

"I still can't think of anyone who would want Mr. Lightfoot to die."

"I understand. That is good to know. I'm curious. You refer to Mrs. Mason and Mr. Casteem. But you call Jorge and Maya by their first names."

Aria looked as if I'd caught her in a transgression. She spoke carefully. "Jorge's parents are from Mexico like me. Maya's mother is from Mexico. When our people come to America, we quickly learn the ways to not cause the wrong attention. Americans are Mr. and Mrs. But we are more familiar with each other."

"You have a flair for social grace."

Aria grinned again. "First a flower artist. Now social grace," she repeated. "I will remember that." She looked again at my card. "Maybe I should have a business card."

"What would it say?"

She shrugged. "My name, I guess. Under my name it would say Housekeeper."

"Not Executive Housekeeper?"

Aria made a demonic grin. She looked like she was dreaming up new worlds. "It would say Executive Supervisor of... Residential Management. Specializing in Flowers. And Social Grace."

"I guess marketing is another skill. You mentioned Joshua. I met him in Tahoe. Seems like a good kid. I wonder if he's around?"

"Yes. I believe he is upstairs. Would you like to talk to him?"

"Please."

Aria stood and walked over to a telephone and pressed some buttons. It was like Gerard Casteem using the house phone in Tahoe.

"Joshua? Mr. Owen McKenna from Tahoe is here. He would like to talk to you. Yes. Thank you." She turned to me. "He is coming down. But he said he is just finishing something on his computer and will be a few minutes."

Thank you.

My phone rang, and she went away.

"Owen McKenna," I answered.

"I got two more emails!" Carston Kraytower was shouting in my ear.

"Try to stay calm. What do the emails say?"

"The first says, 'My burden is to avenge the murder.' The second says, 'Fight back. Try and hit me hard. Give me a challenge, dude. I've practiced enough. Even a sparrow's death is part of God's plan.'"

Kraytower's breathing was very heavy. "This is sick!" he said. "Sick!"

"Please forward them to me. I'll see what I can find out."

As I hung up the phone, I thought about Kraytower's reaction. He was extremely upset, and that seemed reasonable to me. But there was something else that made me uncomfortable. I wasn't sure, but it seemed his personality swings were even wider than what the stressful circumstances might suggest. Anger, then calm, then happy, then angry again. And the anger bordered on rage.

TWENTY-THREE

I could see the front staircase from where I sat. But Joshua didn't appear on the stairs. The doorway from the kitchen opened and Joshua came through. I realized he had come down a back staircase.

I stood. "Hi, Joshua. How are you feeling?"

"Okay," he said. His voice was small and tentative.

"You've recovered from your dive into ice water?"

Joshua nodded, and then quickly sat as if to avoid having to stand before me. His posture seemed formal, his back straight, knees together, hands on his lap.

I sat nearby. "Your father has asked me to stop by. He's gotten some uncomfortable emails. He wants reassurance that all is okay in the Kraytower universe."

Joshua made a single, slight nod. He didn't speak.

"When I met you and Sky in Tahoe, Sky said you're a naturalist."

Joshua looked embarrassed. "I'm not really a naturalist."

"What would you call your interest in the natural world?"

"I just like nature. If one day I become a naturalist, that would be really great."

"What makes you interested? Do you hike in the forest when you're up in Tahoe?"

Joshua looked hesitant.

"I'm not judging, I'm only curious."

"I've learned to be cautious about other people's reactions."

"Because you've been burned on the subject?" I said, filling in a logical explanation.

Joshua spoke slowly. "When I told my father I was interested in ecology and wanted to write about nature, he scoffed like I was a fool."

"Did he want you to study finance or something else that would make more money than writing?"

"Yeah. But mostly, he thought ecology was dumb. To him, it's like poetry or something, not a real-world area of knowledge. A day after I told him about my interest in ecology, his VPs were over to discuss business. They were all in the drawing room drinking sherry and telling jokes. I'd been walking in the Marina district. When I came home and let myself in the back door, I overheard them. My father was telling them I wanted to study ecology, and they told jokes and made fun of me."

"That would be hard to hear."

"It was terrible. I still remember one joke that Mr. Lightfoot told about an ecologist, a banker, and a priest going into a bar. It was rude and mean. Worst of all, my father laughed so loud as if it was the funniest thing he'd ever heard."

"Those kinds of painful experiences burn a scar into your psyche and you never forget it." I was thinking of the contradiction that Lightfoot would tell a joke about ecology when he had also told Nettie Moon Water that he believed all species are equal.

Joshua nodded. "I spent days in a murderous rage." His face turned red. "Don't get me wrong. I would never, you know, murder anyone. I hope you believe that."

"I do," I said, wondering if, in fact, I did. "When you are in nature, do you study the animals or plants?"

"Both. That day at the Marina, I went down to the shore to look at the tide pools. They are a fascinating ecosystem, hundreds of plants and animals that have adapted to a world that oscillates between being submerged for hours and then being out in the sun and air for hours. It's fascinating. The other people down there don't notice or care. They're just taking selfies with the Golden Gate in the background. People think nature is something to conquer and tame. I think nature is something to cherish."

I gave Joshua a long look. He was quite different than the young man I saw when Sky Kool was around. Very different from any other young person I'd met. He showed no dependence on a phone or other electronic device, and he was quickly talking to me, a stranger, about ideas.

"Have you read naturalists?" Joshua asked.

"Some," I said. "But I haven't thought about it much. John Muir is a favorite. Maybe you could tell me who I should read."

"Well, Aldo Leopold is probably the number one naturalist. He had major ideas about nature in his Sand County Almanac. He made a big point about leaving nature alone."

"Like having wilderness areas?"

"That's part of it. In fact, he was instrumental in creating some of the first wilderness areas. But his main contribution to nature writing wasn't just about the need for wilderness areas because in the past they weren't really about wilderness. So he changed what people actually think wilderness is."

"What was there to change?"

"Years ago, people often thought of the wilderness as a place where land wouldn't have buildings but where they could still go to fish and hunt and mine gold."

"I thought one of the major aspects of parks and wilderness areas is that hunting is not allowed."

Joshua was shaking his head before I finished the sentence. "That's a myth. Hunting is allowed in a whole bunch of national parks and wilderness areas. The truth is that the main focus of lots of parks and wilderness areas is to manage the fish and game. Wilderness lakes are stocked with fish just so fishermen can have the fun of catching them. And the same bureaucrats manage big game as a crop to be harvested by hunters. That's why everyone thought that wolves and mountain lions and bears were problem animals that should be killed so ranchers could more easily raise cattle. Hunters killed uncountable numbers of predators. The California Grizzly was hunted to extinction."

I was intrigued not just by what Joshua was telling me but by his thoughtful, intelligent explanation. It was a recitation more fitting to a science writer than a teenage kid.

"Leopold said all this?" I said.

Joshua continued, "Aldo Leopold was the first naturalist to promote a new concept of 'Wilderness' as a place where animals would be left alone and not hunted at all. Leopold was the first to understand that killing all the wolves was a terrible thing. It totally screwed up the natural environment."

"Those carnivores are more than just simple predators?"

"Yes, yes, yes! Up until the early twentieth century, people thought apex predators were merely dangerous pests. Aldo saw the bigger picture. If you take away the apex predator, the game that was their food source explodes in population. Even worse, in the absence of apex predators, the mesopredator population takes over and wreaks havoc in the ecosystem."

"I've never heard of a mesopredator."

"A mesopredator is a mid-level predator. There are many examples of mesopredator population growth, but one that people often notice is coyotes. For eons, wolves kept coyote populations under control."

"Wolves eat coyotes?"

"No. But wolves have always dominated every landscape they're in, and they chased off or even killed coyotes that tried to sneak up and eat the wolf kills. That kept the coyote population in check. But with most of the wolves gone, coyote populations grew fast. While coyotes don't kill many cattle, they kill far more smaller ranch animals than the wolves ever did. Sheep and goats and chickens are much worse off with the wolves gone. And coyotes have spread to places they never were before. A coyote was seen in Central Park in New York and in Golden Gate Park in San Francisco. Coyotes have attacked people. You probably know that house pets in Tahoe are often eaten by coyotes."

I nodded. "I know people who've lost pets to coyotes."

"Well, thank the people who killed all the wolves. Every scientist knows that wolves are critically important. It was Leopold's discoveries that led to the re-introduction of wolves in Yellowstone Park."

"It sounds like you think wolves are a good thing and coyotes are a bad thing."

"No. I think we need a balance. Having man come into a landscape and make fundamental changes is bad. Killing off animal species is as bad and unnatural as paving over wetlands or taking fire out of the forest. The imbalance that results is detrimental in every way."

"What are other mesopredators besides coyotes?"

"Raccoons are a big one. Without apex predators, raccoon populations grow. They eat chickens and ducks, which gives farmers a new problem they never had before. Skunk populations explode as well."

"Skunks eat farm animals?"

"No, but they eat huge numbers of chicken eggs. Worse, they eat large numbers of honeybees, entire hives. You probably know that the decline of honeybees is a serious problem because bees are major pollinators of plants."

"It sounds like we should protect all apex predators."

"Yes, yes, yes!" It appeared to be Joshua's favorite phrase. "We should protect apex scavengers too. For example, vultures are protected by the Migratory Bird Act. But people still shoot them. They think that vultures are just scavengers, not majestic like eagles. So guess what happens when vultures are killed? The local rat populations explode."

"Because the rats eat carrion just like the vultures do, but the rats are scared off by the vultures."

Joshua nodded solemnly.

"The law of unintended consequences," I said.

"Leopold said, we should leave blank spots on the map. Places where we don't build roads and communities, places where we don't dam the rivers and put out the forest fires, places where we don't alter the natural fish and other wildlife populations."

"Places where we simply leave nature alone," I said.

I said, "I'm interested in what you write."

Joshua looked down and showed discomfort. "I'm reluctant to talk about it."

"Why?"

"I guess I'm just not confident."

"Will you tell me about your writing? I'm interested. I promise I won't judge. And I won't tell anyone a joke about a writer walking into a bar."

Joshua grinned, but he still looked skeptical.

The phone next to him rang. He picked it up. "Hello?" Joshua frowned. "Hello?" he said again. He listened, then hung up.

"Another hang-up call like the others?"

He nodded. "I heard the person breathing, then hang up."

"Have you tried the call back options? Star sixty-nine?"

"Yeah. Twice. It doesn't go through. The line is blocked."

"Have you told your father about these calls?"

"No. He pays to have the house staff around, thinking there's safety in numbers and all that. But his focus is a hundred percent on his business. Two hundred percent."

Joshua was silent for some time. "I also read Roxanne Monales," he said. "She took a different approach to nature writing. Her thing is to focus on learning how to make audiences willing to make changes to improve the chances that the natural world survives."

"Science plus communication?"

"Yeah. Monales has had a big effect on me. Ever since, I've fantasized about going to Georgia and being part of her center."

"The one Sky mentioned," I said.

"Yeah. Roxanne Monales started the Center For Nature Writing. It's outside of Atlanta, Georgia. She assembles big thinkers in the world of nature writing and has them give seminars at the center. I've read a lot about it. It sounds so cool!"

"I can tell it motivates you."

He nodded. "Yeah. After reading Roxanne Monales, I started thinking about principles of nature and ways to communicate their importance. If I can write about nature and ecology in simple, effective ways, then those ideas would be relatively easy to communicate."

"Sound bites for people to grasp and remember?"

Joshua frowned. "I'm not saying that people need simple ideas to understand. People understand lots of complex stuff. But they are distracted by, you know, pop culture stuff. If you show people a dense article about ecology and another article with pictures of actors or models, the ecology stuff gets overlooked."

"Ain't that the truth," I said. "I'm interested in these books you read. Leopold and Roxanne Monales. Could I see some of them?"

Joshua looked unsure of how to respond. After a pause, he

said, "I suppose you could come up to my room."

"I'd like that."

He stood and walked toward the main staircase. I followed him up a long, wide flight of stairs to a landing, where the stairs turned 180 degrees and then went up a shorter distance to the second floor. There was a large hallway with a tall ceiling and two upholstered chairs in a little sitting area. A smaller staircase continued up to the next level. The second floor hallway had three doorways that stood open, revealing large bedrooms. One door was closed. Joshua turned and went to the closed door. He opened it and walked inside.

The room was large, probably 18 by 20 feet, with a double bay window on one wall and a large single window on the other. The windows had thick patterned drapes that were pulled back to the sides with gold, braided cords. The room had a high, single bed with ornate posts at the corners.

The main feature of the room was a huge desk against the wall with the bay window. The desk looked like it once belonged to an 18th-century French aristocrat. It was curved to fit into the window bay. It had carved legs and curved drawers. Inlaid designs decorated the top edges and a maroon leather blotter stretched across the center.

To each side of the desk were bookcases filled with books, hardbacks and paperbacks. On the bedposts hung clothes, a hooded sweatshirt, some shirts. There was a beige rain jacket with a sketch portrait across the back.

"I recognize that," I said. "A portrait of John Muir."

"Yeah. Muir is one of my heroes. Like Aldo."

"Don't you have a T-shirt with that sketch on it?"

Joshua gave me a sheepish look as he nodded. "I had the sketch put on a hoodie, too."

The room was the opposite of what I expected for a teenager. The newest furniture was a century old. There were no electronics visible anywhere except a closed Apple laptop on a corner of the desk. Maybe Joshua kept every aspect of modern life hidden. Or maybe he didn't have any.

Joshua reached to one of the bookcases where five matching

books were lined up. He pulled one out and handed it to me. "This is one of Roxanne Monales's books."

I flipped through it and read a passage at random. The writing was dense with ideas yet was accessible and easy to read. There were also illustrations like I'd seen in books by other naturalists.

"Where did you get your love of nature? Are you a big hiker or camper?"

Joshua shook his head. "Not at all. I don't get out much."

"Really? That's curious."

"It's because…" Joshua stopped. His discomfort was obvious.

"You don't have to tell me. But I'm interested in how people like you think, how you come to your ideas. I assumed that nature writers spend a lot of time in the woods."

"I would like to." Joshua hesitated. "But I'm afraid."

"Afraid of the woods?"

He shook his head. "Afraid of people in the woods."

"Something bad happened in the woods," I said.

He nodded. "When I was young, we went on a picnic. Aria took care of the food. I wandered off into the trees, away from her and my dad." Joshua's voice choked. He cleared his throat. "Ever since then, I've never been able to go into the forest without being in a group."

I thought it best to change the subject. "Will your notes eventually be a book?"

Joshua seemed embarrassed. "Actually, I already did that. It's kind of a starter book."

"To test the waters?" I said.

"Yes. I uploaded it to Amazon. So it's now an ebook. You can read it on Kindle."

"Wow, how exciting."

He made a shrug. "Actually, it's not really doing anything. I've learned that just because you write a book doesn't mean anyone will read it. But it's sold a few copies. I guess finding an audience takes a long time."

"What's the title of the book?"

"It's called, 'Essential Principles of Nature.' It's a bad title.

Really puffed-up. Instead of inviting people into the subject, it scares them off."

I agreed with what Joshua said, but I didn't want to say it.

"These are the principles Sky Kool mentioned," I said.

"Yeah. Sky acts likes he's just a laid-back musician. But he's actually very perceptive. He can look at two similar passages of writing, and he'll notice that one is effective and the other isn't. And he can explain why."

"Kind of like a critic?"

Joshua seemed to think about it. "More like a writing teacher, even though he doesn't write much beyond song lyrics. Writing comes easily to him. He could probably plot out a novel."

"Could he plot out a murder?"

Joshua jerked as if he'd been slapped. He turned red. "What are you saying?"

"I didn't mean to be so abrupt. But I'm trying to find a possible murderer. My job is to consider everyone as a potential suspect."

Joshua's complexion paled. "Does that mean you wonder if I could have murdered Mr. Lightfoot?"

"I don't think you're the type."

Joshua looked horrified. Despite his obvious intelligence, it seemed he hadn't thought of the possibility that I could consider anyone he knew as a suspect. "You should have motive and... whatever else before you accuse someone of murder!"

"I wasn't accusing you or Sky. I'm just following up. You said that Lightfoot made fun of you studying ecology."

"But..." Joshua seemed frozen as if his voice had come unplugged.

I waited. People often reveal more when you don't fill in the conversational gaps.

"All this time, it turns out you're not interested in nature writing or ecology. You're just looking for a killer."

"Looking for a killer is my job, Joshua. But I'm also interested in the natural world and nature writing. I'm interested in your writing."

"Sure you are. And now you and my father can both make

jokes about me." Joshua stood up and walked out of the room. He went down the back stairs. I heard a door close hard.

I went down the main staircase. I looked around but saw no sign of Aria or anyone else. I let myself out.

Spot was eager to have me back in the Jeep. He put his cold wet nose on my neck, sniffing out hints of Pacific Heights.

I drove south to Geary, turned west, and headed out to Lands End. I zig-zagged my way south and found a parking place. I let Spot out, and we walked out to Ocean Beach.

There was a thick bank of fog pushing in from the Pacific, muffling the roar of waves that had traveled from Hawaii and more distant places before crashing on the huge expanse of sand. The fog was so heavy it condensed on my face like misty rain.

When we got to the area where dogs are allowed off leash, I let go of Spot's collar. He looked up at me.

"Go fly, Largeness. I'll watch for rogue waves."

He ran off into the fog so thick that I could barely see him. But the fog wasn't as dense as the fog descending over my mood. Joshua was the one person in the Kraytower mix who seemed the most innocent and trustworthy. Yet I'd ignored my instincts and played my detective role by the book, probing everyone for evidence that they might be guilty of a crime. As a result, I'd succeeded in making Joshua think I was just another insensitive adult. I'd driven him away from me. Yet my efforts had not brought me any closer to finding the killer.

TWENTY-FOUR

Carston Kraytower had given me his card with the
business address for Kraytower Growth Assets in the
Transamerica Pyramid skyscraper. He'd written down the name
of Wendell Merchant, someone with the title of investor liaison.
Merchant would supposedly arrange for me to have full access to
the business and its employees.

So I called and introduced myself and explained my desires.

Merchant was smooth and polished. Ninety minutes later,
I'd left Spot in charge of the Jeep in a little-known Embarcadero
parking place I remembered from my SFPD days, and I walked
into the lobby of the tower. As city skyscrapers go, it was as
unusual as they come, a very tall pyramidal structure that had
been configured to accommodate the box-type offices that
people worked out of. I remembered when it was newly built
that people high and low made fun of the building, which was
designed as a pointy tower to minimize the shadow it would cast
over nearby neighborhoods. Many considered it an abomination.
But as with many new concepts, its reputation slowly morphed
from embarrassment to pride. San Franciscans gradually came
to realize that it made the city skyline stand out like few other
buildings did for any city in the world.

Wendell Merchant met me at the lobby reception desk and
took me on a long elevator ride up to the KGA offices. He brought
me in through doors that had inset leather panels and shiny gold
handles and hinges. The carpet was thick, and the air had a faint-
but-elegant aroma of unsmoked pipe tobacco. Every surface,
counter and desk alike, appeared to be made of mahogany. There
was an area of open offices with a dozen well-dressed people—
mostly men—who were working on computers and talking on
headsets. Around the perimeter of the open offices were private

offices. The inner and outer walls all had many windows so one could stand anywhere and see though the offices to the famous views of The City, albeit from far above the street.

Merchant turned to me. "This is it. Mr. Kraytower said you are doing an investigation for him and that I should give you carte blanche. What is your desire?"

"I'd like to talk to a variety of people. I won't take long."

"To whom would you like to speak?"

I worried that I would be manipulated, whether subtly or directly. So I said, "May I wander? Pop in and talk to a variety of people?"

"Certainly. I didn't realize you were coming here today, but that is no problem. I can send out an announcement to the current crew. If any don't immediately see it, and if they seem hesitant to answer any questions, you can use my name and ask them to check their messages."

I nodded.

"Perhaps you would like to word my missive?" he asked.

He turned to a computer, tapped some keys, and then looked at me as his hands hovered above the keyboard.

Again I wondered about potential manipulation of my perception, but it seemed the best approach. Maybe I could be vague.

I said, "How about, 'Mr. Kraytower has hired a consultant named Owen McKenna to explore ways of enhancing internal communications. He will be coming around and asking some questions. Mr. Kraytower requests that we cooperate fully. It won't take long.'"

Wendell Merchant typed. "Shall I hit 'send?'"

"Please."

He clicked and then said, "Would you like anything else? Coffee? Coffee Cake? We have it brought in from a deli near the Ferry Building. Trust me, it is the best you've ever had."

"No doubt," I said. "I think I'm fine. I'll ask if I think of something."

Merchant nodded and then held out his hand, palm up, gesturing toward the financial worker bees.

I nodded and wandered into the small sea of desks.

I spent the next thirty minutes wandering, walking up to strangers, introducing myself, and then asking probing, insightful questions. My technique was obviously superb. My trenchant commentary clearly revealed an impressive grasp of what these people did and how they did it. My casual throw-away lines were designed to catch the most controlled people off guard. And my multi-tasking ability to ask a question and then only vaguely pay attention to the answer while I gave a laser focus to the information on their computer screen was a skill that Sherlock Holmes himself would have envied.

Thirty minutes later I had precisely nothing.

No one revealed anything useful about James Lightfoot or Sebastian Perry. Several people hadn't even met them. Of the rest, they'd only come into contact with the victims once or twice. Several of the people had barely met their boss Carston Kraytower. Some people were new employees, and some had been at the firm for almost as long as Kraytower and his closest associates.

As I thanked Wendell Merchant and left, I felt like a complete failure.

My return trip down the elevator was alone. Once I was out on the street, I began to clarify the few things I knew.

After Kraytower started his firm, he was quickly joined by two of his buddies who went to school with him at Yale, Lightfoot and Perry. It quickly became a business run by a trio of men who were close historically, but were never especially close socially. They had a business relationship that was loosely controlled by Kraytower even though the other men played important roles.

One of the people I'd spoken with referred to those three men as The Founders.

The firm was very successful and eventually took on many employees. But none of those employees really knew The Founders. They only knew the rules of the job and that if they carefully played by those rules and worked very, very hard, they would eventually make a great deal of money.

Now that two of the founders had been killed, it hadn't really changed the jobs or lives of the other workers. Losing two founders was upsetting, but it didn't change the business in any critical way beyond potentially losing the investors who the dead founders had worked with.

So why were two of the founders killed?

The only thing that made sense was that it wasn't about the business. The business streaked forward like a money-making rocketship.

If the murders weren't about the business, then they must be personal. Someone was trying to harm the founders for personal reasons. Or, if they were very diabolical, they were killing founders as an effort to destroy Kraytower.

I drove back to Tahoe wondering about the killer's motive.

TWENTY-FIVE

There were two men in the upstairs hallway when I arrived at my office the next morning. They stood on either side of my office door. They wore navy blue pants with creases and high thread counts. White shirts with button-down collars. No ties but navy blue blazers with three brass buttons on each sleeve. Shiny black shoes. One man was big, the other was very big. Not quite as tall as me, but half again as wide and thick, and all muscle. But for the size difference, they looked alike. They had enough V to their upper bodies that they could both have weapons in concealed-carry holsters and no one would know. Under their arms or at the small of their backs. The men were clean shaven and had matching hair cuts, short enough to require no upkeep, long enough to take a comb impression to telegraph good grooming. The office workers who populated the other businesses on my floor would think they were lawyers for the simple reason that everyone else in Tahoe during the summer wore hiking shoes, T-shirts, and jeans or shorts. Only after later reflection would any observers realize that they'd never seen lawyers that muscular.

As Spot and I came up the stairs, the men stared at Spot.

"Morning, gentlemen," I said. "Help you?" I pulled out my office key and smiled at them. It was the low wattage grin of amusement, the way you'd look at carnival clowns.

The big one pointed at my doorknob as if to say that I should open the door. His eyes were on Spot. Wary. Both he and his partner had their arms at their sides, hands free, the better to grab something, whether weapons or adversaries.

"Name's Spot," I said, addressing their unspoken thoughts. "You can pet him, if you like."

The men didn't move.

I unlocked the door and walked in. Spot walked in with me, turned, and faced the doorway so that the men would have to come past him to enter the office.

Spot did a slow wag. He liked being a doorman, making all visitors undergo a mandatory olfactory investigation before entering our sanctuary.

Big stepped forward first. When Spot sniffed him, he raised his arms as if Spot were going to frisk him. Or maybe chew on a hand. Spot took his time, then looked at the other man. As Big walked past and stood to one side of my desk, Bigger stepped forward and raised his arms, as well. Maybe it was Spot's faux diamond ear stud that gave the men pause.

Spot took more time with Bigger and seemed especially interested in the man's right side, his armpit, his waist, his jacket pocket, his hand.

"C'mon, Largeness," I said. "Let the man into the room. Meat always tastes better if the animal isn't stressed before it's slaughtered."

Bigger didn't react.

I pulled on Spot's collar and got him to lie on his Harlequin Camo bed. He went down reluctantly and stayed with his chest to the bed, elbows like outriggers, rear legs with knees high, the "ready" stance for a dog.

"Have a seat, gentlemen," I said, while I loaded the coffee maker. When I was done, I sat in my desk chair.

The men were both still standing.

"Please, sit."

They didn't sit and didn't even respond except that Big reached behind him and shut the office door. Neither man had spoken.

"Maybe you fellows are mute," I said. "Or maybe this is an audition for a low-budget Harpo Marx sequel. If so, I'm impressed. Give me the casting director's card. I'll call her and recommend she give you the parts."

Big finally spoke.

"We're taking you off the Kraytower case."

"English words," I said, "and good diction and pronunciation. Your message should be obvious. But humor me, I'm slow. What's that mean, taking me off?"

"No more working the case. Go play golf or something."

"You're telling me I'm not to do my job."

"You can work. Just not the Kraytower job," he said.

I looked at Bigger. "What do you think?"

"Just giving you the message," he said.

"What if I ignored your message," I said. "I keep searching for truth and justice, help Kraytower find out why his partners are being murdered."

"Be a big mistake," Big said.

Bigger made a slight nod. "Very big mistake," he added.

"And how would that mistake manifest itself?" I asked.

They stared at me.

"Manifest means to show or make apparent or display in a clear way," I said.

"You got a dog and a girl," Big said. "You wouldn't want them hurt."

"No, I wouldn't."

"That's your message," he said.

"Who sends the message?" I asked.

Their faces were placid and unyielding.

"Let's try a simpler question. Who do you guys work for?"

Big walked to the door. Bigger followed. They turned and looked at me.

"Is that look supposed to scare me?" I said.

They didn't react.

"Got it," I said. "Just like to know where I stand."

They opened the door and walked out.

I watched out the window. They came out into the parking lot down below and walked over to a new, black Range Rover parked four spaces over from my rusted, bullet-hole-ventilated Jeep. Probably didn't want their vehicle too close to my Jeep in case it was like exposing your child to an infectious disease. The Range Rover was polished to a shine and had over-sized, low-profile tires, also polished and shiny.

As they drove off, I wondered what kind of men shine their car tires.

TWENTY-SIX

My phone rang. It was Doc Lee. "You know you only call me when you want macabre medical information."

"Should I drink beer with one of your colleagues instead?"

"No. But I should probably have some advance notice about your twisted focus du jour."

"There's a drug called etorphine. Vets use it to tranquilize rhinos and elephants. I'm tracking a killer who's using it to murder people. I thought the lofty intellectual perception of an exalted doctor would be useful."

Doc Lee didn't respond immediately. Maybe he wondered if he could be a useful etorphine resource. Or maybe he was considering how he should reward me for using the terms lofty, intellectual, and exalted in a single sentence describing him.

"Let's meet at the Cold Water Brewery," he said.

I drove down to the craft beer restaurant in the center of South Lake Tahoe, not far from the hospital on the South Shore. I sat at one of the outdoor tables to wait for Doc Lee. Spot sat next to me. I was tired. I yawned. As all dog owners know, yawns are catching with dogs. Sure enough, after watching me, Spot yawned, his mouth open enough to hold a basketball. I leaned my elbows on the table and lowered my head until the heels of my hands supported my chin. Spot's head was above the table top. He lowered his head until his jawbone rested on the table.

In my peripheral vision, I saw a woman hold out her phone and take a picture of us.

Spot got tired. He turned his head to the side, off the edge of the table, and walked his front paws down until he was lying on the patio stones. He stretched his head forward and rested his chin on his paws. Maybe it was my turn to copy him. But I didn't want to lie on the terrace. People are so picky.

Doc Lee pulled up in his Porsche Panamera. He was very gentle shutting the door, gentle also as he walked up in his Italian, woven-leather shoes. He had never seemed macho like other ER doctors I'd met.

He looked down at Spot. Spot lifted his head but didn't stand up. He knew that Doc Lee wasn't much of a dog person, and Spot was tired, having held up his giant head for several minutes.

Doc Lee gave Spot the minimum touch that could be considered a pet, sat on the chair next to me, and reached out his manicured hand.

We shook.

"Never seen a checkered watch band," I said.

Lee held out his arm so that his sleeve pulled back. "I'm studying up on chess. This goes with my new chess board. Black and Rosewood." He held up his arm and gazed at his watch. "It looks sharp when I'm playing."

"New watch?" I said.

"A Jaeger-LeCoultre. Did you ever think about the fact that a significant feature of chess is that there is no hidden information? Everyone, players and bystanders, can always see everything there is to know at any time. The only way to get an advantage is with brain power."

"No, I never thought about that," I said. "Probably why I'm no good at it. Can't hide an ace anywhere."

"These are critical aspects to game analysis." He sounded very earnest.

"No doubt," I said.

Doc Lee looked puzzled, like a smart kid who didn't get why certain other kids didn't work to ability. "If you paid attention to these qualities," he said, "you could probably be good at chess."

"Maybe," I said. I was thinking about how Spot didn't excel like so many highly trained dogs, unless, of course, excelling produced food treats. "If I had a chess trainer with a pocket full of peanuts..." I said, and then dropped the thought.

A waiter walked up, a hopeful look on his face. Doc Lee and I each ordered different IPAs, in-house brands. The waiter nodded and left.

"You said you had an etorphine killer," Doc Lee said.

"Right. I don't have any close veterinary friends. So I thought maybe you could tell me about such drugs."

"I looked it up," he said. "Deadly stuff. What else do you want to know?"

"I'm wondering why a murderer would choose it for a weapon."

Doc Lee shook his head. "Given a choice, no one would choose etorphine. It's too dangerous, too hard to administer, too hard to acquire. You want to kill someone, there are a hundred easier weapons. A thousand."

"So why do you think someone would use etorphine?"

He drank a big gulp of beer. For a refined guy who was focused on style, his eating habits were closer to those of an NFL player than what one would expect.

"There's only one logical explanation," he said. "Someone didn't have any other good weapon, and they happened to have access to etorphine, and they didn't know how dangerous it is."

"When you say dangerous, do you mean you could accidentally kill yourself with it?"

"Yeah. Yourself or some other person you don't want to kill. Let's say someone finds a tranquilizer dart with etorphine in it. If they scratch themselves with it, they die. If they accidently get a drop of the liquid on any red abraded skin and don't wash it off immediately, they die. If they absorb it any other way—a tiny drop splashed in their mouth or inhaled through their nose— they die."

"Nasty stuff," I said. "So if you had access to etorphine and wanted to murder someone, you would choose a different method."

"Of course." Doc Lee gave me a look like a frustrated teacher gives to a student who is acting especially dense. "There's a reason why people like guns. You can control them better."

"But they're not as deadly as etorphine," I said.

More of the look. "Nothing is as deadly as etorphine."

"How does it work?"

Doc Lee paused, no doubt wondering how to explain something complicated to a philistine. "I looked it up and read some studies about opioid agonist efficacy. The operative consideration is..." He stopped talking. Maybe it was the look on my face.

"Okay, let me take a different approach," he said.

"That would be good," I said.

"Drugs have a chemical makeup, right?"

"Right," I said. "A formula."

Doc Lee gulped more beer. "Morphine is popular because it has many uses. Pain killer, sedative, relaxant, anxiety reducer. Morphine can be made from the poppy plant. Now imagine a clever chemist who analyzes morphine. He figures out the chemical formula. The chemist realizes that he can use a synthetic process to make morphine without needing any poppy plant. In the process, he figures out a way to adjust the formula to make the synthetic morphine a thousand times more potent."

"You always say 'he' instead of 'she,'" I said.

"Of course," Doc Lee said. "In my experience, it's always a he that comes up with such nasty stuff. Women are much less nasty." He paused. "Or men like me. Less hoof-pawing, humpa humpa hetero."

"Humpa humpa hetero?"

"If you have to ask, forget it," he said.

"Got it. Is there no legitimate use for etorphine beyond tranquilizing rhinos and elephants?"

"Not that I know of."

"How does it kill?"

"Etorphine kills many ways at once. It produces hypoxemia, hypertension, respiratory depression, pulmonary shunting, ventilation perfusion mismatch...Shall I go on?"

Maybe my eyes glazed over.

"All I'm doing is answering your question, but you're giving me that look again," he said. "Let's just say that etorphine paralyzes your breathing and stops your heart with a massive heart attack."

"That I understand. You said you wouldn't want to use

etorphine as a murder weapon. But if you did, how would you administer it?"

"Same as with animals. A tranquilizer dart."

"And you'd need a tranquilizer gun," I said.

"No. Tranquilizer guns are used because it's hard to get near a rhinoceros without the risk of the rhino killing you. But with people, you could have a dart in your pocket. Get near the person you want out of your way and then poke them with the dart."

"Where?"

"Doesn't matter. Let's say you're walking along with someone. They look the other way for a moment, you poke them in the back. They feel a little prick, then presto, their heart seizes. They collapse and are dead within seconds of hitting the ground. A typical autopsy might not even reveal the pinprick hole. No one would ever know about the etorphine unless the pathologist ordered a toxicology test." Doc Lee made the explanation with his typical breeziness. No stress, no worry, no anxiety. Just another puzzle for a doctor who sees evil in the ER every day.

"Would etorphine cause a painful death?"

"Sure. Heart attacks are painful. But it would be over really fast. All things considered, if you ranked all the ways a person can die, etorphine poisoning would be one of the less unpleasant ways. Also, it's not gory, so that makes it more attractive."

I thought about it for a moment. "If you're going to die very fast anyway, what difference does gore make in the choice?"

Doc Lee shrugged. "Analysis would suggest it doesn't matter. A death that is not hugely painful and is over very fast would seem a good way to go. But if you ask most people which would be a better way to die, etorphine poisoning or decapitation by guillotine, most would choose etorphine."

"Good point."

We paused, sipped beer, then changed the subject back to chess.

When we were done with our beer, I thanked him, and we said goodbye.

TWENTY-SEVEN

After talking to Doc Lee, I went back to my office. Spot lay on his camo bed, and I sat at my desk and drank coffee. It was a beautiful day in a spectacular place. Yet a powerful malaise came over me, as if my leftover mood from the day before had been intensified. I had no clues about how to find a twisted killer who used poison. I'd learned nothing helpful in San Francisco. First I'd put Joshua in mortal danger up on the snow of Lake Aloha, and I managed to scare his father to death. Then I'd gone to his Pacific Heights house, made some careless comments to Joshua and succeeded in destroying his trust. Joshua was the one person in the mix I cared about, but he might never talk to me again. When I got back to Tahoe, I'd been threatened by two intimidating men who mentioned my girlfriend and my dog as possible targets of violence.

It was a combination of distress that made me doubt my work and my value to anyone. I was accomplishing nothing beyond driving my mood further down into a dark lonely place, a cellar which the brightest summer evening sun can't illuminate.

On my way home, on impulse, I pulled into the parking lot of Street's condo. I hadn't called with advance notice because I knew I'd just sound depressing. As I got out of the Jeep, I worried that I'd spread my funk to her. I told myself that it was my obligation to bring something positive to every meeting with her. But it was no good. I had no good news to offer.

Then her door opened and Blondie rushed out and Street stepped out into the setting sunlight. She walked toward me. The light cast her in a golden glow, reflecting off her auburn hair and highlighting her willowy figure. It was like one of the big heavy switches on a circuit breaker box had been thrown. Electricity coursed through me, and I had an epiphany of sorts like in the

Tom Petty song Here Comes My Girl.

All can be made better simply by the power of a woman's love.

I walked over to her, bent down and hugged her hard, lifting her up off her feet. We stood there, silent, holding each other for a long time.

We spent the evening doing nothing but eating finger food, sitting on her couch, holding hands, talking in low voices, listening to soft classical music. Copeland. Elgar. I told Street I felt as if I'd been saved.

"No, not saved," she said. "Deep down, you have a constitution of granite. You don't need saving. But you do need a little love and kindness."

"I'll say. Thank you so much."

TWENTY-EIGHT

Spot and I were at my office early the next day. I was drinking coffee and doing my email. Spot was sleeping on his camo bed. When I finished deleting the emails, I stood up and drank my coffee at the window.

A black Range Rover turned off Kingsbury Grade and pulled into my office lot. It was newly polished and shiny and drove with an athletic gait.

The Range Rover parked in the far corner, where its occupants would have a view of my building entrance and quick access to the roadway. The doors didn't open. The windows were smoked so I couldn't see how many men were inside. I assumed it was the same as the day before, Big and Bigger, dressed for a San Francisco business meeting, practicing being mute.

I finished my second coffee. The day before, I'd purchased three old-fashioned donuts at the Safeway. I'd eaten just one in service to my Street-inspired low-sugar diet. Today I ate the second donut, which I'd spread out over the two cups of coffee. I savored the last bite as I watched the Range Rover. That left one donut, so I was good for another day. Like having money in the bank.

There was no movement in the Range Rover. They were waiting. For what I didn't know. Probably they wanted to see if I did something that looked like investigating the hedge fund murders, the investigation which they had wanted me to stop. If I persisted, they could catch me red-handed.

They could of course come up to my office like before and plead their case. Because they remained in their vehicle, it made me think they didn't want to plead it within hearing range of other people. They probably felt that they could be more convincing if I were alone at my cabin. Or off in the forest. That would likely end badly for me.

Maybe I could shape the outcome.

My coffee counter is part of a built-in, white, Formica cabinet, Ikea style, with a tiny sink barely big enough to rinse a shot glass and cupboard doors below. To the left of the sink is a tall, narrow closet. I reached in behind a couple of jackets, felt around, and pulled out a canvas-and-wood contraption that I'd been given by a retiring cop on the SFPD. The cop had immigrated from England decades before, and he said it was an example of how the English were less techy but just as effective as Americans.

When I quit the SFPD, I turned in my gun and all of my cop stuff including my Kevlar vest. But I hung onto the low-tech vest because it seemed like it might be useful one day.

The vest was made of heavy canvas that buttoned up both sides. Sewn into the front of the vest was a piece of half-inch plywood fronted with a sheet of 20-guage steel. It was a poor man's bullet-proof vest, ungainly and hard to conceal but suitable for stopping knives and small caliber bullets. Of course, someone could shoot me in the head or throat. But most people aim for the largest part of the body. The vest was one-sided. Shoot me from the front, I might live. Shoot me from the back, the vest still might stop the bullet. But the bullet would have gone through me first.

I slipped the vest over my head. It was bulky and had prominent corners and seemed impossible to conceal. If I couldn't conceal the vest, then any assailant would see it and do their best to shoot me in the head. Or, if they wanted to beat me up, take out my legs with a baseball bat.

Maybe if I had more clothes over the vest.

I pulled my short-sleeve summer shirt over the vest. The plywood corners were still obvious. In the closet was an old sweater. I pulled it on. It stretched over the vest, but it was snug and did nothing to hide the flat piece of plywood strapped to my front. And wearing a sweater on a summer day would look suspicious. I pulled the sweater off and put on a blue windbreaker with a Keep Tahoe Blue logo on the upper left side of the chest. The windbreaker was much looser. It didn't do a good job of hiding the plywood vest, but it succeeded in making it less obvious. The windbreaker also looked like too much wrap for a summer day. So I unzipped the front several inches and rolled up the sleeves. It might look like I was going boating and expected a cool breeze over the lake.

I loosely rolled the sweater and draped it over the back of my neck. I tied the sweater arms at the base of my throat as if I were a yacht club trust fund guy. Some sweater fabric hung down over the area where the plywood corners were most obvious.

The only mirror in my office was a little one over the little sink. I'd never really looked at myself in it. It was just the right size and height for someone 5' 3" to put on lipstick.

Judging by the tiny mirror view, I looked way overdressed for a summer day. And the flat square under my clothes was still noticeable. But I knew the plywood was there, and they didn't. The vest might go unnoticed by the brutes who were focused on scaring me.

I dialed Sergeant Diamond Martinez on his cell.

"Sí," he answered.

"There are two thugs in my office parking lot waiting to roust me. I thought you might like to be there when I roust back."

"Roust back? The wonders of English vernacular are boundless."

"Keeps life interesting for you immigrant English-as-Second-Language types, huh?" I said.

"What kind of thugs are these?"

"The kind that wear dry-cleaned suits, drive a new black Range Rover with high-gloss tires, and are mostly mute. When they do talk, it's obvious that anything longer than a monosyllabic word is a challenge."

"Not the preferred profile Douglas County is trying to attract with its tourist marketing plan," Diamond said. "We want college-grad skiers and kayakers with two-point-three children per couple. Do they have a reason to pick on you? Or do they just take exception to tall guys with beautiful girlfriends?"

"Interesting you say that, considering Street thinks everyone focuses on her acne scars and her excessive thinness and her devotion to bug science. Not the package your average NFL fan would want for chips-and-dip-on-the-couch cheerleader companionship."

"Guess I ain't everyone."

"No, you ain't," I said.

"So these guys in the double R..." Diamond trailed off.

"They stopped by yesterday and said I should stop trying to find out who murdered the hedge fund executives."

"How do you see this playing out?" he asked.

I looked out the window as I talked. The Range Rover was still shiny as ever. "I was thinking that I might drive up the Grade a bit and stop to do some investigating. They will probably follow to make sure my investigating doesn't infringe on their desires. I could talk to them. In the event that something were to happen outside of the parameters of what law enforcement officers approve of, you could be in the area."

"Where you gonna pull over?" Diamond asked.

"I was thinking Middle Kingsbury, not far from the Charthouse Restaurant. There's a road that turns off to the south. Very narrow. Most people never see it. I'll pull in and stop where there's heavy tree cover. They'll follow. You could park some distance away and walk in through the trees."

"These guys carry?" Diamond asked.

"I assume so. Wear your vest."

"You gonna bring His Largeness?"

"Always a good idea," I said. "But now that I think of it, I don't want to put him at risk with enforcers who might shoot first and think later. So I'll bring him but probably leave him in the Jeep. If they see him in the Jeep, and I don't let him out, they'll think that provides them an advantage."

Diamond finished my thought. "As if you rely on him for protection and that without him, you'll be a pushover."

"I can see you'll have a Lieutenant's insignia soon."

"No desk job for this lettuce picker. I'm up at the top of Kingsbury Grade, just west of Daggett Pass. Give me five minutes to get down to your area."

We hung up.

I studied the Range Rover for a few minutes so Diamond could get to wherever he wanted to be.

"Hey Largeness," I said.

He was on his side, sleeping, eyes sealed shut. At the sound of his name, he didn't open his eyes or change his breathing. But his tail made a single thwap on the camo bed. Maybe he was dreaming of a Porterhouse steak and a baked potato, and his subconscious brain thought I was calling him to dinner.

"The mute guys are out in the parking lot. We could engage with them for a little excitement," I said.

Spot didn't move his tail at this further explanation. But I sensed that his breathing was less slow and deep. Probably waiting for a hot-button word.

"It would entail going for a ride," I said.

That last word woke him up, albeit without much energy. He rolled up onto his chest. He yawned, put his front paws out, and walked his legs back until he was in a sitting position. Then he straightened out his rear legs and stood nose to the doorknob, doing a slow wag, still groggy.

I grabbed my clipboard with the yellow pad of paper and opened the office door. We left and headed down the stairs.

Before we pushed out the entrance, I looked to see that the Range Rover was still there. Once outside, I studiously avoided looking in their direction. I kept my head down as Spot and I walked to the Jeep. I was just a distracted, country bumpkin PI who was no match for sophisticated enforcers from The City.

I let Spot into the back of the Jeep. It took some effort to get myself behind the steering wheel, sliding in so that my vest didn't cut into my thighs or jab me in the throat. Then I drove out of the lot and turned up Kingsbury Grade.

The Range Rover followed.

When I got to the place I'd described to Diamond, I turned off on a narrow road. I drove to an area that was some distance from any houses and pulled off where the tree cover was heavy. I parked under some pines and between two boulders.

I grabbed a Bic pen and my clipboard and got out, trying to move as if I were wearing just the windbreaker with no plywood underneath. I tried to keep the sweater arms draped over my shoulders so they would cover the corners of the plywood.

I carried the clipboard at my chest, something like a magician's accessory. It looked like it was important. But its only purpose was as a distraction. If I kept the clipboard in motion, an observer would be less likely to notice my stiff, awkward body movements.

The Range Rover came down the road and pulled off behind my Jeep. Both doors opened. The two men who'd visited me in my office got out. They wore clothes similar to what they'd worn their last visit, but dark gray instead of navy. It was effective. No one would doubt the intentions of men who were so well dressed. Except an observant Tahoe local who knew that fancy clothes and shiny tires in the mountains might indicate that something was amiss.

I looked through the woods toward the nearest house and then turned as if I had just heard a sound and discovered the well-dressed men moving toward me.

"Hey, gentlemen," I said, moving the clipboard in front of my chest, my pen poised as if I were about to make some notes. "I remember you. The two loquacious professors, right?"

The smaller of the two men, the one I thought of as Big, walked forward. Bigger hung back.

"Checking to see if you're gonna drop the Kraytower case."

"The short answer is no. I gotta earn a living like everyone else."

"Then we're gonna force you to quit."

"How you gonna do that? Those steroid muscles are good for show. But they slow you down. You couldn't knock the wind out of a hamster if you jumped on it."

"I can knock the wind out of you with a single punch that'll break you near in half." He raised his fists up in front of his mouth and bent his knees a bit. He looked serious in the way that a professional boxer looks serious.

This was the tipping point. I now knew that they were going to hurt me in a severe way. If I could taunt the man in front of me, maybe I could make him respond without careful consideration.

Maybe I could keep myself from being beaten to death.

"Better be careful," I said. "I can do fifty sit ups. Abs like wood. Hell, the truth is, that's too modest. My abs are like steel. You could hurt your hand."

I waggled my clipboard in front of my chest. I bent forward at the waist as if tensing for a blow. My real reason was to lessen how much the upper right corner of the plywood was projecting. I could see it pushing out from under my windbreaker.

The man hesitated.

"I ain't gonna quit my job just because you don't like it, Mr. Big. I'm ready. Give me your best attempt at knocking out my wind. I doubt I'll even notice it." I tossed the clipboard onto the ground and raised my own fists up near my chin.

The man did a little two-step, his fists still up in front of his mouth. Everything about him telegraphed professional.

"I can see that you puffed-up gym rats don't know crapola about fighting in the real world." I worried that he'd surprise me with a punch to my face. If I couldn't dodge it, I suspected he could kill me with a good head shot. But if his ego was strong enough and his brain stupid enough, my taunt might work.

I did a little footwork of my own, bouncing on my toes. "Real men don't care about all this image crap, fists up, acting like you're a serious boxer. We don't posture and wear those fancy clothes and shine our car tires. You're probably wearing gold lamé underpants as we speak. Am I right? I'll give you a hundred bucks to show me your undies."

He let fly with a gut punch, leaning into it with all his weight, driving his fist out and up as if to fling me into the woods, super-hero style.

It was a heavy, impressive blow, like I'd been hit with a baseball bat. It made my abdomen ache as it drove me backward. Even though I'd hoped for it, the force of impact surprised me. Without the vest, that single blow might have killed me.

The sound of the impact was like hitting a bass drum, while over that sound came the high-pitched snap and crackle of breaking hand bones.

His scream was dramatic, a high-decibel, childlike screech that echoed through the forest and telegraphed physical and psychic pain in near equal, epic proportions. Like a ringing church bell that takes some time for the sound to dwindle, the man's scream lasted a long time.

As he stumbled back and dropped down, knees to the dirt, I heard two voices in quick succession.

"You tricked him, you mother!" the bigger man shouted as he pulled his gun on me. "You're dead!"

"Sheriff! Freeze!" Diamond shouted from behind the man. He had his gun pointed at the man's back. "Drop the gun! Hands in the air!"

Bigger's eyes went wide. But he didn't move. Big was in too much pain to react.

"DROP THE GUN!" Diamond repeated. "NOW!"

Bigger slowly dropped his gun and raised his arms high.

The man on his knees in front of me cradled his right wrist with his left hand. The angle of his hand made me think that he hadn't just broken a number of hand bones but maybe both lower arm bones as well. I stepped behind Big and used my foot to push him forward onto his front. He tried to get his broken hand out of the way, but wasn't fast enough. He landed on it and screamed anew, this time with his face in the dirt.

I kneeled on his back. He whimpered as I patted him down. I didn't have gloves. But I found some tissues. I used them to take a 9mm Glock from a concealed carry holster in the small of his back. The man had no other weapons that I found. I released the magazine, pulled the slide back, and took a round out of the chamber. I put the round and magazine and gun in my windbreaker pocket.

"Hands behind your head!" Diamond shouted at the bigger man. When the man complied, Diamond used his shoe to kick the man's gun well across the forest duff.

Diamond shouted, "On your knees!"

Again the man hesitated. Diamond shouted the command a second time. The man slowly kneeled in the dirt. Diamond kicked him forward onto his face just as I'd done.

"Hands behind your back!"

"Excessive use of force," the man said into the dirt, a phrase he'd no doubt learned from lawyers during past altercations with law enforcement.

Diamond said, "If you don't do as I say, leaving you alive would be excessive tolerance."

The man slowly got his hands behind his back. Diamond cuffed him, then kept his gun in the man's back as he patted him down. He found no other weapon.

Diamond turned toward me.

"Spare cuffs?" I called out.

Diamond tossed them to me.

My man's mangled hand was just visible under his right side. I slid one cuff around his broken wrist and clicked it tight.

"Hands behind your back," I said.

He was slow to respond. Too busy crying in pain.

I jerked on the cuffs. He screamed as loud as before.

"Stop with the baby act." I dragged his broken arm out and up and around behind his back and cuffed it to his other wrist, all the moves accompanied by his howling.

I stood and pulled off my windbreaker and vest.

"Now I get it," Diamond said when he saw what I was wearing. "Clever retro garb."

"Beastly uncomfortable," I said in an English accent as I dropped it. It accidentally landed on the back of the man's head. It thudded hard, but Big was all screamed out.

Diamond holstered his piece. He walked over to Bigger's gun, pulled on blue latex gloves, picked it up, and unloaded it.

Diamond walked over to his SUV, reached into his evidence bag, and came back with evidence bags and a marker. He dropped Bigger's gun into one of the baggies. Then he uncapped the marker.

"What did you say their names were?"

I shrugged. "Don't know." I pointed at the guy who slugged me. "I call that one Big. The other, bigger one, I call Bigger."

Diamond wrote on the baggies with the marker. "We'll see if their IDs corroborate that."

I handed him Big's gun. Diamond put it in a bag.

"Both these idiots have Glock nines and wear the same suits," Diamond said. "Guess they always wanted to be twins." Diamond unbuckled each man's belt and pulled their pants off over their shiny Italian shoes. "Safer to search their pockets," he said.

Turns out that Big's undies weren't gold lamé.

Diamond reached into the men's pockets and emptied the contents into the appropriate baggies.

Diamond mirandized the men and then said, "Let's get these beefcakes into the back of my patrol vehicle," Diamond said.

"I'll help you with your guy first," I said.

The two of us jerked Bigger to his feet and walked him to the Douglas County SUV. As we pushed him, the man looked down and back and tried to stomp Diamond's feet.

Diamond surprised me with the power of his sudden response.

"Bad move, cara de mierda," he said as he slammed the man toward the SUV's hood. As if it were a magic trick, Diamond somehow came down with his forearm on the back of the much taller man's neck. The man grunted as he did a face plant on the hood of the vehicle. Something snapped. A tooth maybe. A smear of blood marred the hood.

"Wow, that was impressive," I said. "Guy's the size of a bull, but you dominate like a matador."

"Easy when they're stupid. Don't like beefcakes stomping my feet. Maybe you can open the back door."

I did as asked.

Diamond got the man somewhat upright, shifted him sideways and ran him head first into the back of the SUV. The man went in until his head hit the inside of the far door. That was another impressive impact. His bare legs stuck out the open door.

"Pull your legs in," Diamond said.

The man didn't move.

Diamond walked around and opened the door next to where the man's head was. He leaned down and whispered into the man's ear.

The man bent his legs until they were inside.

Diamond shut both doors.

"What did you say to him?" I asked.

Diamond lowered his voiced as if telling a secret. "There are some Mexican words, which, when said with the right tone, will get people to do whatever you want."

"What if they don't speak the language?"

"Doesn't matter if they know it or not."

"Mexican words, not Spanish words?"

"Sí."

"Gotta learn that someday," I said.

We got the smaller big man over to the patrol vehicle, opened the rear door, and piled him in on top of the bigger man, then shut the doors.

"Shame they're wearing such nice suit jackets," Diamond said. "Get all dirty and wrinkled." He walked over and picked up both of the men's pants, opened the right front passenger door, and tossed the pants in.

"Could be one of those miracle fabrics," I said. "Blood and slobber wash right off."

"But the stink of stupidity will still imbue the cloth," Diamond said.

"Always knew you were a poet."

TWENTY-NINE

I followed Diamond to the Stateline jail. Two deputies were
there to help.

An hour later, Diamond and I were talking out front. He
handed me a piece of paper.

"Big one's name is Tony Columbo and the bigger one's name
is Luigi Romero. They hire out." Diamond handed me a business
card. "This was in Big's wallet."

I read the type. "'Columbo Romero. We turn hard cases
soft.'" Under the sell line was a Gmail address. I handed the card
back. "Cute. Glad to know I was a hard case."

"Plywood was, anyway," Diamond said.

"So these guys model themselves after Italian blood
brothers."

"Sí. Enforcers who live in Pleasanton."

"East Bay," I said. "Do you suppose they do any kind of work
or just intimidation?"

"According to their sheet, they're old-fashioned brawlers who
tried to go upscale. One statement said they dreamed up the
fancy clothes concept because they thought it was good branding.
Turns out Columbo's great grandfather was San Francisco Mafia
before the Chinese took over."

"Displaced by the Triads?"

"Sí,"

"Any idea who hired them to roust me?"

He shook his head. "My best persuasion techniques aren't
legally permissible. Lots of witnesses in the jail, too."

"All you could do is ask politely," I said.

"Which I did. And they said they don't know who hired them.
They claim it was an anonymous hire through email. Payment by
cash drop."

"Maybe they're telling the truth, or maybe it's a good way to evade talking. Either way, we're left in the dark. I wonder if there is a clever way we could get some info, sneak it out of them."

Diamond shrugged. "One's busy crying in pain. 'Gimme a doctor,' he says. The other's crying about calling his lawyer. Pretty sure they've been around enough to know that if you rat on your client, you never get more clients."

"And you maybe get dead."

"There's that," he said.

"Their addresses on their sheet? Maybe I should pay a visit to Pleasanton."

"It's under their names," he said, pointing to fine print on the piece of paper.

I rummaged in my pockets.

"Here," Diamond said. He handed me a Post-it note and a pen.

"Thanks." I wrote down the address. "Just one address. Maybe they live together."

"Maybe. Italian Americans are like Mexicans that way," Diamond said. "Family is everything."

"Yet your only family is your mother in Mexico City, right? No one has your back."

"If someone got on my case, mi madre would hike down from her apartment, ride the bus and plane to get here, and kick their ass."

"Protective of you?"

"That ain't the half of it. And anyway, I always thought you have my back."

"Me and His Largeness both."

"When you want to give a statement?"

"Now?"

"My kind of citizen," Diamond said.

I looked off over the highway towards the lake. "Have you given them their lawyer call, yet?"

"Gosh, I remember they asked. But I haven't gotten around to it yet."

I grinned. "Maybe I'll find something where they live in

Pleasanton. But maybe not. Probably the guy who hires them stashes their payment somewhere, then emails them the location. He's long gone when Columbo and Romero pick it up."

"So the only way we could find the employer is through the emails he sends them," Diamond said.

I nodded. "I've read that Google will release certain information about a Gmail account if it's 180 days old or more and the requesting law enforcement says it's critical to an investigation."

"What kind of info?"

"Name of the person who signed up for the account and the Internet Service Provider they use. They won't release email content without a search warrant."

"Which we could get," Diamond said.

"But it'd take time," I said.

Diamond said, "You're wondering about offering boxer boys an enticement."

"Nothing specific," I said. "Just a simple presentation. Tell them I'm planning to work with the District Attorney to put them away for the maximum. What would that be?"

Diamond said, "Category B Felony Assault in Nevada with a deadly weapon can result in six years inside and a five thousand dollar fine even when there is no physical injury to the victim."

"Let's say you tell them that," I said. "Then you could say that, in return for them showing you the emails from their employer, you'll lean on me and the DA to go easy. You could say something about a push in the Nevada legislature to only prosecute hard core murderers and rapists in order to cut costs."

Diamond thought about it. "I could even do a little misdirection, like I won't ask for their email password. I'll make that seem like a big deal, letting them keep that privacy. I let them enter it and let them pull up the most recent emails from their employer. Then I print the emails and let them sign out of their account. Who wouldn't be willing to let me do that in hopes that I try to cushion their collision with the Nevada legal system? Only after that will I remember to let them call their lawyer."

"Could be such evidence would be thrown out."

"But you'd get the information, and you could track the man who hired them. I'll go back to the office and make copies of the emails. Maybe you can learn about the sender without having to get a warrant. Hang here for a bit?"

"Absolutely."

Fifteen minutes later, Diamond came out and handed me two sheets of paper. "Check it out," he said. "Home run with the bases loaded."

At the top was the recipients' Gmail addresses. Below those was the sender's address: cork@99EasyStreet.com.

"This is great," I said.

Diamond said, "I checked on the Ninety-nine Easy Street dot com address and no website came up. The address is hosted by one of the big web service companies. So the dot com name may just be parked and used for email."

I looked at the first email. It was time-stamped at 8:30 p.m. on a Saturday. I read aloud. "'Four thousand dollars Sunday morning. Be in Tracy, CA at 5:00 a.m.' The second one was time-stamped the next morning, at 5:05 a.m. Sunday. 'Trash can at the corner of Oak Lawn and Beckman.' So he preps them about the drop to minimize the chance that someone else finds the cash. He drops the cash at, say, four fifty. Drives away and then sends the email."

Diamond said, "And they get four large to drive up to Tahoe and tackle you. Not a bad day's work and pay, except for the little problem that tackling you didn't work."

"Pleasanton, where they live, isn't far from Tracy, where the cash drop was made."

"Right. From Pleasanton, you go east, up and over the wind farm in Livermore, and you're practically there." Diamond turned toward the jail. "I better get back inside and tend to the farm."

"As in farmyard animals?"

"Mean ones," Diamond said. "Unneutered."

"Thanks much," I said. "You want that statement now?"

"Por favor."

THIRTY

To get from Tahoe to Pleasanton in the East Bay, I drove down the Sierra and took Interstate 80 west through Sacramento. I headed across the long bridge over the Yolo bypass, which is designed to absorb massive flood waters when Mount Shasta melts too fast 200 miles to the north.

Spot had his head out the window ever since we hit the valley floor. Meanwhile, I had the AC on, blowing straight at my face. I felt guilty about the wasted energy. But the open window made Spot happy.

Eventually, he realized the truth of Central Valley heat in the summer. You can't just put up with it. You have to escape to a cool environment. He pulled his head in. I rolled up his window. He lay across the back seat, panting with the effort of a dozen toy poodles and using a tongue almost the size of a poodle.

UC Davis's grand Robert Mondavi Center flashed by on the right. Soon I drove by the turnoff for Travis Air Force Base. I remembered reading that it was the inspiration for the name of the character Travis McGee in John D. MacDonald's famous mystery series. As I approached the long crawl up the coastal mountains just before the San Francisco Bay, I turned south on 680 and headed down through Benecia and Walnut Creek and Danville.

Spot's panting sounded like a large bellows. But eventually the bellows turned to the low setting.

At 4000 feet, Mount Diablo is the big imposing East Bay landmark. One of the highest Bay Area mountains, it sports a glorious patchwork of Black Oak trees that grow in winding ravines like dark rivulets through the gold of the grasslands. On a clear day, Diablo is visible from 150 miles away as you come down from the much higher Sierra. Up close, it dominates every view with its beauty.

A few miles past Diablo, I turned off in Pleasanton, a valley town that, while very warm, was cooler than the Central Valley and quite pleasant in manner and attitude compared to its hyper intense Silicon Valley cousins. It took me only a few minutes to find the address where the Columbo Romero boys headquartered their business of turning hard cases soft.

The house was in a planned development of cream stucco houses with terra-cotta tiled roofs. Although the houses were modest in size, all had two-car garages and arched entries that led to shaded front porches. The roof's tiles were largely covered in indigo blue solar panels. On the few windows that faced south and west were large deep awnings. The designs were all about keeping out the hot summer sun.

I pulled up to the address on my Post-it note, parked on the street under a tree, and rolled down the rear windows.

I noticed that the house to one side had two small bicycles on the gravel yard and one tricycle made of red and yellow plastic.

At the house on the other side was an elaborate fence and bush hedge that partially concealed a trampoline.

The Columbo Romero boys lived with children on either side. It was probably a great cover for men plying the intimidation trade.

The garage door had a row of small windows across the top edge. I looked in, cupping my hands to shield my eyes against the glare. Inside was a blue Chevy Tahoe. It looked newish and clean. But it was plain compared to the Range Rover that was now being held by the Douglas County Sheriff's Office. The double R would likely be seized through criminal forfeiture laws because they used it in commission of a felony assault on me with at least one deadly weapon, the Glock 9. The other deadly weapon was Big's meaty fist. But the DA probably wouldn't include that second weapon in his case, as it didn't look very deadly now.

I rang the bell. When there was no response, I knocked. Perseverance may be the singular characteristic of a successful gumshoe.

When no one answered, I contemplated breaking in. Probably

everything I could ever want to know about the Columbo Romero business could be found inside. But there were signs of neighbors, and they might not appreciate my persistence if it came in the form of breaking glass.

I went to the house next door and walked up the drive.

"Hey, mister, wanna see me ride my trike? I can do tricks." The words came from an unseen little kid.

I stopped and turned around. At the side of the yard was a feminine-looking kid with long curly hair. She was sitting on her butt on a patch of grass. With one hand, she had a doll in a strangle hold. With her other, she held a toy truck. I couldn't be sure, but it looked as if she'd been threatening the doll with truck-caused bodily harm if the doll didn't behave.

"Wow, you can ride a trike?" I said. "Simone Biles look out."

"What's Seemobiles?"

"Greatest gymnast in history. But I've never seen her do tricks on a trike."

"I'll show you." She dropped the truck and doll and did a kind of skipping run over to the red and yellow trike, which was lying upside down. She flipped it off its back, got on the seat, and pedaled around in a circle in the driveway.

"Hey, you're good at that. Like a rodeo trick rider," I said.

"Thank you for not expanding your praise," said a woman.

I turned, looking for the source of the voice. She was just inside the screen door, in the shade of the entry, nearly invisible from out in the sunlight.

"Hello," I said. "Not sure I know what you mean."

"We're trying not to fall prey to the excessive self-esteem trend, where every kid gets an award each day for simply existing," she said. "The rodeo trick rider metaphor is kind but on the edge."

"Ah. I'll withhold more praise until she does a triple-twisting dismount."

"Now you're talking. Can I help you find something?"

"I was just looking for your neighbors, Mr. Columbo and Mr. Romero. I see that the Range Rover isn't in the drive. I knocked just in case only one of them had left. But no answer."

"They're a pair, those two. They go everywhere together."

"My experience, too," I said. "Any idea when they're due back?"

"No. They don't have a regular schedule. I don't even know what they do. It must be some kind of heavy-hitter business considering the way they dress."

"They're definitely heavy hitters."

"What is their business, if you don't mind my asking? I am their neighbor, so it seems like I should know."

"They're marketing consultants." I paused. "Persuasion psychology, mostly."

"Persuasion psychology? Wow, I've never even heard of that."

"It's just a fancy phrase for how to get people to do what you want."

"I could use some of that. They must be successful. That Range Rover alone costs as much as my husband makes in a year. And that doesn't count their clothes." She paused. "I'm a stay-at-home mom, just in case you're wondering how I can be here talking to you."

I smiled at her. "Most important job in the world," I said, "raising kids to be good people."

"You got that right. Empathy and just the right amount of self esteem."

"Any chance you would know any of their business associates? The only contact I have for them is an email address. Maybe one of their pals has a faster way to contact them."

She stepped out of the screen door but stayed in the shade of the entry. "No I don't."

"What about the neighbors on the far side? Do they know Columbo and Romero any better?"

"Actually, I happen to know that they don't. My aunt Missy and her husband Joe live there."

I nodded. "The famous trampoline athletes, right?"

"Funny. Their daughter works a second job weekends. She's a nurse and makes good money. But it's still hard being a single mother. The weekend gig at the local urgent care clinic makes all the difference. And the kids get more exercise jumping on that trampoline in one weekend than they do the whole rest of the week playing soccer every day after school."

I turned around and surveyed the neighborhood. Then I turned back to the woman. "Thanks for your help," I said.

"Want me to give them a message the next time I see them?"

"Sure. Just tell them McKenna stopped by. They'll know why I came calling."

"Will do."

Spot was still asleep when I got back to the car. He woke up, stood up as much as was possible in the back seat, and sniffed me. Even though I'd had no contact with anyone, he probably detected hints of little girl and plastic trikes. Bored, he put his head out the window.

I drove forward, made the tiniest of beeps on the horn. The little girl turned and saw Spot. She started jumping up and down with frenetic energy, pointing and yelling, "Look, mommy, look at the dog!"

I waved as I drove away.

THIRTY-ONE

I pulled into the Safeway shopping center near the freeway. I parked at the far corner, took Spot for a walk, and thought about what I knew.

If Big and Bigger were the trained boxers they appeared to be, they would likely spend a sizable amount of time boxing. And the person who hired them might know of them because he or she was associated with a boxing gym. Maybe the person was a boxer himself. So I could look for boxing gyms and see if I could learn about the man that way.

I looked again at the email address. cork@99easystreet.com.

I wondered about cork. Was it someone's name? Or a combo of letters from a name? Did it refer to a wine cork? Was my target a wine connoisseur? Someone who had connections to the wine business? The Central Valley wine growers? People think of Napa and Sonoma when they think of wine. They usually don't realize that the biggest wine producing region in the United States, and one of the biggest in the world, is California's Central Valley.

Back at the Jeep, I let Spot into the back seat and used my phone to Google the word cork. Up came information about the material, the trees it comes from, how it is made into wine corks. Other hits were about the City of Cork and County Cork in Ireland. There were businesses with cork in the name. Explanations of the Middle English roots of the word. There were also…

I stopped scanning down and went back up.

I was looking for a boxing connection. I remembered that there were many famous boxers who had come from Ireland, including some household names.

Was it possible that the person who hired the boxing thugs was Irish? Perhaps even a boxer himself? Someone who identified with County Cork and used it for his email address?

He could still be anonymous. He might have noticed Romero and Columbo as boxers and then kept himself anonymous as he approached them by email and hired them to intimidate me.

Contacting boxing gyms seemed a far-fetched reach. But I had no better idea. As I looked for boxing gyms that might know of Romero and Columbo, I would also look for someone who might have an Irish background.

I used my phone to search for "boxing gym Northern California." I got many hits, none of which were in Pleasanton. I reached into the Jeep and got out my old paper map and made marks for gyms, roughly gauging the distance they each were from Pleasanton. It would take days to drive and visit even a small portion of them.

I had another idea. Why not approach them over the phone? Of course, most businesses aren't willing to reveal information about their clients. But boxing gyms might not think that way. They'd likely assume that promoting their boxers would be a good thing. Seeing that Spot was asleep, I wandered for a bit, thinking up a cover story, then went back to the Jeep so I'd have less wind in the phone when I made calls.

I started with gyms closest to Pleasanton.

"Hello, my name is Joe Robinson," I said to the young woman who answered my first call. "I'm a writer for Boxing Today dot com, and we're doing a feature called 'How Ethnicity Fires Up Boxers.' It's about boxers who use their ethnic backgrounds as an identifier. You know what I mean? Manny Pacquiao from the Philippines, Roberto Durán from Panama, Julio César Chávez from Mexico. So I'm wondering if you can point me to any boxers in your gym who have strong ethnic identities."

"Well, um, we just have, you know, regular guys here. And girls. We have two girls who box here."

"Hey, that's great. Girls boxing. Don't let the guys get all the action, right? Ha ha. But do any of your boxers talk about their background? Where they came from? How they identify? I could feature them in my article, and that would give them a big boost of attention. And of course, your gym would be mentioned prominently. I could probably bring you good business."

"Our boxers aren't really identifying, like, in a certain way. They're all just, you know, Americans. None of them are, you know, ethnical."

"Okay, thanks for your time."

I called the next gym, got an old guy on the phone, went through a similar patter.

"Hey, man, you shouldn't write about foreigners," he said. "This is our country. It's un-American to give press to immigrants. We have to prop those people up, feed them, let them in our schools. The last thing we should do is promote them. I don't care how they throw a punch."

"Sure, thanks." I hung up.

I tried four more gyms. One guy kept me on the phone for over ten minutes, trying to get me to change my story idea to one about gay boxers. I told him it was a great idea and maybe next time...

On the next call, a woman said, "We have a Cuban dude, call him the wasp, 'cuz he's as mean and nasty as you can get. And you know what we call his left hook? We call it the stinger. When the wasp hits you with his stinger, you go down. He's a bantamweight, one hundred eighteen pounds. But his stinger's so bad, he could probably take down your average welterweight or even a middleweight."

"Any other boxers who project an ethnic identity?"

"Well, the other main dude is Angel Garcia. He's from Mexico. We call him Angel the Devil. He's a little guy, too, a featherweight. He fools people just like Satan does. Makes you think he's nice, so you let your guard down. Then he's like ready to knock your head off. It's like evil come calling and you wind up on your ass."

"These are good leads. Thank you so much," I said. "Anyone else?"

"Not really. There's a heavyweight who trains here. Did some professional boxing some time back, but didn't go very far. His name is Cormac O'Connor. He's Irish. I didn't know that at first 'cuz my neighbor when I grew up was named Cormac, and he was totally as American as you and me. And Cormac O'Connor is American, too. Talks like us. But when he was on the circuit, he used to call himself the Mad Irishman."

"Good fighter?" I said.

"Yes and no. He's got good footwork for a big guy. But I don't think his heart's in it."

"What weight class?"

"Heavyweight. Actually, he's way over two hundred pounds. Too big to be a real good fighter, if you ask me."

"Does he still train there? Could I come there to interview him and maybe watch him train?"

"Sure. You want me to give him a message?"

"Let me check my schedule and I'll call back."

"No problem," she said.

"One more question. I met two fighters, names were Columbo and Romero. Do they train there?"

"There's another coupla big guys. Big as Cormac."

"Friends?" I asked

"Nah. We're a serious gym. This ain't where people go to hang with buddies. I don't think Cormac ever talked to Columbo and Romero. And, anyway, Columbo and Romero aren't the talking type. Us in the gym thought maybe Romero got his voice box crushed by a punch or something. But Cormac certainly noticed them. It was like he was sizing them up."

"Any chance you have a phone number where I can reach Cormac? I could set up a meeting at your gym."

"Nah, he's not the phone type. But you can probably find him in Locke. From what I've heard, he hangs out at the bar there."

"Locke? That's the Chinese town?"

"Yeah. On the Delta. Twenty miles up the road from us."

"Thanks. I'll be in touch."

THIRTY-TWO

I drove up I-5 to Locke, a place where Street and I spent some time exploring a few years ago. Locke is a tiny town, built by Chinese immigrants in the early 1900s. That was back when the Chinese were allowed into the U.S. to do hard labor, but weren't allowed to buy land or houses. So a guy named Locke leased his Delta ranch land to them. Most of the Delta land, where the Sacramento River spreads out as it approaches the San Francisco Bay, is under water much of the year. It's a 30- by 40-mile patch of sloughs and channels and backwaters that almost no Californians know about. But it figures large in California history.

The Chinese dug and hauled unimaginable amounts of dirt, created dikes, and created large areas that stayed dry. They built a town with houses and stores and saloons. That charming little town is now a National Historic site. All but a few of the Chinese families have moved away. Their grandkids and great grandkids got schooled and now work in high-tech.

Locke has two short, narrow streets with shops, a bar, a restaurant, and a little park. On both sides of town are waterways, confined by dikes. One is the Sacramento River, another is a series of sloughs. Both have water levels much higher than Locke's streets.

It takes a while to get used to being in a town that sits well below massive amounts of water. But to the locals, it's no different than living below a dam. If the dike is breached, disaster strikes. So you hope the dike isn't breached.

I parked the Jeep on a side street and let Spot out. It was late afternoon. The bar seemed to be doing a big business catering to tourists, most of whom came on motorcycles. I assumed that business would get even better as darkness came.

Spot and I walked the streets. Spot had to endure countless pets and hugs and exclamations and photo ops with children and grandmothers. Eventually, I decided to spare him the rock star treatment to which he is accustomed, and I walked him up one of the big dikes. At the top, we followed the ridge, where there was a well-worn path used by runners and mountain bikers.

I'd once referred to the water-containment aspects of the Delta as levees and was firmly corrected by an old woman who was apparently a grammarian. She explained that levees protect normally dry land from floodwaters. Whereas dikes protect normally wet land from water that naturally sits at a higher level. So The Netherlands in Europe is comprised of land that is below sea level, and the sea is held back by dikes. In contrast, the northern portion of the Sacramento River is adjacent to land that is normally above the river level, and levees were constructed on both sides of the river to keep the river from spilling into farm land when the river floods.

But unlike the northern Sacramento Valley, much of the land in the Sacramento Delta is below the normal river level and in some cases even below sea level. Thus, the grammarian explained, the giant raised roads of Delta dirt that keep out the water are properly called dikes.

Spot and I stopped at the Jeep so I could get Spot's water pan. Then we headed over to a restaurant. I told him to stay and went inside. I ordered two cheeseburgers, a beer, and a water to go.

Spot was besieged by a crowd and loving it when I came back out with the food. I separated him from the adoring masses and walked him to the end of a street, where we climbed up yet another dike. At the top, there were no people, a striking change from the masses of tourists down below. Funny how a little exertion puts off nearly everybody.

It was a lovely afternoon in the Delta. The sun was behind the trees. The waterways were cooling the air. Dragonflies floated on the breeze, darting here and there to grab unseen insects.

I set our drinks and doggie boxes on the ground.

I looked at Spot. "Sit," I said.

He sat very fast. He didn't even glance at me, just stared at the boxes. His drool should be measured the way well pumps are measured, gallons per minute.

"Paw the ground," I said.

Spot lifted his right paw and slapped at the ground repeatedly. His focus on the food never wavered.

"Repeat after me, 'I promise to be a good dog and always do what my master wants.'"

Spot didn't react. Figures.

I opened one of the boxes and lifted out the cheeseburger. I broke it in half to check that the inside wasn't too warm.

"Stand," I said.

Spot stood. The drool flow increased.

"Ready?"

He'd never been more ready in his life.

"Go," I said as I tossed half the cheeseburger into the air.

Spot leaped like a circus performer. The cheeseburger got to eight feet when Spot's jaws chomped down, like a burger raptor swooping up from below. His motion carried him sideways another eight feet. He landed, turned, and looked at me.

"Where's the burger?" I said.

He ran his giant tongue around his chops from left to right, then stared at my hands holding the doggie box. This time I pulled the other half burger out and tossed it even higher.

Like a consummate show off, this time Spot didn't leap, but watched it go up. He took three steps to the side and was ready as it came down. He caught it like Willie Mays in center field at Candlestick Park and swallowed once.

"Insatiable," I said.

I unfolded the water pan and poured in Spot's water.

"Okay," I said. Spot lapped.

After I'd eaten, we lay down on the grass and took a nap.

When I woke, I said, "Ready to go to work?"

Spot opened his eyes but didn't twitch a muscle.

"C'mon, boy, earn your lunch."

He gradually got up and walked with me down the dike and back into the historic district of Locke.

We stopped at the popular bar, which was filled with tourist bikers. I brought Spot in.

Usually, I get resistance. Either the bar's employees didn't care, or they didn't notice. But the tourists did. They lavished him with affection. I walked up to the bar and ordered a draft beer. The bartender set it on the counter. Spot looked at it, then at me.

"I'm bigger than you," I said to him.

I drank for a bit and established a comfort level with the bartender by simply being quiet and polite.

When my beer was two-thirds gone, he came back and said, "Ready for another?"

"No thank you," I said. "Cormac O'Connor around?"

He looked left and right as if O'Connor might be near and then said, "Haven't seen him lately."

I nodded. The exchange established that O'Connor often hung out at the bar, that the bartender knew him, that O'Connor wasn't there now.

"If you think of it, please tell him that Owen McKenna says hi."

"Will do."

"I'll go hike the dike and check back later."

I tugged Spot away from a foursome of laughing, camera phone-toting tourists, and we went out. It was one of those lucky breaks, finding someone who knew O'Connor at the first place I entered.

I walked outside. Three grizzled men in their late fifties stood on the boardwalk. Two were wiry thin. The third was nearly the size of Candlestick Park. All wore old clothes. All had three or four-day whiskers. One sucked on a cigar, the smoke curling up under the brim of a tattered San Francisco Giants cap. One wore a cowboy hat and had a smear of dirt next to a tear in his jeans. He looked like a rancher who'd just gotten off his 1959 Massey Ferguson tractor. They each held a bottle of beer. The fat one leaned back against the bar's front wall, his old, worn boot heel lifted up and hooked on the windowsill of a huge plate glass window. They were as opposite from tourists as you can get.

They glanced at Spot as we approached, then went back to

their conversation. No interest in animals smaller than a young steer.

"The Delta tunnel s'posed to go practically straight below us," one man said. He looked down and stomped his foot on the wooden walk.

"Take our water, fill up those Hollywood swimming pools. Ain't fair," said another.

"Hey, guys," I said. "Sorry to interrupt. Wondering if you've seen Cormac O'Connor recently."

The man with the cowboy hat shook his head. "Try the bar. That's where Cormac hangs out."

"Thanks," I said. I nodded at them and moved on.

Spot and I wandered down the street, around the corner, and back over to the dike. We once again hiked up its steep slope. We paused at the top and looked down on the Sacramento River. Or at least at the portion that wasn't diverted through the deep water channel that was made for barges shipping goods from Sacramento to the Bay and maybe onto ships heading out to the Pacific.

I thought about Cormac O'Connor. I could go back to the bar later and see if he'd finished his day of boxing and stopped by for a cold one.

Maybe I'd get another idea.

As twilight approached, the river was black dark and the air was humid and aromatic with the kind of plants that grow in an area that is naturally under water and only sees air because of the dikes the Chinese laborers built. Much of the Delta was a lopsided world filled with water that spilled from the San Joachin River to the south and the Sacramento River that rushed down from the north. Yet the water had been walled in and forced to follow man-made channels toward the ocean. Even in the dark, from where we stood, we could see that the river and slough and other nearby backwaters were all much higher than the land behind us.

Spot looked down at the water, then looked up at me, not so much wondering about permission to go to the water as trying to divine my intentions.

"Go ahead, boy. It's all dark to me, but you can see with your nose."

I tapped him on his back, and he understood my meaning. He did a semi-sideways crab walk down the steep embankment to the black water. I watched him go. When he got to the river, I heard a sound.

I turned. I saw a vague, dark shape.

"Owen McKenna?" a pleasant voice said.

"Yeah. And you are?"

The punch was like a battering ram, driving through my gut. And there was no steel-clad plywood to protect me.

I bent over, gasping, stabbing pain radiating through my intestines, nausea making me want to vomit.

The second punch came at my head. I had the instinctive sense to dodge it, but I didn't do a very good job. I was already half dead from the gut punch. I moved my head sideways and back, turning it as I moved. The punch caught me on the side of the jaw. My head bounced and rolled, disseminating some of the energy. There was no crack of breaking bone. But the squeaking, squishing sound in my neck vertebrae and the crushing thud on my jaw was severe.

I spun as I went down, flailing my arms, trying to catch something to keep me from tumbling down the steep dike and into the black water below. My fingers caught on fabric as if my hand had gone into the man's shirt pocket. I tried to grasp something, anything. But my world seemed to go black as I hit the dirt with my shoulder and head at the same time and began rolling down toward the river. I was unable to resist the roll. But any movement that could put distance between me and my attacker was helpful. I was a limp rag doll. I couldn't breathe.

Rolling was rough, and it seemed I had a dream that someone was hammering on my head. Maybe the man was chasing me down, ready to strike me a killing blow by stomping on my face. I couldn't tell. My world was black and strangely silent, as if the blow to my head had taken out my hearing. My last realization was that I was on my back, head down a steep incline, dark dirty water sloshing at my hair and washing into my mouth.

THIRTY-THREE

Spot was sniffing me. I couldn't remember how I got there.

Spot cried. He moved around to my other side. He pawed at my leg, his nails raking my thigh, as if to say, stop this scary business and get up.

I tried to see past him, tried to sense where I was.

There was movement. Something dark. I remembered why I was lying at a steep angle. I was on a dike. The black lapping at my head was the river. The movement above me was a man running. Along the top of the dike, far above me.

I still couldn't breathe. I reached my arm up, wavering with lack of oxygen. I was about to pass out. My hand hit Spot. I grabbed onto him. His neck, maybe. I couldn't tell. My fading consciousness made the dark even darker.

I tried to focus. Stay conscious just a little bit longer. Use the fighter pilot's technique to prevent loss of consciousness when doing blood-draining aerobatic maneuvers. Clench the gut. Bear down. Create internal pressure to force blood and oxygen into the brain.

I pulled Spot to me, his head next to mine. My arms were around his neck. My hands gripped his neck fur. But something else was in one of my hands. I squeezed it. Fabric. It made no sense. Why was I holding fabric?

Then I remembered something. It was a vague sense. Like a foggy dream evaporating as you focus on it. I had waved my arms as I went down. My hand hit fabric. Maybe it belonged to my attacker. Some little bit of shirt could have torn off.

I pulled on Spot's head with one hand. I used my other hand to push the fabric against Spot's nose.

"Spot!" I said with a weak, whispered voice. I couldn't think of the right words. I tried to say, "Smell this fabric. Do you have the scent?"

My words seemed like mumbled mush.

I made an effort to repeat myself while I continued to press the little bit of fabric against Spot's nose.

"Find the suspect!" I said. Without air in my lungs, my voice was a whisper. I tried to wave my other arm, tried to point. I managed to turn his head toward the movement at the top of the dike. I got a bit more air in my lungs, volume to drive my voice. "Find the suspect and TAKE HIM DOWN!"

I did the hand drop next to his head, the pointing command. But it was probably too dark for him to see. Then I tried to smack his rear, but my hand slapped his leg.

My last sense before I passed out was the perception of Spot running away from me, up the steep dike. Maybe he was going after the fleeing man. Maybe he was having fun.

Time seemed to float away. The galaxy shimmered. The billions of stars in the Milky Way were all shining bright as if to demonstrate the insignificance of our little planet floating in the vastness of dark space. For some reason I remembered what Carl Sagan said, that our lonely pale blue dot spinning through space was our only home. Dizziness washed over me. The night sky twisted. I suddenly felt I had no home, lonely or otherwise. My brain seemed to stand on end, out of balance, about to tip over and tumble off the edge of the dot into the blackness of space.

A sound penetrated my dreams. Something like a thud. Or a deep grunt. Then came some kind of rattle. Or a growl?

Maybe it was all a dream.

I lay for a long time trying to figure out why there was so much pressure in my head. I was in a dark universe. Strapped down by an invisible force. My pulse was a bass drum in my ears, low volume but high speed. The pounding behind my eyeballs was excruciating.

My lungs felt collapsed. I could only get a tiny trickle of breath into my lungs. I focused on it. Breathe. Expand the lungs. Push down with the diaphragm. Lift up with the ribs. Pull in air.

I smelled stagnant water. The river.

I remembered the dike.

My insides writhed with pain. Someone had punched me.

It came back to me. It was a good set-up. My target would have heard from the gym that I'd asked about an Irish boxer and was told to go to the Chinese town. Locke. So he went there and waited for the hapless investigator. He would watch from a distance. When he finally spotted the investigator, he would follow at a long distance. Then, when the investigator got to the top of the dike and his giant dog wandered down to the river, he struck hard and fast. Two blows, one to the body, one to the head. Hard enough to maim, maybe hard enough to kill.

Except for one oversight. What if the dog…

One of my arms felt numb. I pushed hard with the other and rolled myself over onto my stomach, face to the ground. Now the musty black water was at my lips. With great effort I pushed my head back so I didn't inhale the liquid. I practiced breathing, lips against dirt. In and out. In and out. When I'd gotten better at breathing, I pushed and rocked and got up onto my knees. I was slumped forward, elbows on hard gravel, head still down near the water. From that advantageous position, I might get to a standing position in mere hours. While I worked on the concept, I listened. Everything was still silent. Was it because there was no sound? Or was it because I was deaf, my auditory system knocked out by a crushing blow to the head?

I gradually got one leg lifted up so the foot was on the ground. I stayed in that position for a minute, contemplating what would be required to stand up. To balance on just two feet. The skills of a gymnast.

With great care, I pushed up, using my arms, and got the other leg lifted so two feet were on the ground. With my hands on my knees, I rested and swayed in the darkness. After much preparation, I raised my arms out at my side for balance. Very carefully, I straightened my legs and stood up part way. Not tall. Not straight. But balancing on two feet. I was an athlete. In a minute I was walking. A gold-medal athlete.

The side of the dike was very steep. It seemed the entire world was on a slope and was about to slide off into the same black universe that had swallowed me.

Fight it, I thought. Focus on a single concept. Don't drop into eternity. It was a song lyric. I mouthed the words. I was a bard, a poet, a troubadour.

I kept my arms out for balance, stumbling forward, moving across the steep slope, gradually climbing up. Don't drop into eternity, went the chorus. Over and over.

It was many minutes later when the world straightened.

I was on the top of the dike. The narrow dike top was level. I no longer had to lean, didn't have to crab, didn't worry that I would roll off the edge of the galaxy. I stumbled along, wondering where Spot had gone. Then I remembered that I'd sent Spot on a take down mission.

Maybe Spot went after the man who hit me. I couldn't remember the man's name. Or maybe Spot had given up the mission and was wandering the dikes, searching out the water birds that prowled the night.

If by chance Spot had gotten his target, it seemed important not to call out. Be silent, McKenna. Stealth is good. But where was I going? My memory was lost in a starry starry night. I stumbled on something. A branch or a log. Oh, yeah, try not to fall. Keep my balance. Stay upright.

I kept walking, kept focusing on breathing. In and out. In and out.

There was a sound.

I stopped and listened. Nothing. I put my hands behind my ears, making cups, concentrating whatever sound was out there.

Another sound.

This sound was breathing. My breathing.

I heard another sound. That sound wasn't me.

Someone stressed. Struggling.

Why didn't I have a flashlight? Every Boy Scout knew better.

More sound.

It came from down below me. Not the river. The other direction. Now I heard two kinds of breathing. One animal sucking air through nose and teeth. Another groaning in pain.

Maybe Spot had a suspect after all.

I walked toward the sound. Step by tiny step. Down the slope away from the river. Down toward dark trees. Down toward the back side of the town of Locke.

The sound got louder. I got closer. Soon I saw in the dark the vague shape of Spot and a man next to him. The man was on his back, partially hidden in a thicket of bushes. Spot held the man by the upper arm.

"Good boy, Spot." My voice was just a hint of moving air.

"Get him off me!" the man said, his voice a mix of panic and fear. "He broke my arm. Or worse! I'm bleeding bad. I could bleed out and die. This would be murder."

"Let's have a look," I said. I maneuvered over next to Spot and the man. I let my legs collapse and dropped down, butt first, onto the man's belly.

I weigh 215, and the impact was hard and powerful. The man gushed out air in a gasp and scream. There was a sharp snap of a breaking rib or two. He was unable to breathe back in.

"Oh, I'm sorry," I said, barely able to talk. "Did I hit you hard? Were you unprepared?"

The man choked and tried to gasp. He couldn't get air.

I reached over, rubbed Spot, and whispered in his ear. "You done good, Largeness. You are the best. You can let go now."

I pulled Spot's jaws away from the man's upper arm.

The man was still trying to breathe.

"My job was simple," I said, leaning over, directing my rough whispered voice to the man under me. "I was to find the killers of some hedge fund guys. Catching murderers is a good thing. Isn't that right? Then you came along. You sent enforcers after me to convince me to stop. They tried to beat me up as if they were professional boxers in the intimidation business. When that didn't work, one of them pulled out his gun and was going to shoot me. I thought that was uncalled for. Then you came along and surprised me with your punches, which is really unfair. At least your boys didn't sneak up on me. Straight-up guys, those two. But you can make up for this misjudgment by telling me who hired you to send the enforcers after me."

The man was still trying to breathe. I gave him time. I stood up, testing my legs, doing a hula hoop maneuver to loosen my back. I rubbed my face to see if I was in one piece or if I needed to have surgery to reattach my jaw.

"I'm waiting for my answer."

"Go to hell," he gasped.

I did another butt drop, pro-wrestler-style. This time more of my weight was on his chest. I heard multiple cracks of breaking ribs. Three or four of them. He gasped and screamed again, this time with more feeling. Maybe I ruptured his aorta and he would die in seconds. The thought didn't bother me except that then I wouldn't get the information I wanted.

I turned around so I was kneeling on his chest. I shifted one of my knees up to the base of his neck. I pressured it down a bit.

He screamed, a choking gargle. His scream withered to a toddler's whimper.

I said, "You probably know that the hyoid bone in the neck can't take much pressure before it snaps. If it breaks, it would be the beginning of a cascading series of events, all negative regarding your future. Worse would be if I crush your trachea, which are down lower at the base of your throat. They break with even more of a result. You won't be able to breathe at all. Your last minutes on Earth will be consumed with agony as you try to suck air and only the tiniest amount can get in. A dribble of air mixed with blood. Death can take ten or twenty minutes or more, nowhere near soon enough."

The man was bawling like a baby.

"So I'll ask you one more time. Either you tell me who hired you to send enforcers after me, or I crush your hyoid bone and your trachea and leave you here for the turkey vultures. You should know that they don't wait until you're fully dead. They don't usually fly at night. But if they're roosting nearby, they'll smell your impending death and come for a late night snack. As soon as they realize you can't resist, they'll peck out your eyeballs. Then they go for your gut. It's brutal but very efficient. You'll be reduced to mostly bone and sinew within three days. That will likely happen before anyone finds your body."

The man was trying to howl. His anguish was obvious even though he could barely breathe.

"What's that?" I said. "I can't hear you."

He tried to scream again, a hoarse, scratching, wretched complaint.

"Last chance before I crush your neck and leave," I said.

I turned and put my hand through Spot's collar. "C'mon, boy. Let's you and I get some dinner as soon as I do a knee drop on this man's neck."

"Carston Kraytower," the man rasped.

"What about him?" I asked.

"Kraytower hired me to scare you off."

THIRTY-FOUR

I dialed nine-one-one and reported the attack. I explained where Cormac O'Connor was. I took Spot by the collar and hobbled my way to the nearest street. A sheriff's patrol showed up in minutes. Two deputies got out.

We went through the routine, me explaining the attack in my faint whisper. I gave them the whole truth and nothing but the truth except for the revelation that Carston Kraytower had employed Cormac to assault me. I knew Kraytower would eventually be contacted about the case. But I wanted to be able to talk to him before he knew that I knew he was officially a scum bag crook.

I also gave the deputies my bona fides including the names of sergeants from three counties who could vouch for me, Diamond from Douglas County, Bains from El Dorado County, and Jack Santiago, from the Placer County Sheriff's Office, the man who had initially brought me into the case.

An hour later, Cormac O'Connor was cuffed and loaded into an ambulance, and I was sent on my way with agreements that we would all be talking to one another again in the near future.

I considered the interesting bit of news. The man who hired me to find out who killed his colleagues also hired a tough boxer to convince me to stop finding out who killed his colleagues. He could have achieved the same thing by calling me and telling me my services were no longer wanted.

Except that if he took me off the case, it would look suspicious. Then why did he hire me in the first place?

Maybe he killed his colleagues and hired me to make him seem less suspicious. Perhaps he originally thought I'd never find out the truth. But eventually he came to think that I was tenacious enough to uncover the truth.

Hiring enforcers to try to scare me off the case would keep it looking like Kraytower was innocent and it was the evil murderer who simply wanted me to stop looking for him.

I was about to call the personal number Kraytower had given me when I paused. He may have heard that Columbo and Romero were in jail and that I had survived their attack. But he may have also talked to Cormac O'Connor, who would have assured Kraytower that the next attack on me would be very effective in silencing me. Judging by the severity of O'Connor's attack, it seemed as if his intention was to kill me. Unless news of O'Connor's failure to silence me and his injuries had gotten back to Kraytower, he might be thinking I was as good as dead. No point in tipping him off that I was fine.

So I walked Spot over to the Jeep, got in and, driving very carefully, headed out to I-5 and drove back toward Tahoe.

THIRTY-FIVE

I got back to my cabin in the middle of the night. I decided sleep was my priority. So I went to bed without sending any email to Street or Diamond or anyone else.

In the morning, after two cups of coffee, I tried Nettie Moon Water's phone. Her voicemail message said that she was out of cell range at Fallen Leaf Lake and that it would be some time before she could return a message. She also said that she was easier to reach by email because she had a satellite hookup at Fallen Leaf Lake.

So I left a voice message and also sent an email asking if we could possibly get together for a short meeting. She emailed back a short time later saying she was going to head to South Lake Tahoe. Two hours after that, we met at the Alpina Coffee shop. Spot was pleased to see her again, and he used his snout to toss her hand up and down until she gave him luxurious pets.

We got our coffee and sat at an outdoor table. Spot lay next to her.

"That's a terrible bruise on your jaw," she said. "You look like you should be in the hospital. Or at least in bed."

"I plan to spend many hours there in the future." I didn't tell her that my greatest pain wasn't my jaw but my abdomen.

"Are you having any success finding the killer?" Moon Water asked.

"No. Which is why I wanted to meet you. I've spoken to people who knew the victims. I learned nothing. It appears that the victims had very little social contact with others. The reason seems to be that they were consumed by work. I've been told that people in the financial world of hedge funds often work eighty or more hours a week. One person told me that one hundred hours a week was not uncommon."

Moon Water frowned. "My God, you'd have time for nothing except a little sleep. You'd have to eat all your meals while you were working."

"Right. So the people who the victims worked with didn't really know them well. As a result, I'm focusing my investigation on people outside of their work environment. Because you knew Lightfoot a little—and of course you know Kraytower too—I'm wondering if you can think of anyone else who knew these victims."

She was shaking her head before I even finished the question. "Other than Lightfoot and Kraytower, the only people I knew were some of the house staff."

"I contacted you because I've met most of them and haven't learned anything. You are the designated guardian of Joshua should Kraytower die," I said.

"Yes."

"But it doesn't seem like you are close to Joshua."

Nettie sipped her coffee. "I don't think anyone is especially close to Joshua."

"Can you make a guess why that is?"

"It would only be a guess. I think Joshua is a nice kid. And I was very close to his mother Isabel. After she died in childbirth, I tried to step in and help with Joshua. I stayed in San Francisco for two years just so I could babysit. And after Carston hired what became a long string of nannies, I kept visiting to give Joshua some sense of continuity. I took him places. Plays for children. The Exploratorium. Restaurants that were child-friendly. And even after I'd moved to Reno, I would come back to attend school functions and show support."

"Then why didn't you end up closer to Joshua?"

Nettie seemed conflicted just talking about it.

I waited.

"It gets down to his father. Carston is… I'm not sure how to describe it. He's awkward. He puts people off. Not because he wants to. But because he makes others feel uncomfortable."

"Has he pursued you in a romantic way?"

Nettie was quick to shake her head. "No. He's not like that.

He's not interested in close relationships with anyone. He doesn't go out on dates, and he doesn't go have beer with the guys."

"Was he close to Isabel?"

"No. This sounds really harsh but I think she just married him to have some financial stability in life. She was a bit awkward herself. They made a good pair that way."

"As awkward as Carston?" I asked.

"No. She was much more functional. Carston has always been great at his work. But outside of work, he always says the wrong thing, he always misses the point of any close human relationship. He doesn't understand what a child needs from a father. He can be condescending and megalomaniacal. The simplest conversation turns into a series of commands with no empathy for the person he's talking to. And if you talk to him about his lack of empathy, he acts very concerned and caring. But it's a concept he can only hold onto for a few minutes. Then he's right back to the autocratic ruler, whether at work or at home."

She drank more coffee.

"Hard for a kid to grow up with a father like that," I said.

"And life is hard for the father, too," she said. "It's not easy being Carston Kraytower. In his job, he has to keep up appearances at all costs. So everything is kind of a play. Every setting is kind of a stage set. The pressure is enormous, with investors who've entrusted him with untold millions."

"That would really make him tense."

"Yes. And something else makes him tense as well."

"What's that?"

"I don't know. But it's as if he's always dealing with a background hum of stress. Something basic in his life isn't right. It makes it so he can never relax, never act normal, and as a result, no one else can feel comfortable around him."

"He's never given a clue as to what's wrong?"

Nettie shook her head. "If I were to guess, I would say it's something in his past. Something that only he knows about."

"Kraytower and Lightfoot and Perry all went to Yale. Could it be that whatever is wrong goes back to that time?"

She thought about it. "That would make sense."

"Do you know anything about their time at Yale?"

"No. The only thing that stood out was their closeness. Lightfoot mentioned that he and Kraytower and some other friends all went to the same fraternity. He also said that Kraytower's best friend died. I got the sense that they were close and so the death was very traumatic."

"Do you know the name of the person who died?"

"No. But maybe you could ask Carston Kraytower."

I nodded. I didn't want to explain that I'd already learned that Kraytower had hired someone to convince me to drop the case, a case that Kraytower hired me for in the first place.

"Any chance Lightfoot said the name of the fraternity?" I asked.

Nettie frowned. "I don't remember. The standard three Greek letters. Kappa..." she said.

I waited. "What about Kappa?"

"That was part of the fraternity name Kappa something something."

We talked a little bit more and tried to switch to unimportant social chitchat. Then I thanked her and we left.

As I drove away, I thought once again of Joshua's comment about family secrets.

THIRTY-SIX

B ack at my office, I organized the emails that had been sent to Kraytower and his dead colleagues. I printed them on one sheet of paper.

1 The story would freeze your blood.

2 It was no accident. He poured in the poison.

3 The killer now wears the victim's garlands.

4 My burden is to avenge the murder.

5 Fight back. Try and hit me hard. Give me a challenge, dude. I've practiced enough. Even a sparrow's death is part of God's plan.

I got an idea. Maybe it was the phrase 'freeze your blood.' Or the word 'garlands.' Diamond had said the words sounded familiar but he couldn't place them. That made me wonder if there was a connection to literature.

I found the website for the Lake Tahoe Community College and spent some time trying to figure out who might know literature and how I might speak to them.

The website was very thorough, but it took me a long time to find a phone number.

An automated voice answered and gave me the standard routine about how I could enter my party's extension if I knew it, and then it went through a long menu. I started punching the zero button and saying the word receptionist over and over. To my relief, I eventually got an actual person on the line in the form of a young man.

"Thank you for calling. How may I direct your call?" he said.

"Thank you for answering," I said. "I'd like to speak to someone on your faculty, please. Someone who teaches literature or English."

"I'm not sure how to direct you."

"Just pick the name of someone in your English department that you think is currently at work, and connect me to their phone."

"But I don't know…" he stopped, clearly ill-equipped to handle such a strange request. "You would just get their voicemail."

The new world had become bifurcated. The people who had the skills to do everything on a computer would thrive. The people without the skills would whither. Although my age would suggest I was computer-literate, I feared I was on the wrong side of that divide. What did it reveal about my deficiencies that I wanted to pick up the phone and ask questions of actual people? In some ways, my Luddite skills put me closer to a homeless, phoneless, computerless street person than the new subspecies of homo sapiens who couldn't get out of bed without checking the texts on their smart phone.

"Perhaps you could connect me with someone working in your library," I said. "The library is open, isn't it?"

"Do you have a person's name? There may be a library tech there. But it is lunchtime, and it is summer, and I'm just an intern so I don't know the routine. But I do know you can find everything on the website."

"Thank you for that information. However, I would like to have an actual conversation with an actual person. Just ring the library and let's see who answers."

He put me on hold. I held long enough that I began to think that the library might not have had any humans working there today.

He came back on the line in about one minute. "I've located an adjunct professor who teaches English Lit. Do you think that might help?"

"Yes, please."

"Her name is Louise Murphy. She's currently in the department office. I'll connect you."

"Thank you very much."

The phone rang. It was picked up immediately.

"Louise Murphy speaking."

I gave her my name and a short explanation of why I was calling. "The case we're working on involves some email messages sent to murder victims before they died."

"Oh, my God, that's… That's terrible."

I said, "At first, I just dismissed the messages as the quirky writing of a killer who is full of himself and is trying to put some kind of verbal polish on his crimes. But now I'm wondering if the emails could offer some clue about the writer. They're somewhat unusual in a way that makes me wonder if the writer is educated in literature. I'm hoping I can visit with you and have you look at these. You might see something where law enforcement doesn't."

"Yes, I'd be happy… Well, I guess happy isn't the word in this situation. It's fine with me to talk to you about it. Only I have to get to my job."

"Oh," I said. "I thought you were currently at your job. You teach at the college, right?"

"I do. I just finished one of the classes I teach. But I'm an adjunct teacher. My main job is waiting tables at a restaurant on Ski Run Boulevard. I have to leave here in forty-five minutes or less."

"Where should we meet?"

"Do you know where the college Demonstration Garden is?"

"Yes. My office is on Kingsbury Grade. I can be there in twenty minutes."

"See you then."

I folded the paper with the emails, put it into my pocket, and left.

Louise Murphy and I had neglected to give each other descriptions to make it easy to find one another. When I got to the Demonstration Garden, I looked at the various people, talking, looking, enjoying the summer weather. I knew it was silly to think that an English Lit teacher might have an identifiable look. Yet one woman stood out. She was in her early thirties, tall and thin with short, messy black hair that was the opposite of styled. Which may have meant that it was carefully styled to look unstyled. She wore heavy black-rimmed glasses and black jeans and T-shirt. On the woman's feet were massive black boots that were just one step removed from military jackboots with hobnails. Her fingernails were painted black.

She sat hunched over a laptop computer.

"Ms. Murphy?" I said as I walked up. "Owen McKenna."

"Oh, hi," she said. Her eyes got very wide as she stared at my bruised face.

"Just a fall," I said.

She looked doubtful. She set her laptop on the bench, rose up partway, and shook my hand. "I'm Louise." She sat back down.

Up close, I could see black eyeliner around eyes that were such a dark brown they were almost black. She didn't appear to wear any other makeup. But I didn't doubt that she had black tattoos in secluded places and belonged to a secret English Literature society of Goth intellectuals. She didn't look scary or ghastly, but she wasn't far from it.

"Thank you for seeing me," I said.

"Sure. You're, um, welcome."

For a woman with such a bold physical presentation, she seemed very reserved.

"You said you have to get to your next job soon, so perhaps we can just dive in."

"Yes, please. That would be good."

I pulled out the paper with the email messages, unfolded it and handed it to her.

"You just want me to read this," she said as she took the paper.

"Please."

"What do you want me to look for?"

"Nothing in particular. Just see if anything strikes you in some way or gives you an idea about the writing or the writer."

Louise made a somber nod, hunched over, bony elbows balanced on skinny knees, and looked at the paper, her eyes darting back and forth, going over it quickly.

I sat on the same bench, far enough away that she wouldn't

feel crowded.

After a minute, Murphy paused and looked away from the paper and stared at the nearby forest. Then she looked back at the list and read the first line again slowly, her lips moving silently like a child learning to read. Maybe she was finding a rhythm or something. She frowned hard and long.

She picked up her computer, typed, delicately moved her fingertip on the mouse pad, typed some more. Stared at the screen. She looked back at the list. It seemed she read the next email, and then typed again. She repeated the process a few times. I couldn't see what she was typing. I didn't turn or lean my head. I wanted it obvious that I wasn't trying to see what was on her screen because I didn't want to distract her. I wanted her to focus.

Then she once again paused for a minute or more and stared at the screen. She didn't touch the computer. Her hand seemed to float up, and she began tapping her black fingernail against her front teeth.

Eventually, she turned to me and spoke.

"Well, I can't be certain. But it seems that… Wait, let me take that back. I am certain. These lines come from Hamlet."

THIRTY-SEVEN

I said to Louise Murphy, "Just to be certain, you're saying these lines are from Shakespeare's play."

"Yes. Do you know Shakespeare's Hamlet?"

"The play? Sort of. It was one of his tragedies."

"Right. But do you know it? The lines?"

"No. I saw it once in San Francisco. About twenty years ago. It was a bit hard to follow, what with the older-style language and all. But I liked it. Of course, it was a brutal story, and pretty much everyone is murdered at the end. But it was impressive theater. I remember thinking that I could see why it was still compelling four hundred years after it was written."

"Do you remember the basics of the story?" she asked.

"Let me think. Hamlet was a prince in Denmark, right? His father was king, also named Hamlet. But his uncle Claudius murdered Hamlet's father and married his mother. Much of the play is about Hamlet deciding if and how he should avenge his father's murder. And I recall there was sort of an implied question about whether Hamlet was going crazy or not."

"Right. You remember well." Louise held up the paper with the messages and gave it a little shake.

"Your emails are modern rewrites of lines in the play."

"You're sure of this."

"Yes."

"Are they all from Hamlet, or are some from other plays?"

"No. All come from Hamlet."

"Can you show me?" I gestured at her laptop. "Do you have Hamlet on your computer?"

"Yes. Hamlet is in the public domain. There are lots of websites that publish it." She touched her computer screen. "I'm at one now."

"Can you show me where the words from the emails are?"

She shook her head. "Not exactly. I searched on the words that are written on your paper, and nothing comes up."

"Can you explain?"

"Yes. Let's start with the first email. You've got the number one next to it. It says, 'The story would freeze your blood.'"

I nodded. "I thought the phrase 'freeze your blood' was unusual. Is it in Hamlet?"

"Yeah. There is a scene where the ghost of the murdered King Hamlet is talking about his death. The ghost says,

'I could a tale unfold whose lightest word
Would harrow up thy soul, freeze thy young blood.'"

Murphy turned to look at me. "So it's a little different than this line on the paper. But it's similar in that both the email and what the ghost says is about a story that would freeze your blood. That is unusual to say the least."

"But you don't think it's a coincidence," I said.

Murphy shook her head. "Not when we consider the other emails."

"What are the other similarities?'

"Let's go to the second email," she said as she looked down at the paper I'd handed her. "It says, 'It was no accident. He poured in the poison.'"

She looked at me again. "In the play, the king is murdered by his brother Claudius, Hamlet's uncle, right? Claudius poured poison in the king's ear when he was sleeping. The lines in the play are once again spoken by the king's ghost. He says,

'Upon my secure hour thy uncle stole
With juice of cursed hebenon in a vial,
And in the porches of my ears did pour
The leperous distilment, whose effect
Holds such an enmity with blood of man
That swift as quicksilver it courses through
The natural gates and alleys of the body
The thin and wholesome blood. So did it mine.'"

Louise Murphy paused again, waiting, perhaps, to see if I understood the significance of the similarities between the email text and the play.

"I see what you're getting at," I said. "The email certainly has common ground with the play."

"Then let me continue," Murphy said.

She read from the paper. "Here's the third one. 'The killer now wears the victim's garlands.' In the play, the ghost of Hamlet's father is once again talking to Hamlet. The ghost says,

'But know, thou noble youth,
The serpent that did sting thy father's life
Now wears his crown.'"

"Meaning?" I said.

"Meaning that Hamlet's uncle Claudius, who poisoned the life out of Hamlet's father, took his crown."

I reached for the paper with the emails. "So the killer wearing the victim's garlands refers to Claudius wearing the king's crown."

"Yes," Murphy said. "It's like the writer of these emails was carefully trying to communicate the same information but just do it with different words."

"I see the connection."

"There's more," Murphy said. She took back the paper and read. "The fourth line on your paper says, 'My burden is to avenge the murder.' In the play, Hamlet says,

'Does it not, think thee, stand me now upon—
He that hath killed my king and whored my mother...'"

Murphy stopped speaking for a moment as she silently read ahead a line or two. She picked it up with,

"'Is't not perfect conscience
To quit him with this arm? And is 't not to be damned
To let this canker of our nature come
In further evil?'"

Murphy looked up and said, "When Hamlet says,

'Is 't not perfect conscience, to quit him with this arm,' he means, Don't I have an obligation to kill him with my sword? Wouldn't I be damned if I let him live to cause more evil?"

I nodded, thinking. It was all adding up.

"And the fifth line?" I said.

Murphy read from the sheet of paper. "'Fight back. Try and hit me hard. Give me a challenge, dude. I've practiced enough. Even a sparrow's death is part of God's plan.'" She gave the paper a little shake. "In some ways, this is the most convincing of all. In Act Five, Scene Two, Hamlet is about to have a fencing match with Laertes, who has been persuaded to kill Hamlet by the evil Claudius. Laertes and Hamlet are going to fight with swords. But what Hamlet doesn't know is that Laertes' sword is tipped with poison. Hamlet doesn't want Laertes to go easy on him as if he is just a child. Then, when another character, Horatio, brings up a superstition, Hamlet replies,

'There's a special providence in the fall of a sparrow.'

"This means that he doesn't believe superstitions. He believes God is in charge of everything. The mention of the sparrow is absolutely convincing. No casual writer would ever think to mention a sparrow in that way. These lines all add up to show that the writer is not just aware of Hamlet but is a Hamlet scholar of sorts. The writer knows the lines and their meanings."

She handed me the paper. "Does that help?"

"Yes. Now that you've seen these, I'm wondering what you think this reveals about the writer."

Murphy seemed taken aback. "I have no idea what would motivate a killer."

"I didn't mean that. What I mean is, what kind of background does this suggest? Do you think this writer is an amateur Shakespeare scholar? Or something more than that? A professor of English literature?"

Murphy frowned and seemed puzzled. "I suppose the writer could be an English professor like me. Or an actor. But anyone wanting to base some texts on Hamlet could look up the play and find lines to use."

"Sure, but would they?" I said. "Would a hair salon employee do that?"

Murphy looked affronted. "Of course. I wrote my master's thesis on the blossoming of English as a major language. It was called, 'From Chaucer to Shakespeare, The Rise of English as a Serious Language in Western Literature.' And I'm a waitress."

"Good point. But the question remains. My guess is that most of the people waiting tables at your restaurant are not Shakespeare scholars. How many of them know anything about him?"

She made a single nod. "Most don't have a clue. They've heard the name, but some of them don't even know he wrote plays, never mind when he lived and worked. But that's the case with all occupations."

"So you have no ideas about this?"

"Only what's already obvious. The writer of these lines was, at the minimum, probably exposed to Shakespeare at some point. And it was likely in a significant way, like going to see Hamlet. My guess is that the writer is more of a Shakespeare scholar. But we can't know, right? It's just a guess."

I thought about it. "Figuring out that these lines are from Hamlet is huge," I said. "I really appreciate it. Could you possibly write down the lines that each text comes from?"

"I don't have time for that. I have to leave in a couple of minutes." Louise Murphy thought for a moment. "I can write down the scene numbers and the telltale words that you can Google. That'll make it easy to find the lines and you can print them out."

"Perfect."

She made quick notes after each line of text and handed me the paper.

"Thanks very much." We both stood.

"You're welcome," she said.

"I'll never look at a restaurant wait person the same way again," I said. "Hey, you primarily work for tips at the restaurant, right?"

"Yeah."

"This information is very valuable to me." I pulled out my wallet and gave her a $50 bill. "Thanks very much for your service."

She stared at the bill, hesitated, then took it, turned, and hurried off.

THIRTY-EIGHT

I went back to the parking lot and got into my Jeep. Spot leaned forward from the back seat and put his nose all over me.

"What does a young Goth intellectual smell like?" I said.

He wagged, his tail thumping the rear window.

"That so?" I said as I drove off.

When I got back to my office, I did as Louise Murphy suggested, searched on the words she'd written down, and found the lines from Hamlet. Then I arranged the lines that had been emailed to the victims so that each line of text was followed by the source lines in Shakespeare's play. I printed it all out.

I called Street at her lab. "I've got some news about my case, and I'd like to get your thoughts. Diamond's too. Any chance you could squeeze in a short visit?"

"Sure. Bring His Largeness. No matter how much I try to exercise Blondie, I can never burn off her energy. Spot can run with her while we chat."

I next called Diamond.

"Fighting crime in this county is my job," he said. "I'll be there in un momento."

I pulled up near Street's door at the same time as Diamond rolled his Douglas County Sheriff's cruiser to a stop two parking places away.

Usually, Spot is excited to see Diamond. But the anticipation of running with Blondie was an order of magnitude more interesting than anything else besides steak. Spot ran to the door. It opened and Street's Yellow Lab raced out. Blondie leaped and hit Spot with a hard blow, her front paws to his chest. It barely budged him. She careened away and shot into the forest. He raced after, relatively slow to gain velocity. While she could run fast, it was her quick acceleration and instant turns that made her elusive. For Spot, chasing her was like a big rig truck chasing a small motocross motorcycle. Even though Spot's top speed was greater, he could never turn fast enough to catch her.

Street appeared in the doorway, raised herself up on tiptoes to give me a kiss, then looked horrified. She touched her fingertips to my jaw. "My God, Owen! What happened to you?! You should be in a hospital!"

Diamond came over. He looked at my face and frowned. "That is a very serious injury. You get that chasing boxers?"

"Yeah."

"You return the favor?"

"Yeah."

He made a small knowing nod.

I turned to Street. "I believe you were about to kiss me."

She gave me a kiss that was so light it was as if she worried it would exacerbate my injuries. Then she turned to Diamond and gave him a hug. She stared again at my face.

"What a pleasure for an introverted scientist," she said. "Two kinds of cops come calling at once."

"But only the official public version carries a sidearm," I said.

"Two," Diamond said. "Anything nasty happens, I'll let you borrow my Nano backup."

"Regardless of your armament," Street said, "if I were under surveillance by a bad guy, he'd be making a note to be careful approaching me."

We went inside.

"Iced tea?" Street said.

"Please," I said.

Simultaneously, Diamond said, "Por favor."

"Not just two cops," Street said. "Synchronized cops."

Diamond said, "The two beefcakes were released on bail this morning. It was an out-sized fee set for out-of-state dirtballs. Apparently, they have some change. Thought you'd want to know."

"Sure do," I said. "Crooks who can afford nice clothes can

probably afford bail. Even though you'll keep the double R, they'll still run home to California to skip bail."

"If they skip bail, I'll get a bench warrant."

"You want them back in Nevada?"

"Yeah."

"Because that guy tried to stomp your foot."

Diamond nodded. "That made it personal."

Street handed us each a glass of tea poured over ice cubes. We sat on Street's lab furniture, her on the stool at her microscope bench, me on her old desk chair, Diamond on the collapsible camp chair that Street was given when her chiropractor neighbor closed up shop and left town for a less snowy climate.

I told them about my trek to the town of Locke, about the man who attacked me, and my discovery that Kraytower had hired the boxers to make me drop my investigation.

"But he's the person who hired you," Street said.

I nodded. We talked about the implications.

Street looked very worried. She again touched the side of my jaw where it was swollen.

Diamond asked if my gut felt okay.

"Sore but okay."

Next, I told them about my meeting with Louise Murphy, the English Literature teacher at the college. "I had her look at the lines that were emailed to Lightfoot, Kraytower, and, probably, Perry. It didn't take her long to realize that they were rewrites of lines from the play Hamlet."

Street raised her eyebrows in surprise. Diamond's face was blank, the nothing-fazes reaction of a cop who's seen every version of twisted perpetrator.

"Murphy showed me how they all derived from Shakespeare." I pulled out the paper on which I'd printed the lines. I went down the page, explaining each one.

"This is weird and creepy," Street said.

"Yeah. It's clear that the person who sent these emails found appropriate lines in the play and used rewrites of them to send threats. Two of the people who received the texts have died. But it seems like there might be more motivation in choosing Hamlet than simply finding interesting lines. I wonder if there are other similarities between the play and the murderer's life."

"Like what?" Diamond said. "If the murderer you're trying to catch had a brother who was king-like, that would fit. If that king was murdered and then the king's brother seized the throne and married the king's widow, that would fit better."

"It does seem preposterous," I said.

"The murderer's situation doesn't have to be so dramatic," Street said. "It could simply be that the murderer's life has just one or two components of Hamlet's story."

Diamond made a slight nod.

Street continued, "Imagine that a man was murdered by his brother, and the brother took his place in some simple way. It wouldn't have to be as dramatic as taking over as king. And it wouldn't have to entail marrying the murder victim's widow. Just a simple fratricide with the murderer moving into the victim's home or business would cause one to think of King Hamlet and his murderous brother Claudius. If the murder victim's friends or relatives didn't know of Hamlet, other people would alert them to the similarity."

"And once they mentioned it," Diamond said, "the friends would go through life constantly aware of the fact that the world's greatest playwright had built what might be his greatest play around a similar crime."

"Yeah," I said. "It would dog all your thoughts. My problem is that I can't connect Hamlet's story to these current murders. We haven't found a king-like person who was murdered. We haven't found a brother who took his crown. Metaphorically or otherwise."

"Look at Carston Kraytower's life in these terms," Diamond said. "His colleagues are getting killed."

"How much similarity to Hamlet is there?" I asked.

"Doesn't everyone in the play die?" Street said.

"Pretty much," Diamond said. "Claudius murdered his brother Hamlet and took his crown and then married Hamlet's widow Gertrude. By the end of the play, several others have died from the poison that Claudius supplied."

"So maybe there is a parallel," Street said. "Even without an exact similarity between the current situation and the play, there could be similar themes. Murder and revenge."

Diamond spoke. "Maybe all of Kraytower's colleagues are like Claudius and his pals. Our Hamlet stand-in could be killing them."

"Their deaths being how Hamlet punishes them for their crimes." Street said.

"Could be. According to the texts, it would be by poison, just like in the play." Street said. "That would be the first similarity to Hamlet. The king was killed by poison. These men were killed by etorphine."

"Pretty Hamlettian," Diamond said.

"Hamlettian," I repeated. "Cop talk?"

"'Course," Diamond said. "Or maybe it's Hamlettish."

Street said, "Unlike in Hamlet, etorphine murders look like natural events. What did you call them? Agatha Christie heart attacks."

We three looked at each other, all trying to puzzle out possible connections.

"Hamlet's torment comes from his father being murdered," Street said. "So, to make it like Hamlet, we'd need a precipitating murder that started these current murders rolling."

"Precipitating," Diamond said. He looked at me. "Scientists can't help themselves, can they?"

"No. It's the price we pay for the benefit of their smarts." I turned to Street. "Not only do we need a precipitating murder, we'd need a vengeful relative. Ideally, a vengeful son of the murder victim, whoever that might be. Or at the minimum, a vengeful friend of the murder victim."

"Let's analyze this," Street said slowly, thinking as she talked. "The precipitating murder would have come before these current murders. That might suggest that the current murderer is killing people in Kraytower's world as punishment. These current murders were etorphine poisonings. I bet somewhere in the past is another etorphine murder. If this modern-day killer thinks that one of Kraytower's associates somehow usurped the place of a murder victim from the past, that would also fit."

"Like Kraytower's associates stole the king's crown," Diamond said.

I was drinking tea and had a thought that made me inhale. I started choking and coughing.

"Down the wrong tube," I said when I could finally speak.

"You thought of something," Street said.

"Something I learned from Nettie Moon Water. James Lightfoot had talked to Nettie about his demons."

"James Lightfoot being the guy who died from a heart attack at Kraytower's property," Diamond said.

"Yeah. The Agatha Christie heart attack."

"Even the rich and successful struggle with demons," Street said in a low voice.

"Right. Anyway, I asked Nettie what bothered Lightfoot. She said that he struggled with something that happened in the past. She also said that it seemed that Kraytower had secrets. And when I was in San Francisco, I talked again with the son, Joshua Kraytower. He referred to family secrets, things he was sure existed, but he didn't know what they were. So it could be that something went down years ago, and all concerned are still bothered by it. A murder would fit the bill. I also learned that Kraytower and his business colleagues all went to Yale. They all belonged to the same fraternity. The name was three Greek letters beginning with Kappa. Nettie said it was Kappa something something. Nettie also said that Kraytower's best friend in college died. Maybe that death was a murder."

"Wouldn't it be something," Diamond said, extending the thought, "if that death was someone who belonged to the same fraternity."

Street said, "King Hamlet was killed by his brother. I've been thinking of literal blood brothers. But maybe we're talking about frat brothers. James Lightfoot and Sebastion Perry and Carston Kraytower were all frat brothers in the same fraternity." She paused. "And then there is the curiosity that Kraytower's business is called KGA, for Kraytower Growth Assets. Three letters. Beginning with a K. Like a fraternity name beginning with Kappa."

I said, "It sure looks like these current murders could be punishment for the death of the kid who died."

Street reached over to her computer mouse, moved it, clicked a few times, then typed. She typed some more. Clicked some more. Repeated the process. Then she inhaled sharply.

"What?" I said.

"Here is a story about a fraternity hazing death twenty-two years ago. It was at the Kappa Omicron Upsilon fraternity at Yale. A kid named Edward Lange participated in a drinking contest. Oh my God, listen to this." She read aloud. "'The fraternity brothers celebrated Edward Lange's addition to the fraternity with an alcohol-fueled bash. One participant reported that they were drinking tequila shots with beer chasers. They turned it into a contest to see how fast someone could down a shot and then a beer without spilling a drop. Edward Lange won the contest. He was found dead the next morning. One witness said that his memory of the night was vague, but that he thought Edward Lange had drunk as many as fifteen shots and fifteen beers.'"

"That would kill you," Diamond said. "Frat brothers in a drinking contest is not a pretty picture. The most common cause of hazing deaths."

I said, "So the murderer, whoever he is, could think of Eddie as dying at the hands of his fraternity brothers, just as King Hamlet died at the hand of his brother Claudius."

Street widened her eyes a bit. "And these current murders could be revenge killings for Eddie's hazing death."

"Looks like it."

Diamond said, "Street, you pointed out that the current situation doesn't have to precisely match Hamlet in order for our murderer to think of it in similar terms. But comparing Eddie's death by alcohol poisoning to King Hamlet's death by poison in his ear is another good connection. All victims dying of poison."

"A Hamlet connection," I said.

Diamond nodded. "But this leads to the question of how Eddie's death so long ago could be fueling revenge murders twenty-some years later."

"It certainly is a reach," Street said. "Why such a time gap?"

I said, "Eddie Lange was a young college student. He was probably new to Yale. But he would have had friends. Maybe Kraytower was so upset that he decided to kill his fraternity brothers as punishment. Maybe it took twenty years for him to get up the courage to murder."

"But he hired you to find the killers," Diamond said.

"Right. And then he hired thugs to get me to quit."

"That could be misdirection to take the focus off him," Diamond said.

Street added, "Either way, it seems that a man is avenging the death of his friend by killing the perpetrators."

There was scratching at the door. Street opened it, and Blondie and Spot came in, both panting and smelling of exertion.

"Remember that women kill too," Diamond said. "Not necessarily at the rate or in the same way men kill. However, it might be worth noting that while men usually kill with violent methods, women often kill with poison."

Street looked at Diamond and then turned to look at me. I didn't sense any message in her look.

I said, "But despite the use of poison, the killers in Hamlet were men, right?"

Street's turn to nod. "Not a clear case," she said. "If we want to find any connection to Hamlet, we would hope to discover that Eddie Lange represented some kind of king-like importance to the murderer."

I said, "And that the murderer could think that Eddie's frat brother pals somehow took control of that importance after he was dead."

Diamond said, "Took the rightful king's crown."

I picked up the paper with the email lines on it. "Or, as one line says, 'The killer now wears the victim's garlands.'"

"From what you've said, Kraytower and his colleagues certainly live like kings," Street said.

"Yeah. But they all earned their money. Kraytower started the hedge fund, his pals joined him, and they all grew it into the huge business it is today. A sort of self-earned kingdom. All of which happened long after the death of Edward Lange."

We had another moment of silent thought.

Diamond turned to me. "I can take care of His Largeness. Street knows where to reach me if she should need anything. So we'll be okay with you taking an impromptu trip to Connecticut to find out what really happened at that Yale fraternity party."

THIRTY-NINE

I decided to take Diamond up on his idea that I go to Yale to investigate Edward Lange's death at the fraternity party 22 years ago. I left Spot with him and went back to my office.

I called Kraytower's Pacific Heights home number.

"Kraytower residence, Aria speaking."

"Good afternoon, Aria, this is Owen McKenna calling."

There was a pause. "The tall man." Her voice had a smile in it. "Very tall," she added. "Helping Mr. Kraytower with his… With the men who have died. I can forward your call to his office."

"No, I'm calling to speak with you."

"Me," she said in surprise.

"I have a question that you can probably answer."

"You say probably, and that makes me worry I'll disappoint."

"I doubt that. When I visited and spoke with you before, I also met the gardener Mary Mason and the other woman, Maya something."

"Floros," Aria said. "Maya Floros. Floros means green like a plant."

"May I speak with her?"

"I'm sorry, Maya is no longer employed here."

"Was she let go?"

"No. She… She let herself go."

"She quit?" I asked.

"Yes. Of course. Those are the English words. Maya quit."

"Do you know the reason why?"

"No," Aria's answer came fast. Too fast.

"You must have an idea," I said.

"No, I am sorry, I have no idea." That was too fast as well.

"Aria, I believe Mr. Kraytower told you to help me in any

way you could."

"Yes, that is true."

"Okay, let's take a different approach. Do you know the guessing game where one person knows something and another person guesses what it is? If the guesser gets close, the person who knows something says, 'warmer.' If the guesser gets further from the thing, the person who knows says, 'colder.'"

"Sorry, I don't know this game," she said.

"I understand. But let's try it, anyway. I'm going to guess about why Maya Floros quit her job as a nanny. If I'm wrong, you say I'm getting colder. If I'm right, you say I'm getting warmer."

"But why would someone play this game? I already told you I don't know why Maya quit."

"The reason to play the game is that you will use your intuition. You can sense the warmness or coldness of the answer even if you don't know exactly what the answer is. And if you do know the answer, you never have to state anything specific about the situation. It's just about how warm or cold I am. That makes it easy for you and helpful to me."

"I think I would have to have an example to understand."

"Okay. I'll make a statement. Maya Floros quit her nanny job because Joshua Kraytower was too difficult to be around. Am I warmer or colder?"

The answer took some time. "I see. That would be colder."

"Next statement," I said. "Maya quit her job because the pay was too little."

"Colder."

I said, "Maya quit her job because she came into a lot of money and no longer needs a job."

"Colder."

"Maya quit her job because she doesn't like you."

Aria said, "Colder."

"Maya quit her job because the house is a very unpleasant place to work."

"You keep getting more colder."

"Here's another question. Maya quit her job because of something connected to Joshua's father, Carston Kraytower."

The silence stretched out. "Warmer."

"Thank you, Aria. Can you tell me when Maya quit her job?"

"It was yesterday. Yesterday morning."

"What was her normal schedule?"

"Maya's job was to be around to help with Joshua. When he was young, she was his babysitter. She was around most all of the day. When he was older, she was mostly supposed to be in the house when he was home, to be seen when someone knocks on the door and I'm gone or busy. So she would always be here after his school let out."

"So Joshua wouldn't appear to be alone," I said.

"Yes. This is a safe neighborhood. But Mr. Kraytower is wealthy, and he didn't want to worry about Joshua being—what are the words—what bad people could use to get money."

"I understand," I said.

"Maya also helps me a great deal with my house chores. Helped. She is gone. My life is already harder."

"How long did Maya usually stay during the day?"

"She would stay until Jorge, the garage boy and driver, came. Or if Mary came to work."

"The gardener," I said.

"Yes. And sometimes Mr. Kraytower would come home early, and he would tell Maya that she could go."

"One more question. Do you have Maya's contact information? Phone number or email?"

"The phone number, yes. But I could get in trouble if I gave that to you, no? The concern about privacy. I know that she is an actor in a theater company. That is less of a concern. Giving that number out is advertising, right? Or that other word, what is it? Oh yes, publicity. Maya's theater wants publicity. The theater has a funny name. Hold on. Let me find the business card." There was a short pause. "It's called American Stratford Repertory. They do plays by the famous writer, Shakespeare." She read the info on the card.

"Thank you Aria. You've been a big help."

"You are welcome."

I hung up.

I opened my laptop and searched on American Stratford Repertory.

It was a company that specialized in performing Shakespeare's plays. Their home theater was in San Francisco's Mission District. But looking at their schedule, it seemed they spent most of their time on the road doing performances from Los Angeles to New York.

On closer look, the Los Angeles location was actually to the east in Riverside. The New York location was actually in New Jersey. It was the same for their other venues, which made sense. Few people would be familiar with Arlington Heights, Illinois, but everyone knew where Chicago was. The largest number of theaters was in Northern California.

Their current production was The Merchant of Venice, which was listed as a Sacramento performance. But it was staged at the Harris Center for the Arts at Folsom College, down the road to the west of Tahoe, at the very beginning of the foothills. The program notes listed Maya Floros as Jessica in the play.

The program also listed the running time as 2 hours and 10 minutes.

I considered the driving time from Tahoe and realized that if I left soon, I could be at Folsom College in time for the end of the play. If Maya was like many actors, she might hang around after the performance to chat up the theatergoers. Making a good impression didn't just apply inside the theater. If a moneyed patron was impressed with an actor and got to know them, and if that patron let the director know, it wouldn't hurt the actor's chances of being cast in future productions.

I went back to my computer and found a midnight flight from Sacramento to New York. The timing would work with my plan. So I booked the flight. Then I left in my Jeep.

To get to Folsom College, you drive down the mountains to the bottom of the foothills and head toward the town made famous by its prison and the Johnny Cash song.

Folsom College sits up on a hill with a view that stretches far past Sacramento, 20 miles to the west. I turned and drove up the entrance road as the sun was setting behind the mountains that line Napa Valley another 40 miles past Sacramento.

The Harris Center has three stages. The theater staff and guards were unlocking the outside doors as they prepared for the end of the play and the exit of the crowd. I walked through the lobby as if I were important, and I was able to slip in through a dark door at the rear of the theater without being accosted.

The American Stratford Repertory was doing its thing on the smallest of the three stages, playing, as was the point of having different sized venues, to a nearly full house. It wasn't long before the character of Jessica came on stage. Maya Floros played her with enthusiasm and energy. I had no problem believing that she—Shylock's daughter—was eloping to marry a pauper even as she stole a chest of her father's gold.

At the end, the crowd was pleased. They clapped and cheered.

I went out as part of the crowd and worked my way around toward the stage doors, looking for the green room, the place where performers often met audience members who wanted to personally deliver their compliments.

I found the reception area and quickly saw a group of actors who were still in costume. An elderly couple was crowding in close to Maya Floros, trapping her against a wall as they spoke at length. Maya smiled and nodded and withstood the barrage of appreciation with what looked like a kind of tolerance.

When the older couple moved on, a group of three young people crowded toward Maya. One held an old-fashioned notebook. Another held a phone, thumbs hovering above the screen. They asked questions about her acting. I realized they were likely Folsom College theater students.

Maya soon excused herself and headed toward a door that probably led behind the stage. I politely stepped in her way as I tried to think of an oblique way of getting information.

"That was a good performance, Maya. You have impressive acting chops."

"Thank you."

"My name's Owen McKenna. You may remember that Aria

Ibarra introduced us at Carston Kraytower's house in Pacific Heights. The truth is that I'm not here as a theatergoer. I'm an investigator looking into a crime that may have a negative impact on Joshua Kraytower." Maya immediately looked frightened. "Don't worry, it has nothing to do with you," I said, even though I knew the statement might not be true.

Her fright lessened, but she had an intense look of concern. "Is Joshua okay?"

"Yes. But I'd appreciate it if I could please ask you a question or two."

She stayed silent.

Aria had told me that Maya had quit and left yesterday morning. So, contrary to the information I already had, I said, "Do you remember speaking to Joshua yesterday afternoon?"

"No. I left in the morning. And I haven't been back."

"Oh? I thought you were usually there until after Mary or Jorge come to work. Or until Mr. Kraytower comes home?"

"That was my schedule, yes. But not yesterday. Because I quit."

"Oh, I'm sorry to hear that," I said. "Joshua told me that he likes you."

"And I like him. And Aria, and the gardener, and the driver."

"I see," I said. "Mr. Kraytower was not your favorite?"

Maya made a short laugh that was more a scoff of derision. She didn't speak.

I prodded her. "He didn't..." I said it with a strong flavor of negative judgment.

"Maybe not what you're thinking. But he did everything else. I won't get more specific. I know how people can hire lawyers to make accusations against people who are victims."

"I'm sorry you were victimized."

"You have no idea how sorry I am. He made my life so miserable." Maya's eyes flashed with anger. I wondered if she was angry enough to murder.

"Did any of Mr. Kraytower's business colleagues make you feel victimized as well?"

Maya regarded me carefully. "You're wondering if I killed them?"

I raised my eyebrows.

"Yes, I know about that," she said. "The answer is no."

"I understand you don't want to be explicit," I said. "But did Kraytower simply say or do inappropriate things? Or was it worse?"

She narrowed her eyes as if transferring some of her anger to me.

"Inappropriate things? That's one of the most insidious euphemisms. To try to gloss over vile degradation and public humiliation by calling it inappropriate. Would you call murder an inappropriate response to anger?"

"I'm sorry. I didn't mean to minimize what he did, whatever it was. When you say public humiliation, I assume that means his actions weren't just private between you and him."

Maya clenched her fists at her sides. She was shaking. Her anger had built to rage. "There were the private moments. He would call them awkward. I call them disgusting. Then there were the times when he made jokes about me in front of his friends. 'My nanny, here, thinks she's going to be a famous actress.' And they all laughed at me. He said, 'Joshua's nanny should stick to nannying, her best opportunity to earn a living. Pretending you're going to make it as an actor, that's a one-in-a-million chance, isn't it?'"

Maya's jaw muscles bulged as she clenched her teeth. "When you belittle a person's hopes and dreams, you take away the value of life. You destroy them. Well, I would destroy him if I could." Her lip was lifted in a sneer, but it was vibrating, and her eyes were brimming with tears. She turned, walked through a door and shut it firmly behind her.

I turned and walked out to the Jeep, remembering what Joshua had said about his father making jokes to his business colleagues about his boy wanting to study ecology and write about nature. Public humiliation.

FORTY

I caught the JetBlue nonstop red-eye from Sacramento International to JFK, landed early in the morning, and transferred to a small commuter prop plane that flew at the same speed my Jeep goes down the mountain from Tahoe to Carson City when I'm in a hurry. More disconcerting than the stall-speed flight velocity were the rattles in the structure, not altogether dissimilar from the rattles in my rusty old Jeep.

Nevertheless, we touched down smoothly if loudly in New Haven, Connecticut, and I was in the queue for cabs just 90 minutes after leaving JFK. Having had three hours of poor sleep over Wyoming, South Dakota, and Minnesota, I was functional but not very lucid.

The East Coast summer day was bright and cloudless. I couldn't help noticing that, compared to my home base in the mountains, the sea-level air seemed thick with humidity, and the sun, while uninterrupted by clouds, was merely warm, not the high altitude broil that seared one's skin in Tahoe.

Being in New Haven, I had a brief flashback to my youth in Boston, just 140 miles to the northeast. My early years were a tumultuous time with my three cop uncles who took turns helping my mother raise me. They disagreed and argued about everything except their code of ethics. It was that code—which didn't always align with the law but which was fair and as rigid as concrete—that drew me into the cop profession behind them. After high school in the Fenway-Kenmore neighborhood, I suffered through three years of college at a cheap state school and then quit to go to cop school. When I was done, I had a solid offer from the Boston PD. But despite significant distress at disappointing my relatives, I turned it down. I packed a small backpack with a change of clothes, kissed my teary mother goodbye, and hitchhiked west.

I ended up in San Francisco, the only city I could imagine that would be both more exciting than Boston and more accessible and friendly than New York. An entry-level job as a patrol officer led to a position in the Investigations Bureau, and from there I ended up as a Homicide Inspector a decade and a half later.

Now, as I waited at the New Haven airport, I thought of taking a detour up to Boston to revisit the place of my youth. But something made me avoid it. Fear of disappointment? Worry that I would feel that moving west had been a mistake? I decided it was a simple lack of interest. Nothing about the location of my childhood was notable, so the locale where it took place had no special significance for me. And my mother and uncles were gone, mother and one uncle dead and two uncles retired and living in Florida.

A cab pulled up. I was next in line, so I got into the back seat. "Kappa Omicron Upsilon fraternity at Yale," I said to the driver.

He was one of those dark men from Somalia, who had striking features and deep voices and could be action stars in Hollywood movies if only they spoke English with a Southern California or British accent. This man had some practice yet to do. I had to ask him to repeat himself several times. Finally, I handed him a piece of paper on which I'd printed the Kappa Omicron Upsilon address. He took it and stopped trying to communicate with me.

He took us on a route with far more turns than I'd estimated from the Google map. Maybe he was detouring around road-work delays. Or maybe he was simply following Adam Smith's capitalist principle, that in undertaking tactics to earn more money—however unfair to his customers—the gain to him would in turn promote a gain to society. I could have flown back to New York in the same amount of time it took for him to deliver me to the front of a huge stone mansion just off the edge of the Yale campus. The building was built in the same Gothic architectural style as most of Yale's timeless buildings.

I gave the driver a ten and three twenties. "Two twenties for the fare, a ten for your tip, and another twenty for waiting for me here. I'll be back out in ten minutes or less. At that point I'll either take another ride or send you away."

The man said several things in rapid succession, his musical timbre almost like the bass part in an exotic song. I didn't understand any of it. But it seemed he understood me.

I walked up to a grand door that was more like a church entry than what I expected of a fraternity house. Above the door hung a heavy wood sign that had probably started out with a dark walnut stain. Over the last eighty or hundred years, the wood had darkened such that the stain was nearly black. The letter shapes had been carved out and painted black. So the black letters had barely enough contrast to be legible against the nearly-black background. It was only because it was the middle of the day, the sun was bright, and I knew what it said that I could make out the words Kappa Omicron Upsilon.

Below the sign was another more recent sign, this one made with black marker on a crooked piece of white substrate like an artist's white board. It hung at an angle as if by picture wire. It said, 'Abandon all hope, ye who enter here.' I wasn't certain, but I thought the famous quote came from some story about hell. Santiago's Spanish hero Cervantes? No, probably Dante, another equally famous writer, one of those over-achieving Italians. Clearly, the sign was a joke by a fraternity kid who thought he was very clever. What was clever wasn't the joke, but the fact that he'd gotten accepted into Yale.

I knocked only to realize that my little tap against a massive door could not be heard inside. Maybe a fraternity house was like a small hotel. Guests let themselves into the lobby. If the door was locked, it was because visiting hours were over.

I didn't see a doorbell, so I grabbed the big, vertical wrought iron handle, pushed down on the thumb lever, and opened the door.

I found myself on the slate floor of a spacious entry. On each side of the entry were heavy wood sidebars done in the style of elegant-yet-rustic old country lodge. Above the sidebars were large mirrors framed in heavy ornately-carved moulding the color of ebony. To the sides of each mirror were wall sconces that looked to be wrought iron. The wavy amber glass glowed from pointy, low-wattage bulbs that were probably left on at all hours. On the surfaces of the sidebars were magazines and stacks of local papers and flyers. I shuffled through them. The magazines were mostly Maxim and Esquire, and the flyers were mostly from pizza delivery restaurants. There were enough flyers that one would expect the building to reek of old pizza. Instead, I smelled only pot.

I walked from the entry into a large center hall with a 15-foot-tall coffered ceiling. On the left was a grand dining room with a large dark table. On the windowless wall were double swing doors that likely led to the kitchen.

To the right of the center hall was a living room large enough to have multiple seating areas with old leather chairs and couches. There were low tables with more magazines and higher library tables with straight-backed chairs for playing cards or working on a laptop or maybe even reading a book. On one end was a huge cut-granite fireplace. Because it was summer, there was no fire. Any ashes from the previous winter fires had been swept up. But to one side was a full wood bin, and the fire grate had enough dark char to indicate that the fireplace was well-used and ready for the coming winter.

Along the front and side of the room were large windows. Under the windows were book cases. The shelves were filled with books that looked old, many of them with leather covers and gold-leaf lettering on the spines. They appeared unworn as if a wealthy alumnus had ordered up the Great Books of Western Literature and donated them for the edification of new students. Because the books looked like they'd rarely been cracked open, it may have been that the donor had merely wanted his old frat grounds to look impressive when he visited, especially if he were bringing a business associate.

A few shelves had more recent books, some hard bound with dust jackets, some paperbacks. They too looked relatively unused.

Two young men sat on a couch in front of the fireplace, a laptop angled toward them, the sounds of a movie or TV show quite loud. They each held a can of beer, and they laughed almost

TODD BORG

continuously. Two other kids sat at one of the library tables, one working on a laptop, the other hunched over his phone. Over by the front window paced a kid who talked on his phone.

"I don't care if you agree," he said, raising his voice enough that I could hear him. "I still want to know how to become administrator of my account. Those stocks are mine. I should be able to do with them as I please!" A pause. "I'm over eighteen, a legal adult. And frankly, I don't care if you or my father approve or not." Another pause. "I'll call back tomorrow. I'll expect you to have an answer."

He clicked off, stuffed the phone in his pocket, and kept pacing. His breathing was audible across the room. He clenched his fists at his side, his arms bent a bit as if in a muscle pose, a posture that probably helped blow off his frustration. His biceps and triceps bulged and stretched out the short sleeves of his T-shirt. He was a meaty kid but not a natural mesomorph. His muscles were built on slender bones as evidenced by thin fingers that would be good for playing the violin.

I walked up to him. "Excuse me, please," I said. "I'm looking for a different kind of administrator. I'm wondering if you can give me the name of your fraternity house president or manager."

He had long wavy hair that hung down the sides of his face, obscuring his view of anything that wasn't directly in front of him. He stopped pacing, turned, and looked at me. The kid was tall and didn't have to tilt his head up much to look at my face. He had intense brown eyes and eyebrows that looked to be pulled together by anger.

"The house president is Chad Clancy," he said.

"How would I find him?"

"Depends." He sounded brusque. "Why do you want to speak to him?"

"I'm trying to find out the history of a former fraternity brother, a man who went to Yale around twenty years ago. I'm told he belonged to Kappa Omicron Upsilon. I assume he lived here in this house."

The kid's frown made a subtle change from anger to puzzlement. "Then you wouldn't want to talk to Chad."

"Why?"

"He wouldn't know."

"What makes you think that?"

The kid looked off and sighed as if it were such an imposition to have to speak to an adult. "Look, Chad's, like, real good at scheduling meetings and getting the house chores assigned and dealing with the cleaning help. Organized, that's what Chad is. But he's from Kansas. People like him don't usually belong to a fraternity. I think he might be the first kid in his family to go to college. He certainly doesn't know anything about Kappa Omicron Upsilon's history." The kid leaned toward me and spoke in a lowered voice. "Frankly, Chad isn't real together about, you know, college stuff and city stuff. He only got into Yale because they wanted diversity. He's kind of..."

"An unsophisticated country boy?"

The kid thought about his response. "Let's just say that you should talk to someone who has, you know, a family lineage at Yale."

"You mean rich blue bloods like you."

He frowned very hard. "Are you insulting me?" He spoke in a loud voice.

"I didn't set out to. But when I ask a simple question and your response shows your prejudice against country kids who don't share your pure aristocratic breeding and privilege, it rankles. I'm sure you guys come with American Kennel Club registration certificates. But even the snootiest dog owners know that sometimes a mutt from Kansas is a better dog."

"You SOB!" The muscles were once again clenched. He looked ready to take a swing at me.

One of the kids from across the room said, "Hey, Bayler, you okay?" The kid stood up from the couch. He also had show muscles. He walked over. "This guy giving you grief? I can help you with that." Behind him, the other kids in the room were watching.

"Yeah, this guy's a pompous ass. Let's drag him outside and show him you don't mess with Yale boys."

"Look guys. I merely want to talk to someone about fraternity history. But if you want to fight, you take the first swing. Your pals behind you will be witnesses. They'll testify that I had to defend myself. When I leave here, I'll call my buddy at the Yale Police Department and file assault charges. It will be embarrassing for you to have the police arresting you at the hospital after you regain consciousness. Even worse will be trying to explain it to the authorities who will decide to expel you." I looked at the kid with the long hair. "What will your daddy think?"

One of the kids at the table behind them called out, "That guy might be cop, you know."

The two muscle-bound kids looked at me, a hint of doubt softening their tough exterior.

I answered the unspoken question. "Homicide Inspector San Francisco PD. Twenty years of learning how to deal with self-important wannabe toughs like you two."

Bayler turned to his roommate and said, "Let's get out of here before I break this guy's jaw."

The two young men hustled outside. I could see them through the windows, walking down the sidewalk.

I turned to the others in the room. "Chad Clancy? Can you please tell me where to reach him?"

The kid who'd thought I was a cop said, "He works at Pizza Heaven two days a week. His shift ends at four p.m. But biz slows down after three, three-thirty. So you can probably get some face time with him close to the end of his shift."

"Thanks much," I said. "So how is it that you go to Yale and still act like a courteous, helpful adult?"

The kid looked both ways like he wanted to make sure no one could overhear him. He spoke softly. "I'm kind of like Chad. From the Midwest. Wisconsin. No family riches. I got a scholarship but I still have major student loans and still have to work a job to make it all work."

"You sling pizzas, too?"

"No. I work in a tire store. Just like in high school. I can mount a tire and balance a wheel with the best of them." He lowered his voice even more. "Bayler and Alden don't even know that wheels need to be balanced."

FORTY-ONE

As I walked out of the fraternity, my cell phone rang. I had stepped off the curb to cross the street toward my waiting cab. I took some running steps to get out of traffic and pulled out my phone.

"Owen McKenna."

"Carston Kraytower calling." His voice sounded shaky and had lost its resonance. "Joshua has gone missing. I'm worried. Extremely worried."

I didn't think Kraytower could say something that would take my breath away, but this did. And not just because it ran counter to his efforts to remove me from the case without firing me. "When did you last see him?"

"My housekeeper, Aria Ibarra, said he wasn't in his room this morning. She made some calls to his friends but no one has seen him. So she called me. I was in a meeting. I didn't get her voicemail until fifteen minutes ago. I called her back, and she still hasn't seen Joshua. I'm worried he's been kidnapped!" Kraytower's voice wavered. "So I called the police. They acted like this was no big deal. They said Joshua has to be missing for twenty-four hours before they can do anything. I can't stand it. I asked for a captain, but I was told there wasn't anyone who could help me. Isn't there some way to get to the police chief? I've met the mayor. I could call him. He knows I can influence elections." It sounded like Kraytower was coming undone.

"Carston, please take a deep breath." As I said it, I took a deep breath as well.

I wanted to challenge him about why he hired Cormac O'Connor to send boxers to intimidate me and get me to drop Kraytower's case. Of course, this supposed kidnapping might be an imaginary story to confuse the situation. But if Kraytower didn't know I was aware of what he'd done, I might gain advantage by playing along. And maybe Joshua really had been kidnapped.

I said, "The reason why the police want twenty-four hours to go by is that missing teenagers nearly always turn up. Especially boys who were last seen in their own bedroom. There wasn't a break-in, right? And Joshua wasn't hanging out in the Tenderloin or with bad kids. Almost for certain he went out of his own accord and with someone he knew."

"But Joshua wouldn't disappear like this!"

"The other reason," I continued as if Kraytower hadn't spoken, "is that there is very little the police can do in this situation."

"You don't know that!"

"Yes, Carston, I do. I was on the SFPD for twenty years. So let's try to stay calm."

"Don't patronize me!"

"I'm not. I'm giving you good advice. You're of no use to Joshua if you're so bent out of shape that you can't think clearly. Where are you now? Tahoe? Or The City?"

"Neither. I'm at a conference in Reykjavík, Iceland."

I found myself wondering if it were true. Kraytower had just been in San Francisco. "When will you be home?"

"I don't know. My pilot said my plane has some kind of mechanical issue. I can fly commercial if you think it's important. I'm even willing to fly economy if I have to."

His comment revealed Kraytower's lack of devotion to his kid. It bothered him so much that he was willing to fly economy.

"What else can I do?" he asked, sounding desperate.

"Unmute your phone and take all calls. If there is no caller ID, answer anyway. It could be a kidnapper. Set your text and email the same way. If your email account won't chime when something comes in, then check it continuously."

"Is there a way I can offer a reward for Joshua's return? How would it get publicized?"

"It's too early for that. Joshua will likely return or call soon. Even when kids decide to run away, they usually come back in a day or two. Tell me, who else was in your house yesterday evening and last night?"

"No one except Aria."

"Do you trust her completely?"

"Yes. She holds my world together. She is irreproachable."

"Did your housekeeper know what hours Joshua was home last night?"

"He was home in the evening, at the least. She said he ate dinner in the kitchen and then went up to his room. He told her he was going to do some writing and go to bed early."

"Is that normal for Joshua?"

"Yes. Why the question?"

"Just checking. Joshua didn't strike me as the sort who would sneak out and go to parties, but I still need to ask."

"Joshua is a homebody. Something else must have happened."

"Kids often go AWOL. It's part of growing up. Why would you think he was kidnapped? Did you get a ransom note?"

"No. Nothing. But those poison emails... And the deaths of my employees. They have me on edge. A razor's edge. Now with Joshua gone, it's a huge break from pattern."

"I'll see what I can find out," I said. "I'll call when I learn anything."

We disconnected.

I dialed the number for Kraytower's city house.

"Kraytower residence, Aria Ibarra speaking."

"Hi Aria. This is Owen McKenna."

"The detective. I remember."

"I just got off the phone with Carston Kraytower. What can you tell me about Joshua?"

"Nothing. He was here last night. I gave him dinner. I said goodnight when he went up to his room."

"Where were you after that?"

"I was in the kitchen cleaning up. Then I went into the laundry room to fold the clothes in the dryer. Let me think. After that, I had my tea and read my book, and then I went to bed."

"Where in the house do you sleep?"

"I'm up in the third floor apartment."

"And Joshua was in his room on the second floor?"

"Yes."

"Could anyone have come into the house?"

"No, the doors are locked. I check them every night before I set the alarm."

"Who else has keys to the house?"

"Mr. Kraytower and Joshua and me, of course. The nanny, Maya Floros, still has keys. I forgot to get them from her when she quit."

"Does Ms. Moon Water have keys?"

"Oh, I forgot that. She is—how do I say it—like a substitute mother for Joshua. I have heard some talk from Joshua that Ms. Moon Water is a person who can take over if something should happen to Mr. Kraytower. There is a word. The guardian."

"Does she have the alarm code as well?"

"I don't know. But I suppose she must. A key is no good without the code."

"Does the alarm system have cameras?"

"You mean, like in the movies, where you can be in another country and look at a computer and see every place and every door? No. It's a not-so-fancy alarm."

"I understand. So if someone wanted to get into the house, how would he do it?"

"He would have to smash the window or the door. But the alarm would be very loud. The only other way would be if someone would give him a key and the alarm code."

"Who would do that?"

"No one." She sounded adamant.

"Of Mr. Kraytower and you and Joshua and the nanny and Nettie, who do you think would be the most likely to give someone a key and the code?"

"No one." Even more adamant.

"Please, Aria, I'm not asking for a guilty party. I'm only asking for a priority. Let's say you had to be gone, and someone had to come in to water the plants. Who would be the most trusting family member, someone who would want to be helpful and lend someone a key?"

"I think Mr. Kraytower because he would not have to worry

that he would get in trouble. Everyone else would be afraid of his anger."

"Can you think of any other way that Joshua could go missing?"

"The only other way is Joshua walking out by himself."

"Would he do that?"

"Maybe."

"Can you think of a reason why?" I asked. As I asked the question, my gut clenched. I'd made him very angry with my questions. He'd walked out on me, gone down the back stairway, and left the house.

"Joshua is a good boy," Aria said. "But he is that age where a child likes to... explore."

"Would Joshua go out to meet someone?"

"Maybe. If he liked the person."

"Does Joshua have his own phone?" I asked.

"Yes."

"Have you called it?"

"Yes. All I get is his voicemail."

"Let's say," I said, speaking slowly, "that you have closed up the house for the night and gone up to your third-floor apartment. If Joshua called or texted someone, or someone contacted him, and Joshua made a plan to meet that person out on the street, could he go downstairs and leave the house without you being aware of it?"

"Yes," Aria said again. "And he could lock the door and set the alarm and I would still be sound asleep."

"Do you think that's what happened?"

"I think it is the only possible thing."

"Just one or two more questions, please," I said. "Could you guess who Joshua would meet and go away with?"

"I... It would only be a guess."

"Right," I said. "Just a guess."

"I've heard Joshua tell his Tahoe friend to come to San Francisco to visit. If the friend did that, I can think that Joshua might go out at night and have fun. You might not believe me, but I think that if Joshua had such a visit, it could be the most fun he has ever had."

"He's not a fun-loving kid?"

"How to say this… Joshua is very serious. Not very unhappy. But focused on his writing. He doesn't know how to do unserious things."

"Any idea what this friend's name is?"

"The first time I heard it, I thought it was a heavenly name. Like the blue heavens above. Sky."

I thought about it.

"Mr. McKenna?" she said. "Are you still there?"

"Sorry. I had another question. The nanny who quit? Maya Floros?"

"Yes?" Aria said, her voice now guarded.

"Did she ever help out at Mr. Kraytower's Tahoe house?"

"No. Mr. Kraytower relied on the Tahoe staff to be around for Joshua."

"So Maya Floros didn't come to Tahoe."

"Oh, Mr. McKenna, I didn't say that. Maya didn't ever go there to work. But she went there always to play. What did she call it? Oh, I remember. Mini-vacations. Her best friend's family has a cabin there."

"Any idea of what her friend's name is?"

"No. But I remember that the cabin is on the West Shore. Maya mentioned what the locals there say about how the West Shore is the best shore."

Near the Kraytower palace.

"Thank you very much for your help, Aria. I'll be sure to tell Mr. Kraytower how helpful you've been."

FORTY-TWO

My cabby was still waiting when I got off the phone. I had him take me to the pizza place where Chad worked.

I walked through the front door of Pizza Heaven even though it was probably closer to the beginning than the end of Chad's shift. I ordered a medium-sized Margherita pie and a Sam Adams. The kid waiting tables brought my beer in a minute. The pizza came ten minutes later. When he stopped back later to see if I was happy, I said, "Any chance you're Chad Clancy?"

"Yeah, that's me."

"Owen McKenna, private investigator from California, just arrived to look up the history on a Kappa Omicron Upsilon frat member from twenty-two years ago. I'm hoping you can direct me to someone who might have known him."

"Private Investigator like a PI on TV?"

"Kinda," I said.

"But a real life example. That's pretty cool," Chad said.

"Pretty cool wouldn't be my description," I said.

"How'd you know I work here at the pizza joint?"

"I stopped by your fraternity house and asked." I gestured toward the chair opposite mine. "Have a seat, if you can."

He scanned the restaurant and its few diners. "Only as long as the current diners don't need anything." He glanced back toward the kitchen then turned to me. "You must have talked to Bill."

"From Wisconsin?"

He nodded. "The other stuffed shirts would have directed you away from me. They think I'm a rube straight off the nowheresville farm."

"Not a fun job being fraternity president, huh?" I said.

"When they get drunk playing Animal House and break a faucet and flood the place, or rip the light fixtures out of the ceiling, I get the honor of hiring a plumber or electrician. If it's the middle of the night, which is usually the case, then I get to try and fix it myself. Fortunately, I learned a lot of skills growing up on a farm. The kids who feel entitled because their families have all gone to Yale think they've bootstrapped themselves to success because they got good grades. Of course, the poor kids like me were at after-school jobs while the privileged kids were doing homework. Those well-off kids know that the job of the fraternity president is to be their live-in handyman and house servant." He glanced around at the other diners, checking to see that all was well. "So you came all the way from California. Why?"

"I'm working on an investigation. In the mix is a Yale student and Kappa Omicron Upsilon member named Edward Lange. Twenty-two years ago, he was new to the fraternity and apparently died in a hazing incident. I'd like to find someone who knew him."

"I think I've heard about that. It was a drinking contest?"

"So I heard."

"And this Edward Lange, how does he connect to your investigation? Or maybe you can't say."

"I would say if I knew. Some people have died. They knew Eddie. If I can learn more about him, maybe I can learn more about them."

Chad nodded. "Of course none of us current members were around twenty years ago. Or we were babies. Let me think. I have a fraternity directory in my computer. Hold on."

Chad pushed back his chair and walked toward the kitchen. One of the other diners raised a finger and caught his eye. Chad refilled the man's water, then cleared dishes from another table, then seated a foursome that came in, then answered a phone call, then fetched his laptop from the back and returned to my table.

"Is your pizza okay?" he asked.

"Great, thanks."

"Okay, let me see what I can find." He opened his computer, typed and clicked and started slowly scanning as he dragged his fingers on the screen. He pulled a paper napkin from the table dispenser and wrote down some names and phone numbers and addresses. He slid the napkin across the table.

"Here are three possibles, Kappa frat brothers who are still in the area. I put down their businesses and their graduation dates so you can see that they were here around twenty-two years ago. Whether they knew your guy well or not, I have no idea. But you'll find out when you talk to them, right?"

"Right. This is perfect. Thank you very much. I appreciate your help. I'm curious. What's your major?"

"I'm majoring in computer science. But I'm thinking of shifting to business. I don't like coding, but I love tech. So, who knows, I could even end up on the West Coast some day."

I handed him my card. "Look me up if you do. Next time around, I'll serve you pizza. Thanks again."

Chad got busy with his other customers. I left cash on the table to cover the bill and a good tip and walked out, holding the napkin, looking at the names.

There was a lawyer, a professor, and the owner of a chain of dry cleaners. They all had New Haven addresses and all had graduated nineteen or twenty years ago.

I walked over to campus, found a park bench, and got out my phone. I started with the lawyer, a man named Milton Peabody.

A young woman answered, "Peabody Law."

"Hello, my name is Owen McKenna. I'm a private investigator looking into a death at Yale that happened twenty-two years ago. Milton Peabody was the victim's fraternity brother. I'd like to ask Milton a few questions whenever it's convenient for him."

"I'm sorry. Mr. Peabody is out of the country on indefinite leave on a case in Scotland. I can take a message if you'd like."

"Thanks, I'll try later."

I next dialed the professor, a man named John Manners, who taught Far Eastern Studies at Boston University. I got his voicemail message. Something about his officious tone made me think he wouldn't be forthcoming. I hung up thinking that I could always call back later.

Last, I called Ten Corners Laundry and Dry cleaning. Chad had written down the name Danny Sato.

"Ten Corners," a man answered. "Danny speaking."

FORTY-THREE

Danny Sato had a clipped speaking style, his few words quick and fast, his pronunciation distinct. A man in a hurry.

"Hi Danny, my name's Owen McKenna. I'm an investigator from California. I got your name from a young man named Chad Clancy, who is the current president of Kappa Omicron Upsilon. I'm in New Haven because my current case connects to a former fraternity brother of yours, a man named Edward Lange. I'm hoping you can spare some time to answer a couple of questions about him."

"Eddie, Eddie. Poor Eddie. You want to meet or talk over the phone?"

"Face-to-face would be good," I said.

"A late lunch?"

I was still full from the pizza. "Sure," I said.

"Let's meet at Reds and Greens. Corner of Tillman and Rush. It's kitty corner from one of my Ten Corners. Two o'clock work for you?"

"I'll be there," I said.

Forty minutes later, I was standing outside the Reds and Greens front door when Danny Sato walked up. I didn't identify him by his partial Asian look but by his fast, clipped walking style, the physical parallel to his speech. He was a small man who looked very fit. He wore a crisp white dress shirt tucked into worn jeans that had faded to a blue that went with his light blue sport jacket. On his feet were tattered running shoes.

I reached out as he approached. "Danny Sato? Owen McKenna."

We shook.

"Makes sense an investigator would look me up and know

what I look like."

"I didn't. It's your walk that gives you away."

He raised his eyebrows.

"I recently met an old guy whose career was working as a gait analyst. Since then I've wondered if people walk like they talk. You certainly do. Fast and efficient."

Sato nodded as if he'd always known that his movement and speech aligned.

We went inside the restaurant. A young woman sat us at a window table and gave us menus.

"A recommendation?" I said.

"They specialize in veggie dishes, nearly all of which include reds and greens."

"Sounds good," I said as I tried to imagine fitting in any more food after my Pizza Heaven lunch.

Sato waved at the waiter and gave his order for what sounded like a red and green peppers extravaganza.

"And something to drink?"

"I'll have your Stubborn Beauty Monster IPA," Danny said.

The waiter turned to me.

"Same food, but with water, please." I gestured out the window. "I've never seen a line outside a laundry and dry cleaners before. Is your business always this popular?"

Danny glanced out the window toward his dry cleaner shop and made a little smile. The waiter brought our drinks. Danny took a sip, licked the head off his lip.

"I took a business class at Yale," he said. "One of the central themes that the prof harped on was that no matter how the tides are changing and disrupting the business shoreline, there will nearly always be a demand for service businesses. Even the best robots probably won't do a good job of serving you pizza out of a wood-fired oven or building a custom house."

"Or doing your laundry."

Danny nodded. "I had lots of exciting and wild business ideas. Moonshots, I called them. But they were the kinds of things that were more likely to lose a fortune than make one. So I decided to do something on the side that would be relatively risk free and unlikely to go bankrupt just because of societal changes."

"Laundry," I said.

"A good service business produces income during recessions as well as boom times. So I modernized the laundry concept and it worked."

"Does the Ten Corners name mean you planned ten locations from the beginning?"

He made a single nod.

"You were hoping to get lucky and be very successful," I said.

"No. I was ambitious and confident. Big difference."

"Got it. Ten locations must be a lot of work."

"Actually, I'm up to thirty-one. But I might get out of it."

"Too much work?"

"Partly. Mostly, a national franchiser just offered me twenty-five million for my business. It's tempting. That would help me finance one of my moonshot ideas."

I nodded. "Lot of money," I said.

"Twenty-five million isn't much by some Yale alumni standards. But it's a lot for a kid who descended from six different relatives whose lives were put on hold or destroyed by imprisonment in the internment camps during the forties."

Our food came.

Danny Sato scooped up a heap of veggies onto his fork and momentarily held it in front of his face as he spoke. "Why are you asking about Eddie Lange?"

"I was hired to look into two deaths in Northern California. Both men went to Yale and belonged to Kappa Omicron Upsilon."

"Their names?"

"James Lightfoot and Sebastian Perry. They worked at a hedge fund started by Carston Kraytower, another Yale fraternity brother."

"I remember Kraytower. And the names Lightfoot and Perry ring a bell."

"Did you know them well?"

"No." Sato had taken another bite. He chewed and swallowed

before he answered. "I was older than Eddie and them by two or three years."

"I'm told he died in a hazing incident."

"Yeah." Sato shook his head. "A drinking contest with Eddie and the other new fraternity recruits squaring against the older frat brothers."

"Not you?"

"No, my Japanese DNA makes it very hard for me to metabolize alcohol. I can have just one beer, and I have to sip it slowly with lots of food."

"So you didn't participate in the drinking contest."

"No. When I first joined two years before, they put me through a different kind of torment."

"What was that?" I asked.

"Let's just say it involved a toilet and leave it at that."

"Got it. What was Eddie like?"

"I didn't know him well. He seemed like a typical fraternity recruit. Very smart, very naive, secure about his skills and knowledge, but insecure socially. He was also an erratic scatterbrain. Always jumping from one idea to the next. He was really into Shakespeare. No matter what people were talking about, he could quote something appropriate from one of Shakespeare's plays or sonnets."

That made me pause. I ate in silence for a minute.

"What was Eddie's major?" I asked.

"Math. He was a math genius."

"What does being a math genius mean? Was he one of those guys who got an eight hundred on the math SAT?"

"Actually, he did. But SAT math was like baby food to him. He'd gotten beyond that stuff by the age of six. His math was the real stuff, the physics stuff."

"Like Mozart composing in kindergarten when the rest of us were trying to sing Happy Birthday on key?" I asked.

"Actually, that's a good metaphor."

"So he aced all of his science and math classes," I said.

"I don't think so. From what I heard, he was a terrible student. Barely passing some classes, failing others. Always on academic probation."

"Why?"

"He hated school and the structure. And he had difficulty dealing with professors who didn't even understand the math he was working on."

"Can you explain the math to me?"

Sato thought about it. "Maybe not," he said. "But let's try this. You may have heard of Einstein's field equations."

"Is that the relativity stuff?"

"Yeah. When he published them in nineteen fifteen, some of Einstein's contemporaries immediately saw the genius and sense of the equations. But others had trouble with the most basic of his concepts. That the speed of light is a constant no matter where it is observed or how fast you're moving toward or away from the source when you observe it. That space time is like a stretchy fabric and changes with your mass and velocity. Like that. Some professors of the day not only didn't understand it, they disliked Einstein for his chutzpah."

"So Eddie's math was ground breaking like relativity?"

Sato was chewing and sipped his beer. He nodded. "I think so."

"What does one do with math like Eddie's?"

"I don't know. See the universe in new ways? Develop new kinds of computers? Change the world's economies?"

"Do you understand high-level math?"

"No, not at all. I'm a conceptualist. I can dream up a new way to configure laundry and dry cleaning and the marketing of them. But I have to bring in an architect and an engineer and a business consultant to work out the details."

"Why do you think Eddie didn't just go through the motions of being a good student? It would have been easy for him, right?"

"Why did Bill Gates or Mark Zuckerberg drop out of Harvard to start Microsoft and Facebook? Why did Paul Newman or Oliver Stone drop out of Yale to become an actor and a director?"

"You think Eddie was on track to drop out," I said.

"No doubt. He joined the fraternity at the beginning of his

sophomore year, when I was a senior. Those of us who knew him during his freshman year could see the patterns emerging. The kid wasn't a good fit for school."

"So he joined Kappa Omicron Upsilon and died in the drinking contest."

"Yeah. Any such death is a tragedy. But his death—relative to his potential—was extra tragic."

"Was there any reason to dislike Eddie? Did anyone have a significant problem with him?"

Sato stopped chewing and stared at me. Then he swallowed. "You mean, did someone have motivation to pour more alcohol down his throat and kill him that way?"

"Stranger things have happened. The answer to the question could suggest whether pursuing the notion makes sense."

"Helping Eddie drink himself to death…" Sato's volume trailed off. He lowered his head and stared down toward the table. He seemed to look inward. "That's dark. You ask if anyone disliked Eddie. The truth is that nearly everyone disliked Eddie. Especially the guys. The straight guys, anyway."

"Why?"

"Because Eddie was the geek who got the girl."

"What girl?"

"Julie. Julie Flowers. All the guys had a crush on Julie. She was the scintillating, super-smart girl who attracted jocks and preppies alike. Before she went to Yale, she was a dancer and spent a year at Julliard."

The name sounded familiar. Then I remembered where I'd heard it.

When I'd been talking with Kraytower in his wine cellar, he mentioned Julie and said she was a charismatic dancer and artist who convinced his group of friends to take a ski trip to Tahoe. Kraytower said her attraction to Tahoe had something to do with the lake's blue color.

"Julie went for Eddie Lange?"

"Yeah. Guys understand it when the most desirable girl in class goes for the handsome quarterback or the future movie star. Or the funniest guy who makes everyone laugh. But none of us could figure out why she went for geeky Eddie. But obviously, something about his genius was charismatic. He was the anti-hunk, the anti-charmer, and she fell for him completely. They were planning on getting married."

"Really? One doesn't normally think of a math geek in terms of marriage."

"I agree. It was going to be a New Year's wedding. Julie had this pagan streak. The opposite of a Cinderella. But Julie was never what you'd expect."

"When did Eddie die?" I asked.

"I think the drinking contest was around Presidents Day in February."

"So they were already married?"

"No. Julie was dead by then."

FORTY-FOUR

"Julie Flowers died?" I shook my head as if to shake out the continuing complications.

"Yeah. I wasn't close to them, so I don't know the details, even though everybody talked about it for months. A few days before their marriage, Eddie Lange and Julie Flowers drove out to the Cape for a winter day at the sea. On the way back, they were sideswiped by a truck on the right. Eddie was okay. But Julie died. The police report said that Eddie had done nothing wrong. And the test showed he had no alcohol or drugs in his system." Sato made a slow shake of his head as if, twenty-two years later, he still couldn't believe it happened.

"That must have devastated Eddie," I said, "not just because his fiance died, but that it happened when he was driving."

"Right. More than a few of us thought his guilt factored into why he drank himself to death at that hazing event."

"Didn't the other fraternity members give him support? Help him cope with the loss of Julie?"

"Not really. They blamed him for Julie's death. They thought his driving must have been erratic like everything else in his life. The truth is they were outraged."

"Because they were all attracted to Julie?"

"I think so, yeah. I remember hearing one guy say something like, 'Against all laws of the universe, the weirdo geek got the perfect girl and then killed her with a car.'"

"That's harsh." I tried to imagine the kind of social environment that could produce that kind of severe reaction. "Do you remember that guy's name?"

Sato shook his head. "He was at one of the fraternity parties. I never knew him. He must have been a friend of one of the frat brothers. But I don't know which one."

"What about the names of your frat mates who were attracted to Julie? Guys who would have been dismayed that she fell for Eddie?"

Sato thought about it. "They were all dismayed. You already mentioned the two guys who died. James Lightfoot and Sebastian Perry. Lightfoot was pretty bent out of shape by Julie's death. But Perry was completely outraged."

"All because he was smitten with Julie."

"Yeah. He was an attractive guy, used to getting the girls in high school. He thought it was his birthright to have his pick. He had the proverbial head-over-heels infatuation with Julie. Having Eddie win her attention and love seemed to make him permanently angry."

"Did he act on that outrage?"

"Not that I ever knew."

"Didn't Eddie have any friends? Any supporters?"

Sato was chewing as he answered. "Just the other guy you mentioned. Carston Kraytower. When Eddie died, Kraytower was despondent. He dropped out of school for a while. When he came back, it was as if he had lost all sense of romance about life. Kraytower came from a poor background. Life was hard. College was hope. But Eddie's death seemed like a blow he couldn't take. That combined with a financially-stressed life made Kraytower just double down about earning a living."

I said, "Did you know that Kraytower started a hedge fund in San Francisco?"

"No. Makes sense, though. He was very focused. Success at all costs. Never go back to his childhood." Sato sipped beer. "How'd Perry and Lightfoot die?"

"A bicycling accident, and a heart attack." I didn't add that their deaths might be of the Agatha Christie variety, caused by a poisonous agent.

Sato seemed deeply sad. He stopped eating and hung his head. "So it wasn't just Eddie who died. Two more men are dead, both of whom liked Julie Flowers and didn't like that she was going to marry Eddie Lange. But why kill them in ways that look like accidents?"

"You assume they were killed," I said.

"I doubt that you'd come three thousand miles to investigate accidental deaths."

"You're right. It appears that a drug called etorphine caused the bike accident and the heart attack. What about you?" I asked. "Were you friends with Eddie Lange?"

"No. Acquaintances, nothing more."

"And Julie?" I said.

"I admired her from afar. We never actually met. I doubt she ever knew my name."

"But you remember her name."

"Everyone remembers her name. Her charm, her style, her beauty."

"Got it," I said. "Can you think of anyone who might have known her better?"

Sato looked off, his eyes vacant. "The only person who comes to mind is Ivy Cates. She was also a dancer, although I don't think she went to Julliard like Julie did. Ivy danced with the local dance group."

"Are you a dancer?" I asked, wondering how Danny knew Ivy.

"Me in tights? Not much chance of that. But the dance group rehearsed—or whatever you call it—in the same building as the workout gym, and I belonged to the gym. There was a connecting door between the two big rooms. It had a little window in it. It's embarrassing, but the truth is that us gym rats often gazed through that window when the dancers were doing their thing."

"Looking to see if Julie was there?"

"Pretty much," he said.

"Do you know how I would get hold of Ivy Cates?"

"I think so. She owns a clothing import company. Ivy Imports. The business is all about only working with green suppliers. Every business they buy from has to be green certified or organic or whatever the current environmental standard is."

"Any chance you know her number?"

"No. But it probably shows up on Google."

"Before I go, can you think of anything else that might make

Eddie a target?"

"No. Having Julie die in the car accident was motive enough." Sato pushed his chair back and stood up. "It doesn't compare to Julie dying, but there was another thing that would upset dog lovers."

I stood up and waited for the rest of his words.

"When Eddie and Julie went out to the Cape, they had a dog with them. They were taking care of it for a few days."

I saw where he was going. "The dog died in the same car accident that killed Julie," I said.

"Right."

"Who did the dog belong to?"

"I don't know. It was one of the other fraternity guys. It might have been James Lightfoot's dog."

FORTY-FIVE

I thanked Danny Sato for talking to me. He made a single nod.

I reached for the check. He got it first.

"On me," he said. "You flew a long way to do this job. A lot of stuff went wrong twenty-two years ago. Any chance you can squeeze some justice out of that mix deserves whatever help I can give. The check is nothing."

"Thanks much."

He set the check and some bills down and put a coffee cup on top of them. He went out the door and walked away with his fast, efficient pace.

I walked out and stopped to think. Nettie Moon Water said that James Lightfoot wondered if dogs and other animals had as much right to life as humans. I'd wondered if Lightfoot had killed animals and had been killed in return as an act of revenge.

Now I knew that Eddie's car accident killed not just Julie, but a dog as well, a dog that may have belonged to Lightfoot. Then Eddie died in a hazing incident. People hated Eddie because Julie died. Did anyone also hate Eddie because a dog died? Was Eddie helped into death by someone who thought a dog deserved life as much as a human? Had Lightfoot been the death helper? If so, was Lightfoot's own death revenge, not for killing animals, but for killing a human who was in an accident that killed an adored human and animal?

I looked up the number for Ivy Imports and called it.

Despite my obvious charms and the smile in my voice, the person who answered refused to connect me to Ivy. He said that Ms. Cates was very busy.

"You can send an email request for a consultation. We'll

review it and, if she desires, she will email you back."

I looked up the address for the Registrar of Vital Statistics and then used the map in my phone to check its location and the location of Ivy Imports. The Vital Statistics office was closer.

It took me less than ten minutes to walk there from Reds and Greens. The office was in the City Hall building, a grand old structure on Church Street that looked vaguely like a church. It was across from New Haven Green, a half mile from the Yale campus.

When I walked through the Vital Statistics office door, a middle-aged man with thinning brown hair with 1/8th-inch white roots stood up from a desk, came up to the counter, and asked if he could help.

"Yes, please. I'd like to look up a death certificate from approximately twenty years ago."

"Certainly." He reached into a paper organizer and pulled out a sheet. "We only need you to fill out this form."

He set the paper on the counter and returned to his desk.

The page had horizontal boxes for the name of the deceased, location of death, date of death, my name and address, and my driver's license number. Unlike birth certificates, which, because of adoption records privacy, are protected if less than 100 years old, death certificates are generally public record. I assumed the reason for having to provide my own address was a way to discourage the identity theft of dead people.

I filled out the form. In front of the death date, I wrote the word 'approximate.' I pulled out my driver's license so the man could check my bona fides. "Here you go," I said, turning the paper around to face the man.

He stood up once again, saw me with my wallet out, and said with no small pride in his voice, "No payment is required. Another benefit provided to the tax payer by a public agency."

"Thank you." I put my wallet back in my pocket while he got busy on a computer. He typed and clicked, a printer whirred, and he brought me a copy of the certificate.

There was another worker in the office. She stood up from

her desk and turned to the man helping me. "Gonna take my break, Allen. Back in fifteen." She walked out a rear door.

Allen nodded at her as he pulled a black plastic folder out of a nearby file drawer, set it on the counter, and slid my request sheet into the folder.

"Quite the coincidence," he said. "We had another request for this same death certificate just yesterday."

"Really? Who made that request?"

"It was… I'm sorry, the death certificates are public, but the, um, requesters are private."

"I'm just curious," I said. "A man? Woman? Local person from New Haven?"

The man's face had reddened. I followed an impulse, reached out, and set my hand, palm down, on the plastic folder with the sheets from certificate requesters.

"Oh, no, sir. I'm sorry. That is private information."

"It's clear you spoke without thinking," I said. "You don't know the identity of the other person requesting, do you? You didn't make him fill out a request form." I started to slide the folder toward me.

"Don't do that! Please!"

"We should probably talk to your supervisor."

"No, no! I'd be…"

"I want no trouble for you," I said. "It will cause no harm to you if you simply give me the name. If, as I'm guessing, you don't know who it was, then a simple explanation will suffice." I paused. "But the explanation better be convincing." I slid the folder off the counter and held it up like a bargaining chip.

The man stared at the folder in my hand. His color deepened. "This… This is very embarrassing. I made a mistake. I knew I shouldn't. But I succumbed to temptation."

"I'm waiting."

The man pulled out his wallet. He looked behind him, furtively, as if the woman might come back through the rear door at any moment. He spread the wallet open to reveal some hundred-dollar bills. Allen spoke in a soft, low voice. "The man gave me five of these to show him the death certificate without him filling out the requester form. I spent most of one bill after work last night. Groceries and a bottle of Rutherglen Muscat. It's much too sweet for me. But my sister Betty loves it. If you tell anyone I took a bribe, I'll lose my job. Betty just signed up for Social Security. She only gets thirteen hundred a month. If I lost my job, we'd be in a world of hurt. And I can't sign up for Social Security for years as I'm only fifty-eight."

I gestured for the man to put the money away.

He slipped his wallet back into his pocket.

"What did the man look like?" I asked.

"I'm not sure how to describe him. I'm face blind. I have to see a person many times to learn their face. But I'd say he had dark brown hair cut pretty short. But I don't know how to describe his face."

"How old?"

"I have no idea."

"Compare him to me. My age? Older? Younger?"

"I see what you mean." He looked at me. "I'd say younger but not by a lot. Not at all as tall as you. But taller than me. Maybe five-eleven or six feet."

"What did he wear?"

"Nice clothes. His pants had creases. I don't see much of that these days. Some lawyers have pants with creases."

"Did he look like a lawyer?"

"Oh, I wouldn't know what a lawyer looks like."

"Sure you do. Clothes that are more about pleasing a client or impressing a jury than being comfortable."

"This man's clothes looked comfortable. I don't think he was a lawyer."

"Take a guess at his occupation."

"I wouldn't think he had one. He just looked… I don't know, rich."

"And he bribed you to give him a copy of Eddie Lange's death certificate."

"I printed it out. But all he did was look at it. He didn't take it. He barely touched it. I ended up throwing out the copy after the man left."

"What is your best guess as to what he was looking for?"

"I have no idea."

"I bet you do," I said. "Think about where his eyes went as he looked at the page." I set the certificate he'd given me back on the counter with the writing facing me. "Imagine I'm him. I'm looking at the page." I pointed as I spoke. "Watch my eyes as I look around the page."

"Now that you say that, I don't have to watch. I remember that he glanced at the certificate and put his finger on it, right where it says cause of death."

"Like this?" I said. I put my finger in the same place.

"Yes," the man said.

I looked at the cause of death. I read the words. "Alcohol-triggered acute myocardial infarction." Which I knew meant heart attack caused by alcohol poisoning.

I pulled out my phone, went to Google images, and typed in Carston Kraytower. Up came many pictures. I tapped on one so it enlarged and turned the phone toward the clerk. "Does this look like the man?"

He studied the picture for several seconds. "Yes, I believe that's him."

"Thank you." I took the death certificate, walked to the door, and turned. "No more bribes," I said. "It puts Betty at risk as well as you."

"I know. Oh, how I know. I screwed up."

"Betty's lucky to have you," I said and left.

As I walked away, I wondered why Carston Kraytower would care what his best friend Eddie Lange's death certificate said. Considering what I knew about the other frat brothers dying of etorphine poisoning, the only thing that made sense was that Carston Kraytower suspected or maybe knew that Eddie died of etorphine poisoning, and Kraytower wanted to know if the truth was on Eddie's death certificate. Why did Kraytower wonder that? The most logical explanation would be if Kraytower knew that someone had killed Edward Lange. Maybe Kraytower himself had murdered his best friend Eddie, and he wanted to be sure that there was no official evidence that could reveal that.

FORTY-SIX

After I left the Vital Statistics office, I flagged a cab, gave the address of Ivy Imports to the driver, and was dropped off at a brick warehouse building not far from downtown. It seemed like one of those warehouse districts that was becoming gentrified but in a hipster way.

Inside the spacious entrance to the building was a display case. It had the cheeky title Table Of Contents.

Below were business names. Instead of floor one, two, or three, the sign called them Chapters.

Ivy Imports was on Chapter Four.

There was an elevator and next to it, stairs. I took the stairs two at a time and got to Chapter Four as fast as any elevator.

I came to a large wall of windows that looked in at one of those modern offices where there were no cubicles or dividers. There was just a jumble of desks like in an old newsroom, similar to the central part of the KGA hedge fund office. Only these desks looked to be made of blonde wood, probably something environmentally correct like bamboo. People—mostly women— were at desks, walking here and there, shouting across the large space, sitting at a large conference table. There were no suits. The workers wore unusual clothes, shirts that wrapped like scarves, pants that flowed like dresses, shoes that looked like they were made of thatch and wool. A large number of the women wore their hair long. A few of the men did as well. I saw several dogs and lots of ceramic coffee mugs. Not one Starbucks throwaway in sight.

I opened the door and walked up to a large desk.

"May I help you?" said a young man who was adorned with multiple necklaces made of beads.

"My name is Owen McKenna," I said as I handed him my

investigator card. "I'd like to speak to Ivy Cates, please."

"I'm sorry. She's in a meeting." As he said it, his eyes made just a hint of a glance toward the far left corner of the room.

In the left rear corner were three desks arranged so they touched, two side by side, and one turned 90 degrees. Together, they made a large L shape. Two women stood at the right desk, hands leaning on the desk surface. They were studying some kind of diagram. They gestured and talked. One was in her twenties like most of the people in the room. And she was dressed in similar uniform, rough fabrics with little style but lots of laid-back attitude. The other woman was in her forties and was dressed in what looked like a black leather skirt and black shirt, although I suspected that the leather was imitation, because real leather would spoil the organic, grass-skirt, environmental-green vibe that permeated the office.

"I'll wait until she's out of her meeting," I said.

"Ms. Cates has, um, more meetings lined up. She'll be busy all day. If you'd like to ask for an appointment, you can fill out a request form."

The straight-forward approach obviously wasn't going to work. I had no official status in Connecticut, and despite what I told the kids at the fraternity, I didn't know anyone in local law enforcement. So I resorted to a standard version of the veiled threat.

Although I live on the Nevada side of Tahoe, I knew from experience that lots of East Coast people don't even know where Nevada is. So I pulled out my wallet, flashed my license, and said, "I'm an investigator who's come from California to pursue a murder that took place at Yale twenty-two years ago." I raised my voice enough so that other people could hear. "Ivy Cates was at Yale at the time and was mentioned in connection to the murder. I imagine she is innocent. But I'd hate to go to the police and give them my evidence, and then she'd get called in for questioning because there's no statute of limitations on murder, and, God forbid, the media might get wind of it and connect Ivy Imports to a murder investigation. So I can walk out of here and set those wheels turning, or you can go get Ms. Cates and bring her to talk to me."

The young man was pale. He seemed frozen in place.

As I rotated on my heel and moved toward the door, I said, "I wonder what she'll think about your inability to even grab the fire extinguisher when the building is on fire..."

I reached for the door handle.

"Wait!" The man nearly leaped over his desk in his effort to stop me. "Sir, don't go! I'll go get her."

I slowly turned to see the man sprinting through the office, skidding around desks. He got to the woman wearing the faux leather and started gesturing wildly.

I could see him talking with frantic intensity and pointing toward me at the front of the room.

The woman glanced toward me, said something to the young man, and walked toward me.

"Ivy Cates?" I said to her.

She stepped to my side, put her hand on my elbow, and, with significant vigor, propelled me out the door.

I paused when the door closed, but she continued to push me. We went down the stairs, around and around four flights until we got to the building's Table Of Contents sign, and then headed out to the street.

Again, I paused, but she kept me moving.

"Your tactics are deplorable," she said. "But effective. Now, you can talk." She kept her hand on my elbow and kept me moving at a good pace. "So talk," she added.

"Sorry for those tactics," I said. "But I don't have the time or patience to navigate your appointment protocol."

"You think your priorities are more important than my business responsibilities?"

"I understand that finding a murderer is terribly inconvenient for a busy person..." I trailed off.

"Wow, self-important and sarcastic, too," she said.

"If a Grand Jury sits you down for two or three long days, would their priorities be out of line and self-important?"

I expected her to have a more intense reaction. Instead, she seemed to grow more rigid as she tightened her grip on my elbow and increased our walking pace.

"What's the murder?" she asked. Her breath came in a low-grade huff and puff. She wasn't out of shape. She was merely tense.

"Twenty-two years ago, a student named Eddie Lange died in a hazing incident at the Kappa Omicron Upsilon fraternity."

"So?"

"So Eddie's death appears to be a murder, not a typical hazing. There have been two murders of men in California and Nevada, and both worked for a third man who is still alive. All belonged to Kappa Omicron Upsilon at the same time as Eddie, and all three were present during the hazing incident that killed Eddie."

"That is very strange and unfortunate. But how does this connect to me?" she said. Her voice was measured, but her walking speed seemed to increase.

"Interesting that you show no surprise about the murders. You are obviously a cool character."

"I'm still waiting for the connection to me."

"Eddie's fiancé was Julie Flowers. She was a Yale student who died in a car accident when Eddie was driving, not long before Eddie died. Earlier today, I spoke to one of Eddie's fraternity brothers, Danny Sato, and he said that you knew Julie."

"Yes, of course," Ivy Cates said, her voice like an icy north breeze. "The beautiful dancer Julie. Little miss perfect."

"That's the way you think of her?"

"You would, too, if you had seen her. She looked like Audrey Hepburn. I didn't really know Julie well, but I remember her very clearly. Julie was one of those girls that everyone loved. Men of course. But women too. She was in two of my art classes Freshman year. Art history and painting."

"But you were one woman who didn't love her."

"Actually, I thought she was wonderful. Kind and generous and talented at everything she ever tried. The problem was that she was too wonderful. Her simple existence made me feel like a nothing, like a withered dandelion next to a glorious rose. Pardon the flower metaphor."

"What did she paint?"

"How do I describe it? Her fixation was on the color blue. She studied all the great paintings that are blue. And the artists who focused on blue."

"Like Picasso's Blue Period?" I said.

In my peripheral vision, I sensed Ivy Cates lift her head to look up at my face. "Yes, that and many others. Van Gogh's Starry Night, David Hockney's blue swimming pools. Monet's Young Women in the Boat. That was Julie's thing. She painted blue subjects like skies and ocean. But she also painted stuff you don't think of as blue. Yet she rendered them in blue. She sometimes talked about how when Picasso took an old guitar player and painted him blue, the color made the painting a statement on the subject's mood and the painter's mood. It went far beyond what the image would have done had it been painted in normal colors."

"Why was she so focused on blue?"

Cates paused. We were still walking away from the Table of Contents building, although more slowly. "I only have a vague idea. Obviously, she simply loved the color blue. She bought different blue pigments and ground them up to make her own paint. She was quite obsessive about it. She was always trying to find the perfect blue."

"I've heard that blue is most people's favorite color," I said.

"Maybe. Julie talked about it a great deal. When Julie was young, her family took a trip out west. They did the usual, the Grand Canyon, Los Angeles, Disneyland, Big Sur, Yosemite, San Francisco. But then they went to this place in the mountains called Lake Tahoe. I haven't been there. Julie said that when she saw the blue color of the water, she was transfixed. Or transported. Apparently the water glowed these different blues, and the blues were like an addictive drug to Julie. So she kept telling her parents she wanted to go back. Because they'd already visited in the summer, she pressured them to take a ski vacation in the winter. Eventually, they acquiesced. And Julie said that when she took a ski lift up to the top of one of the mountains above the lake, the blue was even more captivating."

"She had a blue fixation," I said.

"Yeah. She was quite a bore about it, if you want to know the truth. She got some of the kids to take a ski vacation to Tahoe during spring break her freshman year. They flew to Reno, Nevada. I guess Lake Tahoe is in the mountains above Reno."

"Do you know who went on that trip?"

She leaned her head sideways as if it helped to recall a memory. "The only person I knew was Amy, a mutual friend that Julie and I had. There were some guys, too. Eddie, of course, and a guy named Carson something."

"Carston Kraytower?"

"That sounds familiar."

"What do you know about Julie's death?"

"What's to tell? She and Eddie were in a terrible car accident."

"What about Eddie Lange's death?"

"All I heard was that Eddie drank himself to death. It was probably caused by the agony of having Julie die in the car accident."

"Did Julie ever say anything about her plans for the future?"

"You mean, like what was she going to do after she and Eddie got married?"

"Yeah."

"She was going to open a dance school and focus on being a stepmother to Eddie's little boy, and then she..."

I raised my hand to stop her. "Eddie Lange had a son?"

FORTY-SEVEN

M y surprise at the news caused me to stop walking.
"You didn't know Eddie had a son?" Ivy asked.
"No. I suppose I shouldn't be surprised."

"Right. It's not uncommon, you know. Kids have sex, and sex sometimes produces children."

"How old was Eddie's son?"

"I don't know. I never met him. And I didn't pry. Based on Julie's description, maybe two or three."

"What was Julie's description?"

"I don't know. It wasn't significant at the time, so I didn't pay much attention. I got the impression that the kid was bright and engaged. Mostly, I was surprised she wanted to adopt him, because Julie was a dance star. And she was theatrical and charismatic. She could even sing really well. So I assumed that she'd pursue a theater career. I could easily imagine her on Broadway. But of course, every Broadway audition is filled with people who were stars in college and have already had TV roles."

"Stars rise through the ranks until they're in a sea of equally talented people," I said. "So maybe Julie was being sensible."

"Totally. Most of the Yale students were valedictorian of their high school and had perfect scores their entire lives. But when they come to Yale, they have to face the fact that they're just like everyone else. In retrospect, starting a dance school may have been the most practical course for Julie."

We resumed walking.

"Did you know the name of Eddie's kid?" I asked.

Ivy, walking at my side, was not in my direct vision. But I could tell she shook her head. "No. Wait. I want to say Jake. Jake Lange. It sounds both unfamiliar and familiar at the same time."

"Where did Jake live?"

"I believe he'd been living with Eddie's mother."

"The kid's grandmother," I said.

"Yeah."

"Do you remember the grandmother's name? Or where she lived?"

"No."

"Was there a grandfather on the scene?"

"Not that I ever heard. All I knew was that when Eddie died, his mother—the kid's grandmother—lost it."

"What does that mean?"

"Some kind of breakdown. Suicide attempt followed by life in a psychiatric hospital. Jake went into an orphanage."

"And you don't know what happened after that?"

"No. Maybe he was adopted. Maybe he grew up in the orphanage."

"What happened to Jake's mother?"

"We never knew who she was. She was probably one of those high school mothers who's too young for such a responsibility, and they abandon their baby. So Eddie and his mother stepped in to take the child."

"What about Julie's parents?"

Ivy shook her head. "For all I know she didn't have parents who were still alive. I think she was on some kind of scholarship. Or maybe her parents were estranged from her. "

"Like they didn't approve of Julie's plans to get married?" I said.

"Maybe. Certainly, a lot of parents would be uncomfortable with their daughter marrying a kid who had a kid of his own."

FORTY-EIGHT

I thanked Ivy Cates for her help and walked her back to her business.

While I headed to the airport, I Googled Jake Lange and got over 14,000 hits. It wouldn't be easy to track him down. And if he'd been adopted young, he might be going by a different name.

I called Street at her lab.

"Are you at Yale?" she asked.

"Yes. It's been productive." I told her what I'd learned about Eddie's death and his fiance's death and the fact that Lightfoot and Perry felt that Eddie was responsible for Julie's death. Then I told her the revelation that Eddie had a son.

"Oh my God, if Eddie is your King Hamlet," Street said, "you may have found your Prince Hamlet."

"Maybe. The boy's name was possibly Jake. Jake Lange. The information I got is sketchy. But apparently, the boy's mother was a no-show, and Jake lived with his grandmother. Eddie's plan was to marry a girl named Julie, who was enthusiastic about becoming Jake's adoptive mother. Then Julie died and, later, Eddie died. After those deaths, the grandmother fell apart, and the boy was placed in an orphanage. The woman who told me this seemed to know nothing else."

"Maybe you can track Jake Lange."

"I'll try." I paused. "I'll catch the next flight back and see you tomorrow. Love you."

"You, too, sweetheart."

We hung up, and I felt the wash of loneliness. Street was just six hours away, but I always missed her when we said goodbye, whether in person or over the phone.

While I waited for my plane at the airport, I called Aria in

San Francisco to ask if she'd heard anything from or about Joshua. She said no. She sounded very upset.

Next, I called Kraytower to ask him the same question. He'd heard nothing, either. I didn't reveal to him that I knew about his visit to New Haven's Registrar of Vital Statistics to ask to see Eddie's death certificate.

On the plane, I tried to be productive, running through the scenarios on Joshua's disappearance and possible kidnapping.

The most common type of kidnapping was when a disgruntled divorced parent without custody takes the child from the parent who has custody. That didn't apply to Joshua.

In the classic kidnapping, the kidnapper usually chose his victim because there was a person in the victim's life who had money. A ransom demand is given, and, if that ransom is paid, the victim is either returned or killed. Such a standard kidnapping didn't apply to Joshua, either, because there'd been no ransom demand. Although it had only been a few hours. Maybe a demand was still coming.

Perhaps Joshua left or was taken to punish the father for his sins. If so, one would expect a note to that effect. Certainly, there was a lucid, articulate note sender regarding the murders of Kraytower's hedge fund executives. The notes were all about Hamlet. I'd learned from Danny Sato that Eddie Lange had been a Shakespeare buff. And I'd found a young Shakespearean actor who also appeared to hate Kraytower. Maya Floros. I could imagine her kidnapping Joshua to punish Kraytower. Even more, I could imagine her joining forces with Joshua to help him go missing. Both might appreciate the distress that would bring to Kraytower.

But there was no apparent motive to connect Maya Floros to the deaths of Lightfoot and Perry.

That made me wonder if Joshua's disappearance had no connection to the deaths of the KGA men. It could just be a very unusual coincidence.

We learn in law enforcement not to abide coincidences. So I couldn't shake the idea that Joshua's disappearance and the executives' murders were part of one grand plan.

But I couldn't come up with an explanation.

I considered the possibility that Joshua was not just missing, but murdered. But that would really break pattern. From what I'd learned, Joshua hadn't been on the email list for the threatening emails. More significantly, his body hadn't been found, while the other victims had died in plain sight of onlookers.

I went back to considering Joshua as a suspect. At the very least, he disliked his father. It was possible that his antipathy toward his father ran to serious hatred. Could Joshua have killed his father's associates? Could he have staged his own kidnapping to punish his father? Or maybe he simply wanted to hide in order to remove himself from easy questioning by people like me. And if Joshua were part of the crimes, that eliminated the relevance of Eddie's son Jake Lange for the simple reason that Joshua was 16 and Jake Lange would likely be 24 or 25.

Sky Kool's age. If Sky was born Jake Lange, son of Eddie, he would make for an ideal suspect. If not, Sky might have witnessed Joshua being verbally abused by Carston Kraytower. He might have helped Joshua orchestrate a disappearance. It may have been carefully planned.

Until I could talk with Joshua, I had no way to answer any of these questions.

It made sense that I start thinking about where he might be.

He'd gone missing in San Francisco, so it seemed likely that he was in the Bay Area. But the possibilities of his location were too numerous for me to find him without a great deal of research and time spent interviewing neighbors and classmates. It was very frustrating. It seemed there must be something I could do beyond driving back to the Kraytower Victorian and looking for clues to his disappearance.

My return flight to Sacramento got in late. I drove up the mountain and went straight to bed.

My phone rang the next morning.

"Owen McKenna," I answered.

"This is Carston Kraytower." The man sounded panicked.

"What's wrong?"

"I just got a text from the kidnapper."

FORTY-NINE

Of all the things I might have expected, Kraytower's statement about a message from the kidnapper wasn't one of them.

"What's the text say?" I asked,

"I'll read it. It's divided into two parts. The first says, 'Through your cunning, he died. So now more die, bloody, unnatural acts. Your intentions come back to haunt you.'"

"Read it again slowly so I can write it down."

Kraytower did as asked and I wrote.

"Okay, what's the second part of the text?"

"It says, 'I've got your kid. If you want to get him back, be ready to take a drive starting at 2 a.m. tonight. You'll get a text that will tell you where to find your boy. If you tell the cops or try anything funny, your kid dies.' What should I do?" The rich, competent businessman sounded as plaintive and frightened as a lost child.

"Do exactly as the kidnapper requests. I'll be awake and waiting at that hour. Call me as soon as you get instructions."

"The kidnapper still hasn't asked for money. What do you think he wants from me?"

"I think he wants to make you face his pain. Have you seen Sky?"

"Not since he picked me up at the Truckee airport late last night." Kraytower didn't speak for a moment. "I'm very afraid," he finally said.

"That's part of the pain. Be strong for your kid. Give me a call when you hear from him. I've got some stuff I need to do, so I'm going to hang up."

"Okay."

We clicked off. It was better that I hadn't told him what I

knew. That Kraytower was probably supposed to watch his kid die and then die himself as the ultimate punishment for his sins.

I ate some breakfast and drove to my office. I called Diamond, and asked if he could stop by. He agreed. Next, I called Street and asked if she could join us. Street and Blondie showed up in ten minutes. We embraced. Diamond and Spot came a minute later.

"Did he behave while I was back east?" I asked as Spot was all over me.

Diamond said, "Yeah. I remembered that good Great Dane behavior can be enticed by danishes."

I gave Spot a rough rub and told them what Kraytower had said. "I need you both to help me brainstorm on this," I said.

"You want me to be up at two a.m. and be ready to come help?" Diamond asked.

"That would be great. There's a chance that wherever the kidnapper directs Kraytower, we could be there, too."

"What can I do?" Street asked.

"I don't know. I want your ideas."

"If you're going to try to follow this guy, maybe you could get one of those drones with a camera," she said.

"Talk about helpful," I said. "That's brilliant." I turned to Diamond. "Doesn't your department have a drone?"

"Sí. I'll call and see if it's available and charged. It's got a great camera. I could maybe fly it above wherever the kidnapper is going to send Kraytower."

My phone rang again.

"Why would he bring Joshua without demanding money?" Kraytower was nearly shouting in my ear.

I angled the phone so that Street and Diamond could hear. "I don't know, Carston. You'll find out tomorrow morning. Be ready at two a.m. like he says. I'll be ready as well. When you get his next instructions, do as he says." I had another thought. "Do you have a second phone?"

"Why?"

"He may not send you a text."

"Why not?"

"Because you could forward it or email it to me or the cops. He might call you on your phone and have you stay on the line so you can't call anyone else and tell them the instructions. If that happens, you could use another phone to text me."

"I don't have another phone. I can't... Wait, I can use my laptop. It gets cell reception. I could use it to email you. Hold on and let me get the computer." He was back in a minute. "Okay, what's your email? I'll put it into my email address book."

I gave it to him. "Have your laptop nearby when he calls at two. Whatever the instructions are, stay calm. Don't be impulsive. When you eventually see your son, stay under cover if at all possible. Give me a chance to intervene."

"Why? Why can't I go get Joshua? Save my son?!"

I hesitated.

"Answer me!" He shouted in my ear. "I want the truth."

"The truth is that this is a setup. The kidnapper wants you to charge forward."

"Why? He's doing this to bring Joshua back to me."

"No. He's setting a trap and drawing you in so he can kill you in front of your son."

I could hear Kraytower breathing hard over the phone.

"This is a nightmare," Kraytower finally said. "I'm scared."

"Me too. Be strong. But don't try to be a hero. As long as you don't make the kidnapper angry, we'll have a chance to save both Joshua and you. Do as the kidnapper says. I'll be watching from a distance."

We hung up.

Street had wide eyes and white knuckles. Diamond frowned, but otherwise his demeanor was nearly placid. He had the kind of calm that jet fighter pilots get before a crash, all his brain devoted to assessing risks and possible solutions, no computing power left for emotion.

"Kraytower was tense," he said, stating the obvious.

I nodded.

"Does the first part of the text make any sense to you?" Street asked.

"No. I'll call Louise Murphy, the English Lit professor."
Murphy had given me her cell number. I dialed.

"Hello?"

"Hi Louise. Thanks for answering. This is Owen McKenna.
Am I interrupting?"

"I'm working at the restaurant. But I'm on break. I've already
used up half of my ten minutes. They're very strict."

"We've gotten another text from the bad guy. I'm hoping you
can help make sense of it."

"By bad guy, you mean the murderer?"

"Yeah, sorry," I said. "Sugar coating probably doesn't work to
ease your mind."

"No. What's the text?"

"I'll read it to you. It says, 'Through your cunning, he died.
So now more die, bloody, unnatural acts. Your intentions come
back to haunt you.' Does that convey any specific message?"

"This one I don't have to look up. I know it by heart. Like the
other lines you showed me, this is a rewrite of some lines near the
end of Hamlet. It comes right after the climax, when Hamlet's
friend Horatio is talking. He's referring to how everything played
out. We understand that King Claudius, who murdered Hamlet's
father, wanted Hamlet dead, too. So he manipulated Hamlet and
Laertes into a fencing match. To ensure that Hamlet would die,
Claudius put poison on the tip of Laertes' sword. Claudius also
had a poisonous drink. He thought that if Laertes failed to kill
Hamlet, he could get Hamlet to drink the poison. As it happened,
Laertes was able to wound Hamlet with the poison-tipped
sword. In the play, the stabbing was called a hit. A palpable hit.
Then their scuffling caused them to drop their swords. Hamlet
managed to pick up the sword Laertes had used, the one with
the poison, and stabbed Laertes in return. Meanwhile, Hamlet's
mother accidentally drank from the poisoned cup and died. Then
Laertes died. Before Hamlet died, he stabbed Claudius and made
him drink the same poison that Hamlet's mother drank."

She paused. "So nearly everyone dies in the end. Then
along comes Fortinbras and the Ambassador. Horatio tells them
that the people who died succumbed to all manner of evil. He

explains that what happened turned out to be the opposite of what Claudius, the original murderer, intended. In other words, Claudius's actions backfired on him."

"Got it," I said. "Now here's a reach. Is there anything about this scene that suggests a place?"

"What do you mean?" Louise asked.

"Like where did that scene take place?"

"It took place at the castle Elsinore in Denmark."

"Is there any aspect of it that might be like someplace in Lake Tahoe?"

There was a pause on the phone line. "Nothing comes to mind," Louise said. "Horatio talks about 'these bodies high on a stage be placed to the view.' So that could refer to any high place with a view. Like the top of Cave Rock. Does that make any sense?"

"Maybe."

Louise continued, "Elsinore Castle is made of rock, right? So maybe that's also a connection of sorts to Cave Rock?"

"Maybe," I said. "I suppose… wait, I've got it. You're a miracle worker, Louise! Thank you very much!"

I hung up.

Street and Diamond looked at me.

"Louise said that at the end of Hamlet, there is a mention of a high stage where bodies would be placed. Everything about this case is connected to Shakespeare, right? So the meeting place is logically going to be connected to Shakespeare, too. There are two places in the Tahoe Basin that are especially identified with Shakespeare. One is the theater, Shakespeare On The Beach, where they perform Shakespeare plays near the water at Sand Harbor State Park. The other possibility is Shakespeare Rock, near Glenbrook."

FIFTY

"Of course!" Street said. "Shakespeare Rock is that smallish rocky mountain just across Highway Fifty from Glenbrook and not too far north of my condo. It's popular with rock climbers."

"You think the murderer will go there with Kraytower's kid?" Diamond asked.

"I don't know. It makes sense. Everything about these murders, and the messages, makes it clear that the killer has a fixation on Hamlet and Shakespeare. We don't have any facts. But it makes sense to surmise that the killer is probably outraged that someone close to him was killed. I assume that Eddie Lange's death was the triggering event, parallel to Hamlet's father, the king, being murdered. But of course I don't have solid evidence of that, either. I also learned that Eddie was a Shakespeare buff."

"So the killer frames his outrage in Shakespearean terms," Street said. "You said that the death of Eddie was thought at the time to be a drinking/hazing incident that led to a heart attack. But in reality, his death may not have been an accident at all. An Agatha Christie heart attack."

"Right. The death certificate confirms the reports from those who were there, that Eddie Lange died from alcohol poisoning. But Carston Kraytower went to New Haven to look up the official cause of Eddie Lange's death. He bribed the clerk in the Vital Statistics office to show him Eddie Lange's death certificate without filling out the standard form that asks for the name of the requester. That certainly makes it look like Kraytower wondered if Eddie Lange's death certificate suggested that anything other than alcohol was involved. Maybe Kraytower himself helped Eddie to die by using some toxin other than alcohol. So all these years later, he went to New Haven to see if he was in danger of being outed as Eddie's killer."

"The death certificate didn't show another toxin," Diamond said.

"Correct. Maybe there was nothing but alcohol. Or maybe they didn't order a toxicology report. I haven't researched the laws of Connecticut, but in most states, when the cause of death appears obvious, the autopsy is often less thorough or skipped entirely."

"Saves time and money," Diamond said.

Street was frowning, thinking, while she ran her fingertip up and down the bridge of Blondie's nose. Blondie had her eyes shut. Blondie and I shared that knowledge. The simplest touch from Street can be heaven.

Street said, "If the murderer is like Hamlet avenging the death of his father, then that would imply the murderer is Eddie Lange's son."

"Right. Eddie Lange's son was two or three when Eddie died. The son was named Jake Lange. Although we have no idea what name he goes by now. Like Prince Hamlet, he may well be seeking revenge for his father Eddie's death.

Diamond asked, "Is it possible that Jake Lange had a mother like Gertrude in Hamlet, who could have taken up with the man who killed his father?"

"Not that I could find. Eddie's frat brother thought that Jake's mother was a high school girl who abandoned her baby and ran away. So Eddie and his mother were raising the boy. Eddie did have a girlfriend who wanted to marry Eddie and adopt Jake as her son. But she died in a car accident."

"Worse and worse," Diamond said.

"Yeah, and it involves one more bit of suggestive circumstance even if it is nowhere near evidence. Eddie was driving the car when the accident happened and his girlfriend died. She was named Julie Flowers. She was also a student at Yale. Flowers was pursued by several men at Yale. One of them was Kraytower."

Street said. "That might have given Kraytower a motive for killing Eddie Lange," Street said.

"Kraytower and others as well. After she died, Eddie was

ostracized by his frat mates. Some of them even referred to Eddie as the kid who killed Julie."

"That's really mean," Street said.

"Then again, Kraytower was apparently very sad after Eddie died."

"Maybe he acted that role," Diamond said. "Or simply regretted killing Eddie."

I said, "A dog also died in the accident that killed Julie. The dog belonged to one of Eddie's frat brothers, although I couldn't find out which one. Nettie Moon Water told me that James Lightfoot thought that all species were sacred, and he made a point of saying that a good dog might have more right to life than a bad man."

Street said, "Maybe the dog belonged to Lightfoot!"

"If so, he might have blamed Eddie for the dog's death," Diamond said. "That would give him additional motive to kill Eddie."

"What about Eddie's or the girl's parents?" Street asked. "Did they take in the little boy Jake?"

"No. Eddie's father was apparently out of the picture. His mother collapsed when Eddie died. According to a woman I talked to, Julie seemed to have no parents. So Jake Lange was put in an orphanage."

We thought about it.

"It certainly looks like Eddie's son Jake would be the prime suspect," Street said. "But you are still a long way from hard evidence, right? So far you just have speculation and circumstantial evidence. If we knew where Jake was today, that might tell us a lot."

"Here's another bit of circumstantial evidence," I said. "The English Lit teacher I just spoke to referred to the fencing match between Hamlet and Laertes. When Laertes stabbed Hamlet, one of the other characters called it a 'hit.' A 'palpable hit.'"

"Okay," Diamond said slowly. "What does that imply?"

"The kidnapped kid, Joshua Kraytower, has a friend named Sky Kool. Sky is one of Carston Kraytower's drivers. The rest of the time, Sky's a rocker. His band is called Sky Kool and the

Palpable Hits."

"Not only clever word play," Street said, "but a clear pointer to Shakespeare. Is this Sky Kool a Shakespeare expert?"

"Not that I've sensed. He's clearly smart. But I get the feeling that he didn't go to college, or if he did, he dropped out to pursue music. And now that we're talking about Shakespeare, it gives me an idea. When Sky talks, he's often throwing in common sayings and cliches. I wonder if they could possibly connect to Shakespeare."

"Such as…" Diamond said.

"Let me think. He uses sayings like, 'Dead as a doornail.' And 'All that glitters is not gold.' And 'Waiting with bated breath.'"

"I'm pretty sure those are phrases from Shakespeare's plays or sonnets," Diamond said.

"Another phrase he used is, 'Kill them with kindness.' And, 'A rose by any other name would smell as sweet.'"

"Definitely Shakespeare."

"And 'A wild goose chase,'" I said.

"Same," Diamond said.

Diamond stared out the window. He turned back to look at me. "Hamlet's father was the king. Could Eddie Lange have been a king of sorts?"

"Not in a normal sense. But one of his frat mates told me that Lange was a math genius. If his math innovations were substantial enough, that could have made him famous."

"Famous in math is not very king-like," Diamond said.

"No. I was also told that Carston Kraytower and Eddie Lange were best friends," I said. "What if Kraytower used Eddie's math to help create his hedge fund?"

"Innovative algorithms used for new investing strategies," Street said.

Diamond leaned back in his chair, his arms up, fingers laced behind his head. "Thus transferring the king's throne—Eddie's math genius—to Kraytower. And Kraytower made a fortune, which allowed him to live like a king."

Street was looking from me to Diamond. "Having Kraytower fly three thousand miles to look up Eddie's death certificate could be circumstantial evidence against him if he were charged with the crime of Eddie's murder. But it might also make it look like he was investigating Eddie's death to help find the murderer of his colleagues."

"That's what I'm thinking," I said. I stood up, pushed back my chair, and paced the floor. "In sum, this could all be hot air. But it seems likely that the current killer could be Eddie's son seeking revenge for the death of Eddie. It also seems that the current killer sees a similarity between his situation and Hamlet's. The more he draws that connection with his emails and texts and his actions, the more his intentions and actions acquire a kind of legitimacy in his own mind."

"Dr. McKenna, I never knew," Diamond said, his voice betraying nothing except earnestness.

"Psych one-oh-one," I said. "Anyway, the murders have to fit his sense of how Shakespeare depicted Hamlet's revenge, right? It seems that the killer's way to do that has been to enact scenes that are reminiscent of Hamlet. The situation is different, of course. But his messages show that's his focus. Get the principals onto a stage like Hamlet's, there to create a climax where nearly everybody dies."

We were silent a moment.

"Why is it called Shakespeare Rock?" Street asked.

I looked at Diamond.

He said, "The name comes from the north-facing vertical wall, which is nearly always in the shade, and so it has a spectacular coating of multi-colored lichens. In those lichen patterns, one can find a crude image that looks like Shakespeare."

Spot rolled onto his side and made a big sigh.

I leaned over, put my hand on his chest, and whispered toward him, "Whassa matter? You don't like talking about Shakespeare?"

His tail thumped once on the floor, but he didn't open his eyes.

Diamond said, "I agree that Shakespeare Rock would be a fitting place for the killer to have some kind of showdown with Kraytower. But the problem is that it would be physically difficult to pull off. You've probably hiked there."

"Years ago," I said.

"Then you know that it's hard to get to it. The trails are few and very steep. The rock is impressive, a huge, flat vertical wall a hundred or two hundred feet tall. But the base is surrounded by rock falls, big piles of craggy boulders. There is no obvious Hamlet-type stage where the killer would plan his final showdown, whatever that is."

"Horatio talked about a high stage," I said. "What did Louise Murphy say? 'These bodies high on a stage be placed to the view.' I remember that Shakespeare Rock has a roofless cave. You go in thinking you're in a cave, but then it becomes open to the sky. If the killer lured Kraytower into the roofless cave and killed him there, that would certainly be a high stage."

"Sure, the roofless cave would be dramatic," Diamond said. "But the problem is that you'd have to do some serious boulder climbing just to get there. I'm not sure a city boy like Kraytower could even make the climb."

"Good point."

"If his main requirement is a high stage as stated in the play," Street said, "there must be a large number of places around the rock that could serve."

I nodded. "Yeah."

"There's a trail that traces most of the circumference of the rock," Diamond said. "It's below the main rock wall. But in many places it could seem like a high stage. Here and there are views down toward Glenbrook Bay to the north. And to the west is all of Lake Tahoe. So it may be that the kidnapper killer has picked a place that suits him. And he will direct Kraytower to that stage."

"To his death," Street said, her tone somber.

"That's my fear," I said.

"Are you convinced of this enough that you'll go to Shakespeare Rock in advance of hearing from Kraytower?"

"Yeah."

"So you'll be there before the kidnapper shows up," Street said.

"That's my hope."

"Gonna bring your hound?" Diamond looked over at Spot, who was lying on his side, his eyes still shut in an attempt at sleep.

"I don't think so. The advantages he brings are many. But I fear that he might get hurt."

"Doc Lee told me a well-aimed tranquilizer dart loaded with etorphine is more lethal than a well-aimed gun," Diamond said.

"He told me that as well. Like Laertes' poison-tipped sword."

"It hits you anywhere, you die," Diamond said. "Whereas a bullet has to hit you just right to kill. Scary." As if realizing he'd said too much, he glanced at Street, whose eyes were pinched by worry lines. Blondie looked up at Street's face, a connection that was more than affection, something closer to a basic need, like oxygen.

We were all silent, processing the implications.

FIFTY-ONE

"What kind of plan do you have?" Street asked.

"There's a trail in the forest just above my cabin," I said. "It traverses the Carson Range. I can take that to Shakespeare Rock." I looked at Diamond. "Will you come?"

He nodded.

"This trail isn't the Tahoe Rim Trail," Street said.

"No, that trail is up near the mountain peaks. The trail near my cabin parallels the TRT but is a thousand feet below it."

"Hiking in the dark ain't easy," Diamond said, his voice full of doubt.

"I don't think it will be too difficult. It does wind in and out of the ravines and over the ridges. But it's mostly level as if following an invisible topo line of equal elevation. It stretches from Cave Rock on the south to Shakespeare Rock to the north. The trail stays roughly level with my cabin, which is at seventy-two hundred feet of elevation. Where it comes closest to Shakespeare Rock, the trail's about a quarter mile to the east of the rock and a hundred feet above the top of the rock wall. So we'd bushwhack down from the trail to the path that goes around the base of the rock."

"Or you'd bushwhack, and I'll stay up above Shakespeare Rock and launch the UAV," Diamond said.

Street frowned.

"Sorry," Diamond said. "Unmanned Aerial Vehicle. Drone for short."

I asked, "Does it have a good telephoto camera? It could hover high enough up that the killer wouldn't notice it?"

Diamond nodded. "In our practice with it, we've limited its height to four hundred feet up, which is the federal rule. When it is up at that distance, it's very hard to see from the ground, and the buzz is faint. You can't easily tell where it is. And if there is any breeze rustling the tree needles, the noise covers the sound. So it goes unnoticed. The question is if it would do us much good from far up. But it's worth a try."

"What about running it in dark predawn light?" Street asked. "Does its camera work well in low light?"

"Never tried it in low light. But it's supposed to be state-of-the-art. I'll bring it and stay a good distance from both the trail and Shakespeare Rock. Owen and I can communicate by phone. I'm assuming we can get a cell signal there."

I paused. "Is your department's drone here at the lake or down in Carson Valley?"

"Unless someone recently checked it out, it should be in our utility room at the sheriff's office in Minden. I'll call and check."

"How long can the drone stay up?"

Diamond paused. "I think Jayson said that the official maximum was one hour and that we should plan on no more than forty-five minutes."

"I'm thinking that you could be near the trail and be ready to launch the drone. But you could hold off until I sense that something is happening. I'll work my way down the slope in the dark toward the trail that circles Shakespeare Rock."

"A long walk in the dark," Diamond said.

"But doable," I said. "When it seems right, I'll call you, and you send it into the sky."

Diamond shook his head. "You shouldn't talk because you might be close enough that the killer could hear you. So our signal will simply be you calling me and letting it ring a few times. We should both put our ringers on mute. When my phone vibrates, I'll launch the drone and send it up high. I'll watch the video feed on the screen and tell you what I see. You stay silent on the other end and listen. Maybe I'll have useful info, maybe not."

"To bushwhack off the trail down to the circumference trail in the dark would take me awhile, but I'm pretty sure I can do it if I plan enough time. Another concern is how the kidnapper plans to get to Shakespeare Rock. He may try to come directly to the rock from below. Just north of the rock is a small parking area off Highway Fifty. The trail up is very steep. But it's the shortest access point. Otherwise, he may intersect the very same trail we'll be on. So to avoid his discovering us, we'd both have to leave the trail and get to a place where he wouldn't see us. Probably up and away from Shakespeare Rock would be best for you."

Diamond made a single nod. "He'd be unlikely to discover me because there would be little reason for him to go up when Shakespeare Rock is down below."

"Meanwhile, I'll be down by the rock, hiding in the boulders before he arrives."

"Dawn is a little before six a.m. If we want to be in place before the predawn light, when would we leave your cabin?"

"It's about a mile from my cabin to Shakespeare Rock. In the daylight, hiking the trail takes twenty minutes. This week we have a first quarter moon, which means it's up high when the sun goes down, and it sets in the middle of the night. After it sets, we'll be walking in the dark. No light except starlight. That will slow us down a lot. So we should plan at least one hour for the hike. Then another hour for me to get in place before the killer would likely get there."

"We wouldn't want to use any flashlight," Diamond said.

"Correct."

"Is it even possible to walk a hiking trail in the forest with no moon and not use a flashlight?" Street asked.

"Possible but not easy. But we don't have much of a choice. Either we get into position while the moon is still up, or we feel our way through the dark. If we use any light at all, even a shielded phone light, we'll risk being spotted. Walking in the dark is possible, but it takes some getting used to. Your eyes have to be totally night-adjusted. Ten minutes in complete darkness. Then you learn to use your peripheral vision, which is much more light-sensitive than your focused vision. You walk along staring ahead but aware of the general sky glow from the stars. The contrast between sky light and trees and trail is pretty noticeable. The main concern is careful foot placement so we don't twist an ankle. The key is to walk slowly and place your feet carefully. Because the killer believes no one will know where he's going until he calls Kraytower at two a.m., he will likely plan to arrive at Shakespeare Rock a little before dawn. If in fact Shakespeare Rock is his intended destination. He may well think to use the predawn light to see. Five a.m. or so. But we'll already be in place."

"So we'll leave while the moon is still up," Diamond said. "As soon as Kraytower calls. Of course, the kidnapper probably wouldn't see me, what with being brown as a lettuce picker."

"You actually did spend a season or two picking lettuce, right?" Street said.

We all smiled. It was a welcome distraction from our thoughts.

"One season, yeah," Diamond said. "After that experience, being a law enforcement officer—hated by some and shot at by others—seemed a sweet ride. So I went to cop school at night. But you, pale boy, are a whole 'nother matter. Stand out like a vanilla ice cream cone under stage lights."

I shrugged. "Hard for a Scottish Irish dude to be—what did you call it—night blending."

"Not the only thing it's hard for you to do. Too tall to be crowd blending. Too loud to be conversation blending. Too honest to be liar blending."

"So we'll hike in the low light of the moon before it sets. Then we can get into night-blending position before darkness is complete, and we'll only have to wait an hour or ninety minutes before predawn light starts to filter into the forest."

Diamond looked at his watch. "Let me call the department office and see if the drone is in."

"If so, ask them to charge it."

"The drone sits in a wall-mount saddle where it plugs in. So it's always charged." Diamond pressed a speed dial combo, spoke briefly, clicked off.

"The drone is available. One of the deputies is just leaving to come up to the lake. He'll bring it with him."

Street said, "What if, when Kraytower sends an email to you or calls you, it turns out that the kidnapper is directing him to a completely different place? The opposite direction. Down

Interstate Eighty toward the Central Valley?"

"Then we'll have to scramble to come up with a new plan." I turned to Diamond. "Any thoughts?"

"We might be screwed. Even in the middle of the night with no car traffic, we'd be an hour or more behind. Can't have a shoot out at the OK Corral if we're still coming down the mountain."

"This is all very unnerving," Street said.

"Law enforcement always has been," I said.

"I worry."

"Me too," I said.

FIFTY-TWO

Street hugged both of us and took Blondie and Spot home to her condo. Diamond said he'd nap at the Sheriff's Office. I went to my cabin, had a very light dinner, drank a Sierra Nevada Pale Ale, and went to bed.

I was up at 1 a.m., had a cup of coffee and a cup of peanuts, and pulled on dark clothes and a dark hoodie. Because I haven't carried a gun since a tragic shooting I was involved in on the San Francisco PD, my only weapon that has some use at a distance was rounded cobbles I'd collected from a stream bed, 2 inches in diameter, perfect for throwing. I'd never been a very good ball player, but I could throw well enough to unnerve my target. And if I hit him with a well-placed stone, that was as good a weapon as most. I kept the cobbles in a box. I put a few in the pockets of my sweatshirt and more in a shoulder bag.

Diamond showed up at 1:45.

"Coffee?" I said.

"I've only had one, so yeah."

We each had another cup while I spread out my topo maps on the little linoleum, fold-down, kitchenette table.

After we'd memorized the territory, Diamond spoke in a soft voice, "Your computer is on, set to receive emails, right?"

"Check," I said.

We finished our coffee. We waited. The minutes stretched out. I watched the computer.

At 2:15 my phone rang instead.

"McKenna, here."

"He texted me," Kraytower said. "I'm already en route. I'm supposed to head around the South Shore and then back up to Cave Rock. There's an area just before the tunnel where I'm to pull off. Once I'm there, I wait for further instructions."

"Got it. I'll be watching and I'll do my best to be nearby when you meet the kidnapper. Because I will be close, the kidnapper might hear me talking to you. So I won't talk. You can text or call and tell me the location even if I don't talk back. If you're using your computer, you can email me."

I didn't want to tell Kraytower that I was sure the intended destination was Shakespeare Rock because Kraytower might try to go there first, which would surely anger the kidnapper.

Diamond and I left.

The trail is in the woods just 50 feet from the private drive that I share with my vacation home neighbors. We walked across my parking pad, around my old Jeep to Diamond's sheriff's patrol vehicle. He opened the passenger door, pulled out a day pack, and put it on. Then he opened the rear hatch and lifted out a large plastic case that was vaguely like an old-fashioned suitcase.

"The drone is larger than I thought," I said in a low voice.

"The case is big," Diamond said. "The quad copter, not so much. Twenty-four inches across from rotor tip to rotor tip."

"I can help carry."

"The thing about drones is they are very light, so no need. Your thoughts are heavier than my load." He walked across the drive.

I stepped past him and led the way into the forest. The access route to the trail was narrow and twisted around and through a thicket of trees. When we got to the main trail, it was much more open, and the quarter moon was bright. We turned north.

"The drone control unit is in the case you're carrying as well?"

"Sí. Some of the newer ones, you run with a phone app. I don't see how that would work on such a small screen. This drone has a controller like a video game console. I'll be sure not to let the control screen shine toward the trail or Shakespeare Rock."

The moon moved down toward the west side of the lake. The picture-book reflection stripe was dramatic, a broad, shimmering, yellow-white path stretching from Tahoe City across 12 miles of water to the East Shore, one thousand feet below my cabin. The moonlight probed into the forest, giving a general glow to the big trees and an occasional brilliant spotlight on the path and nearby shrubbery.

After our eyes adjusted, it seemed that we were walking in a well-lit environment. The trail was clear, the occasional fallen branch obvious enough that it was no trouble to step over or around.

As usual in Tahoe summers, the nighttime temperature was in the low forties, heading down to the upper thirties. In such crisp air, no crickets or other night bugs serenaded our passage. The air was still, and the night was silent.

Occasionally, we heard the soft air movement of a breeze swishing through the pine needles or the slow rhythmic beating of wing feathers.

"You hear that?" I said. "I think that's a Great Horned Owl swooping through the trees."

"Pity the poor nocturnal rodent who thought darkness provided safety," Diamond said.

As we hiked toward our rendezvous with the kidnapper, I hoped that he wasn't already out there, hiding on a high stage, ready to bring death to us from above.

I walked in front, and Diamond followed.

After forty minutes of slow hiking, the general dark shape of Shakespeare Rock grew in the distance. Although it was slightly below us, it loomed above the surrounding forest, not unlike Cave Rock in shape and size but with its base softened and obscured by trees.

I stopped at a point where the trail curved away from the big rock. I turned back to Diamond.

"This might be a good place for you to head up above the trail," I said. "The forest is quite open. You could find a launching place that's out of sight from this trail but close enough to the rock to get good radio communication with the drone."

Diamond made a slow turn, scanning the dark landscape. He pointed up the slope. "Hard to see in low moonlight. But there's a dark area about fifty yards up, looks like a line of trees. They would give me good cover. I'll try to get above them and look for an open area."

"I'll go the opposite direction, down toward the base of the rock, and look for a place where I can watch for them."

"You still think Sky Kool's the one who took Joshua?" Diamond said.

"Probably."

"If they come close to you, maybe you'll get a chance to take the kidnapper out. Like the night predators. Jump down on him from a tall rock. 'Course, maybe he sees you and shoots you. You want my Nano?"

"No thanks. I don't want to plan to kill anyone." I looked up at the sky. The moon was about to set behind the West Shore mountains. "I better hurry. Once the moon goes down, we'll be in serious darkness until the predawn light. When I sense the presence of the kidnapper, I'll call you, your phone'll vibrate, and you'll launch your drone."

"Sí. Get your butt in gear."

I stepped off the trail and headed down the slope through the forest. Brush and downed wood made my trek difficult. Bushwhacking through the forest in the near darkness that came as the moon was about to set made me wish for a flashlight. But that would advertise my presence.

I walked with my arms up in front of my face, hoping to avoid getting impaled by a stiff dead branch. Most times, I was able to discover branches by feel.

I knew that Diamond would be having a harder time, carrying the large case and having to trudge up the mountain.

Shakespeare Rock loomed as I got near. Like Cave Rock to the south, it projected up into the sky like a miniature mountain that projected from the slope of the larger mountain behind.

I had to choose a direction. I decided to go around it counter clockwise, toward the north and the roofless cave. I found the ill-formed trail that makes a rough circumference of Shakespeare Rock. As I walked along it, I had the sense that the little bit of ambient light was disappearing. The moon was setting.

I was aware that the kidnapper could already be nearby.

I looked around for a hiding place above me so I could look down on anyone coming along the trail. There was no good route up. So I climbed over rocks, up onto a big boulder, across to more rubble. Many of the rocks were jagged. When they had broken off the wall above, they shattered on impact. The sharp edges threatened injury and slowed my passage.

The light was getting dimmer.

I tried to speed up, aiming for the base of the wall. I was just coming over another large boulder when the remaining light blinked out. The moon had set.

I stopped, unable to see. I squatted down, feeling with my hands, and found a small, angled rock I could sit on. It was uncomfortable. But I needed to put up with it while my eyes adjusted.

After several minutes, I started to become aware of the starry sky, a vague milky glow that silhouetted the trees. In time, I began a half crawl, arms out, using hands and feet to find purchase on the rocks.

Once, my foot dislodged a good size rock of 80 or 100 pounds. It clattered down onto other boulders, making several crackling, syncopated impacts like Goliath castanets, then crashing to a sudden, noisy stop.

I froze. One hand was on a boulder in front of me, one hand in the air, my feet in awkward positions.

I waited a minute, listening for any sound. Nothing came to me.

Gradually, I began moving again, feeling my way in the dark, climbing higher, this time slower than before. Five minutes later, I came to a wall of rock. It had sharp-edged ridges across its surface. As I moved to one side and then the other, I realized it was actually a boulder the size of my log cabin. On one side of the huge boulder, the corner dropped away. I reached out with my foot and felt nothing but space. It was as if I were on the edge of a crevasse. I went back the other direction. Again, I reached with my foot, feeling for support, and accidentally dislodged another rock. It made even more noise than the first, crashing down, over and over. Then it went silent. No thud, nothing. I couldn't tell if it had gone over a drop off or disappeared into a soft hole. I decided I'd better not move again until the predawn light arrived and allowed me some vision.

I had no way to tell time in the dark beyond watching the stars arc through the sky. I turned it into a science experiment to pass the time. I focused on a particularly bright star. Perhaps it was a planet. I shifted my position a bit so the planet was in line with the branch of a tree. I waited as motionless as possible.

It wasn't complicated. The Earth makes a complete rotation every 24 hours. That means that over the course of each hour the earth turns one twenty-fourth of a complete rotation. The western horizon to the eastern horizon represents half of the total sky. Which means the sky above me could be divided into 12 parts, and each of those parts would represent the amount the star or planet would move in an hour. To make it simpler, I focused on just half of the sky above me, from the zenith straight up, to the western horizon. That could be divided into 6 parts, each part being an hour.

I was surprised at how fast my planet moved west, away from the tree branch. Sooner than I expected, it had moved at least one sixth of the way toward the western horizon. One hour had passed. My crude clock was effective. I could predict that the pre-dawn light would arrive in about one more hour.

During that hour I heard nothing except tiny forest sounds, movements of the hunters and the hunted, some small creatures and a few large ones, looking for a meal. I hadn't yet heard or seen the deadliest of the hunters, the two-legged animals that I was waiting for.

Soon, I sensed a growing glow coming from behind the peaks of the Carson Range to the east.

My phone vibrated. I pulled it out and looked at it, shielding it from view. It was a text from Kraytower. 'I'm supposed to go to a place called Shakespeare Rock. It's across the highway from Glenbrook. There's a small parking area. I climb straight up a steep slope until I come to the rock.'

Relieved that we had made the right decision, I forwarded the message to Diamond, then put the phone in my pocket. I focused on the dark forest that stretched out and down from Shakespeare Rock.

Many of the human visitors to the rock are climbers, there to test themselves on the vertical walls that, while a half mile back from the water, seem to overhang the lake below. Although rock climbers often get out early, they rarely are in place at dawn unless they're planning to tackle a very long route.

In addition to climbers, Shakespeare Rock draws a few hikers, people who are after exercise and views and want to see the roofless cave, an arched, truck-sized opening in the wall that leads back to a space where the roof had fallen away and was open to the sky. Those hikers would come later than the climbers. I was certain that Shakespeare Rock would be a lonely place until the sun had risen.

The people I expected to show up first were the kidnapper, Joshua, his kidnap victim—assuming the kidnapper intended to bring his victim—and the person I believed was his next target, Joshua's father Carston Kraytower.

If the kidnapper and the others arrived close to sunrise, he could reasonably expect to have no one interrupt the meeting with Carston Kraytower.

With the growing light, I was able to find a way around the cabin-sized boulder. When I got close to the rock wall, I maneuvered to a place with a vertical cleft in the rock. I stood sideways to the wall so that my left arm and shoulder were tucked into the recess. The cleft gave me some cover, and I had clear sight lines to the rock's perimeter trail, which was now 100 feet or more below me.

I could also look up toward the entrance to the roofless cave, although I had no view of its interior.

I waited.

The sky became less dark. It took on a faint red glow. Gradually, the light became brighter but redder still. But it had yet to send much light down through the trees to the area below me.

After 15 minutes of not moving, I heard a soft crackling, popping sound. It was faint and intermittent. It sounded vaguely like car tires on a gravel drive. The source of sound was somewhere below me, but I couldn't pinpoint the position. Then it went silent.

I got out my phone. I had the brightness and volume on the lowest settings but still covered it to minimize its light. I hit the speed dial combo for Diamond's phone. After three rings, it was picked up.

"Silencio," Diamond answered. "I'll talk, you listen. If you need to stop me or register some significant disagreement with what I'm doing, click off, and I'll retract the drone. I'm in position above the trail we hiked. I'm about a quarter mile east of Shakespeare Rock, and I'm at about seventy-four hundred feet, so that I'm a little above the top of Shakespeare Rock. I'm going to turn on the drone and send it straight up into the sky. Here we go. You can probably hear the buzz of the rotors in the phone. But I doubt you can hear them through the air."

Through the phone, the sound was like multiple, low-pitched mosquitoes. The bass section in the mosquito choir. The sound grew in volume and then faded.

"Liftoff," Diamond said in a very soft voice. "The drone is rising straight up into the sky."

Movement caught my peripheral vision. I turned and stared into the dark forest.

There. More movement. Peripheral vision is more light-sensitive than focal point vision, so I looked away a bit.

Two figures moving. Both in dark pants. One with what looked like a hooded jacket, the other more visible. I couldn't make out any details. They seemed to be walking the perimeter trail around the base of Shakespeare Rock. They moved behind a large outcropping. From my perspective, it looked like they would enter a thick group of trees and then reappear on the other side.

The sky grew redder. The air must have been thick with dust and moisture or high clouds that caught the sun's rays from over the horizon.

"What have we here?" Diamond said in my ear. "I already see something on this dimly-lit drone screen. Movement in the little parking area off Highway Fifty on the north. A vehicle is pulling in. Dark gray. Or black. Small. Like a Prius. Someone is getting out of the passenger door. A large-sized person. A man. He's heading up the private road, walking in the wash of light from the vehicle's headlights. As I watch this, I'm remembering the access from the highway. There are two trails. One is behind a gate, well graded and comfortable and on private land with No Trespassing signs. The other trail is very steep and rises straight up from the gate."

I thought about what Diamond said. I hadn't seen any Prius when I'd been to Kraytower's places.

"No, wait, he's not going up the private road. He's turning off the road onto the trail. Reaching out with his arms. I don't understand. Now I get it. The beginning of that trail is real steep, right? He's grabbing onto branches, pulling himself up the steep section. Now he's moving at a good rate. Jogging. No, he's slowing. Walking. It looks like the man overestimated his ability to climb. Now he's stopped. He's bent over, hands on his knees. Probably trying to breathe. Now he's moving again. The vehicle's headlights just turned off. No other movement. Maybe he turned off the headlights with a remote. Or they go off automatically. If not, the driver is staying with the vehicle." Diamond paused.

Diamond didn't speak for a bit.

The sky was now deep, ruby red.

Red sky at morning, best to take warning.

I waited. I didn't hear anything. Despite the growing red light, I couldn't see anything either.

"I'm zooming in the camera," Diamond said in my ear. "The man is still moving very slowly. Obviously, he's not in real good shape. Or used to high altitude."

I kept my phone tight to my ear so that Diamond's voice wouldn't spill out and be heard by anyone near me.

The two people I'd seen had moved into an area that was a bit more open and thus had more illumination from the predawn red glow.

They were still below me, shadows in a dark, maroon forest. Yet I could tell that the one in front was smaller. I sensed that the front person moved with a tentative step. The one behind was taller and thicker and moved in a more robust way. Joshua

Kraytower in front and Sky Kool behind?

The smaller person was still hooded, no face visible. The larger person was just a black shape.

As they moved into an area with more light, the smaller person turned slightly away from me. An image on the back of the hoodie became visible. It was too dark to recognize any details, but I could make out a general shape. Black lines on a gray hoodie. It looked like the drawing I'd previously seen on Joshua's shirt, the sketch portrait of John Muir.

Still, I couldn't make out any detail about the second person. But I thought it was likely Sky.

FIFTY-THREE

It appeared that Joshua wasn't trussed or tied in any way. He moved without restriction.

Yet it seemed like the person behind him held something. The way he moved the object made me think of a walking stick. Whether the second person was Sky or not, the stick could be enough of a weapon to keep Joshua from suddenly running and escaping.

The pre-sunrise light was now so dramatic that it made me think of blood.

The two hikers turned off the perimeter trail and began going up the boulder field. They weren't coming toward me, but more toward the roofless cave. Joshua went first. Despite the low light level, he looked agile. He used his hands on the larger boulders, a good way to steady oneself when the footing was unreliable. Sky, whose face I still couldn't see, stayed behind Joshua, careful, it seemed, to keep Joshua close in front of him. I couldn't imagine a scenario where Joshua could get the best of Sky, because Sky was obviously larger and more muscular, and, most of all, had the kind of commanding presence that would intimidate Joshua.

As they got higher, I saw that Sky had a cone-shaped object hanging off the back of his belt. It looked like a small version of a road-work cone. I had no idea what it was.

Soon, they had come up high enough to be even with me. They were thirty or forty yards to my side. I stayed motionless against the dark rock. If they happened to see me, Sky would likely flee. Maybe he'd be able to take Joshua with him. If so, I'd never have a chance to understand what was really happening.

"Lost my view of the big guy," Diamond said in my ear. I pressed my phone tight against my ear, trying to keep Diamond's words from spilling out toward Sky and Joshua.

"Last I saw, he was hiking up into a heavy stand of trees. He paused a few times. To breathe, I'm guessing. I think he'll arrive at the trail that goes around the base of Shakespeare Rock in four or five minutes."

I kept my eye on the dark silhouettes of Joshua and Sky. They were now about ten yards above me and still off to the side another thirty yards. Despite the growing dawn light, I still couldn't see their faces. I was trying to anticipate the best route for them to get to the roofless cave when they stopped climbing up and hiked sideways toward a steep face of vertical rock about the size of a small office building. They went just below the steep face and disappeared around the other side.

I dared not move from my position. It was best to wait. They'd reappear eventually.

A couple of minutes later, Diamond spoke into my ear, "Still no movement anywhere."

I continued to look off to where Joshua and Sky had gone behind the rock. After several moments, there was movement on the top of the rock face. Joshua had climbed up and over from the back side. He came forward to the edge of the vertical face. Above and behind him loomed the face of Shakespeare Rock, a huge vertical wall. Joshua squatted down and sat on the rock. Then he scooted forward, moving very slowly, until he was sitting on the edge of the precipice. He let his feet hang off the edge. The drop off was about 60 feet, maybe more. The landing was sharp rock. No one could fall 6 stories to sharp-edged boulders without being killed. He had his hood pulled forward and down, shading his face from the growing dawn light, making him look dark and ghostly.

I immediately understood the concept. Joshua was sitting on the edge of a vertical drop off. If he fell he'd likely die. Sky could come up behind him at any moment and push him off. Kraytower would eventually arrive below. He would look up and see how precarious Joshua's position was. I didn't know what demands Sky would make of Kraytower. But whatever it was, Kraytower would give in to whatever Sky wanted. It was either that, or watch his son fall to his death.

I waited. The red sky above us was lightening. Less like blood. Moving toward an orange-red sunrise. The contrast with the dark forest below was dramatic. I scanned the woods for any sign of Kraytower. There was no movement. When I looked back up at the small cliff, Joshua was still visible, sitting on the edge. But Sky was not.

Diamond spoke in my ear. "Driver of the Prius just got out. He's walking toward the gate. Now he's turning off, going up the steep trail, following the first person."

I stared down at the forest, trying to see when Kraytower would appear, wondering who was following him.

I heard him before I saw him. His heavy breathing was extremely labored, like a man struggling to stay alive.

In another minute, there was movement. He came up the steep slope one slow step at a time. Gradually, the crackling of twigs and branches on the forest floor became apparent. When he got to the perimeter trail, he stopped and looked both ways. His son was perched almost directly above him, but Kraytower hadn't seen him. It was an effective position. If Joshua fell—or was pushed—he'd land just in front of where Carston Kraytower stood.

Kraytower started to move counter clockwise on the trail.

"Halt, Kraytower," came commanding words. The sound of the words seemed to boomerang all through the forest, although I knew the words came from the far side of the rock that Joshua sat on. The sound had a familiar quality, but I couldn't place it. Then I realized it was a megaphone. The conical object that Sky had carried. It made his voice loud and clear even as it disguised his location. It also gave it a booming resonance that made him sound different. It was like an effect for a theatrical stage.

"Where's my boy?" Kraytower called out, his voice plaintive. The authority of the rich financier was gone, like a king stripped of his clothes.

"He's straight above you. Look up on the rock face."

Kraytower turned his face up. He looked left and right, searching. Then he saw his son high above.

"Joshua!" he yelled. "Oh, my God. You're on the edge of a

cliff! Stay calm. Don't move. Are you okay? Don't worry, boy. I'll get you down! I'll do whatever your captor wants." Kraytower reached up to a boulder and started to climb.

"Don't move," the voice boomed.

Kraytower stopped. "What do you want from me? I'll give you money. I can pay whatever you'd like. I can make you rich."

It sounded like the hollow entreaty of someone who'd always gotten what he wanted with money.

"I don't want your dollars," the booming voice said. "I want your confession."

"I don't understand. What do you mean?"

"Twenty-two years ago. Back at Yale. You and your fraternity brothers got Eddie Lange drunk at a frat party and he died."

There was a pause as if Kraytower was shocked. "Yes, Eddie drank a lot. We all drank a lot." Kraytower was speaking up into the forest. He looked left and right, unable to see his accuser. "It was a terrible night, a terrible experience. No one was more upset about Eddie's death than me."

"You and your stupid fraternity boys killed him!" the voice in the forest yelled.

"I'm so sorry about that. Were you his friend?"

"More than that," the voice said. "I hold you responsible for his death."

"I admit that the drinking was serious," Kraytower said. "That's the terrible truth. It was a drunk fest. Fraternity boys get crazy sometimes. We were idiots. All of us. Eddie died. That's a scar on our souls. We'll all carry it to our graves. I'm so sorry."

"It wasn't just the drinking, Kraytower. Was it?"

"I don't know what you mean."

"Yes you do. You killed him with the drug."

Kraytower didn't respond.

"You killed Eddie with the same drug I used to kill James Lightfoot and Sebastian Perry, your co-conspirators."

"Are you Eddie's son? I wondered about that." Kraytower sounded broken. "I thought you'd made the connection. I'm so sorry. But you don't need to hurt my son. Joshua is innocent. I'll do whatever I can to make it better. I'll pay whatever you want."

"SHUT UP! You can't just buy your way out of trouble. If you say one more idiotic thing, I'll push Joshua off the cliff."

"What can I do?" Kraytower said.

"Admit what really happened."

"I just did."

"No," the booming voice said, "you didn't. You gave Eddie the poison! Say it."

"I..."

"Admit it, Kraytower! Admit it or Joshua dies! You gave Eddie the veterinary drug. The Rhinoceros sedative. Tell the truth, or I push Joshua off to his death!"

Kraytower hesitated.

"LAST CHANCE!"

"It was an accident!" Kraytower suddenly said.

"You don't accidentally poison someone with rhinoceros sedative!"

"The paper insert with the drug said it was a powerful sedative. That's why we only gave Eddie a tiny fraction of the amount. We dipped a tranquilizer dart into it and got a micro drop. We didn't even think he'd notice. It was a practical joke gone very badly."

"You poured the poison in. Just like Claudius did with King Hamlet. You killed him. Then you took his math formulas and used them to analyze investments. I have one of his notebooks. I read what he wrote about formulas that could be used to analyze data fluctuations in financial markets. You took it! You killed him and then used his genius to build your giant company!"

From where I stood against the dark rock, I could hear Kraytower hyperventilating. He was panicking.

A new voice spoke loudly from just down the slope below Kraytower. "The best way through this is to admit it, Carston."

It was a familiar voice. It took me a second to realize who it was. Nettie Moon Water. Kraytower must have called her for a ride to the kidnapper rendezvous.

"Telling the truth is the first step," Nettie said. "Everyone can begin to heal when people stop lying."

Sky shouted in the megaphone, "Polonius said, 'I will find where truth is hid, though it were hid indeed within the centre!'"

Kraytower spoke in a lower, softer voice. "I can't tell you how sorry I am. We meant it as a practical joke. A very mean joke, I admit. But we did not mean to kill. When Eddie died, we were devastated."

Diamond spoke in my ear. "It seems the main players have all arrived. Maybe I should land the drone and come down in case you could use help. Then again, if someone runs, the drone could help us see where he goes."

I wanted to respond, but I didn't dare. Even my lightest whisper would bounce off the wall behind me and project out. I could only hope that Diamond would make his best decision.

I wondered if I should reveal myself to the others. Or would that crank up the tension? My appearance would likely cause Sky to panic. Whatever his intentions were, he felt in control now. If I stepped out, he'd feel he was losing control. That might drive him to harsh action.

I stayed quiet. The emails had instructed Kraytower to come alone. But Sky hadn't reacted to Nettie's presence. Nettie was probably the calming influence everyone needed.

"Where'd you get the drug?" Sky asked over the megaphone.

"I found it," Kraytower said.

"Tell the truth!"

"I did find it! When I was at Yale, there was a burglary at a veterinary pharmaceutical distributor in Brooklyn. I'd been down in New York visiting a classmate in Brooklyn. I got off the bus and walked through the area where the burglary had taken place. I found a few dozen boxes that were scattered in a parking lot like they'd fallen off a truck. I looked in one or two. They contained bottles of distilled water that were to be used with certain drugs. Maybe the burglars tossed them thinking they weren't valuable. I walked along, kicking the boxes like I was kicking a can. Then my foot hit one that was light instead of heavy. I opened it up and found vials of the sedative and tranquilizer darts. I took it as a curiosity. I never thought I would use it for anything until we got stinking drunk at the party. Then I got the stupid idea to try a bit of it on someone. Just the tiniest bit. I never knew… I recently went to the office in New Haven where they keep death records. On Eddie's death certificate, it says the cause of death was alcohol poisoning. So maybe the sedative had no effect."

"Only one person at the hazing party got the drug, and he was the only person who died!"

"I know. I accept that it may be the drug that killed Eddie. Please let Joshua go. I'll make it up to you somehow."

"You could never make it up."

There was an awkward silence.

"I think there's more to tell," Nettie said.

Kraytower said, "I kept the darts and drug in a Château Mouton-Rothschild wine box. In my cellar. After our party, I found the wine box had been broken open. When Jim Lightfoot and Sebastian Perry died, I worried that they'd been killed by the sedative. So I hired a local detective to look into their deaths. I thought that hiring him would direct attention away from me. But he was more stubborn than I thought. He learned about the drug that killed Lightfoot and Perry. I realized that he was probably going to find out what happened to Eddie. I worried that he'd figure out my connection to Eddie, so I tried to have him warned off. But that didn't work. I could have called him and told him to quit, but that would have revealed my culpability. So I'm guilty of a thousand bad things. The only thing I didn't do was use good judgment."

"The punishment for that is your own poison," came the booming voice, echoing through the forest.

"NO," Nettie called out. "If Eddie Lange actually died from the drug, then Carston's crime was manslaughter, not premeditated murder. The murders of Jim Lightfoot and Sebastian Perry were first degree murder. They don't balance out."

"Eddie Lange was killed. Alcohol and rhino tranquilizer. He was killed by the combined efforts of Kraytower and his frat boys. Eddie's life work in mathematics was stolen and used to make millions. There's no mercy for that kind of sick crime."

"This can stop!" Nettie said. "It can stop right now! We can work it out."

Nettie walked around Kraytower's side and tried to step

above him.

Kraytower grabbed her and tried to move her behind him.

She twisted out of his grip and scrambled up the slope and stood between Kraytower and the rock wall. Joshua was almost directly above them. Sky was out of my sight on the far side.

"Let Joshua go!" Kraytower shouted as he tried to pull Nettie away from the rock. "Please!"

"Maybe I will. But not for you."

I heard a whoosh of air come from the far side of the rock wall.

"Ouch," Kraytower said. He reached up to his shoulder and pulled out a dart.

Joshua rolled back from the edge of the big rock and disappeared down the back side.

I slipped my phone into my pocket and started scrambling down from my perch. There was another whoosh of air. I climbed over boulders, slid off the big ones, jumped down the smaller ones. I came to a huge slab of rock tipped up very steep and slid on my butt down its surface. There was a sixpack of giant rocks. I did a boulder-hopping run over them. I leaped onto the perimeter trail. I was about one hundred yards from where Kraytower and Moon Water had been standing.

I sprinted. From the time I left my hiding place a full minute or two had elapsed.

When I reached them, Kraytower lay on his face. Nettie Moon Water was crumpled on her side, her foot against the side of Kraytower's hip. Her arm was raised up, draped across her head, obscuring her face. I kneeled next to Nettie and put my fingertips on her neck just to the outside of her throat. There was a weak pulse in her carotid artery. She moaned.

I quickly checked Kraytower the same way. He had no pulse. His color, even in the dim light, was grayer than Nettie's. His skin was less supple. The contrast between life and lifeless was dramatic.

Nettie moved. She reached her other arm up to her head. Felt above her left ear. Her fingers picked up blood. She must have fallen and hit a rock.

I could do heart compressions on Kraytower. But Doc Lee had told me it would be pointless. The drug was as toxic to humans as anything invented. Deadlier than bullets. Deadlier than hand grenades.

FIFTY-FOUR

I pulled out my phone. Diamond was talking.

"Diamond, I haven't been able to hear you," I said. "Nettie Moon Water is injured, barely conscious. I think she hit her head. She needs an EMT. She's on the perimeter trail on the north side of Shakespeare Rock. Carston Kraytower has been shot with at least one tranquilizer dart. He's dead. Call it in, then call me back." I clicked off.

I took off my jacket, folded it into a pillow, and gently raised Nettie's head to put the jacket underneath. Her hair was wet near her left ear. The blood wasn't flowing. But it was seeping.

When Kraytower had been darted, Nettie probably tried to catch him as he fell. But he weighed twice or more what she weighed. When they went down, she hit her head.

She tried to say something, but the words were mumbled.

"Help is on the way, Nettie. Stay here."

I heard my phone, tapped it, heard Diamond's voice. "I can see two people running down the mountain," Diamond said. "They're moving west from you." It was classic Diamond. He had the same emotional response as everyone else. But he was able to prioritize and subordinate his feelings to the most important task.

"I'm on it," I said. I didn't disconnect because I needed to hear Diamond.

I leaned over next to Nettie's head. "The medics are on the way. The boys with the poison darts have left. You'll be okay. Just be patient." I caressed her forehead, then stood up and started running along the trail toward the west. I clicked my phone to speaker so I could hold it in my hand as I ran. The sunlight had just touched the top of Shakespeare Rock. It bounced light down into the dark forest. For the first time that day, there was enough light to see.

I ran counter clockwise along the perimeter trail beneath Shakespeare Rock. It wasn't a maintained trail, and there were lots of fallen logs and other obstructions. But I was able to run fast. As it curved toward the south, I turned off it and headed down the mountain to the west.

"They're still running," Diamond said. "The smaller one is in front."

"Let me know when you can see me," I said, huffing hard. "Then you can tell me where they are in relation to me."

I ran down the mountain, trying to see through the forest. Despite the lightening pink glow in the sky above, the trees were still dark and foreboding. And in those trees, the branches were sharp brambles at head level. Run into them in the dark and they would tear the skin off your face.

I tried to anticipate, slaloming around and between the trees. My feet hit low brush that felt like flexible steel. I went down head first, flipped a somersault, and ended sitting on the ground. I still held my phone with my right hand. I felt the branches with my left. They were smooth and hard. Manzanita. Nearly impenetrable without a bulldozer or chain saw. I got up, found my way around them, and continued running.

"I see you," Diamond's voice said from my phone. "Your targets are about fifty yards below you. They're pausing. One is in the bushes. Now the other one is, too. Oh, I get it. They stashed mountain bikes. They've got them out. They're up and riding. The trail they're on goes to the south. It looks like it angles down to the highway. The bigger guy is in front. The smaller is right on his tail. You'd have to run like a superhero to catch them."

I slowed my running. I was feeling the pressure of trying to breathe, trying to catch two bad kids, and trying to face the stress of a wounded woman and a dead man up on the mountain.

"Wait," Diamond said. "Man down. The smaller guy caught a wheel on something. He skidded and landed on his side. He's struggling to sit up. Must have been quite a blow."

"Give me directions," I said, breathless as I ran.

"Straight west of you," Diamond said. "Keep going straight

down the mountain. No, angle more to the south, your left."

I adjusted my line.

"Perfect," Diamond said. "Keep going. Another twenty yards. Hurry, he's up and walking his bike back up to the trail."

"I see him," I said in a low voice.

I watched as Joshua got one foot in the toe clip of his pedal. He made a half rotation and lifted his other leg over the bike. He stood up and pedaled hard, moving away from me on the trail. He was accelerating fast when I hit him.

We both went down hard. His bicycle hit the dirt and slid into the bushes. Joshua flew off to the front in a half somersault.

I scrambled up and dove onto his body. He hit the ground stomach first and seemed stunned into inaction. I was thinking about poison darts that he might still have on his person. I dropped down on his back, my chest hitting squarely on the sketch of John Muir's face. I reached out and grabbed each of his wrists, pinning him in place. He made a high-pitched cry.

I was rough as I turned him over, keeping my fingers locked on his thin wrists so he couldn't pull out a poison dart and stab me with it.

Once on his back, his hoodie dropped away a bit, and the light of dawn fell on his face.

Only it wasn't Joshua Kraytower.

It was a woman. It took me a moment to remember. It was the woman who did Kraytower's gardening. Mary Mason.

FIFTY-FIVE

I patted Mary Mason down and found no weapons. I pulled her fanny pack off of her waist. There were two poison darts inside. I loosened the strap of the little pack and put it around my waist. I walked her back up the mountain.

"Why?" I said after we got to the trail that traced the perimeter of Shakespeare Rock. "Why so much hatred of Carston Kraytower?"

She didn't respond. But her breathing was heavy and choked as if emotion was suffocating her.

I said, "Carston Kraytower killed Eddie Lange all those years ago at Yale. Was Eddie Lange your son?"

No response other than tears and difficulty breathing.

"How did you come to work for Kraytower?" I asked.

But she didn't answer.

I asked other questions.

"Was Sky your grandson?"

She didn't answer.

I continued as if she'd said 'yes.' "Where did Sky live after his father Eddie died? Does he remember his father?"

She stayed silent.

Nettie Moon Water was sitting up at the edge of the trail when we returned. Her elbows were on her knees, and she leaned her head into her hands.

Kraytower's body was nearby, a heavy presence in death.

We waited. Mary Mason still didn't speak. She appeared very stressed. There was sweat on her forehead and tears in her eyes. She shook as if shivering from cold. I guessed she was having a severe nervous attack. If my guess that she was Eddie's mother was correct, she was the mother who collapsed when her boy had been killed 22 years ago, and she was put in a psychiatric hospital. She probably spent 22 years struggling with anger as her son's fraternity brothers got rich off his math genius. Now her mission of revenge was suddenly over.

I kept a firm grip on Mary's arm as I knelt next to Nettie and asked how she felt, and if she had a bad headache beyond the site of her injury, or if she was nauseated or dizzy, signs of concussion. She claimed she was just shaken.

I knew better. She had brought Kraytower from his home, in effect giving him a ride to his death. Even if they hadn't been close, she'd known him for a long time. It would be hard to have him dead, hard to watch him die.

Nettie looked at Mary.

"It was your boy who died all those years ago," she said, figuring out the relationships immediately. Knowing what I did of Nettie, she would have empathy for Mary.

Mary didn't answer.

I tried to think of things to say to ease the tension and discomfort of a murder scene. Street would have known how to do it. I felt helpless.

Diamond came down through the forest. He didn't have the drone case, having left it to make hiking through the forest easier. He saw that I was holding Mary Mason's arm. He raised his eyebrows.

"This is Mary Mason, Kraytower's gardener and one of two killers pursuing Carston Kraytower, James Lightfoot, and Sebastian Perry," I said. "Mary was wearing one of Joshua's sweatshirts. I thought she was Joshua until she crashed on her mountain bike."

"And the other person with her?" Diamond asked.

"He got away."

"You ID him?" Diamond asked.

"No. But it makes sense he was Sky Kool. Nettie and I guessed that Eddie Lange, the guy who died in the fraternity hazing at Yale twenty-two years ago, was Mary's son. I'm reasonably certain that Sky Kool was Eddie's son and Mary's grandson."

Diamond would know that I'd patted Mason down. He pulled out his cuffs and cuffed Mary's hands at her front rather than her back, a gesture of kindness for a person who had to hike a long distance through the forest. Hiking any distance was difficult with hands cuffed behind.

"Mary Mason," Diamond said, "you're under arrest for the murder of Carston Kraytower." He then mirandized her.

Two EMTs showed up twenty minutes later, laboring up the steep trail. They took a quick look at Kraytower's body, then spent some time with Nettie, looking at her head wound, shining a light in her pupils, taking her blood pressure, asking questions. They cleaned and dressed the wound. When they said they would bring a litter to carry her down the mountain, she assured them she could walk. Their relief was obvious. But they still had to get a litter to bring Kraytower's body down the slope.

After the EMTs assured us that Nettie would be okay, Diamond said, "You think we should call for backup to haul our suspect away? We'd have to hike down to the highway. And we'd need more than one vehicle to take her and us. That might take awhile."

"Almost faster to go back the way we came. Then we could pick up the drone."

Diamond nodded, and we escorted Mary up the mountain to the trail we'd come on. Mary Mason stayed silent.

When we got to my cabin, Diamond put Mary into the back of his sheriff's vehicle, and they left. I drove my Jeep down the mountain and stopped at Street's condo. Spot sniffed me with much focus.

"It's a relief that Nettie seems okay," Street said after I explained what happened. "You can tell me the details later."

I said goodbye and left. Spot had his head out the window, staring at Street and Blondie as we drove away.

The power of their charisma.

I pulled off the highway a mile away and parked such that I could see the vast expanse of lake glowing in the morning light. The pink of the sky was shifting to blue.

My thoughts seemed aimless. I'd caught one of the murderers. But now that I knew that Joshua wasn't there, I worried about his fate. Was he okay? Was he held captive? Or was he a co-conspirator in a fake kidnapping?

Mary Mason had been working at the Pacific Heights house when I first went there. Aria had told me that Joshua was kidnapped from the Pacific Heights house. How did it happen?

Did Sky's grandmother Mary, conjuring up a scheme to punish Kraytower, simply ask Joshua to come with her in her car? Maybe to help her pick up supplies at a gardening store. Joshua would have felt comfortable going with the family gardener, a woman he'd probably known for much of his life, known from both San Francisco and Tahoe.

As I sat in the Jeep and thought through the various scenarios, I looked across the lake. If I'd had binoculars, I might have been able to see Kraytower's lake house and sculpture gardens looking like an elegant Italian villa.

It occurred to me that if Mary wanted to kidnap Joshua and stash him someplace where Kraytower wouldn't find him, she'd take him a good distance from Pacific Heights. But to where? Why not take him to Tahoe? Ever since the kidnapping, Kraytower had been in San Francisco or New York or London or Reykjavik.

For Mary's purposes, it would be like hiding Joshua in plain site.

And if her grandson Sky was present to any degree, Joshua would feel very comfortable. Maybe Mary and Sky could even convince Joshua to lay low while they did their evil deed. Maybe he was hiding at Sky's rented cabin. Or held prisoner there. As soon as I thought about it, I realized I'd missed the obvious.

I pulled back out on the highway headed north around the lake.

It was still early morning. The tourists were still asleep or eating breakfast. Traffic was light.

Ninety minutes later, I pulled into Kraytower's drive and parked under the trees. Sky's blue Nova wagon was parked next to Kraytower's black Suburban limo. The Italian sports cars were in the garage. The house was dark. No sign of any people at all.

It could be that the alarm had sensors and cameras that alerted inhabitants to a trespasser. But I didn't have much choice.

I quietly tried the front door. It was locked. No doubt the doors on the lake side would be locked as well. I didn't want to ring the bell if I didn't have to. Whether Sky heard me come in or discovered me once I was inside didn't make much difference.

The gate that Sergeant Santiago and I had used to access the main yard was unlocked. The irrigation system had recently watered the grass. I walked through cold wet grass over to the sculpture garden that was closest to the house. One of the marble maidens was near the corner of the living room. She had her arm stretched out, lifting her flowing robes, her posture imploring me to join her.

Near her was a smallish Jeffrey pine, its trunk 12 inches in diameter, its lowest branches six feet above her head. As with most pines, the branches were spindly. But they were often strong.

I raised my foot and put it on the 3-foot pedestal that held the maiden. With my arms hugging her cold marble knees, I boosted myself up so that I was standing next to her. She was sculpted on four-fifth's scale so that her entire height was rendered four feet tall. As I stood on the pedestal, her face was at my abdomen. We hugged each other for a moment while I got my bearings.

When I'd been to the Kraytower mansion before, the maidens had all looked to be of marble. Marble was tough stuff but prone to fracture. Many of the marble sculptures left over from antiquity were missing arms.

Yet her outstretched arm seemed the only good way to reach the tree branch above her head. So I put the toe of my shoe in the curve of her flowing robes, put my hands on the top of her hair and crown of flowers, and boosted myself up so I could step on her outstretched arm.

Gingerly, I transferred my weight, trying to stay near her shoulder, nevertheless anticipating the crack of breaking marble and my fall back to Earth.

The crack never came, and the maiden proved to have super-human strength. I got my other foot on her opposite shoulder and slowly straightened up, standing on that slender beautiful figure that glowed white in the morning sunlight.

I was very obvious. Anybody looking out a window would have seen me. Anyone looking through a telescope from twelve miles across the lake would have seen me.

I gripped the tree branch above, did a pull up, hooked the edge of my sole onto a nub of wood that remained from a long-missing branch, and climbed up farther. Moving carefully so I didn't misjudge my movements, I was able to stand on the branch. The marble maiden was now far below, her entreaties directed toward an imaginary suitor in the yard.

I got a good grip on a large branch above my head and walked hand-over-hand several feet toward the house. From there I could almost touch my foot to the edge of the roof eve. I visualized how I might propel myself across the gap, did a mental rehearsal, and then swung my legs and pushed off.

My feet landed on the roof eve. I teetered for a bit, nearly losing my balance and falling off backward. But I was able to drop to my knees on the roof. When I felt steady, I crab-crawled up the sloped slate to the wrought iron fence that marked the perimeter of the roof-top sculpture garden. The fence was short, and I was over it in seconds.

A new group of maidens beckoned me. I ignored them and walked over to the rooftop door, the glassed entrance that I'd seen earlier when Kraytower took me to the second floor of the house. Unlike the ground-floor doors, this one had no dead bolt. But the door knob was locked and felt strong.

I cupped my hands against the glass, shutting out the little bit of light, and tried to see in. There was only darkness inside. Or maybe the inside of the glass had blackout blinds.

In the cargo pocket of my jeans was my Leatherman tool, a sort of heavy-duty version of a Swiss Army knife. I tried inserting the knife blade between the door and the strike plate to slide the bolt. No luck.

I might have been able to force the jamb if I'd had a tire iron, but that would break the glass and alert anyone within 500 yards. But one needn't force a door jamb if the keyed lock could be forced. It didn't work with top-quality locks. This lock brand was in the middle of the quality scale. Worth a try.

I unfolded the large slotted screwdriver and slowly inserted it into the key hole, pushing it in hard enough and far enough to grind past the brass tumblers. Then I gripped the tool very hard with both hands and rotated it. Internal metal sheared, the lock gave way, and the door opened.

I waited for the shriek of an alarm. It didn't come. Perhaps there was a silent alarm. Either way, it didn't change my plan.

I slowly shut the door behind me. It had dark brown slatted blinds that swung and banged against the glass. Going from the brilliant sunlight outside to the darkness inside was a shock. I paused inside the house, trying to sense my bearings, waiting for my eyes to adjust. I didn't look back at the door I'd come through. I didn't want to re-establish night blindness.

Gradually, I become aware of blue carpet on the floor, lit by little sharp slivers of light that came in through the blinds on the door and the drapes on the windows. I stepped forward, sliding my feet on the thick, smooth-nap rug.

After my eyes became more sensitive, I saw a glow some distance away.

I felt my way forward step by step, moving slowly, taking care to be silent. As I got closer to the glow, a vertical stripe of light appeared. There was a doorway, and the door was ajar, swung in an inch. I tried to peak through. The door crack revealed nothing except that the dim light fluctuated as if it came from several candles.

I very slowly touched the door and eased it inward. The door opened to the dark study that Kraytower had shown me before. The room had bookshelves and reading chairs. There were large windows with drapes shut like all the rest. The only light in the study was the yellow, flickering gas flame in the fireplace. It was a setting for respite from a cold dark winter, not a brilliant summer day.

Gerard Casteem sat in a big leather chair. To his side was an antique wooden table that held an unlit lamp with an ornate shade. Next to the lamp was a bottle of brandy and a snifter glass, lit up by the firelight. The glass was two-thirds empty.

I quietly stepped through the doorway. I don't think the man heard me. But he might have expected me to show up.

"'There's a special providence in the fall of a sparrow,' right?" I said.

Without looking up or even moving a finger, Casteem spoke in a voice that sounded like what I'd heard from the megaphone up on Shakespeare Rock. "Eddie Lange was murdered. He was my son and Jake's father. Like Jake, Hamlet lost his father to murder. Jake and Hamlet share that misfortune. It's the simplest rule in the world. Kill someone's child, expect that they may kill you in revenge."

FIFTY-SIX

I said to Gerard Casteem, "Jake Lange was your grandson."
"Mine and Mary Mason's. Jake is the boy you know as
Sky. Mary is his grandmother. And he knows that. We thought it
would be best if he didn't know that I'm his grandfather. It would
have given him too many questions to grapple with. Nevertheless,
that's why I let him call me gramps."

"You and Mary are obviously close."

"Not at all. She and I never saw eye-to-eye on much. We
were only married for two years. But Mary and I were equally
devoted to Eddie and, later, to his son Jake. AKA Sky. When
Kraytower pretended to be Eddie's best friend and then killed
him and stole his math equations, we both lost our minds. From
the beginning, we wanted revenge, mostly for Eddie's murder.
But also because Kraytower and Lightfoot and Perry used Eddie's
economic theories to build a giant hedge fund. Mary was eager to
help me. We've both had revenge simmering in our minds since
Eddie's death."

Casteem drank brandy. "We alternated with the victims so
that one of us always had an alibi. Mary killed Perry on the Rim
Trail when I was here at the house. It was easy for her to ride
by and poke him with a dart. I killed Lightfoot when she was
in San Francisco. No one suspected us. It's easy to fool people
with a cane and a fake tremor. But we stopped thinking about
an alibi when we both went out to get Kraytower. And now that
he's dead, it doesn't matter that we've been caught. We achieved
justice."

"Justice by your measure," I said.

"One's perception, whether or not others agree, is all one
has."

I asked, "What was the point of the emails, the references to

Hamlet?"

"More justice. A poetic response suitable for our fury. Eddie was a Shakespeare fanatic. Shakespeare was a daily part of his life. His killers put us through agony. So we made Shakespeare a part of their death."

"You succeeded. But you never intended to kill Joshua," I said.

"Of course not. Just because the rule would suggest that we might kill Kraytower's boy in exchange for him killing our boy doesn't mean we'd do it. Joshua never did anything but ask someone—anyone—to love him. I would never kill him. But we used him to get Kraytower's attention and to make Kraytower come to us at a place and time of our choosing. I blew two tranquilizer darts at Kraytower. You should know that I didn't mean to hit Moon Water. She was being heroic, trying to protect Kraytower. I respect that even though he didn't deserve protecting."

"You didn't hit Moon Water. The second dart must have missed Kraytower. Moon Water fell and hit her head. She'll probably be okay."

"What?" Casteem said. "Oh, good. Very good. That would have tormented me for the rest of eternity. I'm so glad you found me and reported that news." He drank brandy. It wasn't a delicate sip. More like a slug of medicine he wanted to get down. He reached for the bottle and refilled his glass. The firelight made the amber liquid glow.

Casteem said, "Mary Mason will corroborate what I've said. That is, if she is speaking. She often goes silent in times of stress. It's a kind of mental shutdown, like a thermal cutout to protect equipment from overheating."

"You have no more targets?"

Casteem took a moment. "No. Just the men who tormented and killed our son and stole his genius to fuel their own gain. Now they're gone."

"You believed Jim Lightfoot and Sebastian Perry were as guilty as Kraytower?"

"They actively conspired with Kraytower to get Eddie

excessively drunk. That was reported from multiple witnesses who also said no one else at the hazing party was actively pushing to get Eddie drunk. It makes sense that they were all in on the injection of the tranquilizer."

"Do you think they intended to murder your son? Or could it have been a stupid accidental death, a prank gone wrong, like slipping a pill into someone's drink and not realizing it would kill?"

Casteem drank more brandy. "If Kraytower and company hadn't built a giant hedge fund based on Eddie's math innovations, I might have considered that. But these were smart guys. They would know that people might have a dramatically different reaction to a drug than a rhinoceros would."

"And you think Lightfoot and Perry were also in on the theft of the equations from the beginning?" I asked.

"Our son Eddie was quite boastful about his math discoveries. He talked a lot. Partly, it was self-aggrandizing. Partly it was enthusiasm. He knew he had done ground-breaking work. Because he freely talked about it, everyone else knew it, too. It wasn't long after his death that Kraytower started the hedge fund. Almost immediately, he hired Lightfoot and Perry to work for him. There's no question they all knew that the math that powered the company's growth was Eddie's. They were complicit in every part of the theft of Eddie's intellectual property. It wasn't like the trivial theft of a valuable diamond or some other material object. For a creator like Eddie, having his work stolen and used for profit by others was like the destruction of everything he lived for. It was the theft of his very essence. But of course, he was already dead."

I wondered if it was true, that the whole thing was premeditated. Kraytower had made the claim that it was a sedative prank gone bad. Using Eddie's math—uncredited— after an accidental death was very wrong. But it was nothing like a plot to kill a man in order to steal his work. But Kraytower had said it was a practical joke when he was under threat of death out at Shakespeare Rock. People often scramble to make excuses when they're afraid. And he'd repeatedly lied and connived and was devious by any measure. He even had me assaulted after he'd hired me. An evil man.

I thought of what James Lightfoot had talked to Nettie about, a subject that increasingly looked like an effort by Lightfoot to justify his own rage after the death of his dog in Eddie's car, and, probably, an effort to justify his participation in Eddie's murder.

Lightfoot himself might have said that they were all bad and thus had less right to live than any decent dog.

Casteem never changed position, never looked away from the gas fireplace, never glanced toward me. I felt like my presence in the room was trespassing on sacred memories of Eddie and his genius. The man before the fire was a cold-blooded murderer, and yet I didn't want to add to his stress and pain. I remained standing in the doorway, behind him, largely out of his sight if he should look up. I could duck behind the door if he should blow a dart my way.

Casteem said, "I don't expect you to believe any of this. But I don't care whether you do or not. I made my decision, and I'm comfortable with it." Casteem drank more brandy.

"I believe you. I heard about Eddie from Nettie Moon Water. I went to New Haven, Connecticut to learn about his life," I said. "In the process, I found out that Kraytower had gone there too, to look up Eddie's death certificate, probably to learn if they'd ever found a hint of the etorphine. That told me that Kraytower was fully aware that he'd caused Eddie's death. Accidental or not, he knew he'd killed Eddie with the tranquilizer."

"Like poison in the king's ear," Casteem said. He drank more brandy. "Years after Eddie's death, when I arranged to get hired by Kraytower, I sent for Mary Mason. I told her that there were jobs to be had. But my real wish was to get help with my plan to punish Kraytower as he had punished us." Gerard paused, then said, "I made some hints about what I was thinking. Mary figured out my intentions and decided to help."

He drank more brandy.

"It turns out she'd found out where Jake lived and that his new name was Sky. When Sky turned twenty-one, she talked him into coming to Tahoe as well. We never told him that Kraytower and company killed his father. Maybe we dropped hints. But Sky was clueless. He's a smart boy, but naive. He actually believes in the goodness of people. He's similar to Joshua that way, although they are very different personalities."

"How did you figure out where the poison and tranquilizers were hidden?" I asked.

"For years, Kraytower had spoken of his prize wine that once belonged to Thomas Jefferson and which he kept in a locked antique box inside the wine cellar. Things he said made that story sound phony to me. He made too much of a point of wanting the house staff to think the box contained special wine. I suspected otherwise, so I arranged to have a look before his party. The box held tranquilizer darts and several vials of etorphine. The labels had twenty-two-year-old dates. It didn't take much research to reveal a burglary that took place at a veterinary pharmaceutical warehouse in Brooklyn, New York, not long before Kraytower killed Eddie. Maybe Kraytower kept the etorphine in the cool wine cellar to preserve it for future use. Or maybe he just kept it there to minimize the chance that someone would find it in the garbage somewhere and turn it into law enforcement."

From my three-quarter rear view, the edge of Casteem's face was lit by the flickering firelight. Even though I couldn't see his eyes or mouth, he looked enormously sad, his flesh seeming to sag from his cheekbones.

"How did you kidnap Joshua?"

"We didn't. Mary brought him up from the Pacific Heights house. I simply told Joshua that I needed to confront his father about something he did years ago. Joshua didn't know why. But I think he didn't mind the idea of throwing some stress his father's way. After all, Carston Kraytower was his father in name and biology only. Most of the other aspects of parenting were missing. And yes, I know you're wondering if I wasn't much more of a father to Eddie than Kraytower was to Joshua. But I was. Mary and I were utterly devoted to Eddie. So I asked Joshua if he would stay in the wine cellar for two days. I knew that Kraytower didn't really care about his son. But it would, nevertheless, make him feel a small portion of my pain, make him rush in where

I could get a good shot with the dart." Gerard sipped brandy. "Joshua's a good kid," he said. "With Kraytower gone, he'll probably blossom."

"Where's Joshua now?"

"Still in the wine cellar. From the time this house was built, the wine cellar was designed as a rudimentary apartment. A small bathroom. A kitchen with a sink and mini fridge and hotplate. Joshua told me he welcomed the chance to spend some time in solitary, work on his nature principles, think his way through his next book of essays. Be somewhere safe where his father couldn't mock him and humiliate him." Casteem paused. "You don't need a key to get into the wine cellar. It doesn't even have a lock on the door. Now that you're here, I'll let you do the honors of telling him it's time to come out."

"Do you know where Sky is?"

"I gave him permission to take Kraytower's Lamborghini to the grocery store in Tahoe City. He's never been so excited in his life. He should be back soon."

"What's next?" I asked.

"Laertes' sword was tipped with poison. What killed Hamlet and Hamlet's father and mother killed the others around him, as well."

"Considering the circumstances, you can probably avoid a death sentence and get life in prison."

"No thanks. I've completed my mission." Gerard drank more brandy. He set down the glass, took a deep breath and sighed. Then he picked up something else that I hadn't seen in the shadows on the table.

A tranquilizer dart. He pushed the end of the syringe, and it clicked as if it was now loaded and cocked. Then he stabbed it into his leg at the inside top of his thigh. Perhaps it hit his femoral vein. Just ten seconds later, he reached a hand up to his chest. Twenty seconds after that, he shuddered and slumped to the side.

I left Casteem where he died. I walked out of the study, found some lights, and walked down two more flights of stairs to the basement level. Ironically, the basement was filled with light from floor-to-ceiling windows that faced the lake. It was relief from the darkness of the upper floors with the drapes all shut. The wine cellar was in the northwest corner of the house. I opened the door.

A wafting breeze of cool humid air come out. The main room of the wine cellar went far back because it was partly underground. I didn't see Joshua. But there were two doorways that led to the apartment rooms. I didn't want to intrude on Joshua's space, and I didn't want to shock him. I simply leaned in through the open doorway and called out.

"Hello, Joshua. This is Owen McKenna. Your ordeal is over. Feel free to take your time. Come out when you're comfortable, and I'll fill you in on what's happened."

FIFTY-SEVEN

When Joshua came out of the wine cellar, I took him outside. We walked around the back of house. I sat Joshua down in the sun and told him what happened. I didn't sugarcoat it. He was too smart for me to attempt to put any gentle spin on his father's past.

Although Joshua had trouble breathing, he took it well. When I told him that his father had been killed by Gerard Casteem and Mary Mason, he swallowed hard and narrowed his eyes. It was a surprise and a shock. Most kids would collapse for a long while. But Joshua seemed to understand the motivation that Casteem and Mason felt.

I did not tell him that Mary Mason had used his John Muir sweatshirt as a way to masquerade as him.

"My father died at Shakespeare Rock just a few hours ago," he said. "Where is his body now?"

"The EMTs treated Nettie Moon Water and then removed your father's body. It's probably at the morgue in Minden, Nevada."

"What will happen to Mrs. Mason and Mr. Casteem?"

"Mason is in custody. Casteem told me that you were in the wine cellar. Then he stabbed himself with a tranquilizer dart. He died in seconds. His body is upstairs in the study."

Joshua's eyes flashed as he jerked his head up toward the upper windows of the palace. Then he turned and stared across the lake. His jaw muscles bulged as he clenched his teeth. I worried about him. In the space of a minute, his world had morphed into something he didn't recognize.

"Sky is the son of the man my father killed at Yale," Joshua said as if to be certain he wasn't mistaken.

"Correct. Eddie Lange, the math genius."

"And it was supposed to look like Eddie died in a fraternity hazing."

"Right."

Joshua squinted his eyes against the sunlight shimmering off the lake.

"In a twisted way, Sky and I are like blood brothers. My father killed his father. And his grandfather killed my father."

"Yeah."

"If my father and his fraternity brothers hadn't stolen Eddie Lange's math knowledge, they wouldn't have built a big company. And if Eddie had done it instead, all of this wealth would have been in Sky's family."

I nodded.

"Does Sky know all of this?"

"Almost none of it. All he knows is that his grandmother is Mary Mason. They were keeping that information to themselves so it wouldn't jeopardize their employment with your father. The cops know about your father's death. But you're the first person I've told about Casteem."

Joshua's eyes looked like they stung. "I'm going to make certain that Sky gets all this wealth. I can do that, right? When I turn eighteen."

"I think so," I said. "I don't know the details, but your father told me that he had, long ago, made his choice for your guardian should he die."

"Nettie Moon Water," Joshua said. "He told me."

"Are you okay with her?"

He made a single nod. "Nettie is a good person. I think she will look out for my best interests. Do you agree?"

"Yes. And Nettie will help you make things better with Sky," I said. I stood up. "I need to call the sheriff's office and report Casteem's death."

Joshua nodded.

"Then I think you should come and stay with me for the next day or so, while some of this stuff gets sorted out. This house might be uncomfortable."

Joshua paused. "Okay," he said.

I dialed Santiago and walked across the lawn while I told him what happened.

"I'm taking Joshua with me. We'll head to my place."

"Sounds like a good idea," Santiago said. "I'll try to get to the Kraytower house before Sky Kool finds Casteem dead."

Next, I called Nettie Moon Water.

"It's Owen McKenna. Sorry to leave you on the mountainside. But we needed to bring in our suspect. And I wasn't thinking very clearly. Are you okay?"

"I'm a little woozy. But I'll be fine. The EMTs escorted me down to my car. After much protest, they finally let me drive home."

"To Reno or Fallen Leaf Lake?"

"Reno. That way I'll be closer to medical help if I need it. Were you able to apprehend Sky?"

"No. The other killer was Gerard Casteem." I told her the details.

"Joshua will need help," she said. "Especially over the next few days. But I can't help right now. I need some sleep to clear my head. Is that okay?"

"Of course. Joshua will come with me. You call when you feel better."

"Thanks."

That evening, Joshua sat awkwardly in my rocker, reaching out so he could pet Spot on his big bed next to the wood stove. I made small talk from the kitchen nook while I chopped up veggies for homemade pizza. I popped the top on a Sierra Nevada Pale Ale.

"Beer?" I asked.

"No thank you. I'm too young," he said.

I nodded, thinking that his whiskey-fueled sledding might put off any drinking for some time.

"I have The Mountains of California on the little bookshelf," I said as I spread my fixings over a crust.

"John Muir? I have that book." Joshua stood, pulled it out, and flipped through it. "My favorite passage is his chapter on the forests.”

"Where he describes Sequoias," I said.

"Yes! Yes! Yes! A tree that appears to never die a natural death, not disease or fire. They just live on for thousands of years, getting bigger and bigger, until they're struck down by lightning or men's saws."

I realized that this subject was a way through Joshua's current distress. I said, "I read that in nineteen seventy-eight, a branch broke off the General Sherman sequoia from one hundred thirty feet up."

Joshua immediately interrupted to continue what I was saying... "And it was one hundred-fifty feet long and seven feet in diameter, a single branch that was, by itself, bigger than any tree that grew east of the Mississippi!"

"Yes, yes, yes," I said, using Joshua's phrase.

He grinned at me. "Sequoias are a perfect example for why we need nature writers."

"Because, without the writers, the Sequoias would have all been cut down?" I said.

"Absolutely. Muir realized it as soon as he studied the trees. There were all these loggers planning to take the trees. It's been documented. Many of the sequoias date back to before the Roman Empire, and there were no protections for them! Finally, in eighteen ninety, they established Sequoia National Park. If not for that, the trees would all be gone. Like the California Grizzly."

We talked trees for the rest of the evening while we ate pizza.

I pulled out my backpacking pad, and Joshua slept on it with my sleeping bag for a blanket and Spot next to him for extra warmth.

The next morning, I brewed coffee and was pleased that Joshua wanted some as well. We sat on the deck and took in the view and talked about wide ranging subjects. Neither of us mentioned that somewhere among the trees that we could see 12 miles across the vast lake was the Kraytower palace.

I cooked up pancakes and eggs and bacon. Joshua said he was

a vegetarian, so Spot and I got all the bacon.

Nettie called that morning. I invited her to my cabin. Joshua called Sky. Nettie and Sky both arrived within minutes of each other. We four sat on the deck and spoke of the situation without ever focusing on the macabre details.

Sky showed distress at the news that Casteem had died and that Casteem was his grandfather. But he kept impressive control over his emotions.

When Joshua told Sky that he was going to get the wealth he deserved, Sky waved his hand in dismissal. "We'll talk about that some other time. Our main priority now is to figure out your life."

EPILOGUE

Street and I and Spot parked among a dozen vehicles, mostly luxury brands that didn't go with my rusted Jeep or Sky's old blue M & M Nova wagon. Sergeants Jack Santiago and Diamond Martinez were already there, talking by the marble maiden who'd let me use her outstretched arm in the commission of my home invasion. Santiago leaned his hand on her bare foot. It seemed oddly forward, his touching her pale bare foot like that.

When I let Spot out into the back yard, he trotted over to the swimming pool and looked at the diving board. That made me worry. Around the pool were tables with food. A single Spot splash had the potential to destroy the party, if that's what it should be called. I ran after him and took hold of his collar.

Joshua appeared at my side. "Hi, Mr. McKenna."

"Hey, Joshua. Please call me Owen."

"Owen."

"I read your book last night," I said.

"You did?!"

"I downloaded it online."

"You bought my book! I'm amazed!"

"No, don't be amazed. Your book deserves to be read."

"It's just that the only people who usually care about that kind of naturalist stuff are those who study at places like the Georgia Center for Nature Writers. People like me who aren't normal."

"I think you're normal, Joshua. And I'm kind of a regular guy, and I care about such writing."

Joshua shook his head. "Normal people watch TV reality shows and play Frisbee. They don't care about what weirdos like me think about the principles of nature."

"I think you're wrong about that. Are you writing anything new?"

"Well, I'm working on a new premise about how ecosystem awareness spreads. If we try to get good things to infect the population in a way that's parallel to how infectious diseases spread, we can quickly raise awareness. It's my premise that the only way to save the planet is..." he suddenly stopped. "Oh, sorry, I'm doing it again, being a bore."

"No, I'm interested."

"Thanks. But I should bore you at a different kind of occasion."

We walked over to a small stage set. Sky had his Stratocaster plugged into an amp and was adjusting the levels.

"Hey, Sky. You gonna play us some rock 'n roll?"

"That's what Sky Kool and the Palpable Hits do."

"Cool. By the way, I found out that 'Palpable Hit' comes from Hamlet. When Hamlet and Laertes are fencing and Hamlet was hit by the poisoned sword tip, one of the other characters called it a palpable hit."

"Yeah. I learned that from Gramps. He was always quoting Shakespeare. So I borrowed it for my band's name."

Joshua wandered off as Sky strummed a chord and held it, then adjusted the amp controls with his right hand. Then he played a blues riff, held a note, stretched the string with his left fingers, bending the note up in pitch, made another adjustment, looked at me.

"Sounds good," I said.

Sky said, "Joshua told me that you knew about our drinking when we went sledding. Don't blame Joshua at all. He'd told me he wasn't going to ride on the sled and he didn't know how to tell you. I was just trying to get him to loosen up. The drinking was my idea. A really bad idea. He could have died." Sky looked at me intensely for a moment. "It was amazing that you didn't yell at me. You didn't even mention it."

"Not my place to judge." I said.

"Well, I learned my lesson. I threw away the flask. And I won't ever drink around Joshua until he's much older if ever, if ever."

"Good call."

Later, after Sky Kool and the Palpable Hits had played a set of songs, and the wait staff had served gourmet food and poured wine, and Nettie Moon Water had read a poem about understanding life's troubles with the help of the nature spirit, I found Joshua sitting by himself, making notes in the small sketchbook that he seemed to always carry. I brought Spot and a woman over to Joshua.

"Joshua, remember how you told me about the Georgia Center for Nature Writers?"

Joshua looked up at us. "Yes of course. The Georgia Center is huge. And the founder, Roxanne Monales, is like a god. I've read all her books. She's single-handedly made nature writing into a force that changes societies and governments and laws and... Oh, there I go again, spewing words. I'm sorry."

"It's okay, Joshua. The reason I brought up the subject is I wanted to introduce you to someone." I held my hand out palm up and flexed my fingers several times to indicate that he should stand up.

Joshua looked at me and the woman who stood beaming next to me. He closed his sketchbook and got to his feet.

I said, "Joshua, please meet Roxanne Monales."

The woman reached out her hand. "Hi Joshua. I'm Rox. I'm very pleased to meet you."

"Oh, I'm... I'm..." Joshua shook her hand. He was speechless, and his face was rapidly turning pink. He held onto her hand as if unable to let go. It was the first time I'd seen him voluntarily touch anyone other than Spot. Then he realized the awkwardness and pulled his hand back as if it were burned. "I'm Joshua. And you're... You're my hero, Ms. Monales."

"Thanks, Joshua. But I'm just a normal person with a strong conviction. Call me Rox."

Joshua nodded but didn't—maybe couldn't—say the name Rox. He just stared at her.

"I read your book," she said. "I really enjoyed it."

"You read my book, too?" Joshua sounded like he was choking. He could barely get the words out.

"I found it compelling and interesting. I think you're onto some good original ideas. And your writing mechanics are professional as well. That is no small thing."

"What does that mean, writing mechanics?"

"Your essay structure. Prose style, syntax choices, grammar. And you have a persuasive ability with few equals."

Joshua was speechless again.

"So I've conferred with our board of directors, and we'd like to offer you a visiting fellowship."

"I'm sorry, I don't know what that means."

"It means that because of your exceptional scholarship, we'd like you to come stay with us for a six month residency. In addition to pursuing your writing, you'd teach some classes in nature observation and nature writing. Maybe you'd even give an occasional lecture elsewhere about your insights. The residency provides credit at nearly any university. We'd give you a monthly stipend along with room and board. It wouldn't be much. But you'd have your own small cabin in the forest outside of Atlanta, which is perfect for writing. Meals are served in the main hall, breakfast and dinner each day and a help-yourself buffet for lunch. The food is nothing inspiring, but it's quite good. And, of course, you would have lots of contact with other scientists and writers."

Joshua's eyes flooded with tears.

"But I'm only a freshman at UC San Francisco. I won't even start school until this fall. I'm just a kid."

"A brilliant kid whose insights could help preserve the natural world."

Joshua was shaking his head in disbelief. "I don't think you understand. I skipped two grades in grammar school, so I'm only sixteen. I'm not allowed to even make these kinds of adult decisions. I'd have to ask my... My guardian if it's okay."

"Sure," Roxanne smiled. "But for what it's worth, I asked Nettie Moon Water before I approached you. She gives you permission, and she's hoping you'll say yes."

Joshua wiped his tears. He acted puzzled and then suddenly bent down and hugged Spot. Spot was used to sudden affection from humans who find it easier to connect with dogs than people. After a long moment, Joshua straightened up, looked Roxanne Monales in the eye, reached out and shook her hand again, and said, "Yes, yes, yes! I accept your amazing offer."

"Thank you for your enthusiasm," Monales said. "My world is rich with intellectual resources but not so much with enthusiasm. The timing can be flexible. We can plan for you to join us next spring. But we also had a cancellation for this coming fall semester. It's probably much too soon for you to decide. But if by any chance you wanted to start in ten days, we have an opening then."

Joshua's eyes, full of surprise, got wider. "Ten days from now," he said.

"Actually, you'd have to be there in seven days to be ready for the start of the program. Depending how you traveled, you'd probably have to make arrangements tomorrow."

Joshua looked like he was in medical shock.

"I'll just check on refreshments while you two talk," I said.

I pulled Spot away, and we walked over to the linen-covered table with a punch bowl of pink liquid. I filled a glass.

We walked over to a highly realistic marble statue of a young man, who stood surveying the lawn and the giant lake beyond. I sat on a marble bench next to the statue. As is a Great Dane trait, Spot sidled around so that he stood to the marble man's side. I sipped lemonade flavored with grapefruit. Spot leaned sideways against the statue the way Danes do with living people. But when his side hit cold marble, he turned and looked at the statue as if he only just realized it wasn't a mostly-naked, albino person, but was stone.

I considered the crowd, a few executives from KGA, a few West Shore and Pacific Heights neighbors. They were a well-dressed, well-educated, well-traveled group. They probably all had wine cellars. They'd probably all graduated from elite schools. I wondered if any of them had children like Joshua, raised with the illusion of having everything and yet missing the most important thing a child needs, an involved parent or two who is interested in their pursuits and is devoted to helping them prosper.

In time, I wandered back to Joshua and Roxanne Monales.

"I'm curious," Joshua was saying to Roxanne. "How is it that you even found out about my book? I mean, I've told almost no one about it. It's practically a secret."

Roxanne glanced at me and then looked back at Joshua. "As you might know, I got my PhD in environmental science at UC Berkeley. There is another scientist I've been in contact with who also got her doctorate at Berkeley. Her field is entomology."

"The study of insects," Joshua said.

"Yes. We've never met, but we know of each other's work. She sent me an email saying she'd read your book and thought I should read it. So I did, and I immediately realized the quality of your writing. It made me want to meet you and entice you into joining us at the Georgia Center. I was in the Bay Area for a conference, so I contacted her, and she arranged for me to come to this soirée."

"Soirée," Joshua repeated slowly as if he'd never had the pleasure of pronouncing the word.

He asked, "What is that scientist's name? Anyone I might have heard of?"

"Her name is Street Casey, a friend of Owen McKenna. I think you've maybe even met her."

Joshua looked at me. "I have, but I didn't think she even knew I had written a book." He looked back at Monales.

"This is what happens when your expertise is remarkable," Monales said. "People talk about it."

Roxanne Monales gave Joshua a card, said she'd be in touch with details, and excused herself. Joshua took Spot by the collar and walked off, saying he had a lot to think about. I found Street with Diamond and Santiago. The three of them were sitting at a table by the pool, sipping wine. The sun was hot but filtered through the pines, and the lake breeze was cool. I pulled up a chair and sat with them.

Santiago said, "Street told us you were concerned about

Kraytower's kid."

"Joshua," I said. "Yes, I was very concerned."

"You think he'll be okay?" Street asked.

"Yeah."

I saw Street turn and look off across the yard. Joshua was beckoning her. She got up and walked toward him.

Diamond, Santiago, and I couldn't hear them, but we understood the communication. Joshua was talking and gesturing. He looked very earnest. Then he leaned toward her and shook her hand.

They separated, and Street came back to us.

She said, "Diamond, what was that Shakespeare quote you told me a year ago or so, the one about hope?"

"I don't remember the exact words. Something about hope being the best medicine there is."

After the gathering, Sky invited us to what he called a Departure Concert at the Truckee train station. The stated date was three days away and the time was 2 p.m.

Street and Diamond and I arrived just before the appointed hour.

Sky and two band mates had set up their instruments and amps on the train platform. I had no idea how they got permission. Maybe they didn't ask.

A small group had appeared. In addition to Street and Diamond, Sergeant Santiago and Nettie Moon Water were there.

Diamond and Santiago stood in a corner with Street and Spot and me. Just after the music started, Joshua joined us. He didn't speak, as the music was too loud in the small space. Joshua took Spot by the collar and turned to face the band. Sky Kool and the Palpable Hits played a blues song.

After it was over, Joshua said, "Your dog changed my life a little," he said. "It used to be that I couldn't think of anything fun. But he's sort of all about fun, right?"

"And eating."

Joshua nodded, bent over, and hugged Spot.

Sky picked up his microphone.

"Hello everybody, I'd like to make a special announcement. My best friend Joshua has been given a residency at the Georgia Center for Nature Writers. This is a big deal, folks. He's gonna do nature writing and teach classes and give lectures and basically be a star. I'm lucky because I get to go with him and help him move in. So we're singing a celebration. Gladys Knight and the Pips, move over. Amtrak's California Zephyr is due to arrive from Sacramento in a few minutes, and Joshua and I will get onboard. Joshua's never ridden on a train before, so this will be extra fun. It's a long ride to Chicago. And then we have to make a few connections to get to Atlanta, Georgia. So here's a song for Joshua's future. The original title for the song was The Midnight Train to Georgia. This new version is The Afternoon Train to Georgia."

Sky's band played, and Sky sang a vocal that would have impressed Gladys Knight herself. Even the band's harmonies were impressive.

Joshua looked unsteady, but he remained composed. He was probably contemplating a future where the past with his lousy father was reduced to background noise, replaced by a future that was about to begin with his first train ride. He was jumping into an academic world that had already judged his writing and found it desirable.

Most importantly, he had discovered that he had a friend, a blood brother who would stand by him.

When the song ended, the small crowd clapped and whooped. It was followed almost immediately by the whistle and honk of the approaching train. Sky's band mates collected their musical equipment.

Ten minutes later, I once again held Spot's collar. Joshua and Sky hauled their luggage onboard. Joshua came back to the door, jumped down the steps, and ran over to Street and me and Spot. He shook Street's hand, pet Spot, then reached up his arms toward me. I bent down, and he grabbed me with surprising force and held on a long time. Then he turned, wiping his eyes, and ran back up the steps into the train.

When he rejoined Sky, they slid the nearest window open. We walked closer to the windows.

Sky was all smiles, confident and cool. By contrast, Joshua looked small and tentative. But he waved and smiled.

The train gave a huge blast on its horn.

Joshua leaned toward the open window. "Hey, Owen," he called out in a soft voice. "Street told me that some time back you were possibly working on a limerick about Spot. Did you ever finish it?"

"Well, I'm not a writer like you. But, yes, I did. I'll tell you if you promise not to judge."

"I won't judge," Joshua said. "Promise."

"Tell us, Mr. Detective!" Sky yelled with great enthusiasm.

I recited it.

"There once was a Great Dane named Spot
Whose faux diamond ear stud was not
What one had expected
Yet all had accepted
That the Great Dane named Spot was hot."

"Whoo hoo!" Sky shouted. He pumped his fist up and down.

"Very good!" Joshua said. "You are a writer!"

The train gave another blast of its horn and started to move. We all waved again. As Joshua and Sky pulled away from us, Spot looked up at me, then back at the receding train. He wagged.

About The Author

Todd Borg and his wife live in Lake Tahoe, where they write and paint. To contact Todd or learn more about the Owen McKenna mysteries, please visit toddborg.com.

A message from the author:

Dear Reader,

If you enjoyed this novel, please consider posting a short review on any book website you like to use. Reviews help authors a great deal, and that in turn allows us to write more stories for you.

Thank you very much for your interest and support!

Todd